Off the Mark

Off the Mark

Will Stebbings

Matador
9 Priory Business Park,
Wistow Road, Kibworth Beauchamp,
Leicestershire. LE8 0RX
Tel: (+44) 116 279 2299
Fax: (+44) 116 279 2277
Email: books@troubador.co.uk
Web: www.troubador.co.uk/matador

ISBN 978 1780881 522

British Library Cataloguing in Publication Data.
A catalogue record for this book is available from the British Library.

Typeset in 10pt Aldine401 BT Roman by Troubador Publishing Ltd, Leicester, UK

Matador is an imprint of Troubador Publishing Ltd

Printed in Great Britain by the MPG Books Group, Bodmin and King's Lynn

CHAPTER 1

A Momentous Day

'Grey skies are gonna clear up. Put on a happy face,' sang Mark Barker, at the top of his normally quiet voice, not caring who would hear him. They couldn't touch him now. He couldn't remember the next few words, so he lowered his voice a touch and continued 'Da da da da da da da dum. Put on a happy face.' Then he shouted out 'Freedom! I'm free!'

It was Friday July 23rd 1965. A truly momentous day. It was Mark's last day at school and he knew his life would never be the same again. The school was the Parkside Grammar School for Boys, in the small market town of Sanford in Norfolk. He had some mixed emotions as he collected his cranky old bike from the dilapidated bike shed. He couldn't wait to get away, because his time at school had been absolutely miserable and he hated the place. But there was a very slight tinge of sadness, as it was the last time he would see all those familiar sights which had played such a major part of his life for the last five years.

At no time had Mark ever considered the option of staying to take 'A' levels. His parents had not discussed the matter with him. His elder brother and sister had both left school at that age, so it was accepted that he would follow suit.

He looked round as he pushed his bike towards the school gate… and freedom! There was a rule that you didn't ride your bike on school premises. Why on Earth was he still bothering to obey the rules? Surely no one would dare to try to chastise him on his last day? No, he was just taking a mature attitude to the question of safety. And setting a good example to the younger pupils. But in a few seconds, he would no longer be a schoolboy.

He had sat his GCE 'O' levels a month earlier and was reasonably confident of a handful of passes, but it would be a few weeks before he learnt the results. Until then, what chance did he have of getting a job when he didn't know what his qualifications were? The career guidance at school had been no help. If you didn't have a very clear idea of what you wanted to do, their stock answer was to suggest the Civil Service (after all, weren't they Civil Servants themselves?).

So following their suggestion, he had applied to join the Civil Service and had been granted an interview. What a disaster that was! Wearing his father's only suit (which had seen better days, was several sizes too big for Mark and was brown!), and a brand new pair of stiff leather shoes that quickly gave him blisters on each heel, he made his way by train and tube to Saville Row in London. He had allowed plenty of time to find the building where he was to be interviewed. So with over an hour to spare, he found himself slowly walking up and down Saville Row in pain on a sweltering July afternoon, gasping for a drink.

With fifteen minutes to spare he announced his arrival and was led to a room where several other hopeful young candidates were still waiting from earlier appointment times. This was going to be a long afternoon! No one dared to speak. This was a daunting experience for a shy sixteen-year-old and he sat looking at his nice new shiny shoes – and then across to the other candidates' shoes. Then at their suits (for they were mostly male). Oh dear! Their suits fitted their owners and were dark blue or charcoal – not brown! He wished he could go home straight away.

Eventually, it was Mark's turn to be interviewed. He was directed into a large wood-panelled office, where several austere people sat behind a large desk. The only light was coming from the window behind the interviewers, highlighting the minute particles of dust that hung in the air. He was invited to sit on a chair strategically placed about ten feet in front of the desk. The floorboards creaked loudly as he made his way to the chair. Surrounded by so much space, he felt like he was a hundred yards from the large desk. His head was swimming round and he was struggling to breathe. He found it impossible to look up and make eye contact with any of the interviewers, especially as they were only silhouettes against the afternoon sun. He couldn't even manage to count how many interviewers there were. He had never felt so nervous. He wasn't the most self-confident person in the world, even with friends. With total strangers, he was a quivering bag of nerves.

As he continued his ride home from school, the only question he could remember from that dreaded interview was 'Which newspapers do you read?' He answered quite truthfully the Daily Express and the Daily Mirror. After all, they were the newspapers that his parents had delivered, so that is what he read. It was no good saying the Times or the Observer, because he had never read them in his life, so any follow up question would have certainly caught him out. Mark had been brought up to always tell the truth.

He had decided he wasn't cut out for the Civil Service if it meant you were judged by the newspaper that you read. Not that they had accepted him anyway! But what was he going to do? Probably something clerical. He was good at Maths and English; useless at Art and Woodwork, so manual work was out. On Monday, he would go down to the local Labour Exchange to sign on and get his National Insurance card. And see what jobs were on offer.

Meanwhile, he had to tackle the three-mile bike ride home for the last time. Would his bike actually make it? It was clanking and making all sorts of strange noises. His father had bought it for him as a reward for passing the eleven-plus. It was a lovely shining black Raleigh back then, bought on the 'never-never' at ten shillings per week. But, apart from the fact that it was falling apart, he had outgrown it several years ago, so the first thing he would do when he got a job would be to buy a new bike.... a three-speed bike with racy-looking straight handlebars.

He contemplated the few happy times he had known during the last five years. He had played football and cricket for both his house and the school at under-thirteen and under-fifteen level. Had he stayed on, he was sure he would have represented them at senior level, as well. Beyond that, he was struggling to find good things to say about his time at school. In fact, it had been thoroughly miserable for most of the five years.

Mark had always been a sensitive child and couldn't handle the never-ending teasing that he had had to endure. He had started his time at the Grammar School with his elder brother's hand-me-down school blazer (a bright crimson colour) with leather patches at the elbows. During the next five years, very few of his clothes were new. School assembly involved the majority of the pupils sitting on a hard wooden floor for nearly half an hour per day (except for the few Catholics who were admitted once Prayers and hymns were over, to stand at the back). That hard floor took its toll on a chap's trousers. As well as the patches in his elbows, he soon had patches on his posterior. This meant that whenever he walked across the quadrangle, he was aware of sniggering behind him as all the boys competed for a new witticism. One of his nicknames was Steptoe, after the television series about a rag and bone dealer that was popular at that time.

Even when the lads were not sniggering at him, he imagined that they were. He became quite paranoid whenever anyone was behind him. He ran up stairs to expose his patches for the least amount of time possible. His 'friends' were actually the worst. On one occasion, his mother had run out of dark thread and used white cotton. This made the patches stand out even more than usual. In her day, everyone had patches. She considered she had done well by him. After all, he had his football gear and his white P.E. kit, so he couldn't really complain, could he? Mark wasn't the only person in the family and he should have a little more consideration for others! But she had never had to attend a Boys' Grammar School.

The other thing he disliked about Parkside Grammar was the masters. Mark didn't understand why so many of them had taken a dislike to him. He'd been in his share of scrapes, but he wasn't a perpetual miscreant like some. It was true that some masters didn't like any pupils, so with them it wasn't personal.

Punishments were varied. A Prefect or a Master could issue 'Punishment Parades'. This involved staying behind after school for half an hour under the jurisdiction of one of the Prefects. It was up to the Prefect to decide the activity of a 'Parade'. Some liked the miscreants to stand to attention on the quadrangle for half an hour. Some got them to write out 'lines'. There were even some prefects who did no more than take offenders into a classroom and let them do whatever they wanted as long as they were well behaved. Many pupils managed to get another 'parade' while they were serving the first one!

Detentions could only be issued by a master, but if anyone got three or more 'Parades' in a month, this led to an automatic one-hour detention. Three detentions in a month led to the 'cane'. Only the headmaster was allowed to implement the cane as a punishment, but that didn't stop some of the other masters from inflicting their own variations of corporal punishment.

Mr. Underwood, the History teacher, seemed to take great delight in the use of a large black plimsoll applied ferociously to the posteriors of offenders, who had to bend over in front of the class. Mark made a point of not misbehaving in Mr. Underwood's class unless he had some new trousers!

Mr. Washington, the Geography teacher, on the other hand, liked to administer instant reprisals there and then. Blackboard wipers (those wooden blocks with a felt pad) would be thrown violently at anyone who didn't appear to be paying attention. People talking could be dragged to the front of the class by their hair or ears and made to endure the ritual of chalk being rubbed into their gums.

Although that was a little barbaric, most boys preferred this instant punishment to the approach taken by Mr Medwell, who regularly gave out detentions for any offence from missing homework to low marks in tests. Detentions were read out during Monday morning assembly and they had to be served on Tuesday afternoons. Tuesday afternoons were traditionally reserved for inter-house football or cricket matches. If you failed to turn up for detention, a further hour was added next time. Nobody told Mark this, so the first time he got a detention, he thought he'd leave it a week, only to find it doubled the next week.

Mr Medwell was Mark's housemaster, so they had a mutual interest in Mark staying out of detention. Not that Mr. Medwell ever showed any favouritism towards Mark.

The French teacher, Mr Knighton, was definitely an eccentric. He insisted on speaking with an exaggerated French accent, even though he was born and bred in Norfolk. He translated everyone's name into French. So Pete Williams was Pierre Guillaumes. Or Monsieur Guillaumes. Mr Knighton tended to ignore those people whose name he couldn't easily translate. He constantly smoked some horrible smelling French cigarettes that left revolting nicotine stains on his fingers and he had a very jaundiced looking complexion. He was tall with a large crooked nose. He walked with a stooped gait and Mark thought he looked remarkably like President De Gaulle.

Then there was Mr. Forrester, the Latin teacher. All around the walls in his room were pictures of classical statues of nude men. On the shelves, in between the Latin Primers, were books of classical art – again all nude men. Mr Forrester was a quietly spoken man who didn't seem to mix much with the other teachers.

Mr. Charles (nicknamed 'Elsie', because his initials were 'L.C.') was the Physics teacher and when he didn't have lessons of his own, he would volunteer to help out with the football. He insisted that everyone had a shower after the game and he stood in the shower area, watching, supposedly to ensure everyone complied. Although if Tony Riley was in the shower, you could be fairly certain that Elsie wouldn't notice you. Tony was a big lad for his age.

Elsie was another bachelor. There were lots of bachelors at Mark's school.

The one master who was universally disliked by all pupils and masters alike was Mr. Tucker – the P.E. teacher. He would occasionally start a lesson in a quite jovial mode. But for no apparent reason, he could suddenly turn. The boys would be going about their vaults or head-springs and making a certain amount of schoolboy noise when gradually more and more people would notice that Mr Tucker's face had turned to thunder. Everyone would stop what they were doing and move to the edge of the gym. It would go deathly quiet. It would stay like this for five minutes – sometimes longer. The only noise being the occasional shuffling of nervous feet. Everyone knew how frightening Mr. Tucker could be in this mood, so no one dared move. He had been known to knock a boy to the ground for very little.

Then it happened. With a voice like a thunderstorm he would explode. 'WHAT DO YOU THINK YOU ARE DOING?' he shouted to the whole class.

Naturally no one replied. 'THAT'S NOT WHAT I ASKED YOU TO DO!' Actually, it was, but that didn't matter. He'd flipped and was now out of control. Every class would suffer his terrible wrath for the rest of the day. The word would get round to any class due to take P.E. that day and each class would creep into the gym as though walking on eggshells. The headmaster was afraid of him, so what chance would a small first-former have of standing up to him?

Once Easter was over, Mr Tucker took the swimming lessons in the unheated outdoor pool, joining the dead insects and rotting leaves, and regardless of the weather or temperature. He showed no mercy. His method of teaching you to swim was 'Do it or else!' Mark wondered if one day, there would be a tragedy with Mr. Tucker.

Of course, not all the teachers were perverts, eccentrics or sadists – just most of them! Or so it seemed to Mark. The one teacher he quite liked was Dave Jenkins – who took Biology. Dave actually seemed to enjoy his work. He had a good stock of jokes he would recycle for every new intake. He talked about the 'Plat-billed Duckypuss' and the 'Anti-Spine Eater'. All the teachers had nicknames, mostly derogatory, but Mr. Jenkins was known as 'Dave', which just happened to be his first name! Dave was married and lived with his wife three hundred yards down the road from the school. It was a great disappointment to Mark, when he heard some years later that Dave had been dismissed for homosexual activity.

As he came within a mile of his home, Mark could see his 'little girlfriend' on her bike in front of him. He had no idea of her name, but she lived a couple of streets away from him and he saw her most days, either on the way to school or on the way home. On a good day, he would see her in both directions – some days not at all. He had plucked up courage a few months earlier to say 'Hello' as he overtook her, but so far, no more than that. She attended the local Girls' High School and wore a bright green blazer, a green beret and a green and white striped frock. There was little or no interaction between the two schools, which meant a chap like Mark grew up in isolation from the opposite sex. To him, they were a different species.

She was lovely. She had long auburn hair tucked up under her beret. She was tall and of medium build. Mark guessed she was good at sports, because she had very shapely legs. She seemed to ride along so effortlessly whatever the weather conditions. At first, he was too shy to even overtake her, preferring instead to ease up if she appeared in front of him. Then he started approaching a little closer until he decided all he had to do was say 'Hello' as he overtook. The first time he did it, he felt very pleased with himself. She gave him a polite smile and said 'Oh, hello' with just a hint of surprise in her voice. After that, he knew he couldn't overtake without speaking, so some days he overtook, some days he didn't. This was no great hardship, because he could hang back just enough to admire her legs and the way they changed shape as they pedalled up and down. Yes, definitely good at sports.

Today might be the last time Mark would see her. Could he say a little more than just 'Hello'? No, of course not. He considered that his horn-rimmed National Health glasses made him an ugly youth. She wouldn't welcome being seen talking to someone like him. Her friends might see her. But he would ride past and say 'Hello' for the last time.

His clanking bike announced his presence and as he got beside her, he slowed and said 'Hello. Is this your last day, as well?' He couldn't believe he'd done that, but he had and now he could feel his heart beating faster.

'No', she said. 'I've still got another year of my A-levels' Oh, dear! That meant she was a year older than he was, so she definitely wouldn't want to talk to him.

However, she carried on. 'What are your plans, now?'

'Well, I've still got to find a job. The Careers Officer was no help, although I did get an interview with the Civil Service,' Mark replied. 'I don't think that was for me. My uncle keeps telling me to go into the RAF. He flew in Wellingtons in the war.' Then Mark hesitated for a few seconds, before adding 'And he wore 2 pairs of socks. It gets cold when you fly at altitude, you know.' He paused to see if his little joke got a reaction. His lovely companion looked across at him; then she smiled and started laughing. The family joke had worked.

"Very good,' she said, still amused.

But now Mark didn't know what to say next. His head was racing and he was starting to feel a little breathless, even though they were only pedalling at a modest pace. He hoped she might say something else, but she didn't. He contemplated racing on ahead, but decided that would look very odd. What did he talk about when he was with his mates at school? Then he said, 'Do you like jokes?'

She looked across at him with a bemused look on her face and he wondered if this had been a good move. But she replied 'Yes,' but without any great conviction.

'Right then,' he began and then paused while a heavy lorry went passed.

'A stranger entered a saloon in the old Wild West and ordered a drink. He remarked that the er, bar …, the er, saloon was empty.' Mark's companion was just looking ahead and his mouth was starting to feel dry. He wasn't sure she was all that interested and now he wished he hadn't started.

But he continued 'The bartender said "They've all gone to the hanging."

"Who are they hanging?" the stranger asked.

"The Brown Paper Kid," came the reply.

"That's a strange name. Why do they call him that?"

"Because all his clothes are made of brown paper. He has a brown paper shirt; brown paper trousers; a brown paper waistcoat and a brown paper hat."

"What are they hanging him for?"

"Rustling!"

Mark was aware that he had rushed the joke, but then his companion burst out laughing and he felt so relieved.

This was going well. He was just starting to overcome his nervousness. 'By the way, my name is Mar….' Just then his pedal came off and as his left foot flew round where his pedal should have been, he lost his balance and fell against his young friend's bike. She managed to control her fall and with an amazing amount of dignity, she remained upright and came to a controlled stop. Whereas Mark fell over in a heap on the kerbside and rolled under a privet hedge, with the wheels of his bike still spinning.

She obviously wanted to laugh, but she made an effort to show some concern for his predicament. However, when she saw him crawl out from under the hedge with an old bird's nest on his head, she couldn't help herself. She was still laughing as she parked her bike and asked him if he was hurt.

'I think I've ruined my dignity,' he said, trying to act as though it was nothing. Actually his left leg was throbbing, but he wasn't going to make a fuss. 'Are you all right?' he asked her.

'Yes, I'm fine. What happened?'

'My pedal came off. Can you see it?' he asked, looking round.

'Yes, here it is,' she said, picking it up from the gutter. 'And this looks like the nut that should hold it on? Can you fix it back on?'

'I'll need a spanner to do it properly. I'll have to walk home. You carry on.' He hoped she might walk home with him, but he could hardly expect it. In any case, he was now feeling so embarrassed that part of him welcomed her probable departure.

'Well, I do have to hurry home to help get ready for tomorrow. We're going on holiday. So I hope you don't mind if I carry on.'

'Of course not. Where are you going?'

'We're off to Cornwall.' she replied.

'That sounds nice. I hope you have a good time.' Mark suddenly had a vision of her lying on the beach in a swimsuit.

'Thank you. Bye!' and she elegantly mounted her bike and glided off into the distance.

And that was it. Mark had talked to a girl – and she had talked back to him. Why hadn't he tried to talk to her before? He might never see her again. And he still didn't know her name. She probably didn't know his, because he didn't quite complete his name before he toppled over.' Still, she was very friendly to him and when she had laughed at him, it wasn't really malicious. 'Damned stupid bike!' he thought. God, she was lovely! He'd have a fantasy about her that night; especially with those legs. He would repeat that image of her lying on a beach in her swimsuit.

Mark had never had a proper holiday. His Aunt Dorothy and Uncle Len had a beach hut on Heacham beach, so the family sometimes caught a bus or a train to visit them on a Sunday. Several of his relatives would turn up. His mother had eight sisters and four brothers, so this was a popular venue for the family in the summer. Heacham beach is all shingle and there was little in the way of amenities, but his parents weren't interested in holidays, so it had to suffice.

When he was six years old, Mark had spent a fortnight with Aunt Irene and Uncle Ted who owned a pub in Thetford. Uncle Ted always made fun of Mark. At six years old, Mark's teeth were a little crooked, so he couldn't say 'six' without a bit of a lisp.

'How old are you?' Uncle Ted would keep asking.

'Thix', said the young Mark. Laughter all round.

'Stop teasing him, Ted' said Aunt Irene. 'He'll soon be theven!'

Nevertheless, Mark enjoyed much of his stay at Thetford, because at the back of the pub was a huge amount of land, lots of interesting outbuildings, a small copse, chickens and ducks and a large hole in the ground, which everyone called 'the pit'. No one knew why the 'pit' had been dug out. Perhaps it was to extract flint. A lot of the older properties in Thetford were made of local flintstone.

Uncle Ted had a cruel sense of humour. One day, he convinced Mark that there was buried treasure under the little mossy tussocks that proliferated on the far side of the 'pit'. So Mark spent many hours digging amongst these, only to end up sadly disappointed.

He enjoyed collecting the chicken eggs and preparing the feed twice a day. And he loved climbing up Castle Hill and rolling down into the dried moat below. But he couldn't do this on his own, because he was so young and most of the time, his aunt and uncle were too busy running the pub to take him. So he had to spend hours on his own, in and around the 'pit.'

The next year, he declined the offer of a second holiday on the grounds that he wanted to be with his friends. But it was mostly because he didn't like Uncle Ted making fun of him. Mark's elder brother had only ever had one holiday at Thetford.

Mark continued to push his tired old bike home, feeling hot and bothered. As he passed 'her' house, he saw her bike parked against the garage wall. She spotted him from her bedroom and leant out to call to him, 'I'm Janice,' she said. 'Did you say you were Mark?'

'Yes, that's right,' he replied and his heart starting thumping all over again.

'Good luck with the job hunting'. That was nice. He wondered if…. No, of course not!

And then he was home. To his parents' semi-detached Thirties-built home with its peeling paintwork, metal windows and overgrown garden.

And there was his mother talking over the low fence to Mrs. Nichols, the next-door neighbour. They had both lived there for over thirty years and had benefited from each other's company when the children were at school and their husbands at work. Once they got 'gassing', it was very hard to separate them. They never went round each other's houses, but would stand talking over the fence for hours on end. Their kitchen windows faced each other and at a given signal, they would both go outside for a natter.

As Mark leant his bike against the shed, they stopped talking. 'That's it, then?' said his mother.

'No, I thought I'd go back next term. I'm missing it already. There's bags of life left in this blazer.' His mother didn't appreciate his sarcasm.

Mrs. Nichols asked 'Any luck with a job, yet?'

'No. I'll have a look in the today's local paper to see who's desperate enough to give me a job. If not, I'll be down at the Labour Exchange on Monday.'

Mrs Nichols continued, 'My nephew's got himself a job at that canning factory over the river. He's earning twelve pounds a week. Why don't you give them a try?' Mark was not impressed. Her nephew had gone to the Secondary Modern School and didn't have to take GCE's. He might be earning twelve pounds a week now, which was a good wage for a sixteen-year old, but in five years' time, he would still be earning twelve pounds a week and probably still doing the same job.

Mark went inside, took off his blazer for the last time and tried to wash the bicycle grease from his hands, with only partial success.

Then he sat down in front of the television. He picked up the Radio Times and the TV Times. In those days, you needed both magazines to find out what was on the two channels available to U.K. viewers. It was 4.15 – too early for anything decent on television. So he opened the local paper instead and turned to the 'Situations Vacant'. He scanned past the 'Farm workers', 'Accountants' and 'Secretaries' and his eyes fell upon an 'Office Junior' position at the Water Board'. He read it carefully. It read –

'Office Junior required to work in busy accounts office. Age 16 – 19; Male. Must be good at figures and have a neat hand. £7.10s.0d per week. Three weeks holiday after six months qualifying period. Must be of smart appearance. Good prospects of promotion. Minimum qualification four GCE 'O' levels, including Mathematics and English Language. Written applications must be received by 3rd August 1965. Address correspondence to –

> R.J Thompson,
> Accounts Manager,
> Anglian Water Board,
> 20 – 24 Bridge Street,
> Sanford,
> Norfolk.'

'That sounds like a good match,' thought Mark and after checking that there were no more half-suitable vacancies, started writing a letter on rough paper. He wouldn't mention the 'O' levels at all. He could explain the situation at the interview. When he had finished the letter, he left it on the sideboard. He would get his father to check it when he returned from work.

Mark then went into the front room where he had his old Dansette record player and his small record collection. He picked out a few singles and placed them on the auto-stacker. Nobody else in the family shared his taste in music, so he always went into the front room to listen to his records. They were mostly 45's, but he now had eight LP's. They were all 'mono' records, because you weren't meant to play stereo records on his old Dansette. For a few years, he was into American pop music, such as the Beach boys and the Four Seasons. When his uncle gave them their first second-hand record player, the first record he ever bought was 'Sherry' by the Four Seasons. When he bought the Record Mirror, he was always more interested in the American charts than the British. This meant he would be aware of the titles of records by his favourite artists long before they were ever released in Britain.

One day back in 1963, Mark was in the local record store, listening to a couple of new releases in one of the small record booths, when he picked up a record by the Impressions called 'It's All Right'. He had seen this listed in the American charts, but had never heard it, so he gave it a spin. He was overwhelmed. The lead singer (whom he later found out was the young Curtis Mayfield) had a sort of falsetto voice like the Four Seasons or the Beach Boys, but there was something else which moved him. The arrangement was perfect, with a lovely clipped brass effect and infectious rhythm, but it was that voice and the harmonies that did it for him. He listened to the flip side, a lovely emotive ballad called 'You'll

Want Me Back' – more of that same lovely soulful voice and those close harmonies. He bought the record.

After that, he had explored this particular genre, which he later found was described by some journalists at that time as 'New Wave R & B'. Over the course of time, the term 'R & B' has been used confusingly to describe several different genres, but at that time it was a fairly generic term for almost anything from Black America.

The record stores didn't always stock Mark's type of music, so Radio Luxembourg (The Station of the Stars) was usually Mark's key to hearing his music. The reception was poor and sometimes non-existent, but if you were serious about your music, you put up with that. At that time, most of the programmes on Luxembourg would be sponsored by a particular record company, so if they went to the trouble of issuing a record in Britain, they made sure it was aired to some extent.

Back on the Dansette, the first record Mark had selected was 'You're No Good' by Betty Everett. This triggered off memories of his disputes with his mates at school, who had bought the cover version by the Swinging Bluejeans. Since the fifties, there has been a long history of British artists (and even white Americans) taking R & B songs and turning them into pop hits. This had always annoyed Mark who had a greater awareness of the originals than his friends and cringed whenever he heard these pale imitations. Because without exception, to him they were always pale imitations – never adding anything original, but always removing the soulful element of the original.

Mark's friends considered him to be a little eccentric and narrow-minded. He felt they were the ones who needed to open their minds. It wasn't just a matter of taste – it would be a funny old world if everyone had the same taste – but they were locked into accepting what everyone else accepted. All he wanted was a level playing field where all versions of a song could get equal 'air' time. Pirate radio might have helped the situation a little, but it also marginalised Radio Luxembourg, so Soul and R & B continued to attract only a minority interest.

While he listened, he contemplated his future. Today *was* a momentous day. Not just because it was the end of an era, but also because it was the beginning of a new one. He had to start considering himself as an adult and he would now have more control over his life. He decided to set himself some objectives. He didn't write them down, but he would commit them to memory. They were –

To get a worthwhile job (not necessarily the first one offered) within 2 months.

To get a half-decent set of clothes, both for work and for casual use (no more patches!).

To gain more experience of girls (a date would be nice, but let's not get too carried away!).

To get a new bike.

CHAPTER 2

Home Comforts

Just before six o'clock, Mark's father, Frank, arrived home from work and collapsed in his well-worn armchair. By trade, he was a coach painter and sign-writer, but he worked at a local food-processing factory where his main activity was general painting or decorating, with just the occasional sign to paint, mostly on lorries or vans. Before the Second World War, he was in partnership with another man, running his own successful sign-writing business called 'Barker & Howell'. The partner, Geoff Howell, contrived to avoid the call-up. So he continued the business during the war, taking over sole ownership. With the shortage of skilled labour during the war, the business went from strength to strength.

When he returned from the war, Frank Barker had been unable to buy back into the business, which made him very bitter about his ex-partner. He had no trouble finding work, but with no working capital, he could no longer remain self-employed. At first, he worked for companies that allowed him the opportunity to pursue his specialised trade, such as local hauliers or motor traders, but over the years, he had been made redundant several times as new spraying techniques superseded his skills. He had been with his current employer for the last six years. It wasn't a brilliantly paid job, but there were little perks, such as cheap tins of food.

He occasionally did a little private work at home, mostly as a favour for old friends. Frank saw such jobs as his beer money.

Mark told him about the letter. 'What do I know about applying for an office job?' was Frank's gruff response. That was true.

'Well just read it through, anyway. It's important for me to get a job and I'd hate to miss out because I said something stupid or ambiguous or anything'

His father replied, 'I've got a sign to paint tonight, so I won't have time.'

Mark could feel himself getting annoyed. 'Well that's typical. It would only take a couple of minutes. That just shows how much you care about my future. You're always the bloody same!'

His mother intervened, 'Frank, it won't take you long.'

Mark could tell that his father wasn't very keen, so he stomped off into the front room to listen to some more records. He always did that when he needed to cool down. 'Your tea's nearly ready,' said his mother, calling after him.

The front room was originally intended to be used for special visitors and only to be used occasionally. However, as the family had grown up, an overflow room was definitely required. In any case, 'special' visitors had been non-existent. So Mark and his brother were now the only ones to use the room. It was no longer fit for special visitors. The settee was the same one that had been in use for thirty years. Springs and horsehair were protruding from various openings in the upholstery. Moreover, the room was very cold in winter and too hot in summer as it caught the afternoon sun.

Mark played one record, but he was too angry to enjoy it so he returned to a plate of sausages, eggs and chips with a slice of white bread.

'I'll have a look at your letter, once I've done the first coat,' said his father.

'Thank you,' Mark replied, trying to sound a little grateful, but still feeling a little aggrieved that he hadn't got a better reaction, first time.

Life in the Barker household was prone to these little squabbles. Sometimes they blew over quite quickly, like this one. Other times they could be really fierce and fester for days on end. The usual cause of disagreement was the television.

Each person in the family had different tastes in entertainment and with only one television in the house (these were the days before video recorders), it was a real powder keg situation. The family would sometimes have an amicable agreement at the start of the evening as to what they would watch, with some attempt at 'give and take'. But this seldom worked out satisfactorily, because favourite programmes would often clash – and all this with only 2 channels!

Comedy programmes such as 'Steptoe and Son' and 'The Likely Lads' and a few game shows were universally accepted. Mark was the only one to enjoy Science Fiction and 'The Man From Uncle'. His mother liked 'Coronation Street' and a 'good play'. His father insisted on watching 'The Black & White Minstrel Show' as well as documentaries and political discussions. Mark's brother liked detective series, such as 'No Hiding Place' and pop music, which usually annoyed the rest of the family.

When Mark lost out and went off into the front room to play records, he might find his brother had beaten him to it, so he would be doubly confounded!

This being a Friday meant his mother would be going to Bingo and his father would be off down the pub. His parents never went out together. With a little luck, Mark's brother would be going out as well, so that would give Mark a free rein to watch whatever he liked.

The main living room also doubled as the dining room. After everyone had finished their meal, finished off with a cup of tea, and while Mrs Barker did the washing up, Frank set up his painting gear on the table. Mark loved to watch his father at work. He was a real craftsman and produced work of the highest quality. He could sign-write in any script, which was ironic because his handwriting was practically illegible.

The job that night was a house name. The wooden plaque had already been gloss-painted in black, which left the wording to be applied. This was to be 'MILL VIEW' in capitals. Frank laid the plaque flat on the table and measured the position of the letters, which would all be the same height. He chalked up a piece of string with a loop in the middle. He held the 2 ends against the designated position for the top of the letters. Then he clenched the loop in his teeth and pulled back his head. When he was sure everything was in the correct position, he released the loop and the string hit the sign, with a soft thwack. Once the small dust cloud had cleared, this left a perfectly straight guide line in chalk. He repeated this process for the bottom guide line. Had the letters included lower case characters then a third and possibly a fourth line would have been needed, but not this time.

He looked at the lines for a few minutes and decided they were spot-on. Sometimes, he had to wipe off the chalk and repeat the process several times, but this time, he'd got it right first time.

Now he chalked out the rough outline of the letters. This was to ensure the text was positioned centrally and correctly spaced. When he was satisfied, he placed the sign on top of a few books to give him the required height and then leant it against a couple more, making sure there was no risk of it slipping. He opened a tin of light grey undercoat and stirred it for a few seconds. Then selected his finest brush and picked up his mahlstick (pronounced 'maulstick') in his left hand. The mahlstick acted as a bridge to support his right hand and prevent fatigue. Mark watched every stroke with total admiration, until the operation was complete. Every edge was razor sharp and all letters were of a uniform size.

17

Frank would leave it to dry overnight and the next day he would apply the gloss coat, which was to be a golden yellow. Sometimes, he would use gold-leaf, but that was expensive and probably not appropriate for an external sign. He cleaned his brush with thinners and tidied everything away. He was not the tidiest man on the planet, but when it came to sign-writing, he was meticulous about putting everything away in its proper place.

Then he was ready to read Mark's letter. Mark suggested that Frank should read the advertisement first, which he did. Then he read the letter. After a little consideration, he said 'That looks fair enough to me. Of course, this time of year, there'll be lots of people applying. But you stand as good a chance as anyone.'

'Can you think of anything I can say that would make my letter stand out?'

'Just make it as neat as you can.' That was ironic coming from Frank.

As Mark prepared to write out the letter again, he discovered there was neither writing paper nor envelopes in the house, so he would have to fetch them from town tomorrow. But his bike would have to be repaired before then, so he gathered up a few tools and went outside to do just that. He discovered that the thread on the pedal was slightly damaged so he wasn't sure how long his repair would last. He decided a road test was in order.

It was still a fine warm evening as he headed off down the lane. On any summer evening, you could be sure to find a small group of neighbours having a chat somewhere down his road. Most of them were friendly and Mark said 'Hello' to one group of three. In the other direction, he could see Mrs. Cooper and Mrs. Pettit standing at Mrs. Cooper's gate. Both had given Mark a bad time over the years whenever his football had gone into their gardens, so he didn't bother to speak to them.

Mr Pettit was now retired. He owned a Morris 1000, which he'd owned from new and was his pride and joy, although he spent more time polishing it than actually driving it. When he did go out in it, he would drive the complete length of their road (about 300 yards) in first gear. All the neighbours would cringe to hear the car screaming up the road. When he returned, he would take a good ten minutes to park the car. It had to be in exactly the right position outside his gate and exactly the right distance from the path. He had a narrow driveway, but parking in that was a major undertaking, which he only tackled when he was sure he wouldn't be going out for a while. He was incapable of performing a three-point turn in the quiet road. He had to drive to the end of the road (a further three hundred yards) where there was a very small T-shaped lay-by. Even then, he took several minutes to perform the simple manoeuvre. He had never had to pass a driving test and it showed!

Mark's pedal seemed to be holding up quite well, so he ventured down Hall Lane, which is where the lovely Janice lived. She lived in the first of a small development of ten modern houses where there used to be a small orchard. This at one time had been an illicit source of apples, greengages and plums for Mark and his friends. He'd seen many of his old haunts disappear during the last few years, particularly the old hollow oak tree in the meadow down Sandy Lane, which used to be in the countryside. Now it was part of a large Council Estate and Sanford was gradually creeping out into the countryside like a large malignant growth.

Mark couldn't see any sign of Janice as he rode past. Not that he looked too hard. He wouldn't want her to think he was riding past just to get a glimpse! He decided to call in to see his old friend Podge, who lived a few doors down from Janice. Podge (real name Roger) and Mark used to be very good friends, but had ended up in different classes at school and had drifted apart recently. This was not helped by the fact that 'Mrs Podge' was a bit of a snob who didn't approve of her two sons associating with the Barker brothers. Mark wasn't sure what Podge would be doing next year, so he wanted to see him. Unfortunately, when he knocked at the door, there was no reply and the house looked deserted. On a Friday, the family often dashed off to the coast in their caravan.

So he headed off back home, again glancing sideways, but not too obviously, towards Janice's house. Still no sign. If he rode up and down the road enough, he might eventually spot her, but he couldn't do that, could he?

A little further on, he passed his father who was heading towards the pub on his bike. Mark's mother had already left to catch the bus to take her to Bingo. His father didn't stop, but as he passed he asked if Mark's bike was all right now. Mark just said 'Yes'. He didn't have too many long conversations with his father.

Then he was back down his own road – New Street (It was new, back in the 1930's). All the houses on the left-hand side were built to the same semi-detached design, while the houses on the right had been added slightly later and were all different in size and style. Mark's own house – number 21 – was easily the worst decorated in the street. Frank Barker wasn't going to spend all day painting at work and then come home only to start all over again on his own property.

It was a three-bedroom property, with a small kitchen, the living room, the front room and a small bathroom. The toilet was outside, next to the coal shed. Both formed a lean-to attached to the kitchen and faced Mrs Nichol's kitchen, so any visit to the 'seat of comfort' could be observed by their neighbour. There was no light or heat in the toilet, so during the winter months, visits were not a pleasant experience. On one occasion, during a heavy storm, Mark had not engaged the latch fully and the door blew wide open, revealing his predicament to the astonished Mrs Nichols, who was busy at her kitchen sink. The toilet roll was attached to the door, so that came streaming out onto the path.

The house had one coal fire in the living room and one in the front room, but the front room chimney had not been swept in years and Mark's mother was paranoid about the chimney catching fire, so fires were not permitted in this room. Mark had decided he would buy an electric fire when he started earning. There was a back-boiler to the living room fire, but this had gradually become furred up, so was now very inefficient. This meant that it was not possible to have a proper bath. Hot water was obtained by boiling up a kettle on the gas stove in the kitchen. Personal hygiene was achieved by having a 'strip wash' in the kitchen, with the curtains drawn so that Mrs Nichols couldn't see. When Mark had been much younger, his mother would wash him standing up in the large porcelain sink (Mark was in the sink, not his mother!).

Mark occupied the front double bedroom, which faced north-west and was extremely cold in the winter. Ice would often form on the inside of the window and it was not unusual for Mark to see his breath condensing as he exhaled. He used to share the double bed with his brother Brian, but once his sister married 3 years earlier, Brian moved into the smallest bedroom overlooking the back garden.

Their parents' bedroom also faced the back garden and was the warmest of the bedrooms due to its position above the living room and the fact that it included the airing cupboard and the hot water cylinder which retained what little hot water that might be generated by the back-boiler. The only room in the house that had a carpet was the front room. All the other rooms had cold linoleum on the floor.

But now it was summer and Mark returned from his little ride down the lane, happy that his bike would stand a trip to town the next day. His brother had not come home from work at tea-time, so he must have gone straight out with his friend Ian who had his own car. The house was not locked. In fact, the house was never locked. In the sixties, people of their class did not fear burglaries. There was nothing of real value in the house. The next day, Mark would park his bike in a side street in town, without any kind of lock, confident that it would be there when he returned. Life was different in the sixties.

The rest of the weekend was uneventful in the Barker household. For Frank Barker, this consisted of him finishing his sign on Saturday morning, and then nipping down the pub. In the afternoon, he settled down to watch the horse racing on television. Then after tea, he was off to the pub again. On Sunday, he went to the pub at lunchtime, came home to a delicious Sunday roast, eaten an hour after everyone else, then slept till teatime, in front of the television, stirring only to make his usual Sunday afternoon smells and noises.

Mark went into town on Saturday morning to get his stationery and then later, he posted his letter. He spent the rest of the weekend reading newspapers, magazines and books (he was currently into H. G. Wells), watching television and listening to records. And of course, had an argument with his brother over television.

Mark's mother went into town on Saturday morning, using the excellent Eastern Counties bus service. She came back fully laden with two heavy shopping bags. She had also ordered a delivery of groceries from The International. These would be delivered by bike on Monday. On her way home, she picked up some fish and chips for the family's lunch. After Frank had finished watching the horse racing, she sat down to watch the wrestling, with Kent Walton doing the commentary. Her favourite wrestler, Les Kellet, was wrestling that day. Unfortunately, he lost. She would get very agitated by the antics of these wrestlers. 'It's all a fix,' Frank would keep saying. Or 'It's just a farce!'

After tea, she was off to Bingo again. When she returned, she emptied some dried peas into a bowl of water to soak overnight, ready for Sunday lunch. She spent Sunday morning preparing the Sunday roast. This was Yorkshire Pudding served as a starter followed by roast beef, roast potatoes, cabbage and those dried peas. On Sunday afternoon, she sat in the chair next to Frank to watch an old black and white film, only stirring to nudge

Frank when he snored or made disgusting smells ('You smelly old bugger, you! I'm going to stop giving you marrowfat peas!'). Sunday tea consisted of potatoes and vegetables left over from the lunch, fried up as 'bubble and squeak.'

Everyone sat down in the evening to watch 'Sunday Night at the London Palladium' and the Sunday play.

In fact, this was a fairly typical weekend in the Barker household. This was supposed to be the start of a whole new life for Mark, but nothing seemed to have changed.

On Monday, Mark went to the Labour Exchange to get his National Insurance card and register for work. But there were no jobs suitable for him. There were loads of jobs for factory workers, shop assistants, female typists and building workers of various skills, but no clerical positions for someone of Mark's age and (lack of) experience. He was not entitled to unemployment pay, so for the next few weeks, life for Mark was not that much different to being on his school holidays. He went to the Labour Exchange several times a week, without success. He found 2 more possible jobs in the local paper and duly sent off his applications, but the only reply he had was from the Water Board, who rejected him without an interview. No reason was given.

When he saw Janice in town with another boy, he felt very despondent. The boy was obviously much older than Mark and Janice wore make-up. This was further proof that she was out of his league, which he considered was probably Third Division South! However, he still managed to have a fantasy about her that night.

He didn't bother to go and see Podge again. He figured if Podge wanted to see him, he would come round. His friends from school all lived quite a distance away, so he knew he couldn't see them. He would just have to make do with his own company, but Mark had become used to this.

That Friday, in the local newspaper, he saw an advertisement for a clerk's position at the Electricity Board, which he optimistically applied for. It occurred to him that he was working his way through the Utilities on the Monopoly board.

This time, he did get an interview, so he donned his father's brown suit and borrowed one of his ties (he didn't think his school tie was appropriate) and he duly attended the interview. He was still a little nervous, but he settled down after a while. There were three interviewers and apparently twelve applicants, so the odds were against him, but it was a useful experience.

Again, when he received his rejection letter, there was no explanation of where he was falling down, so he had no idea what he ought to work on before his next interview. Being nervous was certainly not going to help him, but he knew how important it was to get a job, so he was bound to feel anxious. These people always kept him waiting for a while and that didn't help! A tailor-made suit would be a very big plus. But for that to happen, his father would have to go without cigarettes and beer for a few weeks, and his mother would have to forego her Bingo for a similar period, so it wasn't going to happen.

He told himself it was still too early to be getting despondent. He still had a few weeks left before he could say he hadn't fulfilled the objectives he had set himself a few weeks earlier.

CHAPTER 3

First Objective Met

During the last 2 weeks of August, things started looking a little more encouraging for Mark. First of all, he got his GCE results. He had achieved 6 passes – Maths (grade 1), English Language (grade 2), English Literature (grade 4), French (grade 5), Spanish (grade 5) and Physics-with-Chemistry (grade 6). Grade 6 was the lowest possible pass mark.

Now at least he could quote 6 'O' levels on any application form and this included Maths and English which seemed to be preferred by a lot of advertisers.

He also got another interview. He was in the Labour Exchange one day, talking to a member of staff, who said 'We've just had this job in. It's on the new industrial estate at West Sanford at a company called Gresham Installations.' That name rang a bell with Mark. 'They've just moved up from London as part of the overspill.'

'What's overspill?' asked Mark.

'It's a government initiative to relocate businesses out of London to various parts of the country. The businesses get subsidies to encourage them to relocate. The local authorities also get government assistance to build new council houses to encourage the employees to relocate as well. They've targeted several towns in Norfolk – Thetford, King's Lynn and Sanford are amongst them. All the new houses being built in North Sanford have been earmarked for overspill employees. Greshams are still in the process of relocating and their offices have only been open a few days. We've had quite a few vacancies from them this week – mostly in their factory.'

That's why it rang a bell with Mark. His cousin George had been working for them down in London for several months, in preparation for their move to Sanford. Mark mentioned this to the man in the Labour Exchange, who asked 'Would that be George Harris?'

'Yes, it is.'

'Well he's our contact at Greshams. Shall I give him a ring, now?'

'You might as well. Tell him I've just got 6 GCE passes. He probably doesn't know, yet. What is the job?'

'It's a Junior Costing and Wages Clerk, whatever that means. £350 per year.'

He dialled the number and asked for Mr George Harris.

'Hello Mr Harris. This is the Labour Exchange here. We have an applicant for your Junior Cost Clerk position. He's got all the right qualifications and he's with me at the moment. He's got 6 'O' levels, including Maths and English. What's more, you both know each other. It's your cousin Mark.' Mark could hear his cousin's voice, but couldn't quite make out what he was saying. 'Now?' asked the man. 'I'll find out.'

He turned to Mark. 'Can you get over there straight away?'

'Well, yes, but I haven't got my suit on. Tomorrow would be better.'

The man spoke to George again, then turned to Mark 'Your cousin says the building is still in a mess, so it would be better not to wear anything too smart. A lot of the staff are wearing jeans at the moment.'

'Well I can go straight away. It will take me about twenty minutes on my bike.'

And it was all arranged. Mark didn't have to wear his father's old brown suit and he didn't have time to get nervous. He liked George, so he didn't feel at all anxious about an interview with him. It didn't seem too long ago that George would have been seen walking around town in his Teddy Boy outfit sporting long sideburns and wearing drainpipe trousers and winkle-pickers. He was about thirty years old. After completing his national service in the RAF, he had worked for several years at a firm of Chartered Accountants in Sanford, while studying for his Accountancy qualification. This had been very good experience for learning his trade, but that particular company was notoriously bad at looking after their staff. So George had seized the opportunity to further his career at Greshams, who had offered very generous incentives to work in London until they were ready to move to Norfolk.

Mark was soon on his way. He just had to find the place. He rode over to the other side of town where the new industrial estate was taking shape, with many new buildings at various stages of construction. Mark remembered the area as a large farm and open countryside. It all looked completely different now and he had difficulty getting his bearings. He found the road he needed, but he couldn't see Gresham Installations anywhere. After riding up and down three times, he noticed just one office building without a sign. Outside, there was a man laying turf and he saw Mark looking lost. The man confirmed that this was the correct building and pointed Mark to the entrance.

Once inside the building, Mark was still struggling, because the reception had not been completed and was not manned. He asked one of the workmen if he knew how to find Mr. Harris. The workman was very blunt and said he didn't know anyone. Mark remembered the man in the Labour Exchange had said to go along to the end of the corridor, but nothing looked like a corridor or an office. There were workmen all over the place and wires dangling from the ceiling. Half of the floor was missing. He was starting to get anxious after all. He wandered through the incomplete building, wondering whether he should be there unaccompanied. Then he noticed four small offices at the far end, two either side of what could loosely be described as a corridor. As he got nearer, he could hear someone using an adding machine – entering figures and pulling a handle continuously. The first two offices he looked in were completely empty, but there, in the very last office sat George, bashing figures into the adding machine. Mark barely recognised him, as he no longer had his side-burns nor his extravagant quiff.

He spotted Mark and said, 'Mark. Come on in. Just give me a minute while I finish these figures.' Mark felt very uncomfortable standing there and was starting to feel nervous after all. Eventually all the figures were entered and the handle pulled for a last time. George tore off the tally roll and stapled it to a batch of papers.

'Right,' said George. ' If I hadn't just finished off that little bit of adding I would have had to have started again. I've only got one chair at the moment, so you take my seat.' George perched himself on the edge of his desk and looked down at Mark. From this position, Mark found it very difficult to look up and make eye contact. It was a very warm day and he was sweating from a combination of his bicycle endeavours and the anxiety of finding George. He rubbed his sweaty palms against his jeans. The sun was streaming through the large picture window on one side of the office. On the corridor side of the room was a frosted glass partition. George's desk was covered with invoices and petty cash vouchers all stapled together with tally rolls from the adding machine. There was no carpet and the telephone was precariously perched on top of a metal filing rack. Opposite Mark was a metal safe, with a very substantial looking handle. The safe was slightly ajar and Mark could see a cash box and several important looking packages.

'So you got 6 'O' levels, then. What subjects and grades did you get?'

Mark went through them and the interview continued in a very informal vein, which helped Mark relax a little, but he still felt awkward looking up to his cousin. George asked if Mark was intending to attend night school. Mark's response was non-committal, stating that any future education would depend on the route his career took. That seemed a very sensible answer without making promises he had no intention of keeping. He'd had enough of school.

George explained the role, which was to be split between two separate departments. The Wages Department was staffed by two girls (Mark's eyes lit up at this!) and was very busy at the start of the week, so they needed some help Monday to Wednesday, but they were very slack the rest of the week. So on Thursdays, Fridays and the occasional Saturday morning, the Junior would work in the Costing Department, and his duties would include costing up the wages, so the two roles were connected. This didn't really mean very much to Mark. George also explained the type of work carried out by Greshams. Again, it meant very little to Mark. George had mentioned the term 'demountable partitions', as though everyone knew what a 'demountable partition' was. Well Mark didn't, but he didn't want to show his ignorance.

George asked Mark if he had any questions. Mark was brought up to speak to adults only when spoken to, so although he knew he must now view himself as an adult, old habits meant he declined the chance to find out more. The interview was very one-sided with George doing most of the talking and Mark's answers to George's questions being very brief. George wound up the interview by saying he would be in touch when he had seen all the applicants, but they needed someone as soon as possible. The building would be fully operational in two to three weeks. 'Really?' said Mark, sounding very surprised.

'Yes, that's the beauty of demountable partitioning. Once you get the shell of the building established with a floor and a ceiling, you can erect these walls in a few days.' He patted one of the walls to illustrate what he meant. 'You can also take them down and reposition them quite quickly if you need to re-organise your office space.'

George showed Mark out of the building via the back fire escape, which saved him having to tiptoe around all the workmen, and then shook his hand. It seemed strange shaking his cousin's hand, but it made Mark feel really grown up.

George had found the interview very hard going. Mark was very quietly spoken and had very little to say for himself. George knew he was intelligent, as his GCE's indicated, but he feared for his ability to interact with others. George couldn't even be sure how much Mark wanted the job and he had gained no insight into Mark's career aspirations (hardly surprising since Mark didn't know either). Perhaps it was all a question of getting more experience in the adult world. Mark was still quite young.

But Mark was enthusiastic and he rushed home to tell his mother. He would actually be doing two separate jobs, so that was twice the experience. And this certainly seemed to be his best chance of getting a job. George was looking for a school leaver, who was good at figures, so Mark couldn't see why he shouldn't get the job. And he would be working with a couple of girls! Moreover, he wouldn't be judged on his father's old brown suit.

His mother said 'I'll see Aunt Louise at Bingo on Friday. I'll talk to her to see if she knows how you got on.' Aunt Louise was the second eldest of his mother's many sisters and she was George's mother.

When Mark's mother returned home from Bingo on Friday, Mark asked her if she'd remembered to talk to Aunt Louise. She had, and Aunt Louise already knew about Mark's interview, but she wasn't able to comment on his chances, but she knew no decision had been made, yet.

A week later, he got exactly the same response. And the week after that. So much for wanting someone quickly! There were no other opportunities on the horizon, so Mark felt he was running out of time to fulfil his first objective. He had attended another interview at an export company near the quay, but that didn't go very well.

He really wanted that job at Greshams. So what could he do about it? He could go round to see George, but that seemed a little presumptuous. As it happened, it would have been the right thing to do, but Mark didn't realise that.

Instead he went round to see Aunt Louise. He used to go and see her regularly when his bike was still brand new, so perhaps it was time he visited her again. She lived in the small village of Manningford, about five miles away on the edge of the Fens. Her cottage backed onto open countryside and from her back garden, you could see for miles, with barely a tree in sight. As Mark pulled into her road on his poor old bike, he could see the little block of four terraced bungalows built after the First World War. They were called Memorial Cottages and just in front of the dyke on the other side of the road was a small black marble memorial stone with the names of the villagers who fell during that war.

Aunt Louise was a mountain of a woman with a huge heart. As she opened the door to him, she bellowed, 'Why, it's the boy Mark! Come you on in, my beauty' in her lovely broad Norfolk accent. 'It's lovely to see you. Have you just cycled over? That's good of you to come and see your old auntie. I'll just put the kettle on and we'll have a little natter.' He sat himself down on Uncle Fred's huge soft armchair beside the range, which was always blazing away, even in the middle of summer. She carried on talking as she filled up the kettle from the tap outside in the yard, shuffled slowly across the room and placed the kettle on top of the range. 'I'm a poor old thing, these days. My old bones are giving me gyp, you know. It's a good job Fred has got a car to take me to Bingo, otherwise I'd never get out. The boy George fetches my shopping. Bless his old heart. Would you like a nice piece of fruitcake? Of course you will.'

'Well actually, I've just had my lunch, so I won't, thank you.' Aunt Louise made some lovely pastry, but her fruitcake was always very dry and Mark had a lot of difficulty swallowing it, especially as he didn't much like fruitcake, anyway. They had a good old natter about the old days; visits to Heacham and Thetford; and various members of the family. Mark couldn't help noticing that Aunt Louise's moustache had become even bushier than he remembered. She'd made the mistake of shaving it a few times when she was much younger and now it had turned into a thick dark growth that any macho man would be proud of. It matched the colour of her hair, which was jet black, with only the occasional white hair. She did most of the talking, but Mark didn't mind that. She always had a few yarns that were made even more interesting by her exaggerated body language and her use of the local vernacular. Her enormous bosom would shake as she laughed at almost anything.

She started a typical yarn by saying in a very low voice (as though someone else might be able to overhear) 'You remember the girl Spencer that lived down Marsh Lane. The girl Barnes, that was. A mouthy little mawther. Yes you do. She married Albie Spencer who went to school with your sister. Your mother would know her. Anyway, we all saw her at Bingo the other night, palling on with that Roger Clough, who's just got out of prison for breaking and entering. He's a nasty bit of stuff. Tell your mother, will you?' Mark hadn't got a clue who she was talking about, but it was still very amusing the way she put it across. Her yarns usually followed that style.

They got round to talking about how Sanford was changing, which led nicely on to the new industrial estate, the overspill and how well Greshams were treating George. 'He's going to get a company car soon, you know. It's a white one! When he was in London, Mr Gresham would take him out for a meal in a big swanky hotel and paid for everything. Everything! Even the taxis. They paid all his hotel bills and all his meals. Mind you, he's worked hard, the boy has. Bless him'. Then they discussed Mark's job application. Mark was able to make the point that he really wanted this job and was concerned that the way it was dragging indicated to him that George didn't want to give him the job.

'Well, I don't think that's the case. I know the offices are still in a mess and he wants to be sure he isn't showing any favouritism. I'll tell him how much you want the job, though.' Aunt Louise knew that George was hoping to find someone with the same qualifications as Mark, but able to show more enthusiasm. So far, the only people he'd seen were also quiet like Mark, but with fewer GCE's.

'Let's have another pot of tea.' This time, the cup of tea was served up with a huge slice of fruitcake, which seemed to take forever to eat. She always wanted to feed Mark. She said he looked like a matchstick with the wood scraped off. He knew he wouldn't leave without being given a few little items from her larder. Halfway through eating his cake, he said he'd have to be on his way and could she put the rest of it in a bag for later? She told him how lovely it was to see him and to come round again, soon. 'Wait a minute. I've got some lovely home-made jam, here. There's strawberry and raspberry. Here, have some plum as well. Would you like it in a bag? Your mother always liked my plum jam. Tell her I'll see her on Friday.' Then he was off on his bike again, wondering if calling on Aunt Louise was the right thing to have done.

His visit must have had an effect, because two days later, George came round to see him to tell him he'd got the job and could he start on the 1st of October? Mark said he could start straight away, but George felt it would be easier to calculate his salary if he started at the beginning of the month. The 1st of October was a Friday, which seemed an odd day of the week to start a new job, but then he'd have the weekend off to get over the shock of having to work for a living. So it was all agreed. George reminded Mark to bring his National Insurance card when he arrived.

So Mark had met his first and main objective – just in the timescale he'd set himself. He told his mother he needed a jacket. He could use his old charcoal grey trousers from his school days (this pair didn't have any patches), but he couldn't go to work in his school blazer, nor his father's brown suit. Her response was that now he had a job, he could buy his own clothes. And she was expecting him to give her some housekeeping money every week, just as his brother had to do. Mark pointed out that he would be paid monthly, so she wouldn't get anything until the end of October. After a very heated argument (the first of many over his housekeeping money), she agreed to pay the deposit on a new sports jacket, but he would have to pay the future monthly payments. His £350 per year wasn't going to go very far at this rate!

The next couple of weeks went very slowly, but at least Mark felt the pressure was off him now. He wanted to make the most of his last few precious days of freedom between school and work, but at the same time, he was anxious to start earning money, to buying new clothes and a new bike. And to meeting some girls.

He had seen how his brother had developed some kind of social life since leaving school. Brian was now taking driving lessons. But he still didn't seem to be having any luck with girls. Like Mark, he also wore glasses, which seemed to Mark to limit your chances of getting an attractive girl. But girls wore glasses, too. Perhaps if Janice had worn glasses, things might have turned out differently. It wouldn't matter to Mark if a girl wore glasses and had legs like those!

It was the start of the football season and for the first time ever, Mark wasn't playing at all. Perhaps he would never play again. He wasn't too bothered about not playing cricket, but never to play football again? Perhaps he ought to add that to his list of objectives, especially as he had now reduced the list by one.

CHAPTER 4

First Day at Work

And so the great day came. Mark's first day at work. He arrived at 8.50 and asked at reception for Mr. Harris. There were still a few workmen around, but the building looked much more like a working office block. The reception was very smart and was enhanced by the receptionist, who was very elegant. She had red hair and the most welcoming smile. She noticed Mark was holding his National Insurance card and asked 'Are you starting work here, today?' Mark gave a nervous nod.

'Friday's a funny day to start, isn't it?' asked the receptionist.

'Well, George wanted me to start on the first of the month.' She noticed he had said 'George', rather than 'Mr Harris', but said nothing. She always called him Mr. Harris, because he was in quite a senior position. All the directors at Greshams were also addressed by the staff as 'Mr.'

'I'm Ellie,' she said. 'Mr Harris isn't in, yet. So take a seat. Is that your bike outside the door?'

'Yes.'

'You'd better move it round the side of the building. That's where Mr. Hopkins parks his car. He's the Managing Director and has a slight disability, so that front area has to be reserved for him.

'I'm sorry, said Mark, going red, 'I didn't realise.'

'Don't worry about it', said Ellie, realising his discomfort. 'He often doesn't arrive till 9.30. He has to take his children to school.' Nevertheless, Mark felt very embarrassed about making such a mistake. At least he found out before Mr. Hopkins arrived. How embarrassing would that have been?

After moving his bike, Mark returned to take a seat opposite Ellie, with his back towards the main entrance. He sank into the plush leather. As he sat there, he was aware that all the staff looked at him as they came in. They all said 'Morning, Ellie' and then looked across at him, quite deliberately, but he didn't look back. Most of them had London accents, but Ellie didn't. She had just the merest hint of the Norfolk burr. As well as manning the reception, she also answered the switchboard. She had a delightful telephone voice.

'Good morning. Gresham Installations. Yes, of course. I'll just put you through. Hello, Ian. I have Tom Askew from the London office for you. Thank you.' In a very short space of time, she answered three other 'phone calls, which she handled with the same degree of confidence and professionalism. Mark knew he couldn't cope with her job. He had very little experience of using the telephone and would be very uncomfortable at meeting and greeting complete strangers.

By ten minutes past nine, all the staff seemed to have arrived, except George and Mr. Hopkins.

'He is expecting you, isn't he?' asked Ellie.

'Yes. Mind you, it was two or three weeks ago when we agreed my start date. I hope he hasn't forgotten.'

'Where are you going to be working?'

'Wages and Costing.'

'That's two separate departments.'

'Yes, I'm going to spend half the week in Wages and half the week in Costing.'

'Do you know where you should be today?'

'I think it's Costing, today.'

'I could talk to Bob, if you like? He's the Cost Accountant.'

'I don't know,' replied Mark, shrugging his shoulders. He didn't know what was right and proper.

'Let me have a word with him.' She dialled Bob's extension. 'Bob, do you know if Mr. Harris is due in today? I've got your new chap in reception. All right, then'

She turned to Mark and said 'Bob said Mr. Harris is expecting you, because he was talking to Bob about you yesterday. So we'll leave it a few more minutes. He may have got stuck in traffic. He often gives Margaret a lift and she's not in, yet, either.'

A few minutes later, George did appear with a quite elderly lady who Mark decided must be Margaret.

'Morning, Mark,' he said quite gruffly. 'Just hang on there a few minutes, will you? I'll come and sort you out in a minute. Morning, Ellie.'

Mark was still sitting there ten minutes later when he heard Ellie 'phoning someone to ask them to come and stand in for her for a few minutes. A short squat woman appeared and took Ellie's place on Reception. She took a call. She had a very thick London accent. 'Mr.

Bland? Do you know where 'e works, love? I can't see 'im on the list. 'Ang on a min'te.' She pushed a plug in. 'Derek? It's Marge on Reception. 'Ave you got a Mr. Bland workin' with you? 'E's in Buyin'? I wish someone would tell us. 'E's not on the list. O.K.' She pulled out one plug and pushed in another. 'Ello. Yes, I think I've farn' 'im. Just 'old on.' More pushing of plugs. 'Mr. Bland? I 'ave a call for ya. No, I didn't ask who it is. Dya wan' me to fine' art? Here 'e is, then'

Mark didn't think Ellie's job would be under threat from Marge. Ellie returned and thanked her. Ellie looked even more elegant standing up. She was wearing a tight knee length turquoise skirt, high heel shoes and she had long slender legs. She must have been nearly as tall as Mark and he was six feet. Marge was about five feet three inches. She had thick ankles and wore flat shoes. She wore a tight beige sweater that showed off her figure, but Mark didn't think she should have bothered. She had large saggy breasts that seem to point sideways and she had round shoulders. Mark wasn't very good at estimating ages, but he thought Ellie was probably in her late twenties and Marge would be about thirty-five. In actual fact they were both twenty-six years old.

Eventually George re-appeared and told Mark to follow him down to his office. He seemed very stressed and had a face like thunder. As they walked down the now completed corridor towards George's office, George explained that Margaret wasn't ready when he went to pick her up and then three people had called into his office as soon as he arrived.

Once inside George's office, Mark handed him his National Insurance card. 'Can I have your bank details?' George asked.

'I haven't got a bank account.'

'Well, you'll need to open one.' It sounded like an order. 'I'll pay you by cheque, this month.'

'Can't I have cash? I've got no way of cashing a cheque.' His parents had never had a bank account, so he didn't know what to do with a cheque.

George looked at him for a moment, obviously not pleased. 'I'll get some extra petty cash in, but you will have to sort out an account, soon. I hear there's a small Midland Bank opening up on the estate soon. That will be handy. If you need a sub to keep you going until the end of the month, let me know.' Mark didn't know what a 'sub' was. He was seeing a side of George he'd never seen before. He'd previously only seen him in family circles, when he was always very jovial. After all, this was the chap he'd seen singing along to Little Richard and Jerry Lee Lewis.

'Anyway, you'll be working with Bob Walsh today in Costing, but we'll have a chat with the girls in Wages first.' Mark was filled with trepidation at the thought of meeting the girls for the first time. The 'girls' were working two doors down from George's office and as Mark entered their room, he realised that the term 'girls' had been used very loosely. The one on the left was enormous. She was about forty years old and obviously didn't care much for her appearance. Her long dark hair probably hadn't been brushed that day. Under the desk, her skirt had risen up way above her knees and her huge thighs were wide apart. It was not a pretty sight. She would certainly not win any beauty contest. She was introduced as Josie and was the senior of the two women. She had a cigarette burning in an ashtray that was already overflowing, even though it wasn't yet ten o'clock.

Penny was blonde, better looking, of neater appearance, late twenties, and about half the size of Josie, but still a little overweight.

'This is Mark,' said George. 'Your new junior.' There were polite 'hellos' all round. 'He's going to spend today with Bob and then join you Monday to Wednesday next week. That's what we agreed, right?'

'Mr Harris. You know the pressure we're under in here on Mondays, Tuesdays and Wednesdays. We'll be too busy to show him the ropes,' barked Josie. 'It would make more sense if he came in here on a Thursday and Friday, when we're just a little bit quieter.' She emphasised the 'little bit'. George knew they were very quiet at the end of the week. Josie had originally pushed for an experienced payroll clerk full time, but George knew how lazy she was. He also knew how badly she reacted to the pressure of the job. In any case, Bob needed some help as well, so he had decided to employ one junior and then evaluate the situation after a while.

Just then, Bob was passing. So George called him in. 'Bob. Come and join us for a minute. This is Mark.' Bob shook Mark's hand warmly and welcomed him to Greshams. 'We were just discussing where Mark is going to be working.' Bob looked surprised. 'The girls don't want him until they've had time to show him the ropes. How about if you have him from now until next Thursday, when he'll come in here, until the Thursday after? On that Thursday, we'll carry on with the pattern we *all* originally agreed.' He emphasised the "all" in a sarcastic tone.

They carried on discussing the pro's and con's of all this, while Mark just stood there, not contributing anything. He decided that there was no love lost between George and Josie, but Bob was an outgoing and very amenable chap who was only too willing to accommodate everyone's wishes. Penny suggested Mark could join them that day, but Josie gave half a dozen reasons why this was not practical, so Penny backed down. All the time, Mark could see that George's patience was wearing thin.

'Right then,' said George, deciding it was time to end the discussion. 'You go with Bob, then, Mark. I've got work to do. I'll see you later.' He stormed out. Josie slammed a drawer shut and uttered a bad tempered sigh.

'Welcome to the 'ell 'ole, Mark!' said Penny. 'It's not as bad as it seems, is it Bob?'

'Nah! You'll be all right, mate.' Bob was another Londoner. He was a bit older than George, about five foot six, medium build and wearing a green sports jacket, white shirt with a red and white striped tie. He turned to Penny and said, 'A woman goes into a dentists and said "I keep thinking I'm a moth."

The dentist said, "You need a psychiatrist, not a dentist."

"Yes, but your light was on!"

Penny giggled. It was obvious to Mark that Penny liked Bob. She looked across to Josie who was not even smiling. 'Oh, come on, Josie. Have a larf.'

'I don't think this is funny, Penny. I told Mr. Harris we needed someone experienced. And we've got a school leaver who needs to be shown everything. I don't know how we're going to do it. This is nothing against you, Mark!'

Obviously not. He felt as welcome as a cat in a dog kennel. He was not looking forward to working in the 'Hell hole.'

'Come on Marky boy,' said Bob, patting him on the shoulder. 'I've got lots of things you can do. We'll see you girls later. Cheers!'

Penny said 'Cheers!' back. Then added 'Welcome aboard, Mark.'

Bob's office was just next door. 'Let's start with a cup of coffee, shall we? Do you know where the coffee machine is, yet?'

'No.' said Mark, with no further elaboration.

Bob looked at him and thought he sounded a little abrupt, but continued, 'Right. It costs tuppence and it only takes pennies, so you'll need to keep a stock of pennies. I've got some for now,' he said opening his top drawer and rattling a small box of loose change. The coffee machine was upstairs in a little rest room, which was thick with smoke. They sat down in the rest room. Bob offered Mark a cigarette, which was declined. He then lit up himself and tried to break the ice with Mark. It was hard work. Mark was still unsure of himself and felt uncomfortable in these strange surroundings. He sipped his coffee. It tasted revolting.

'What interests or hobbies do you have, mate?' asked Bob, trying to make Mark relax.

'I like listening to records – mostly Soul and R & B. I like playing football and cricket, but I haven't done any of that since leaving school.' Mark's response was all in a monotone and he blushed at the effort of having to speak to an adult.

'There used to be a factory football team when we were down in Balham, so they may start a new team, once they all get settled here. What position do you play?'

'I played in goal for my House. But was right-half for the school team. Sometimes inside-right.'

Bob realised he was going to have to do most of talking, so he continued, 'I'll mention your name to Woody. He works in the Wood Machine room in the factory. I know he played in the factory team, before. There's also talk of starting up a Sports and Social Club. Mr. Gresham has indicated that he would make some funds available. With so many people being new to the area, he thought it was important for morale. I've been asked to join a committee. We'll have some dinner dances, perhaps put up a table tennis table in the canteen. It's even been suggested that we have a special family day in the summer, when some of the London mob come and play cricket and tennis for an annual cup.'

'That sounds good,' said Mark. He thought it might help him make some new friends, but there probably wouldn't be too many people of his age. 'Are there any other people of my age at Greshams?' What he really meant was 'Are there any nice girls working here.'

'Not too many. There's a new trainee draughtsman, started a week ago. There's an apprentice joiner came up from London. His father is one of the site foremen. There's a few young girls in the typing pool. Don't know much about them. They keep themselves to themselves. Do you have a girlfriend?'

'Not at the moment.' His thoughts went to Janice. If only he could have boasted of her as his girlfriend.

'Anyway,' said Bob, 'let's get you started on some work.' They stood up and started walking toward the stairs. Bob continued talking. 'I'll take you round the building a bit later and you can meet a few more people. I'm sure it's all a bit daunting at the moment.' That was an understatement.

'Our function is to provide costs for all the materials and the labour that goes in to making the products, as well as the cost of erecting them on site. This helps the Estimators to get the sums right. At any given time, there are probably about twenty to thirty sites on the go. The smallest may only have a few small partition walls, right up to the largest office blocks you can imagine.'

The partitions are made by a system of specially designed anodised aluminium posts into which we slot the panels. These panels can be made of a variety of materials, from something like chipboard at the lower end, right up to really solid fireproof panels. All covered by a special PVC covering that is made under licence exclusively for us. Or some of the walls may be glazed or half-glazed, as our offices are. You may have noticed.'

Mark kept nodding or saying 'Right' or 'O.K.'

'Some of the posts are hollow, so light switches or electrical sockets can be accommodated. Then of course, some of them are designed to take door hinges. These things are all cut to size in the factory over the way.' At that point, they had reached the stair landing, where there was a large window. He pointed out of the window to the factory.' I'll take you for a walk round there later. And then everything gets loaded onto our own fleet of lorries and despatched to site. Once on site, the actual erection is quite speedy.' At school, the word 'erection' would have resulted in titters all round, but Mark decided to be mature about it, now.

Just then, they passed through reception again and the lovely Ellie. She smiled at them both and said 'Hello.'

'Hello darlin'.' Said Bob. 'When are you going to run away with me?'

'I'll ask my hubby when he thinks it might be convenient,' she said.

'I'll take that as a 'no', then.'

'I hope this dirty old man isn't leading you astray, Mark,' she said.

'Not yet. But there's plenty of time.' Mark was pleased with his reply and it got a smile from Ellie.

That made two ladies (Penny and Ellie) who had gone out of their way to be friendly to him and make him feel welcome.

They carried on towards Bob's office. Mark was now noticing the partitioning along the corridor. There seemed to be a strange mixture of glazed, half-glazed and solid partitions. He mentioned this to Bob. 'That's so that if the Salesmen bring customers round, they can show some different options, but I think it just looks a mess. Upstairs, the Drawing Office is mostly open plan and that looks a lot better. I'll take you up there, later.'

They were now back in their office. 'This will be where you sit, Mark.' Mark looked at his 'desk'. It was actually a shelf built into a recess next to the door and facing a frosted glass partition. The shelf was covered in black vinyl and didn't even provide a smooth writing surface. Bob had a proper desk with drawers. 'I've got to disappear for about half an hour. What I'd like you to do is to sort these invoices into alphabetical order of customer site. These are all invoices for site materials and they are supposed to quote either the site number or the site name. Here's a list of site numbers for you to tie them all up. If you can't find either a name or a number, put them to one side and I'll show you later how we get that info. Is that all right? Cheers, mate.'

Mark suddenly felt deflated. His first task was to sit down at a shelf for a desk and sort some invoices into alphabetical order. Do you really need 6 GCE's for this?

And why does everyone keep saying 'Cheers?' Mark thought you said that when you were drinking someone's health. Was this a Londoner thing?

His little task took him about ten minutes. About a third of the invoices did not have a site name or a site number anywhere on them. Mark recognised some of the site names – BOAC, New Scotland Yard, several large insurance companies and Rolls Royce. It appeared that Greshams were not a tin-pot little organisation. They had some very prestigious customers.

The telephone rang. Was he supposed to answer it? He left it for a little while. Then as it continued ringing, he got up and looked at it. That didn't help. Eventually he picked it up and tentatively mumbled 'Hello.'

A man's voice asked if Bob was there. 'No,' answered Mark.

'Do you know where he is?'

'No.'

'Don't be so abrupt! We all have pressure to deal with. That's no reason why you can't answer the 'phone politely! Who am I talking to?'

'It's Mark. I'm new, here.'

'Just get Bob to 'phone Ted, will you?'

'Okay.'

Oh dear! What was all that about? Mark had just answered the questions he had been asked. He didn't realise he was being abrupt. Ted sounded like someone really important.

A few minutes later, Ted came storming into the office. He was a dark-haired thickset chap, with a face that didn't look like it had ever smiled. 'Are you Mark?'

'Yes.'

'Can you just make sure Bob sees this note I've left on his desk? It's very important. And please be a little more pleasant on the 'phone, will you? Okay?'

'Yes, okay.'

'Cheers!'

Mark sat there looking at the glass partition. He didn't know what to do with himself. He sat there for fifteen minutes doing nothing. He had a swivel chair. He'd never sat in a swivel chair before. So he amused himself by twizzling round. Then back again. Then he got his foot wrapped round the leg of the chair and nearly toppled over.

George came in and saw him sat there doing nothing. 'Where's Bob?' he asked.

'I don't know. He said he'd be about half an hour.'

'Haven't you got any work to do?'

'I did have but I've finished.' George pulled a disapproving face and then walked out without saying anything else.

What was Mark supposed to do? He'd done the job he was asked to do. He didn't know what other tasks he could be expected to perform. Things were not going well and Mark was taking it all to heart.

George reappeared with a wire filing tray, containing some invoices. 'File these in alphabetical order of supplier, will you?' and then left him to it, without saying another word. Invoices were obviously very important around here. Mark wondered if he would be asked to sort the same batch into site order in a day or so.

He quickly re-organised the tray of invoices and double-checked them. He wasn't sure where to place '3M'. He didn't realise that George just wanted to keep him occupied. Mark thought this might be an important task and he wanted to impress George with his speed and accuracy. So as soon as he had finished, he rushed down to George's office and as he walked through the door, he said 'George. I've done that but I wasn't sure...' George pushed the tray away with Mark on the end of it. Mark hadn't noticed that George was talking to someone important-looking. George glowered at Mark, but said nothing. 'Sorry,' said Mark and made his exit.

Now what had he done? He just sat at his 'desk' looking at the glass partition again.

After a few more minutes, George re-appeared. 'I'm sorry,' said Mark. 'I didn't realise you had someone with you.'

'That was Mr. Gresham. If you see me talking to him, don't come in. The same goes for Mr. Hopkins. I take it you've finished the invoices?'

'Yes. I wasn't sure whether to file '3M' under 'T' for three or put it at the end.'

'It doesn't matter,' said George picking up the tray. 'So you still haven't got any work to do?'

'No. I don't know what I'm supposed to do, yet.' Mark sounded genuinely concerned about it, but even though the filing was not at all important, at least George knew he was keen to impress.

'Well, I'm sure Bob will be back, soon.'

And he was. 'Have you done that, mate?' he asked.

'Yes. There's a few here that didn't have a site name or a site number on them.'

'We'll sort those out later. The next thing is to get you to enter these invoices into the Cost Ledger. But first, I fancy a bun and a cup of tea. Let's go over to the Works Canteen and I'll show you round the factory at the same time.'

Mark remembered the note from Ted and told Bob about it. 'It can wait,' said Bob.

'But Ted said it was important.'

'It may be important to Ted, but it's not important to me. He always wants things done in a hurry. That's what he's like, but it's not important and neither is Ted. Ted's a difficult person to ignore, but it's worth making the effort!'

Mark smiled and felt relieved he hadn't offended someone important, but he would have to be more careful about answering the 'phone in future. Next time, it might be someone important.

So off they went to the Factory. They visited the Joiners' Shop, the Wood Machine Shop and the Metal Shop. In the Metal Shop, Mark observed that there were a few women manning some of the machines.

Bob stopped next to one of them and said 'Hello Jenny. How's things?'

'Busy as usual. I've got to get this batch out by lunchtime.' She was working a plastic injection machine, pouring plastic pellets into a mould and then pulling down on a handle, which she held for a few seconds. She emptied the mould into a box on the floor. Then she held down the handle and emptied the mould again. She was a tiny woman, with dark hair and lots of make-up. She wore a full-length navy blue coat-style overall, but perched on a small stool, she was revealing a few inches of slim but short thigh.

'Who's this, then?' she asked looking round at Mark.

'This is Mark. He's joined us today.'

'If you want me to show him what's what, bring him round here,' she said with a broad grin. 'I'll gladly take him under my wing.'

'Mark, I think you've just pulled,' said Bob. 'She's a married woman, but you won't mind that, will you?

'That depends how big her husband is,' said Mark, blushing.

'Your ol' man's only a little chap, isn't he, Jenny?'

'Yeah. Little all over,' she laughed. 'See you 'round, Mark,' she added as they moved away. She was local. That was the first time that someone had ever flirted with Mark. Although he didn't fancy her and he knew she was just a married woman having a bit of fun, he still enjoyed the experience, despite feeling embarrassed by it all.

As they moved out of the Metal Shop, Bob pointed out that the women only did the lightweight work, such as drilling and injection moulding. The men did the heavy work such as operating the saws or the routers, where they machined out the slots in the aluminium posts for hinges or door locks.

Mark asked how many people worked at Greshams.

'About half of them,' replied Bob.

'Right,' said Mark. Then he realised Bob's little joke and tried to laugh out of politeness, but his efforts just made the joke fall flat.

They entered the canteen. The only people in the canteen were the staff – 3 ladies behind a counter, all wearing white overalls and hats. 'Are you serving yet, Betty?' Bob asked the nearest lady.

'Yes, What would you like?'

'Do you want a tea, Mark?'

Mark said 'Yes, please.'

Bob took a bread roll from a glass cabinet and said 'Help yourself if you want anything, mate.' Mark picked up a ham roll on a plate, sat down and started eating it. He was aware that everyone was staring at him. He didn't know why. Bob took the teas and paid for everything. He then placed Mark's tea on the table in front of him. 'Nice roll, is it?' he asked.

'It's fine, thank you.' Mark was half way through it when he realised that food and drink were not free and Bob had just inadvertently bought him a cup of tea and a roll. Well, he had said 'Help yourself, mate.' So he did. He wondered if he should offer to pay for them. But he didn't have any money on him. He'd brought a packed lunch and didn't really need the roll at all. By then, he was feeling totally embarrassed, not helped by the fact that everyone kept staring at him.

This was not a good day. He'd parked his bike in the wrong place; upset Josie by being a school leaver; annoyed Ted by being too abrupt on the 'phone; angered George by not looking busy, as well as not having a bank account; been embarrassed by a flirty married woman; and now inadvertently conned Bob into buying him a bread roll.

What else did this day have in store for him?

As it happened, the rest of the day went off a little smoother. After lunch, which Mark spent alone in the office, Bob took him round the rest of the office building, where he found out how to get the information that was missing from the invoices. This involved asking Ted and his colleagues in the Buying Office, who had raised the original Purchase Orders, to match the invoice with the Purchase Order. This time Ted was very polite and helpful. In fact, he seemed like a very nice chap, although he still didn't look as though he'd ever smiled in his life. Mark also met his boss, the Chief Buyer, whose name was Barney Briggs – an energetic man, short and slim, wearing a dark pinstriped suit with a light grey waistcoat. He had a small dark pencil moustache. He would not have looked out of place playing the part of a cockney spiv in an Ealing comedy. His conversation was peppered with the phrase 'All right, my son?'

When he was introduced to Mark, he asked 'Are you the young chap who got our Ted in a lather? It's easily done, my ol' son. Don't take any notice of 'im. 'Is bark's worse than 'is bite.'

Around the corner, Bob poked his head into one medium sized room and said 'This is the Typing Pool.' All the typists looked up and Bob addressed the lady at the front, saying 'It's all right, Gail. I'm just showing our new lad round. This is Mark.'

'Hi, Mark,' she said.

'Hello,' replied Mark and blushed. Then he continued to look at his feet. He'd never seen a typing pool before. He was aware that there were six girls, who quickly returned to their work after giving Mark a quick look over. Being a shy sensitive lad, Mark thought he must have disappointed them. He didn't actually look at any of them, even though he really wanted to see if there were any that he could imagine as a possible girlfriend.

'Haven't you got a joke for us, today, Bob?' asked Gail.

Bob repeated his dentist joke and it got a few laughs and a couple of groans.

'What about, Mark? Do you tell jokes?'

'What has a bottom at the top?' asked Mark.

'We don't know,' came the reply.

'A leg!'

'Oh very good,' said Gail, without actually laughing. 'Did you learn that one at school? You and Bob are going to be a great double act. I'll have to come and visit you both in your little den when I need cheering up'. Mark wasn't sure whether that was sarcasm or not. It probably was.

As they walked back down the stairs, Bob said, 'You want to watch Gail. She's a real man-eater. She'll have you for dinner, mate. She's only been with us a few months and she's already had the Works Manager and one of the Foremen that I know of! You should be all right, though. She seems to prefer married men.'

There was a visitor sitting in reception as they passed through, so they only got a friendly 'Hello' from Ellie.

Back at the office, Bob showed Mark how to record the materials cost in the Costing Ledger. When Mark had done that, Bob introduced him to Margaret who wanted the invoices back now that they had finished with them. Margaret worked on her own in the Accounts office next to George. She looked after the petty cash when it wasn't in George's safe, so Bob pointed out that she could often be a useful source of change for the coffee machine.

This prompted Bob to ask Mark to fetch some coffee. And indeed, whenever Bob wanted a coffee, that was Mark's job. Mark apologised for not having any money to pay his way. Bob asked if needed a sub. 'What's a sub?' Mark asked.

'It's an advance on your pay. Any sub you have will be deducted at the

end of the month when you get paid. Go see George if you want one.'
Mark noticed he said 'George' and not 'Mr. Harris.' Why did some people
use his first name and some use 'Mr?'

A steady stream of visitors came to see Bob during the day. Some
were introduced to Mark, some weren't. Those that Mark recognised as
Londoners always seemed to be complaining about something. Most of
them had moved into the new housing estate and there were problems
with carpets, kitchen units, plumbing, damp, lack of telephones and the
state of the roads, which were still being constructed. At first, Mark just
regarded them as a bunch of moaners, but after due consideration, he
realised it must be difficult to relocate en masse to a new town, where the
only friends they see are work colleagues.

Penny was one of the visitors. She didn't seem to moan as much as
the others. There was definitely some kind of mutual affection between
Penny and Bob, but they both mentioned their respective spouses, so
Mark knew they were both married. Penny asked Bob if he had any more
jokes. 'Mark's got one. Tell Penny your joke, mate.'

Mark repeated his 'bottom' joke. Penny gave a very short but genuine
laugh. 'Oh, very good,' she said. 'We need a comedian in that office, next
door.' The look on her face indicated to Mark that she was not too fond
of Josie.

Mark thought he might like working with Penny, but wasn't looking
forward to working with Josie.

Bob had to leave at four o'clock that day, as he was going 'home' for
the weekend.

Mark said he thought that Bob lived on the new estate. He did, but
going 'home' meant going back to London to be with friends and family.
A lot of the Gresham employees went 'home' at the weekend and some
shared lifts.

Mark asked if he was required to work on Saturday. 'Not this week,
mate. We'll work out a rota sometime' said Bob.

Before Bob left, he showed Mark a 'Take-off'. This was a 5-part
document that was raised by the 'Take-off' Department. The five parts
were on NCR paper, which meant they acted like carbon copies without
the need to use messy carbon paper. Each of the five parts was a different
colour and went to a different department. The Costing Department's
copy was blue. A 'Take-off' contained details of the materials that had
been extracted from the site drawings. One copy went to the Buyers so

they could order the materials. One copy went to the Works so they could prepare the necessary materials at the appropriate time. One copy went to Despatch, who co-ordinated the delivery to reach site at the right time. And one copy was retained by the 'Take-off' Department. Some of the staff in the 'Take-off' department were joiners who had spent time on site erecting the partitions.

There was a huge backlog of 'Take-offs' to be costed and at the moment, Bob had several piles awaiting attention. But first, they needed filing. Guess whose job that was? Mark spent the rest of the day filing these in a large metal filing cabinet. Being the bottom copy, the writing on the blue copy was very faint. This did not help Mark's task. Many of the sites did not have files, so he left any 'take-offs' for these to one side to sort out with Bob on Monday. By the end of the day, he had several minor cuts on his fingers from the sharp metal edges on the files and his feet were aching from standing up so long. And yet again, he'd been given a task to perform, which he was unable to complete through no fault of his.

At five o'clock, Mark could see and hear movement outside his office, so he tidied up his work and made for the front entrance. Marge was back on Reception, so because he hadn't yet been introduced, Mark ignored her as he left the building. While pedalling down the road, he passed three young factory girls cycling in the opposite direction, possibly cleaners or shift workers, he thought. They were laughing and one of them called to Mark, 'Hello Handsome. My mate fancies you.' He put his head down and ignored them. As Mark didn't have a very high opinion of his looks, he decided they were just being cruel and he could do without that after the day he had just experienced.

There was lots of traffic trying to exit the estate as he threaded his way through some of the cars at the junction. And then he was out onto the main road and on his way home. He contemplated his first day at work and all the little mistakes he'd made. He didn't like making mistakes and he wanted to be popular, but some of his actions today would not have helped his cause.

It would have been nice to share his troubles with a friend, but he had now lost touch with his friends from school. He had given up on Podge who had made no effort to contact Mark. He suddenly felt very lonely. He hoped in the weeks to come that he might make friends with some of the people at Greshams. There was the possibility of football.

And what about Penny? Can you have a friendship with a married woman?

On Monday, he would go and ask George for a sub. Then he could make a start on fulfilling some more of his objectives. He would get some new clothes and a new bike. He would have to buy things on the 'never-never' to start with.

CHAPTER 5

Blisters and Thighs

Monday seemed to come round all too quickly

Ellie was busy on the 'phone as Mark walked through the Reception area, but she gave him a little wave and a nice smile. He had arrived well before Bob, so he carried on with his filing.

When Bob did arrive, he greeted Mark very warmly and asked him about his weekend and they both discussed their weekend activities, which in Mark's case weren't very much, but he had prepared a little joke for Bob. He said 'I watched "Brigadoon" on television yesterday afternoon. I didn't want to miss that. They only show it once every one hundred years!'

'Oh, good one, Mark' said Bob, as he gave a little chuckle.

Mark mentioned the 'Take-off's' that didn't have a file. 'They're probably new sites, so we need to start some new files. If you go and see Anne in Filing, she looks after all the stationery. She can give you some new files. Get some of those file tabs as well, will you? She's in the room next to the coffee machine. While you're there, get yourself kitted out with any other stationery you need – pens, pads, etc.'

He hadn't met Anne yet and felt a bit nervous about the prospect. He needn't have worried. He found Anne in the Filing room. She was about twenty years old, medium height and slim with pink glasses. She had ginger hair that was tightly permed and she gave Mark a very friendly smile as he entered her room. 'Are you Anne?' he asked.

'That's me.'

'I was told that you could supply me with a few items of stationery?'

'I certainly can. What do you need?'

Her warm response made Mark feel more comfortable. He told her what he needed and as she collected his items from the stationery cupboard, she asked 'You're new here, aren't you?'

'Yes. I joined on Friday. I'm working with Bob Walsh.'

'I haven't been here that long, myself. I suppose it's too early to ask if you're enjoying it?'

'Well it all seems a bit boring and menial, so far. I suppose you have to expect that if you're a junior. So far all I've done is filing and fetching coffee.'

'Well, my job title is Filing Clerk, so I have to expect all that.' Mark wondered if he had offended her by insinuating that filing was menial, but she carried on 'I find the people very friendly, on the whole. Although I have to say, the Londoners always seem to be complaining.'

'Yes, I noticed that. I decided it must be difficult for them to be uprooted from a place like London and be relocated to a small Norfolk town like Sanford. All their friends and family are probably still in the London area. They've been used to certain amenities, which they're not going to find up here.'

'Whereabouts do you live?' she asked. Mark told her. 'Oh, that's not too far from me. I live at Kensington Drive. Just off Downham Road. How do you get to work?'

'On my old bike.'

'Me, too. Although I'm not looking forward to doing it in the winter. My boyfriend's got a car and he works on this estate. But he has to leave a lot earlier than me in the morning and he finishes earlier, as well.'

'Can't you work the same hours as him?'

'I did ask my boss. That's Paul O'Connor. Do you know him?' Mark shook his head. 'He's a Contracts Manager. He insists I'm here till five o'clock each night.'

Mark gathered up his new stationery and said he'd have to be getting back before Bob wants his coffee.

'I'll see you around then. I hope you enjoy working here,' she added.

Mark had enjoyed meeting Anne. She was pleasant company and he felt relaxed in her presence. She was very down-to-earth. She had a boyfriend, but that didn't matter, because Mark didn't really find her sexually attractive – just nice to be with.

Over the next few weeks, he had many opportunities to see Anne. If he felt like a break, he would discover another item of stationery that he needed. Sometimes, he saw her on the way to work or on the way home and they chatted quite freely. With some girls he felt a little nervous, but with Anne, he was totally relaxed. He liked Anne a lot, but he couldn't help still wishing that it was Janice he was with. But he was gaining a little more experience of the opposite sex – not quite the experience he would hope for, but it was a start.

When Mark returned to his office, Bob said 'Well done, mate. Would you like to fetch some coffee before you get too comfortable?' This time Mark had some change for the machine, so after leaving some of it in Bob's little pot, he trudged off upstairs again.

During the next few days, he was shown how to record the labour costs from the timesheets and how to cost up a series of 'Take-off's'. He also had to do lots of filing and fetch lots of coffee.

On the Tuesday, Mark approached George for a ten-pound sub, which was duly granted. He rode into town that lunchtime and bought himself a raincoat on 'HP'. He decided that on Saturday, he would catch the bus into town to get himself a new bike.

Then the day he had been dreading came around. It was Thursday and the day he was due to start work in the Wages department. Although he was dreading it, he told himself that at least it couldn't possibly be as boring as the work he had been doing.

When he arrived at work, Penny was already there, but Josie hadn't yet turned up. He wheeled in his chair from next door and planted his belongings on the shelf that was to serve as his desk. It had been decided that Penny would be showing the ropes to Mark, so she invited him to sit next to her, which was very uncomfortable, because there was nowhere to put his legs.

She described the weekly routine. On Mondays, the timesheets would be received in the post from all the building sites. The factory foremen would also bring along the clockcards for their workers. Both the timesheets and the clockcards had to be sorted into alphabetical order of surname. Mark guessed whose job that would become.

Then the employee's wages would be calculated by taking the hours worked, adding the appropriate overtime premium where applicable and multiplying all this by the employee's hourly rate. This would be written at the bottom of the timesheet or clockcard. Of course, in 1965, there was no such thing as a pocket calculator, so they would each use a ready reckoner. This was a large volume containing a page for each possible monetary value from a halfpenny up to nineteen shillings and eleven pence three farthings. This task normally took all of Monday morning and most of Monday afternoon.

Travelling expenses would also have to be recorded. For employees living and working in the Greater London area, this was derived from measuring the distance from their home address to their place of work. This was facilitated by a large map mounted on the wall, with a large wooden ruler that had cash amounts marked on it, corresponding to the mileage. Penny demonstrated how to use this.

Once the timesheets had been actioned, the Wages staff had to enter these figures onto the payroll sheet, calculate Income Tax and Graduated Pension. National Insurance, in the sixties, was a flat rate, rather than a percentage of your pay, as it later became. Also on the payroll sheet, they would enter expenses, make any other deductions, such as 'subs' and record the Holiday stamp. This whole process was known as a 'Gross-to-Net'. Penny demonstrated this by showing Mark the payroll sheets, which were attached to a large purpose-built board. On top of this was placed an employee record card and some carbon paper. She pointed out how important it was to press very firmly so that the bottom copy, which was the employee's payslip, could still be read by the employee when he or she received it in his or her pay packet. All the columns on the payroll sheet had to reconcile to be carried forward to the next page. If it didn't reconcile, you might have to go through every employee again until you found the error, so it was a good idea to double check as you went along.

When the 'Gross-to-Net' was completed, the bottom copies (the payslips), which were perforated, were torn off and folded up. They were then slipped into the pay packets (which had been prepared on the previous Friday) with the net pay figure protruding. On Wednesday, the cash would be collected from the bank. George had to 'phone the bank beforehand so they could prepare the cash in designated denominations. When the cash was received, the office would be locked all day for security reasons.

The cash would be inserted into the pay packets. The packets for each site would then be collected together and inserted into a registered envelope. All the registered envelopes would be delivered to the Post Office to arrive on site on Thursday. Penny pointed out that Wednesdays were very pressurised, because the money could not be collected from the bank before ten o'clock, when it opened, but the registered post had to be delivered before five o'clock, when the Post Office closed. The foremen from the Factory came to collect the pay packets for the Factory workers. She warned Mark not to expect a proper lunch-hour on a Wednesday.

Thursdays and Fridays were used for miscellaneous tasks, which included preparing the pay packets and the payroll sheets for next week, as well as some administrative tasks for leavers and new starters. It was also the best time to address queries from the employees or their foremen. 'Some of the calls can get quite testy,' she explained.

'Can I assume you and Josie will handle the men's testy calls?' Mark asked, with a glint in his eye.

'Oh, you're quick,' laughed Penny. 'And very rude.' Mark wasn't sure if his remark was out of order, but he was pleased to see Penny enjoyed it. He was known at school as a bit of a joker and he didn't see why he shouldn't renew his reputation at work. Penny carried on explaining the payroll procedures.

This all sounded to Mark as though he would at last get a chance to use his brain. He liked working with figures and it wasn't all filing. Thursdays and Fridays sounded a little more mundane, but he would be back in Costing on those days.

While Penny was describing all this, Josie arrived. She interjected occasionally with little remarks or instructions that seemed to Mark to be designed to make him feel uncomfortable about his role.

Penny said she would go into more detail as he carried out each of these tasks for the first time.

'So where do we start today?' asked Mark.

'Ah!' said Penny, slowly. Mark didn't like the sound of that. 'There's one other little job I 'aven't told you about. As you probably know, every employee 'as a National Insurance card. Well, we 'ave to stick the stamps on the cards. We usually only 'ave to do this about once a month. And guess what? This is the week.

Not only that, but we also 'ave to do the same with the 'oliday stamps. The idea behind 'oliday stamps is that we pay for a stamp for every employee who turns up for work. We buy these from the Builders' Federation. If an employee wants to take 'oliday, we cash it on 'is behalf and pay it with 'is wages. If 'e leaves our employment, we give 'im 'is 'oliday card, so if 'e goes to work for another company in the building industry, 'e can use 'is 'oliday card to get 'is 'oliday pay. The 'oliday stamps also need sticking on, this week.'

Mark thought to himself that this wasn't fair. That was a Thursday or Friday job and he wouldn't normally be there on a Thursday, but somehow, he didn't think that was going to make any difference at all. He was right. Penny did the factory workers and Mark did the sites, which included about three times the number of employees as the factory. Josie didn't do any. She occupied herself by answering the 'phone whenever it rang, making personal 'phone calls, smoking or generally complaining. She did fetch the coffee on one occasion, which Mark decided was her conscience telling her to make some kind of contribution to the day's efforts.

On Friday, Mark was asked to prepare the pay packets and payroll sheets for next week, while Penny actioned three leavers and four new starters. Josie did much the same as Thursday, including disappearing for long periods of time. Although she did handle a pair of testy calls!

Penny and Mark got on very well together and had a laugh or two. Mark saw another opportunity to build on his reputation of being a joker. While looking at the names of the employees, he said 'There's one chap here with the name 'Denis' who spells his name with one "N" and another with two "N"s'.

Josie said she thought that you could spell it with one or two "N"s.

Then Mark added, 'I know a chap down our road who's got loads of 'ens. He's a farmer!'

Not only did Penny chuckle, but even Josie gave a light-hearted groan. However, it was made perfectly clear to Mark that they might enjoy a little laugh now, but this was the lull before the storm and that next week would be a different matter. Or as Penny put it – 'A different fettle of kish.' She had lots of little interesting phrases, especially when something went wrong. 'Everything in our favour is against us!' was one of them. Or 'Every silver lining has a cloud.' Something that was 'disastrous' was described as 'dixarsterous'.

★ ★ ★ ★ ★ ★

On Saturday, Mark went into town to buy his bike on the 'never-never'. The owner of the shop, Ben Robbins, recognised Mark as Frank's youngest. Frank had often painted a little sign or two for Ben, so as a gesture of friendship, Ben said he wouldn't add any interest for taking the bike on H.P. Mark paid a small deposit and was given a payment card. He would have to pay off one pound a week for another eighteen weeks.

While he was in town, Mark bought himself a new LP. He thought that as he was now earning money, he could graduate from singles to LP's. But he had an interesting experience with the man in the record shop. Mark started by asking if they had Ben E. King's new LP. The man just replied 'No.'

'That was rather blunt,' thought Mark. He then asked for another record that he couldn't find in the rack.

'No, we haven't'. Again, quite bluntly. Instead, Mark fetched another LP from the rack, which he duly purchased and this time, the man was polite and helpful and said he could order the others if Mark wanted. Mark declined.

As he walked back to his new bike, he thought that that was how he must have sounded to Ted last week when Ted accused him of being blunt. If the man in the shop had just said, 'No, I'm afraid we don't have that record.' or 'I'm sorry, we've just sold out.' It would have sounded so much better.

So Mark should have said to Ted, 'No, I'm afraid Bob's not here. Can I take a message?' or something similar. It was a valuable lesson learnt.

Monday soon came round again and Mark arrived at work in his new raincoat, as it had been raining. Josie and Penny were both there already, opening the mail and piling up the timesheets. It was decided that Mark would concentrate on the Factory payroll.

While he was waiting for the clockcards to arrive, Margaret brought in her new assistant, whose name was Blodwyn. She was duly introduced to everyone. It soon became clear that she was Welsh. She was a pasty faced, but quite attractive young girl, about eighteen years old, with darkish blond hair over her shoulders. She was five feet five inches tall, but appeared taller due to her high heel shoes, which served to accentuate her very shapely calf muscles. She had quite broad shoulders, a narrow waist and wide hips. But the most stunning thing, as far as Mark was concerned, was the length of her tight brown skirt. This was the heyday of the mini-skirt, so short skirts were not that unusual, but they were usually worn by girls with long slim legs. Blodwyn's legs were anything but long and slim. She had her back to Mark for most of the time, so he was able to have a good look at her legs without her knowing. She leaned forward to shake hands with both Penny and Josie. Her skirt rode up a little further and her ample backside swelled. It was a very solid looking backside.

Then Margaret turned and introduced Blodwyn to Mark. He stood up to shake her hand. 'Oh, a gentleman,' she said in her delightful Welsh singing voice. She had the most beautiful green eyes that Mark had ever seen.

He just said, 'Pleased to meet you, Blodwyn.' He stood there not knowing what to do or say next. Blodwyn looked at him, but he looked away. Mark always had difficulty maintaining eye contact.

After a few seconds, which seemed like an eternity, Penny rescued him by saying 'You don't sound local, Blodwyn?'

'No, I'm from Swansea. My father had to relocate with his job, so we've just moved into the area.'

'Well, welcome to Greshams,' added Penny. Then Margaret and Blodwyn left to meet some more people.

'You all right, Mark?' Penny asked. 'You can put your eyes back in, now.'

'I don't know what you mean,' he blustered.

'Oh, come on,' said Josie. 'You've gone all unnecessary. Haven't you seen a girl in a mini-skirt before?'

'Not one as short as that, he hasn't,' said Penny. 'You could see what she'd had for breakfast!'

'What does that mean?' asked Mark.

'Haven't you heard that expression before?' asked Josie.

'No. What does it mean?'

'You'll have to work that one out for yourself!' she replied. 'Do you have a girlfriend?'

'No, not at the moment.'

'Well get in, there,' said Penny. 'She was impressed by you standing up like a gentleman. They're very passionate, you know, the Welsh. Have you ever had a girlfriend?'

'No. I went to an 'all boys' school, so I don't know too many girls.' It was clear that Mark was very embarrassed by all this and Josie urged them all to get stuck into their work.

Penny sat with him at his shelf while he worked on the first two clockcards. When she was happy he had grasped what was required of him, she left him to it. He was quite slow and deliberate at first, but he started to speed up and had finished the clockcards by lunchtime.

After lunch, Penny sat with him again while he started on the payroll sheet for the Factory. She had to show him how to use the Tax Tables for recording free pay, based on a person's tax code, deducting it from his taxable pay and then looking up the tax due. She explained the difference between an employee on a normal cumulative tax basis and one on a 'week one' basis. She showed him how to enter the National Insurance contribution, as well as Graduated Pension. Graduated Pension was a wonderful way of taking a little extra from an employee, based on his or her earnings, to store away as a little extra pension for his or her retirement. Many years later, it was discovered that this scheme would only ever add a few pennies to someone's pension, but at the time, it seemed like a good idea.

Penny re-iterated the need to press very firmly, so that the bottom copy would be legible, and reminded Mark to reconcile each payroll sheet. He found this whole process very slow going. There were so many tables to look up and he kept getting confused between them all. Sometimes he forgot to press hard, so he went over them again, but this could have the effect of smudging the bottom copy. His index and middle fingers were starting to ache from the pressure he was applying with his pen. When he mentioned this to Penny, she pointed to a callus on her own hand. By the end of the day, he had a blister in the same place and he was getting even slower.

To make matters worse, his first payroll sheet wouldn't reconcile. After spending three quarters of an hour failing to find the problem, he had to ask Penny. She wasted another half-hour herself before she found his error. All the time, Josie was getting annoyed because they were getting behind schedule. She was concerned that if Mark had made mistakes on the payroll sheet, had he made any mistakes on the clockcards? She decided that it would be necessary to check them all before they went any further.

Mark felt that he had already double-checked all these before starting the payroll sheets, so he didn't think it was necessary. After all, he'd only made one mistake on the payroll sheets, but he knew how important it was to get an employee's pay right. It had been stressed to him how difficult it was to correct an employee's money after he had been paid, particularly if it was an overpayment. It also resulted in a loss of confidence in the Wages Department, which would lead to all sorts of unnecessary queries.

But he was disappointed that Josie had already found an excuse to have a dig at him. No doubt, she would be banging on George's door at the first opportunity. As it happened, Penny found no errors on the clockcards. She said 'Well done' to Mark, but Josie didn't.

At the end of the day, Josie had a review of their progress. She decided that they were behind schedule and it might be necessary to work late tomorrow night to catch up. She was not a happy person.

Mark was glad to go home that evening.

The next day, he came in early to create a good impression. Josie and Penny were already there. There were polite 'Good mornings', but the atmosphere was not good. He wondered if Penny and Josie had had words. He picked up his payroll sheet and board and carried on where he left off. He had a lot of difficulty holding his pen, letting alone pressing hard.

Penny asked him to fetch some coffees. She was a little abrupt about it. He had run out of change for the coffee machine. No one else had any, so he went to see Margaret to see if there was any in the Petty Cash box.

Margaret wasn't there and Blodwyn was sitting there on her own. He noticed she had her own desk, not a shelf to work on. She was sitting sidewards on to him and was wearing a tight V-knecked light blue sweater that revealed a few inches of well-rounded bosom. She was also wearing another short skirt, which, in her seated position, was revealing several inches of her wonderful thighs.

Mark asked if she could let him have some change for the coffee machine from the Petty Cash box. 'The box is still in the safe and Mr. Harris isn't in yet to open it. But I might have some change in my purse. I don't like coffee, so I don't need it. She stretched over to the far side of her desk to reach her handbag. As she did so, her skirt rode up even further, revealing the very tops of her thighs and a glimpse of bright red underwear. Mark tried to avert his gaze, but his eyes were drawn to the wondrous sight before him.

As she returned to her seated position with her purse in her hand, she said, 'Oh, look at me, showing my legs off. Never mind. Everyone's wearing mini-skirts, these days. My boyfriend says my legs are too big and fat to wear a mini-skirt. What do you think?' She had a very mischievous glint in her eye as she asked the question.

'No, no. They're not fat. They are very shapely, if you don't mind me saying so. Very shapely.' He was trembling as he said this, wondering whether it was right and proper to be discussing her legs. He actually agreed with her boyfriend that her legs were too large to be wearing a mini skirt, but it was fine by him. As she stared at him, he felt uncomfortable and he found the few seconds of silence unbearable, so he added 'In any case, it's the shape that's important, not the size.'

'Well, thank you. Yes, I suppose they are shapely. They're very strong you know. I sometimes have a little wrestle with my boyfriend. He's much stronger than me, but if I get him in a head-scissors, there's no way he can escape. I can just hold him, there, without any effort. When I really start squeezing, he begs me to let him go.' Again she stared at Mark to see how he would react to this.

'Wow,' said Mark, still trembling. 'That's really impressive.' He wasn't sure where this conversation was going. He was thoroughly embarrassed, although he was genuinely impressed at the thought of her wonderful strong thighs giving some poor soul a head squeeze. Looking at the shape and size of them, he could believe every word she had said.

'Yes, you don't want to be messing with me,' she added as Margaret entered the room. Mark wasn't sure whether Margaret's arrival was a blessing or not. He was totally unprepared for such a conversation. Blodwyn handed over her six pennies, and Mark gave her a sixpenny piece, thanked her and left.

'Good morning, Mark!' said Margaret as he left.

'Oh, sorry, Margaret. Good morning'. He nearly walked into the door that Margaret had left slightly ajar, while out of the corner of his eye, he was aware of both of them staring at him.

He was still shaking when he returned to the Wages office. He sat there for a minute, unable to concentrate on work. The conversation with Blodwyn had only lasted a minute or so, but it had a profound effect on him.

'Were you going to fetch some coffee, Mark?' demanded Josie.

'Oh, yes,' he said, 'Sorry, I was miles away.'

Penny said, 'I don't think your mind was just wandering. I think it had left the building!' At any other time, she might have meant this as an amusing remark, but Mark could tell she was in a bit of a mood, so it sounded more spiteful than amusing.

When Mark got to the coffee machine, there were two people ahead of him. He didn't know them at all so he didn't speak. As his legs still felt weak, he sat down for a minute until it was his turn. He hadn't actually had an erection, but he was aware of a certain moistness in his underpants. He'd never experienced a sensation like that before. He wanted to go back for more, but of course, he wouldn't – not yet, anyhow.

Mark took the coffees back and told himself he needed to concentrate on work and not make any more mistakes. He finished off the Factory payroll, which reconciled first time. He announced this to Penny and Josie. 'You can do page three of the Site payroll, now,' said Josie. 'It's all the same procedure as the Factory, but you might find some expenses, which go in that column there. '

He was aware that he was still taking a long time to do this task. His finger was in pain. He was still struggling to remember the correct sequence of tables to use and his mind was still a little pre-occupied with Blodwyn. He was trying to think of an excuse to go and see her, but he'd already cleaned her out of change. In any case Penny had later announced that she'd got some change from the canteen when she went to buy herself a bread roll for lunch. Mark was longing to see those legs again.

By lunchtime, he had finished page three, but he was again having difficulty getting it to reconcile. This time, he was determined to find the error himself. Lunch breaks had to be staggered, so he volunteered to take a late lunch, so he could finish this off. After half an hour, he had found his error, which he corrected, but he'd made a bit of a mess with the payroll sheet and one employee's payslip was totally illegible. Penny told him to get a blank payslip and write it out again. They kept a sheet of blank payslips just for that purpose, so he obviously wasn't the first person to do it.

He didn't take a full lunch break. He sat and ate his packed lunch, by which time Josie had returned from her lunch. He told her he'd finished page three and she told him to do page eight. He worked out that at that rate, Penny and Josie must have both completed two pages to his one.

By now, he was really struggling to hold his pen and this next sheet took even longer. In fact, Penny and Josie had finished all the other sheets before he finished his and they had to wait for him, before they could finalise the payroll.

Penny showed him the last task of the day, which was to perform a cash analysis. This involved working out how many of each coinage denomination was required. Again this had to be reconciled with the total net pay from the payroll sheets. George was then informed of the figures so that he could get the payroll cheque prepared and signed by a director ready for the morning. All that was left then, was to tear off the payslips, fold them and insert them into the pay packets.

They had finished in time – just, but Josie was far from pleased. She addressed Mark – 'Now, young man. You've got to speed up and cut out the errors.'

He felt very hard done by. It was his first payroll and he was in a lot of pain. By now, his blister had burst. He hadn't made that many errors, especially considering it was his first time and they'd met the deadline, so what was the problem? He thought Penny might have stood up for him, but she had been in a bad mood all day, herself.

'Now tomorrow,' Josie continued, 'will be very hectic. I don't think we can afford the time to show you what to do, do you, Penny?' Penny considered, and then shook her head slowly. 'So it's best if you go back to Costing tomorrow. We'll have to find another way of introducing you to Wednesdays.'

Mark just said 'O.K.' collected his things together and wheeled his chair back into Costing. Bob was still there. It was just after five o'clock. 'How's it been going, mate?' he asked.

'Well, we got the payroll ready for tomorrow, but it hasn't been a particularly enjoyable day. Josie thinks I've been too slow and she doesn't want me in there tomorrow when they do the money.'

'Well, that doesn't seem fair. It's your first payroll. You're bound to be slow until you get into the swing of things. Don't take any notice of her. She'd have complained whatever you'd have done. You were on a hiding to nothing. What have you done to your finger, mate?'

'That's my blister. That's where I've been pressing as hard as I can with my pen.'

'No wonder you were a bit slow. We'll keep you away from any writing for a day or two.' That probably meant more filing.

That night, in bed, Mark considered the events of the day. He tried to think about work issues, but it was his experience with Blodwyn that was uppermost in his mind. He wondered why it had affected him so much and he also considered the other girls he had met in the last 2 weeks. Ellie was obviously gorgeous. She was attractive, elegant, warm and friendly. If she were a little younger and single, would he want her as a girlfriend? He wasn't sure. She wouldn't want him, but that's another 'fettle of kish', as Penny would say. She would be good company for an evening out, but Mark didn't actually fancy her physically. He ought to have done, but he didn't.

Anne was a lovely person, but he felt nothing but friendship for her. But why was that? She was very feminine, dressed well and had a neat slim figure. He felt very much the same for Penny, except that she was married, older and a little overweight. And it was now clear that she could be subject to moodiness. But Blodwyn! Yes, he certainly fancied Blodwyn. He had always been led to believe that men lusted after women's breasts.

60

So if he was more interested in their legs and bums, did that mean he was perverted? And if the thought of Blodwyn's strong legs excited him, did that mean he had homosexual tendencies? He thought about that for a minute, but satisfied himself that this was not the case, by realising that he had never at any time found any man attractive. But are you meant to get excited about a pair of strong legs? After all, Josie must be capable of crushing him with her enormous thighs and he certainly couldn't get excited about that prospect. He shuddered at the thought.

In any case, why was Blodwyn talking to him about her legs, like that? Was she attracted to him? Was she trying to get him excited? Was she one of these 'prick-teasers' he'd heard his old school mates talking about? Was she getting some kind of satisfaction out of embarrassing him? And she had a boyfriend, who thought her legs were too fat. If she was new to the area, did that mean she had only been going out with him a short while, or was he still in Swansea? And if they were having these little wrestling sessions, it wasn't just a casual relationship. But why had she talked to Mark like that?

So many unanswered questions.

He relived the conversation he had had with Blodwyn. This time, he did get an erection. Oh well. It was a shame to waste it.

CHAPTER 6

Hopelessly in Lust

Wednesday came round. Mark arrived before Bob and noticed a large pile of 'Take-offs' on his 'desk', so he thought he'd show some initiative by making a start on filing them. When Bob came in, he said 'Oh, well done, mate. We need to keep on top of all these. We're slipping behind badly.

I've got some good news for you, though. We're getting some help in for you. There's a young girl starting in a few weeks. She'll be full-time. You'll like her.'

'What's she like?' asked Mark.

'She's nineteen; been working at a shipping agents in town, doing various office tasks, including some costing. She's quite good looking; nice figure; wears glasses. You'll like her. She lives in a little village – is it Manford or something?'

'Manningford. It's where George used to live before he got married.'

'How did you know that?'

Mark hesitated for a few seconds. 'George is my cousin. Didn't you know?' Mark had been wondering if he should try to keep this a secret, but someone was bound to find out sooner or later. Although he would rather Josie didn't find out just yet – at least not until he had got himself established and proved himself.

'No, I didn't realise. Anyway, her name is Karen and she's single, so who knows, mate?' He gave a little wink as he said this.

'She's not Welsh, then?' asked Mark, thinking he might open up a certain line of conversation.

'No. Cor, she's an old slapper, that Blodwyn, isn't she?'

Mark wasn't too sure what an 'old slapper' was, but it didn't sound like a complement. 'Her skirts are interesting, aren't they?' was Mark's next question.

'What with those ball-crushing thighs?' Bob obviously didn't find her legs attractive. 'Now if it was Ellie wearing a short skirt. That would be a different matter, wouldn't it?'

Mark said 'Yeah.' It seemed to be expected, so he didn't draw attention to the fact that he would rather look at Blodwyn's legs than Ellie's, although he could well understand why Bob would find Ellie attractive. The fact that Bob had made such remarks about Blodwyn put Mark off considering the possibility of going out with her, even if there was the slightest chance that she would be interested in him. For some reason, he felt a little deflated by Bob's comments. Still, he was going to be working with another young girl. That would be nice. And she wore glasses, so Mark might stand a chance with her.

'The other thing I wanted to tell you, Mark, is that there is going to be a meeting in the canteen tomorrow, after work, to discuss starting up a football team. Can you make it?'

'Definitely. What time?'

'It'll be soon after five o'clock. I'm going. I haven't played for a few years, but I need to get some kind of exercise. I've put on a few pounds, lately. They're going to try to organise a few friendlies and if they get enough people, they'll put a team into the local Sunday League.'

That was two bits of good news in quick succession. Then Bob suggested it was time for some coffee and gave Mark some money out of his 'pot.'

When Mark returned, Bob had disappeared. He reappeared a few minutes later and said 'Hey Mark. Do you fancy a little ride into town?'

'I don't mind. What's this about?'

'We have to go and get the payroll money from the bank. Greg is driving. It's his company car. Drink your coffee up, we need to get going.'

Four people crammed into Greg's two-door Vauxhall Viva. Greg was a senior surveyor and he had a company car. They had to use a company car for insurance purposes. The other person was introduced as Mike. He was also a surveyor; about six feet four inches tall and built like a tank. He was jokingly described as the deterrent for potential thieves. Bob quipped that when you saw him getting out of the car, he just seemed to keep coming. Mike sat in the front, next to Greg and told lots of little yarns. He also broke wind and belched at regular intervals. He had apparently had a few drinks the night before. They drove with the windows open all the way. He had his own vocabulary. One of his favourite adjectives was 'pissbodical.' Mark thought this was a wonderful word to use in the right circumstances. It sounded like a swear word, but it wasn't really.

Mark asked what they would do if there was an attempt to rob them. Bob said, 'Well, I'd shit a brick and throw it at them!' There was lots of amusing banter like this and everything was pissbodical.

Mark discovered that both Greg and Mike frequently visited customer sites and they mentioned various towns and cities that they had visited recently. 'You seem to get everywhere,' said Mark.

'Everywhere but Liverpool,' replied Greg.

'Why not Liverpool?'

'We had one customer there, a year or two ago. We weren't able to use any of our own labour force. It all had to be local and approved by the unions. Liverpool is a completely closed shop. It was only a small site, but we lost lots of money. The workers were forever coming out on strike or working to rule – mostly nothing to do with our site at all. The contract should have been completed in two weeks. It took ten!'

We won't bid for anything there, now – not at any price.'

When they arrived at the bank, Greg stayed in the car, as it was on a yellow line. The other three went in. The bank had the money ready and as soon as the clerk had verified the cheque, they went back to the car, carrying several bags of money. Mike carried most of it. Mark didn't have any. He decided to act as lookout and kept looking around for anything suspicious. He couldn't believe they were entrusted with all this money.

They had instructions to vary the route each week, so they started off in completely the wrong direction and the return journey took ten minutes longer than the outward journey. Greg dropped them off right outside the front door to the office building. As they walked quickly through Reception, Bob held up one of the money bags and said to Ellie 'Now will you run off with me?'

'Oh Bob. You suddenly seem more attractive.'

They delivered the cash to the Wages office. Josie gave it a quick look over and said 'Cheers, lads.' They all said 'Cheers' back and she locked the door behind them.

After that little excitement, it was back to the filing.

Half an hour later, Bob asked Mark to take some invoices back to Margaret. Mark had been looking for an excuse to go and see Blodwyn again. Margaret's office was only two doors down and it would have taken Bob about thirty seconds to do it himself, but that was what a junior was expected to do – and Mark certainly didn't complain.

Mark was pleased to see that Margaret wasn't there again, but Blodwyn was, wearing her tight brown mini-skirt. They said 'hello' to each other. Mark had no idea what to say, but he found Blodwyn certainly wanted to chat again.

She said 'Did I embarrass you, yesterday? I didn't mean to, you know. It was just that you made some very kind remarks about my legs. That was nice. My boyfriend says I've got fat legs and a big bum, so you made me feel better.'

'Well, it's not the kind of conversation I was expecting and I did feel a little uncomfortable. But there was no harm done.'

'Did you mean what you said? You weren't just being polite, were you?'

'Of course I meant it. You've got great legs.' He was starting to tremble, again, but it gave him the opportunity to legitimately have another quick look at her legs. Yes, they were still as lovely as he remembered, if not more so. 'Why do you go out with him, if he's always saying nasty things about you?'

'Well, he's lovely really. I'm very fond of him.'

'I think he should treat you with more respect.'

'Do you have a girlfriend?'

'No, not at the moment.' He wondered how many more times he would be asked this question before he could say 'yes.'

'Well, get yourself a nice Welsh girl.' Was this some kind of invitation? He decided not. She was just a tease.

'I hear they're very passionate,' said Mark, consciously rising to the bait.

'I don't know about that, but they are very warm and caring.'

'Do they all have shapely legs?' Where did that come from? Not a very clever thing to say at all, but he couldn't think of anything other than her wonderful legs.

'It's a pity you're not my boyfriend. He doesn't like my legs. I can tell you do by the way you look at them.' She seemed to close her legs tighter together, as she said it, drawing attention to the full curves of her upper thighs. And she had that mischievous glint in her eye, again.

Now Mark was really trembling.

'Well, I'm sure I'm not supposed to keep looking at your legs,' he said, as he felt himself turning red.

'I don't mind. I quite like it,' she replied

Then after another few seconds of embarrassment, he added, 'I think I'd better get back to work.'

'I've embarrassed you again, haven't I? Don't take any notice of me. I just like to talk. Come and have another little chat, sometime. We won't talk about my legs, again.'

'Right'.

'Unless you want to,' she added with a mischievous grin.

'She's done it again,' he thought as he returned to his filing. His legs felt weak again as he stood there next to the filing cabinet. This wasn't normal behaviour for a young girl and it surely couldn't be normal for a shy seventeen year-old youth to be so affected by it. He wondered if he had the courage to call her bluff and ask her out. He'd never asked anyone out before. If only she didn't have a boyfriend, he might find the decision a little easier. Her boyfriend didn't sound as though he deserved her.

After about an hour, Bob asked, 'Can you do me a favour, mate? We've had to revise our list of materials costs. I've written them on this old list. Can you take it up to the Typing Pool and ask them to re-type it for me? Give it to Gail. You remember Gail, don't you?'

'Oh no,' thought Mark. 'You can't really want me to go up to that room, with all those girls?' All his old fears of girls being an alien species returned. A whole roomful of nothing but girls! If it was just one girl, he might just be all right. But a whole roomful!

He gritted his teeth and walked off down the corridor.

He decided to make the most of this experience. He would have a quick look round the Typing Pool to see if there were any nice looking quiet girls (perhaps one with glasses?). When he got there, the door was open. He gently knocked and crept in. Gail wasn't there! Now what would he do? Everyone looked up as he walked in, stared at him for a few seconds and then got on with their work. They now ignored him. He addressed the nearest one – a twenty-five year-old who wore too much make-up and was chewing. 'Is Gail around?' he asked.

'Don't know where she is at the moment.'

'I've got some typing here.'

'Just leave it in her tray on her desk, love.' She said it in a way that indicated it was obvious to anyone what you did with typing.

He did as she said and left without looking back. He had forgotten to have a good look round at the other girls.

Towards the middle of the afternoon, Gail came down to see them. 'Was this your stuff you brought up for typing, Mark? There was no name on it.'

'Well, it's actually Bob's, but I took it up.' She gave the documents to Bob.

'Thanks, Gail,' he said. 'Here Gail. Have you got any nice young single females in your team for our Mark? He's looking for a girlfriend.' Mark tried to look annoyed, but was nevertheless interested to hear what Gail had to say in response.

'I think they've all got boyfriends or husbands. I'm not sure about Sheila. I know she packed up with her boyfriend last week, but she's probably too old for you.'

'Or I'm too young for her,' thought Mark to himself.

'What do you look for in a girl?' she asked.

'Preferably one with a pulse. Apart from that, a nice personality is the main thing.' In other words, 'Beggars can't be choosers', he thought.

'What about me?' she asked putting her arm round him and nestling her head against his shoulder. 'I've got a nice personality.' This threw Mark completely. He knew she was teasing him, but how could he say 'no' without being offensive or say 'yes' when he knew he would be leaving himself open to more teasing.

He put down the file that was in his hand, put his arm round her shoulder and said 'That's a very nice offer. Can I leave it 'til the end of the month and see if I get a better offer in the meantime?'

Bob burst out laughing. 'Nice one, Mark.'

'You cheeky bugger!' she cried as she slapped his arm. 'That's the last time I deliver your typing.' She wasn't really annoyed, but she was a little surprised that this quiet unassuming lad had got one over her.

'What about that new girl in Accounts?' she asked, after a few more seconds.

'What old 'Thunderthighs'?' said Bob.

'Old Bill Connell thinks she's got a great pair of legs. "Something to get hold of" is what he says about her,' replied Gail. 'And "Imagine that wrapped around you." He says what he thinks, does Bill.'

So Mark wasn't the only one round here who liked the look of her legs. Bill Connell sounded like a man after his own heart.

'What about it, Mark?' she added.

'She's already got a boyfriend,' mumbled Mark.

'You don't want to let that stop you, does he Bob?'

'Well, it would depend upon whether she insisted on bringing him along on the date. It can cramp your style a bit, you know!'

'Anyway, I've got work to do,' she said. 'I'll see you two around.'

'Cheers, Gail,' said Bob.

Gail popped back in again and whispered. 'She was just walking by. I hope she didn't hear what we said!'

'What, old Blodwyn?' asked Bob.

'Yes, Blodwyn! Oh, well it's too late to do anything about it, now. She shouldn't creep about.' Mark was really hoping Blodwyn hadn't heard what they'd said.

Bob's telephone rang. It was Penny asking him to take the wages to the Post Office. 'Is it that time, already. Right, I'll get it sorted.' He put the 'phone down. 'Mark. Fancy another ride? I'll just get the others.'

It was the same four people as before. Greg brought the car round to the front door and Bob carried a large metal filing tray full of registered envelopes and a record book. There was the same level of banter for this journey. Bob told the others what Mark had said to Gail about waiting to see if he got a better offer.

'I was assuming that she wasn't seriously making me an offer,' Mark said.

'You can't be too sure with Gail,' said Mike. 'She's anybody's. She'd suck you in and blow you out in bubbles.'

'What a lovely expression,' thought Mark.

'She's been around the block a few times,' added Greg. 'I can think of at least four people she had in the few months she was working in London.'

They carried on discussing her various conquests until they reached the Post Office. Again, Greg stayed in the car, while the others went inside. There were four tills open and they all had long queues. It occurred to Mark that with all this money in their possession, they should be able to go straight to the front of the queue, but they had to wait their turn. At that time of night (about 4.30), there were several people determined to get their business mail in the post before the close.

Once the wages money was all handed over, the packages checked against the book and everything duly stamped, they returned to the car with a certain amount of relief. They entered the office with just a few minutes to spare before leaving time. Mark tidied up his things and left.

As he was about to mount his bike, Anne appeared, so he asked if he could ride with her. Anne had discovered a short cut round the back of the estate, but it involved going down a very quiet path, so she was glad of the protection. Mark wondered if her boyfriend would be bothered if he knew she was with Mark, but she seemed pleased to have some company.

They chatted about so many things and there was never a lull in the conversation. Mark told her about the trips to the bank and the Post Office and his conversation with Gail. Anne had also heard about Gail's reputation. He toyed with the notion of telling Anne about his experiences with Blodwyn, but thought better of it. Anne shared some of her day with him and the journey seemed to take no time at all. She really was good company.

That night in bed, he relived the latest conversation with Blodwyn. The end result was the same as the previous night.

The next day, having warned his mother that he would be home a little later than usual due to the football meeting, he set out on his bike, hoping he might see Anne on the way. Instead, he passed Janice. He recognised those lovely legs as he came round the corner and she was just ahead. She seemed as lovely as ever and she seemed genuinely pleased to see him.

With all his vast new experience of women, he felt a lot more confident than on his previous encounters with her. He found out that she had had a very enjoyable time in Cornwall. She was currently finding her second year of 'A' levels to be much harder than before and was wondering if she would be better off working like Mark.

He told her that he still hadn't been paid, so financially he was no better off. He also told her that being a junior was no fun, so if attaining 'A' levels could help her avoid that, it would be well worthwhile. She did not have a clear idea of a career, but definitely wasn't going to University.

Mark told her he had seen her in town a few weeks earlier. 'Was that your boyfriend with you?' He wouldn't have dreamed of asking such a question a few weeks ago.

It was her boyfriend. He was working in a bank in town. Mark had just been considering whether he could ask her out, but now he thought better of it. Why do all these girls have boyfriends? Still, it was nice to see her again. She was as lovely as ever.

The rest of the day passed off uneventfully. The only time that day that Mark saw Blodwyn was when he followed her down the corridor. She was about twenty yards ahead of him and he was carrying a tray of coffees, so he couldn't catch her. He noticed she was wearing a tight knee-length skirt rather than one of her mini-skirts. She had a very shapely pair of calves, probably even better than Janice's. And her tight skirt revealed much of the shape of her behind. She had a delightful

69

movement, so he was quite content to admire the view and resisted the urge to say 'Hello' to her.

At five o'clock, Mark went over to the football meeting in the canteen. He sat next to Bob, who was the only person he recognised. Most of the people there were wearing overalls. A man named Nobby introduced himself and did most of the talking. He had run the team in Balham, so he knew most of the people at the meeeeting, but he asked the names of those he didn't recognise. He turned to Mark and asked his name.

'Sid,' said Mark.

'Hey?' said Bob, looking at him questioningly.

'Damn!' he thought to himself. 'I didn't mean to say that.' This had been his nickname at school and he had hoped he would lose it when he left school. His brother Brian had been given the name first. Brian had been so named after an old tramp who could frequently been seen shuffling around town. Everyone knew the tramp as Sid Mason. When Mark joined the school, Brian's class mates decided to call him 'Little Sid.' Mark's own classmates eventually shortened this to just 'Sid.'

'It's just a nickname,' said Mark to Bob, but the damage had been done. He couldn't bring himself, in front of a canteen full of people, to say 'Sorry. Did I say Sid? I really meant Mark.' So in the football fraternity, he would now be known confusingly as 'Sid.' He could kick himself. Why didn't he stop to think before he opened his mouth?

It was agreed that Nobby would act as the team manager and Woody would captain the team. They would try to arrange some training one night a week, when they had found a suitable venue, and they would organise a few friendlies with local teams.

Meanwhile, it was suggested that they have a bit of a 'kick-around' on Sunday morning, if anyone knew of a suitable playing field. Most of the people in the meeting were new to the area, so Mark suggested the local Recreation Park, which was fairly central. He gave out directions and pointed out that there was only one goal, so it was always possible some local kids might get there first. They agreed on a start time of 10.30.

Someone called Toby, wearing a white coat, said he could get there nice and early to reserve it. Mark thought Toby looked and sounded remarkably like Dudley Moore. He was about five foot two, with thick curly black hair, a slight speech impediment and a London accent. His favourite phrase was 'Yeah. I agwee with you one hundwed per cent.' Mark reckoned he had used this phrase about eight times during the meeting.

Bob told the meeting that he had spoken to Mr. Gresham who had promised a sum of money to buy some kit and a few balls to get them started, but after that they had to be self-sufficient. Nobby stated that everyone would be expected to pay match fees and a signing-on fee to cover insurance. Mark wondered if he should ask for a reduction for under eighteen's, but he thought he'd tackle that another time.

One chap, Terry Roberts, was currently playing for a local league side and would continue to do so for the rest of the season, but would help out whenever he could and might join them next season if things went well. He was local, so his knowledge of local football matters would be very useful. Bob Nichols used to play for Chelsea (mostly the Reserves) and although now in his forties, he had kept himself fit and would help out with the training.

There was lots of cheerful banter, but Nobby was adamant that if he was going to be involved with the team, they would take it all very seriously and that included regular training. Mark had never trained for football before. He just turned up and played. Then they adjourned, with everyone promising to turn up Sunday morning for the 'kick-about' at the 'rec.'

When Mark got home, he checked that he still had a full set of football kit. He had, but the socks had holes and his boots were still dirty from the last time he had played, which was nearly six months previous. He promised himself he'd give them a good clean on Saturday.

The next day, when he rode to work, he kept a look out for both Janice and Anne, but he saw neither. While riding along, he toyed with the idea of asking Blodwyn to come out with him, but then he thought he'd just take it easy for now and see how things went. In other words, he lacked the confidence to do it and was afraid of being rejected.

The morning was again very uneventful. Mark did a little more costing and a lot more filing. During the afternoon, Bob disappeared to a meeting, leaving Mark to file a whole new load of 'Take-off's'. While he was standing at the filing cabinet by the open door, Blodwyn walked past. She spotted him standing there and came in for a chat. She was now wearing a pair of dark brown corduroy trousers. Mark was very disappointed. Not only could he not look at her thighs, he couldn't even admire her calves.

'What are you doing in here?' she asked. 'I thought you worked next door.'

'I work half the week here and half next door.' Then it went quiet. He had the feeling she had something on her mind, so he let her speak next.

'I've stopped wearing mini-skirts,' she said.

'So I've noticed. Is this because of your boyfriend?'

'No. I was passing this office the other day, when I heard you all talking about my legs and I heard someone call me 'Thunderthighs.' I found that very hurtful, especially when my boyfriend keeps telling me my legs are too fat.'

Mark wasn't too sure of the best way to handle this. He thought about pretending they had been talking about someone else, but she probably wouldn't believe him. 'I don't know what to say. I was angry when I heard that term used. Especially when I think that you've got such fantastic legs. I should have defended you, but I didn't want everyone to know that I fancied you.' Did he really just say that?

'Do you fancy me?'

'Of course I do. You've got a lovely pair of eyes and a great figure. Who wouldn't fancy you?'

'Well, Bob by the sound of things!'

'I get the impression he goes for very slim girls. The sort that I always think are totally lacking in shape. No one could accuse you of lacking in shape. I've noticed that the people who can get away with wearing a mini-skirt are the ones with very thin legs. If anyone has a decent pair of legs, you notice them that much more.'

She smiled at him and said 'I'm glad I came to see you. You always make me feel good about myself. I'm glad you like my legs.' She looked thoughtful for a few seconds. Then she gently closed the door. Mark wondered what she was up to.

'Let me show you something,' she said. 'Give me your hand.' She took his left hand and placed it between her upper thighs. 'I'll show you how strong my legs are.' She crossed her left leg round her right and said 'Now you try to pull your hand out.'

He had never felt a woman's thighs before and it felt wonderful. They were deep, soft and warm. And surprisingly firm. But he didn't think he would have any difficulty removing his hand... until he tried. She wasn't squeezing very hard – just enough to retain his hand and the corduroy added some grip. 'This is silly.' he thought. 'She isn't even trying.' So he braced himself to give a really hard tug. Sensing this, she dug her feet firmly into the floor and placed a hand on the filing cabinet to steady herself.

He gave an almighty tug. Not only did his hand stay firmly wedged between her legs, but she hardly moved. He had half expected to pull her over.

'Wow,' he said. 'But you're not really squeezing are you?'

'No. Just enough to hold you. This is what it's like if I start squeezing' and she did. He felt her inner thigh go hard and felt an enormous pressure gradually being exerted. Even so, it wasn't painful. Her thighs were so deep and smooth that all he felt was this enormous pressure. She really was strong. She held it like that for about twenty seconds and smiled at him as she did so. Then she relaxed and he went to free his hand, but she resumed the pressure.

'Where do you think you're going? You're my prisoner. I'll let you go when I'm ready,' she said mischievously. She was really enjoying this and he certainly wasn't complaining, although he was hoping no one would come in. He gave another little tug, but he knew it was hopeless. She eventually uncrossed her legs. He reluctantly removed his hand.

'You have incredible legs,' he panted. 'You enjoyed that, didn't you?'

'I think you did as well,' she said looking at the pyramid in his trousers.

'Oh, I'm so sorry,' he said, looking thoroughly embarrassed.

'Don't be silly. It makes a girl feel good to know she can have that effect on a man.' She had called him a man!

'I don't understand how your boyfriend can say you have fat legs. There's not an ounce of fat on them.'

'"Fat legs and fat bum" is what he says. You feel my bum and see what you think.'

Was he dreaming? Was she really inviting him to feel her bum? He hesitated.

'Go on. It's all right!' she said.

He cupped his right hand and placed it gently on her left buttock. It felt so round and so firm. Surely this was a perfect bum? Then she clenched her cheeks together. It was suddenly rock-hard. He moved his hand across her cheeks. The gap between them was firmly closed. He swept his hand round the whole arc of her left buttock again.

'There. What do you think of that,' she asked.

'Absolutely incredible. There's not an ounce of fat on there, either.'

He still had this pyramid in his pants and he didn't know what to do about it. 'And you're telling me your boyfriend doesn't like your legs or your bum.'

She nodded.

'He must be balmy. Have you always had strong legs like that?'

'I first discovered how strong they were when I was about fifteen. There were these two boys at school who kept trying to pinch the ball we were playing with. "We" being me and my friend Megan. Now Megan is strong. She was about three or four stone heavier than me and several inches taller. But Megan is strong all over. My legs are strong, but my arms aren't.' She felt her arm as she said this.

'One of the boys grabbed our ball and Megan chased him. She cornered him against a wall. Then she grabbed his arm and swung him round several times till he fell over in a heap. She fell down on top of him and pinned him to the ground. His friend tried to grab hold of her and pull her off, so I got hold of him and tried to pull him off. I was struggling to free him, but Megan gave a big jerk and threw both of us off. I fell to the ground with him between my legs, so I squeezed as hard as I could. He started yelling that he couldn't breathe and was letting out cries of pain. I felt so angry and wanted to carry on hurting him.

Both of them were made to say "sorry" in front of a crowd of other people and they felt thoroughly humiliated.

They never teased us again.'

'Wow,' said Mark. It was his favourite word at the moment.

'After that, everyone treated us with the utmost respect.

A few weeks later, an older boy came up to me and said he'd seen what had happened and wanted to know if he could have a go at escaping from my leg scissors. At first I declined, but he was quite insistent and I have to confess that I wanted to see for myself if it was just a fluke or a heat of the moment thing. But he wanted to do it in private, because he didn't want his mates to know some young girl might have shown him up. I was a bit naïve in those days. He could have been trying to rape me for all I know, but he wasn't.

We went behind the tuck shop and did just as he had asked. I found it wasn't a fluke and he was helpless. Without the anger of the previous occasion, I was able to experiment and apply just the right amount of pressure to hold him, hurt him a little or a lot. Needless to say, he had no chance of escaping.

The funny thing was that he enjoyed it and so did I. When you've been brought up to believe that women are the weaker sex and then you find you can do that with a chap, you do enjoy it. I did anyhow. He asked again a few weeks later, but I didn't like him very much, so I didn't think it was right.

That was a few years ago. I've grown a little since then, so I'm probably even stronger now.'

Mark was in awe. He had been keen to increase his experience of the opposite sex, but he had never envisaged anything like the last five minutes. He couldn't really think straight, but he simply had to seize the moment and ask her out.

'This boyfriend of yours – is he local?'

'No, he lives in Swansea. We've been going out together for seven months.'

So he wasn't local. That was all the encouragement Mark needed. 'Would you consider going out with me sometime?'

'I don't know. What did you have in mind?'

'You mean apart from going round the back of the tuck shop?' She laughed and he continued. 'This is still my first month at work and I haven't been paid yet, so I don't have a lot of money. At least, not until the end of the month. Perhaps, at the end of the month, we could go to the pictures, but meanwhile, I could take you into town, tomorrow – just have a wander round and get to know each other better?' His voice was trembling as he said all this and it showed.

Blodwyn smiled at him, realising that he was nervous and that asking her out had been quite a trial for him. She said 'We're going back home for the weekend, so I can't go out with you tomorrow. I'll be seeing Gareth tomorrow. We need to sort out one or two things. Can I give you an answer on Monday or Tuesday?'

'Of course.' Well at least she hadn't rejected him out of hand. He wondered what these "one or two" things were. Perhaps she wanted to find out how they could make their relationship work when they were nearly three hundred miles apart? Perhaps she was going to finish with him?

'And thank you for asking,' she added. 'If I didn't already have a boyfriend, the answer would definitely be "yes".'

'That's nice to know. I didn't think you'd want to go out with an ugly chap like me.'

'Who says you're ugly. You're not ugly.'

But before he could pursue this conversation, Bob's silhouette appeared in the frosted glass and he opened the door.

'Hello,' he said, poking his head round the door. 'I'm not interrupting anything, am I?'

'No,' said Blodwyn. 'We were just having a little chat.' Bob came in and sat at his desk.

Mark sat down and partly crossed his legs to hide his pyramid, which was at last starting to subside. He was also trying not to act sheepishly and felt he had to break the silence, so he said 'Blodwyn's going back to Swansea for the weekend.'

'Are you now? Going back to Welsh Wales, eh? Do you speak Welsh, Blodwyn?'

'Only a few words. It's in North Wales where they mostly speak it.'

'Can you say the name of that famous railway station?'

'What, you mean Llanfair-pwllgwyn-gyllgogerychwyrn-drobwllll-antysilio-gogogoch?'

'No, not that one.' He looked thoughtful for a few seconds. 'Cardiff! That's the one!'

Mark and Blodwyn both groaned, but Bob's little joke had broken the awkwardness of Bob interrupting them.

'I'd better get on with some work,' said Blodwyn. 'I'll see you all next week.' She gave Mark a lovely smile and he gazed into her lovely green eyes.

'Have a good weekend,' he said, but he was hoping she would have a horrible weekend with Gareth and come back on Monday with some good news for him.

After she had gone, Mark stood up again, happy that his pyramid had completely subsided and resumed his filing. Bob gave him a strange look and asked 'What have you been up to with Blodwyn, you dirty little devil, you?'

'We were just having a little chat.'

'Yeah, right! With the door closed. You looked as though I'd interrupted something.'

'She just wanted to tell me a little personal story.'

'I bet you've been trying to get your end away, you randy little git!' After a few more seconds, he enquired, almost seriously, 'Do you fancy her, then?'

'I'm still getting to know her. I think she's got lovely eyes, though.'

'That's not what I asked. Do you fancy her?'

'I suppose I could do.' Mark was now expecting Bob to make some disparaging remark about her legs, but it didn't come.

Instead, he just said, 'Well, get in there! I reckon she fancies you.'

'What makes you say that?'

'It's just the way she looked at you when she left.' Yes, it was a nice look.

He carried on with his filing. He would be back in the Wages office on Monday, so he would dearly like to clear up all these "take-off's" before he went home. He looked at his blister. He hadn't done much writing for the last three days and it was starting to heal. His mother had told him to use surgical spirit on it. That was meant to harden the skin. He hoped it would harden before next week.

And then it was time to leave, but he hung around for a few minutes to finish off the last bit of filing and to let Anne get off before him. He didn't want to ride with her that evening. He just wanted to think about Blodwyn.

As he rode home, he considered what had happened that afternoon. Blodwyn was clearly a little obsessed with her legs – hence the mini-skirts and these weird conversations. This was not helped by a boyfriend who didn't appreciate them and so she probably felt frustrated enough to mess about with a shy and innocent young lad who knew no better. He never realised a girl could so enjoy demonstrating her strong legs like that. It was all new to him, but, apart from all the embarrassment it caused him, he loved every minute of it. He didn't kid himself that this was love or anything silly, but he found her totally and utterly physically attractive. He would dearly love to explore her legs and bum again. He remembered reading an expression that perfectly summed up his feelings – he was hopelessly in lust.

That night in bed, he had a wonderful fantasy about her. In this fantasy, he was walking her home from town across the park when they stopped for a rest on a grassy bank. As they lay there, she saw him eyeing up her legs and she just said 'Come here' and proceeded to wrap those gorgeous thighs around his head. He managed to say 'Wait, my glasses,' and she let him remove them otherwise they would surely have been crushed to bits. She proceeded to toy with him with a series of little squeezes and big squeezes. Just when he thought she had released him,

77

she slapped her legs together again and laughed all the time. It was a glorious fantasy and had the desired effect. Normally this was his way of getting off to sleep, but his mind was still racing away.

He kept telling himself to keep his feet on the ground and just be pleased he had been able to expand his experience of girls, albeit not the way he had anticipated. But he convinced himself that this was his best chance yet of getting a date. After half an hour of turning this all over in his head, he repeated his previous fantasy and then he did sleep.

CHAPTER 7

Disappointments and a 'Nutter'

On Sunday, Mark headed off down the Park with his nice clean boots for his 'kick-about'. He was the first person to arrive. No Toby; no Nobby; nobody!

He wondered if everyone had misunderstood his directions. It was two minutes before 10.30 – the time agreed that they would start. Mark always liked punctuality and he expected it from others. He decided to hang around the goalmouth to stop anyone else grabbing it.

After five more minutes, Bob Nichols arrived. He told Mark not to be surprised that no one else had arrived yet. He hadn't expected Toby to get there early. He was 'all mouth and trousers'. Mark thought the expression was 'all mouth and *no* trousers,' but he wasn't sure. He asked Bob if he had played with anyone famous at Chelsea. Bob confessed that he'd never played in the first team, but he had played with a few big names in the reserves. He mentioned a few, but they meant nothing to Mark. After all, that would have been back in the fifties, and Mark would only have known the stars from that era if they had been included in his set of 'Famous Footballers' cigarette cards, which he used to collect.

A few people gradually drifted along and someone had a tired-looking football, which they kicked around for a while. Mark volunteered to go in goal and his handling was quite good, although he felt a little rusty.

At 10.50, Nobby arrived with a couple of better balls, but around eleven o'clock he told everyone that they'd all do a proper warm-up and proceeded to lead them through a set of squats, shoulder twists, trunk turns and sit-ups, all interspersed with lots of 'running on the spot' and star jumps. 'Come on! Open up your legs. That's what you say to the girls' There were lots of painful groans and stiff limbs. Woody, Bob Nichols and Mark were the only ones who managed to keep up with Nobby. Only half the expected number actually turned up. Notable for their absence was Bob Walsh and Toby – two people who had appeared to be the keenest at the meeting.

The 'warm-up' was more like a half-hour keep fit session. At the end of it, Nobby told them they it was no good trying to arrange friendlies if they weren't fit enough. 'If you think you can just turn up and play, without first getting fit, you've got another think coming. I don't mind losing a few games while we find our feet, but I want no part of a team that is an embarrassment. You can pass the word on to those who haven't bothered to turn up. There'll be no friendlies until I think you're ready.'

Then they divided themselves into two teams and had a game with Mark as the only goalkeeper, in the only goal. They were wearing a variety of shirts and shorts, so no one really knew who was in which side, but it didn't seem to matter. The quality on show varied enormously from 'totally uncoordinated' through to 'obviously played before', with Bob Nichols being in a class of his own.

Whenever he got the ball, he controlled it instantly, looked up and found a team-mate. When he tackled, he won the ball. When he dribbled, he beat everyone, then released another accurate and perfectly weighted pass. And when he headed the ball, it stayed headed. He chose not to blast the ball at Mark in goal, preferring instead to pass or try long-range efforts.

Mark gave a good account of himself in goal and saved one of the two penalties awarded by Nobby, who acted as referee, as well as participating in the game when it suited him. A few people said 'Well done, Sid!' The final score was 11-8 to Bob's team.

As he rode home, Mark felt quite confident of getting into the team if there was to be a team. No one else seemed interested in playing in goal and he didn't make any bad mistakes.

That night, he hardly slept again. He knew there was every chance that Blodwyn might not go out with him, but he had to hope. He contemplated the best way to approach her. He felt it unlikely that she would come and find him to tell him her decision. Equally, he didn't want to appear too eager and go storming in to see her straight away. In any case, he wouldn't want to discuss the matter in front of Margaret or anyone else. Sometimes, he could make out people's silhouette in the frosted glass in front of his desk (shelf), so perhaps he could keep a look out for her and then follow her down the corridor. 'Mind you, the corridor is a little public,' he thought.

After due consideration, he decided to just play it by ear and not get too desperate if he didn't actually get the chance to speak to her the next day. He didn't want to frighten her away. Even if her answer was 'No', he'd like to be friends with her and have the occasional chat. Although, if they were anything like the previous chats, this could get very frustrating for him. He hoped she would still wear her mini-skirts, even if it were only on the odd occasion.

Mark got to work in very good time the next morning. He beat Josie to work, but Penny was already there. Her husband worked on the same estate and he always dropped her off at 8.30.

She told Mark that, this week, he would do the Factory payroll again and as some clock cards had already arrived, he made a start.

When Josie arrived, she gave him another stern talking to. 'Now, young man. You need to quicken up your pace this week… AND… there were a number of errors on last week's payroll. You'd entered the wrong man's details on the payroll sheet at least twice. We had a Hell of a job sorting it all out. One chap threatened to go to the union unless we telegraphed him the correct money. I've still got to make all the adjustments on this week's payroll, so I'll do his payslip. So pull your socks up or I'll have to go and tell your cousin. He doesn't know about your mistakes, yet, so let's keep it that way by eliminating them all.

Now go and fetch some coffee.'

Penny followed him out of the door to go to the Ladies. 'Don't get downhearted, Mark. We usually have a few corrections to make. It was a very easy mistake to make.'

'How did she find out about George being my cousin? Did Bob tell her?'

'No, Margaret knew before you got 'ere and she let it slip, last week.'

'It wasn't favouritism, you know. I don't think George wanted me to have the job. He took a long time to make up his mind about me.'

'I know. We kept badgering 'im about it and 'e kept saying 'e wanted to make sure 'e'd got the right person. If it makes you feel any better, I think we have got the right person. Considering last week was your first week, we didn't do that badly. Don't take any notice of Josie.'

'Thank you,' he said as they went in separate directions.

Back in the office, Josie was busy sorting out the timesheets and there was a steady stream of foremen from the Factory, bringing their clockcards.

One of them was Toby, who was the Metal Shop Foreman, closely followed by Nobby, who was in charge of the Maintenance Department.

Nobby asked Toby where he had got to the day before. Toby made an excuse about his wife having other plans for him. 'Well, we can't run a football team based around our wives' requirements, can we?'

'Nah, I agwee with you one hundwed per cent. If it had been a match, I'd have been there.'

'Not if you hadn't been to training, you wouldn't. 'Cause you wouldn't have got picked!'

Josie intervened, 'Nah then, boys. This is a Wages office. Would you like to take your squabbles somewhere else?'

After they'd gone, Penny asked Mark if he played football.

'Yes, I was there yesterday. I was one of the few who did turn up.'

'That's good. It's nice to see you mixing in. It's a good way to make friends, I should think.' That may have been true except that there was no one anywhere near to Mark's age. He couldn't see himself making friends with older married men.

Mark was making good headway with the clockcards and was on target to finish them well before lunch. His blister was not too painful. All this time, he had been keeping a watch out for Blodwyn, but he hadn't seen her walking past. Just after eleven o'clock, Margaret came in. She told them all that she had a 'phone call from Blodwyn to say she wouldn't be returning to work. She'd gone back to Swansea.

Mark felt devastated. His head was swimming around. He wanted to ask Margaret more about her conversation with Blodwyn, but he just sat there listening as Margaret added 'I think there's more to it than we know. She never looked too good in the mornings. She kept talking about needing to see her boyfriend this last weekend. He still lives in Swansea, you know.'

'Do you think she is pregnant, then?' asked Mark.

'He's quick, isn't he?' said Josie.

'I'm not saying anything else,' said Margaret. 'But I'm not too sorry. She never seemed very interested in her work. She was always on the 'phone to her boyfriend and personally, I didn't take to her at all. And I found her skirts very embarrassing.'

Then Josie changed the subject and Mark turned round to continue his clockcards – except that he couldn't concentrate. He came in prepared for the possibility of being rejected, but he never imagined he would never see her again. Was she pregnant? That didn't seem to fit in with her behaviour. She certainly didn't look pregnant. In fact, he had noticed that she had a very narrow waist, but someone like Margaret would know better about these things than he would. It might explain why she was staying in Swansea, but there were a lot of things he couldn't explain.

He told himself that there was nothing he could do about it and to just get on with his life, but he really was so disappointed... so very disappointed. He might well find himself a nice little girlfriend over the coming months, but he could be sure she would be nothing like Blodwyn. She really was a 'one-off'.

He realised he had only known her for one week, but in that time she had had such an impact on him. He tried to console himself with the thought that Karen would be starting soon. At that moment, however, it was no consolation. He was totally devastated.

Mark finished off his clockcards and continued with the Factory's payroll sheets. Despite his distraction, he was picking up speed and by mid-afternoon, he had finished the payroll sheets and they had all reconciled first time. He had decided to throw himself into his work to keep his mind off his disappointment.

He was then trusted to work on some site timesheets.

A little while later, the 'phone rang and Josie answered it. Mark heard her say 'Sid? There's no one here called Sid.' Mark jumped up and pointed to himself. 'Wait a minute,' she said into the 'phone, then turned to Mark. 'Is this for you, then? Who's Sid?'

'That's me. I'll tell you about it in a minute.'

It was Nobby telling him they'd found a venue for mid-week training. It was at an old boxing gym, near the quay. It was called the 'Lads' Club' and to be there for 7.30 Tuesday evening. Mark knew roughly where it was.

He handed the 'phone back to Josie. They both looked at him enquiringly.

'Sid?' asked Penny.

'It was my nickname at school.'

'Would you rather we called you "Sid" then?' she asked.

'No, no, no. It was a big mistake. They asked me my name at the football meeting and through force of habit, I blurted out "Sid." I regretted it straight away. Please don't call me "Sid!" It's not my name.'

Ten minutes later, Josie said 'Sid! Will you fetch some coffees, please?' He just gave her a dirty look. His mother always used to teach him that if you don't take notice of people teasing you, they'd soon get tired of it. In any case, he wasn't in the mood for silly games.

By the end of the day, they had all made very good progress with the payrolls and Josie was happy that they were well ahead of schedule.

Mark felt the need for someone to talk to. So that evening after work, he saw that Anne's bike had already gone, then chased off after her. He soon caught her. They started off with some small talk. Then he asked her if he had heard about Blodwyn leaving.

'Yes, I heard, but to be honest, I'd only met her very briefly for a few minutes when Margaret brought her round on her first day. We'd hardly spoken to each other. Well, she hadn't been here long enough.'

Mark said, 'I had a few short conversations with her and we seemed to be getting on quite well. I was thinking of asking her out. I knew she had this boyfriend in Swansea, but I couldn't see that working with her living in Norfolk. So I'm a little disappointed.'

'There's plenty more fish in the sea!' Anne said.

'Yes, but this fish seemed to find me attractive. She actually said so in not so many words. Other girls find me unattractive.'

'You're not unattractive!'

'Course I am!'

'No, you're not. You mustn't think like that.'

It was nice of her to say that, but he still thought that any chap who wore glasses wouldn't get very far on his looks. He had to attract a girl by other means – wit, intelligence, charm or better still – money! After all, his brother still hadn't got a girlfriend and he wore glasses, so that proved his point. But as Anne wore glasses, he kept these thoughts to himself. He didn't regard Anne as attractive, although he certainly wouldn't have called her ugly. She was a lovely *person* and that was what mattered. Even though he didn't fancy her, he considered her boyfriend to be a lucky chap. His ride with Anne had been therapeutic. He needed to get Blodwyn out of his mind and talking to Anne had helped. He had heard that it takes a long while to get over someone you loved. He hoped that the same didn't apply to lust.

That night, he resisted the urge to repeat his favourite fantasy. He was afraid that dwelling upon Blodwyn's charms would just drag out his feelings of despair and he had to move on. However, he had no control over his dreams and Blodwyn duly appeared in one erotic dream, which also included room for Megan and Karen, both of whom he'd never met, but he was able to recognise them and they certainly seemed real enough in his dream.

Everything was going well in the Wages department on Tuesday, except that in the afternoon, when they came to split up the payslips, Josie and Penny both noticed that Mark's payslips were too faint to read. In his determination to speed up and eradicate mistakes, he had forgotten the need to press hard. All three of them pitched in to reload the sheets onto the payroll boards with fresh carbon paper and go over them again.

Needless to say, Josie was not a happy person.

Nevertheless, they agreed that Mark should join them on the Wednesday to help with the money.

Towards the end of the afternoon, the 'phone rang. Josie answered it as usual. 'It's for you, Mark. He says it's a personal call.'

Mark took the 'phone, expecting it to be Nobby again, and said 'Hello.'

The person on the 'phone had a Welsh accent and he sounded rather angry. 'This is Gareth Flynn. I understand you've been asking my girlfriend for a date?'

'Who would that be?' asked Mark. He felt a surge of anger – not so much at this weirdo, but at Blodwyn for telling him.

'Why, do you make a habit of trying to date other blokes' girls? I'm talking about my Blodwyn, of course! I take a very dim view of such behaviour. And she tells me you've been paying her all sorts of compliments about her legs. She's my girlfriend and I'm the only one who can talk to her about her body.'

Now Mark was even more annoyed at Blodwyn. He felt no great desire to stick up for her honour, but he didn't want to make a scene in front of Penny and Josie. He was shaking with anger, but he just asked 'Are you sure she's not just saying all this to make you jealous?'

'I've got nothing to feel jealous about. She's my girlfriend and she doesn't want anyone else.'

'What are you trying to achieve with this 'phone call?'

'I'm just warning you off, pal!'

'Well, I hope you feel you've done your bit. Now I'm going to put the 'phone down. I've got work to do' and he passed the 'phone back to Josie. 'Thanks, Josie,' he said. She noticed his hand was shaking.

'What was all that about?' she asked, putting the phone back. 'He sounded like a bit of a nutter.'

'Yes he did, didn't he? It was just some weirdo got the wrong end of the stick about something.'

'Are you getting mixed up with strange women and their boyfriends?' asked Penny, who would probably have heard some of what Gareth was saying. But she didn't sound as though she disapproved.

'Chance would be a fine thing,' was all that he wanted to add and went back to work. He was hoping she hadn't heard Gareth using Blodwyn's name or his reference to her legs.

He couldn't believe Blodwyn would do such a thing. He felt even more puzzled about her behaviour, but decided it wasn't worth worrying about.

In the evening, he turned up at the gym for the football training. This time, there was a better turnout, although Bob Walsh still wasn't there. The gym was dark, very dirty and dilapidated. There was a lot of dust in the air, as well as the smell of cigarette smoke. Several of the players had lit up before Nobby put them through their paces. The same people were gasping for another cigarette at the end of the session, which consisted of more of the same exercises as Sunday, but for even longer this time. There were also a few dusty old medicine balls lying around, so Nobby had them all throwing these to each other. Mark wasn't sure what that was going to achieve, but it was a break from 'running on the spot.'

After an hour of this, most people were ready to drop. There was no room in the gym for a game of football and several people complained about this, so they arranged another 'kick-about' down the 'rec' for Sunday morning. Hiring the gym was costing them money, so everyone was asked to pay half a crown towards the cost. Mark asked for a reduction for his age, so he paid one and sixpence.

Several people were talking about going for a drink, but no one thought to invite Mark, so he made his way home.

Wednesday came round and Mark was pleased to have been allowed to help with the cash. It meant he would have taken part in every activity in the weekly payroll cycle. It also meant one less day of filing in the Costing department. While they were waiting for the money to be collected, they were given details of where each pay packet had to go. A man named Dave Taylor, whose title was Labour Controller, furnished them with this information, but right up until the time the door was locked, he kept coming back with late amendments.

Mark found him to be a very congenial man who took his work very seriously. Penny told Mark that Dave had served in the Korean War, but he never liked talking about it. She knew he had killed people and seen several colleagues killed. Mark told her that his father was the same about his experiences in the Second World War. Even twenty years after the end of the War, Frank still woke up with terrible nightmares.

Bob came in to get the cheque for the money run. He asked Mark to join them again, but Josie said they wanted him to stay there and see all the preparations. 'You never know when one of us might go sick,' she said. Mark was disappointed not to have a little ride and enjoy the banter, but he understood what Josie meant.

Josie suggested that they all made a point of visiting the toilet and get topped up with coffee before the money arrived, because they didn't want to be unlocking the door more than was absolutely necessary.

The money was delivered and the door was locked. They stacked up the money into racks. Unfortunately, there were only two racks, so to start with, Mark was asked to watch what the other two did and then later check that the correct cash had been inserted into each pay packet. At the end of the exercise, there should be no money left, otherwise they had to go through every packet again until they found the error. Despite coming straight from the bank, a lot of the money was dirty and their hands soon got grubby. Penny advised Mark to wash his hands before eating anything.

Mark could see what they had meant about the pressure of Wednesdays. Apart from the responsibility and security of all this money, they also had a very tight deadline to meet. Even so, Josie and Penny seemed quite capable of talking while they worked and Mark only found one mistake. Josie even said 'Well done' to him. 'If we had gotten to the end before finding that, it would have been an 'ell of a job to find.'

Mark noticed that the 'phone was much quieter than usual. He guessed that most people knew what happened on a Wednesday and kept out of Josie's way. When it did ring, it was Dave Taylor with another amendment. Mark thought it might have been Gareth again, but he never called again.

When all the money had been inserted into the pay packets and there was no money left over, they began the task of sealing the packets with the payslips pushed inside. Then they gathered together the packets for each site and wrote out a registered envelope for each one. The size of the envelope varied according to the number of employees at a particular site. The Factory pay packets were kept separate and sorted according to their locations. Finally, every registered envelope was weighed and appropriate postage stamps were applied. Details were then entered into a special book that would be taken to the Post Office with the packets.

When all was ready, Josie 'phoned Bob to tell him. It was only 3.30. The earliest the Wages had ever been ready. This time, Mark was permitted to join the Post Office run.

They used George's new company car. It was a white Vauxhall Victor. Company cars had to be either white or that horrible dull blue like Greg's Viva. Bob drove, with Mike in the front passenger seat. The fourth person was Bill Connell. Mark remembered the name from their conversation with Gail.

As they came into town, Bill was constantly straining his neck to look round at various young girls in their mini-skirts. Mark decided he must have been in his late forties or early fifties. He asked Mark if he was a 'leg and bum' man or a 'breast' man.

'I didn't know you had to be one or the other,' replied Mark.

'You can like both if you want. Just don't tell me I'm sitting next to someone who doesn't like either.'

'No, you're safe. In any case, even if I was queer, I don't think I'd fancy you.' He could hear Mike and Bob chuckling in the front.

Bob said, 'I think Mark had his eyes on old Blodwyn.'

'Phaww! What a pair of legs that girl had,' called Bill, holding his hands up as though he was grabbing hold of her. 'I'll shall be sorry to see her go!'

'You're obviously a "leg and bum" man, then?' Mark asked him.

'Absolutely!'

'Are you married?'

'I was. I got divorced two years ago. The best thing I ever did!'

Bill was a Londoner and Mark noticed that the Londoners at Greshams were more likely to be divorced than the local people were. They also seemed more inclined to get involved in affairs. Gail's conquests seemed to be mostly with Londoners. Somehow, he couldn't see Gail having an affair with Bill. He struck Mark as being a 'dirty old man' who didn't have a lot of respect for women.

Just then they passed another young girl in a mini-skirt. She was very tall and particularly thin. Bob said 'How about that one, then, Bill?'

'Nah! There's nothing to her.' Mark agreed.

Mike was busy looking at a dark-haired woman wearing a tight sweater. He was obviously a 'breast' man.

Once they had got rid of the money, Bob suggested they give George's new car a 'good test', so they went back to the office through the countryside. Mike said 'I think we're only meant to vary the route when we've got some money in the car!'

It wasn't a lot of fun in the back. There were no seat belts in the car and everyone was getting thrown around. Mike was encouraging Bob to put his foot down and kept saying things like 'You can have him, Bob!' or 'Push him off the road!' Somehow, Mark didn't think he would drive his own car like that. He was glad he hadn't endured the journey straight after a heavy lunch.

Back at the office, Josie thought they'd been a long time. 'Yes, there was a big queue in the Post Office and a lot of traffic in town. It was all a bit "pissbodical", if you ask me,' replied Mark.

Penny said, 'If it was "pissbodical," Mike must have been with you.'

Penny and Josie looked remarkably relaxed. Penny was reading a book and Josie was just smoking and looking out of the window.

'What shall I do now?' asked Mark.

'Nothing,' replied Josie. 'Just have a rest. We've done well today and it's time to relax.'

One of the foremen came in to fetch his department's payslips. He said one of his men was off sick and asked if they could keep his pay packet in the safe until he returned to work.

Mark didn't like doing nothing and he looked fidgety. He kept swinging round on his swivel chair. Then he said, 'Shall I make a start on next week's pay packets?'

Penny said 'If you don't know what to do with yourself, why don't you go and do some costing?' So he gathered up his stuff and wheeled his chair next door.

Bob was glad to see him, because they were getting further behind with everything. He said he would be glad when Karen started. So would Mark. He was looking forward to meeting her.

Mark found Thursday and Friday particularly boring. Working in the Wages Department gave him a sense of purpose. There was an end-result. Getting the money out to everyone was the culmination of a week's hard work. To Mark, the work he did in Costing, apart from being very boring, didn't seem to achieve anything. Bob was good company and whenever anyone visited them, there was always some little amusement, but the work itself was thoroughly BORING.

To make matters worse, he was asked to come in to work on Saturday for a couple of hours. You didn't get paid any extra for this. It was just expected. Bob said he would be there and he was, but Mark didn't see him do any work. He spent most of the morning wandering around to see who else was in the building. There were no women at all. It was a 'bloke' thing to work on a Saturday and you had to show willing.

The next week followed a very similar pattern to this one and Mark was back in the Costing Office on Thursday when he received his payslip and some cash in a pay packet. He checked it all carefully. There was a mistake. He now knew enough about payrolls to check everything. He was paying tax, which he didn't think was right as he hadn't started work until October, so he should have had six months free pay before tax should be calculated. But even worse was that his gross pay was based on £325 per year, rather than £350.

He went to see George, who explained that as he hadn't been given a tax code yet, he was being taxed on 'Emergency'. This meant he wasn't being taxed cumulatively at all. It might get it sorted out later when the Tax Office got round to it, but in the meantime, George had no choice.

As for the salary, George had never mentioned a figure of £350. Mark realised it was the Labour Exchange who quoted that figure and he had never discussed it with George. There was nothing in writing to support his case. Mark felt very angry, but it was his own fault for taking things on trust. Another lesson learnt.

After the deduction of his 'sub' and the tax, he didn't seem to have a lot of money left to see him through the month. And he still had to give his mother her housekeeping money. He was not a happy chap.

On Friday afternoon, a new desk was carried in for Karen.

'So she gets a desk, while I sit at a shelf,' he thought to himself, bitterly. As far as he knew, he was the only person in the building who sat at a shelf. The corresponding shelf in Margaret's office was stacked with Ledger books and filing trays – in other words, it was used as a shelf!

Mark felt as though he'd had a bad week. He'd lost Blodwyn, been twice told off by Josie, been screwed with his salary and now this new girl was getting better treatment than he was.

Nevertheless, he was looking forward to meeting her, except that he wouldn't be working with her until Thursday. He had made the mistake of forming a preconception of her. Bob had told him she was quite good looking, had a nice figure (although Bob's taste did not coincide with Mark's) and she wore glasses.

From this, Mark had decided she was quiet and unassuming, friendly, had a good sense of humour and that her and Mark would get on like a house on fire.

The only question now was would she be more appealing to a 'leg and bum' man or a 'breast' man – or possibly both!

CHAPTER 8

A Change of Heart

It was Monday 2nd of November. Mark arrived at work in good time and was eagerly looking forward to meeting Karen for the first time. He didn't have to wait too long.

Bob was soon in the process of showing her round the building and he made the Wages Department his very first call.

Because of the position of Mark's desk, his first view of Karen was a rear view, as she was introduced to Josie and Penny on the other side of the office, although he had been aware of her looking at him as she came through the door. Mark turned to watch the introductions and to gain his first impressions.

She was about five foot nine and, wearing high heels, she appeared to be a few inches taller than Bob. She had very dark brown hair and was wearing an olive green knee-length knitted dress with a lemon coloured cardigan draped loosely around her shoulders, as though she was cold – only it wasn't at all cold in the office. Mark was very pleased to see she had shapely legs – not quite in the same class as Blodwyn's and perhaps a little larger, but perfectly acceptable.

As soon as she started speaking, Mark's preconception of a nice quiet girl went straight out the window. She had a very broad and somewhat coarse local accent. She was very keen to tell everyone that she had some experience of working in a payroll office, so she knew all about tax tables and graduated pension, etc. Penny and Josie did not look particularly impressed.

Then Bob pointed her towards Mark and she turned to him. Mark didn't think she was the least bit attractive. Her glasses were very thick – both the lenses themselves and the dark frames. She had a rather jaundiced complexion and a few dark spots on her face.

She held her hand out to shake hands. Mark had originally intended to stand up, but suddenly changed his mind. He reached for her hand. It felt limp, cold and clammy. It wasn't exactly a handshake, at all. She dived straight in before he could speak, 'Hello Mark. We've met before, haven't we?'

'I don't think so.' Mark felt sure he would have remembered. After all, he didn't know that many girls.

'Yes, we have. You came for an interview at Lemons.' This was the name of the Export company where he was unsuccessfully interviewed. The only person he had spoken to that day was the manager who interviewed him. However, the interview was conducted in an open plan office, so it was possible that Karen had seen him, but he hadn't noticed her – especially as he would have been far too nervous to look around him.

'You were wearing a baggy old brown suit and a grammar school tie. My friend Jean said you'd got your clothes from a jumble sale.'

'It was actually my father's suit. I didn't have anything else to wear. It's nice of you to mention it. Do you and your friend get your clothes from jumble sales, then?'

'Oooh!' went Josie, Penny and Bob together.

This was hate at first sight. Far from being the nice quiet little girl he was looking forward to meeting, she was a very tactless individual. It wasn't her fault that she was plain, but she really did need to learn some manners and a little humility.

Penny said, 'I can see you two are going to get along just fine!'

'I'm sure we'll be all right, won't we Mark?' said Karen. 'I'll see you on Thursday, won't I?'

'I'm sure I'm looking forward to it no end!' The sarcasm seemed to be wasted on her. She didn't seem to have detected the animosity that Mark felt towards her. He'd have to work on that.

As she walked out of the door, Mark couldn't help noticing her awkward gait. She was struggling with her high heels and seemed to be making hard work of the simple process of placing one foot in front of the other. In every respect, she was a very uncoordinated person.

'You weren't very nice to 'er, were you, Mark?' asked Penny, after Bob and Karen had left. 'You were much nicer to Blodwyn when you met 'er. I 'ope it's not because Karen didn't have a short skirt on?'

'That's got nothing to do with it. I thought she was a very rude person.'

'I've got to admit,' added Josie, 'that I found her a little forward. Apart from what she said to Mark about his father's suit, I thought her comments about knowing all about payrolls was out of order.'

'Well, perhaps she was just a little bit nervous on 'er first day,' was Penny's contribution.

Mark said 'She didn't strike me as a person who suffers from nerves. She seemed too sure of herself for my liking.' Mark felt very disappointed with his new colleague. Now he would regret not seeing Blodwyn again.

A few minutes later, it was time for Mark to fetch some coffee. As he walked down the corridor, he could see Bob and Karen ahead of him, still making the rounds. He had another look at her legs. At least they were nice to look at, but she was still making hard work of walking in her high heels. And she was still talking ('Probably without putting her brain in gear,' thought Mark).

It was funny how some women, like Ellie for example, enhanced their elegance by a pair of high heels, while others just looked ungainly and totally inelegant. Here was a prime example. Not only was Karen struggling to walk in a straight line, but her whole posture was wrong. Her shoulders and back were all bent over. As she turned to enter another office, Mark could see that she was very flat chested and he thought she was probably, consciously or subconsciously, adopting a body posture to disguise this fact.

The problem with Mark was that once he had decided he disliked someone, he disliked them with a vengeance. For her part, Karen still wanted to be friends. So when Thursday finally came round, there was one person in the Costing Department determined to keep the relationship at arms' length and another doing all she could to improve things. Only Karen was still inclined to say the wrong thing, even though she didn't always mean to.

She was not classed as a junior, but Mark was. So she thought it perfectly in order to tell him what jobs he should be doing and they were, on the whole, the more menial tasks like filing and fetching coffee. Mark bitterly resented this. He felt he knew the work as well as she did and was probably a more able person. She was about a year older and had more overall experience than him, but he could see no justification for her higher status. He told her that he didn't take orders from her, so she took up the matter with Bob, who told Mark that she had a case. Bob did quietly tell her to be a little tactful about this, so her method of giving orders to Mark became more like 'Mark, darling, would you like to fetch some coffees, please?'

It didn't make Mark feel any better. He hadn't been enjoying his time in Costing before she arrived, but now he really was getting all the boring jobs. And he objected to being called "darling" by someone whom he disliked.

However, he was pleased when she asked him to fetch some stationery, because it meant he could go and have a chat with Anne. He hadn't seen her on her bike lately and he found out the reason why. Now that the clocks had reverted to GMT, she didn't fancy biking home in the dark, so she had arranged to get a lift to and from work with Gary, who worked in the Drawing Office. Mark didn't know who Gary was and felt disappointed that she had stopped using her bike, but he could understand it.

She also told him that she was transferring to another job. Her boss, Paul O'Connor, was to become the new Works Manager and he needed an assistant. As she already reported to him, she would transfer with him. That would happen at the end of the month, so she would no longer administer the stationery. Her current position was being advertised. Mark said he hoped her new job worked out for her. He also hoped her replacement was going to be unattached and looking for a shy young boyfriend.

Mark told Anne about Karen. Anne was very understanding and sympathetic. She had already met Karen and had formed a similar opinion to Mark.

Later that day, Mark asked Bob if he had any intention of playing football. 'Yes, I want to. There seem to be so many things happening at home, that I never get round to it.'

They chatted generally about the team and the people involved. Karen had to have her say. 'Do you play, then, Mark?' she asked.

'I certainly do,' he replied.

'I play, you know,' she announced. 'I play with my brother in the back garden. I usually beat him.'

Mark was a little surprised, but didn't consider this proper football. He asked with his usual sarcasm 'Do you play in your high heels?'

'Now, don't be silly, Mark!'

He admitted to himself that it was a silly remark, but he had only ever seen her in high heels and struggling to walk, so he couldn't imagine her doing anything remotely energetic.

'I've always been good at sports. I played hockey and netball at school – and athletics,' she added.

Perhaps that explained her shapely legs. 'My best event was the hurdles. I came second on the school sports day. I was also quite useful at the long jump.

You look surprised, Mark?'

'Well to be perfectly honest, Karen. You seem to struggle to walk in your high heels, so I can't imagine you running or jumping.' He couldn't be bothered to spare her feelings. After all, she didn't spare his when she had talked about his brown suit.

Bob intervened. 'Why don't you two make an effort to get on with each other? You're always bickering.'

'Yes, Mark,' said Karen. 'Why don't you try being nice to me for a change? You've always being horrible to me.'

'Well don't take it personal,' he said.

'Why, are you horrible to everyone?' she asked.

'No. I mean everyone wants to be horrible to you.' She didn't appreciate his attempt at humour.

Then he added 'I'll try being nice to you if you can make the effort.' Unfortunately, he didn't really mean it. He still disliked her and that was that.

He did admit to himself that he was surprised that she might be a little athletic and wondered whether his first impressions had coloured his judgement, but he only had her word for this athletic ability. Still, her legs were a good clue.

Over the next two weeks, Karen continued to try to be friendly and Mark continued to avoid being friendly, but he did make some effort to cut out the nasty remarks. He wasn't always successful, but he did try.

One day, he was working in the Wages department when Karen came in for a chat with Mark and the girls. As usual, Mark was being a little unfriendly towards Karen. Penny said 'I feel for Bob. You two can't be much fun to work with. You're not very nice to Karen, are you, Mark?'

'No he's not, are you Mark?' said Karen as she walked slowly and deliberately towards him. 'He's horrible to me. I'm going to have to change that.' She sounded as though her patience was wearing thin.

She perched herself on his 'desk' a few inches from his face. The shelf-cum-desk wasn't designed to take this sort of weight and it bowed slightly. He wondered how much she weighed and whether the shelf could take her weight. She crossed her right leg over her left, right under his nose. Her dress was a little tight, so this action wasn't easy for her, but it meant she showed very little flesh above her round knees. Was she trying some kind of seduction technique on him? He had to admit it was having some kind of effect on him. Being this close to him made her seem quite imposing. Her calves appeared to be quite long and full from this distance and he was aware of her dress straining around her thighs. He wasn't sure where to look. He really only had two choices. He could either look ahead at her legs or at her face above. He decided to look at her face, but looking up at her put him at a distinct disadvantage and he felt a little intimidated. He noticed that underneath her thick glasses, her eyes were quite attractive. Her mouth was a little thin, but she had good cheekbones, when you could see them beneath her glasses.

'Now, Mark. Are you going to be nicer to me from now on … or not?' It sounded like some kind of challenge.

'Why, what are you going to do if I'm not?' He thought he'd rise to the challenge.

'I'm going to be so nice to you that you'll have to give in.'

'Is this you being nice to me – sitting on my desk?' He was weakening and didn't really know how to handle the situation.

She changed position. This time, crossing her left leg very deliberately over her right, a few inches closer to his face and the shelf bowed again. He heard the faint rustle of her tights and it really felt intimidating to have a girl sitting this close to him. He felt compelled to watch her change of position and quickly looked at her legs. It was what she wanted of him and he duly obliged. She did have very nice calves and he secretly yearned to touch them.

She said 'I'm not moving until you say something nice to me.'

He thought about this for a minute or two. He couldn't say 'Stay there, then,' because he wouldn't be able to do any work with her in that position. He was hoping for some help from Penny or Josie, but it didn't come. He considered physically trying to push her or lift her off, but she looked so self-assured that he wasn't sure how easy this would be with any degree of dignity. The way the shelf was bowing made him think she was no lightweight. After due deliberation, he said 'All right, then. You've got nice legs.' It sounded a bit lame, but at that moment he couldn't think of anything else to say; and after all it was a true statement.

'That is a nice thing to say.' But she didn't move immediately. It was as though she knew she had some kind of power over him and she wanted to milk it for all it was worth. She then eased herself down from the shelf and then put her arm around his shoulder and gave him a little squeeze. He wasn't sure why. Did she fancy him or something? The funny thing was, at that moment, he quite fancied her, but he wasn't going to let her know that.

'Perhaps I can get on with some work, now?' he said, picking up some clockcards to work on.

'I'll see you on Thursday, Mark,' she said.

After she had gone, Mark tried to work out what had just happened. He really didn't understand women. They do and say funny things. He was still coming to terms with his little escapade with Blodwyn and now Karen was managing to mess up his mind. He was sure he still disliked her, but now he was feeling some kind of physical attraction to her. And he had to admire the way she manipulated him into paying her a compliment. Moreover, she had just defeated him in some kind of psychological battle and she now held the upper hand. That on top of being able to order him around when work dictated.

As he didn't relish another similar battle, he made up his mind that from that point on, he was going to make more of an effort to be amenable. Nothing special. He wasn't going to be extra nice or go overboard in any way, but Penny was right in that Bob must have been getting fed up with their (his) antics.

That evening, Mark went round his sister's to baby-sit. Barbara had a very broad taste in music, but she shared Mark's love of Soul and R & B. She talked about seeing the Temptations on television recently and she asked if Mark had seen them. Of course he had, despite having to battle with the rest of the family for viewing rights. Then she said 'That lead singer's a good looking chap, isn't he?'

'You mean David Ruffin?' he asked, looking puzzled.

'Yes, the one who sang "My Girl". The one with glasses!'

'How can he be good-looking? He wears thick glasses!'

'So! That doesn't mean he can't be good-looking.'

This was quite a revelation for Mark. Maybe he wasn't as ugly as he thought. Maybe Blodwyn and Anne meant it when they said he wasn't ugly. More to the point, perhaps Karen did fancy him. After Barbara and her husband had gone out, he looked at himself in a mirror. He had never understood what it was that made one chap good looking and another ugly. He had heard Karen say that Charlton Heston was her favourite film star, but he looked ugly to Mark. As he looked at himself, he thought that, like Karen, his eyes might be attractive, but they were hidden under his glasses.

On Thursday, he made every effort to fetch the coffees before anyone had chance to ask him. Somehow, that made him feel in control of the situation instead of being at Karen's beck and call. He even asked if anyone wanted a bread roll from the canteen. As soon as there were some "take-off's" to be filed, he filed them. He didn't ask, nor wait to be asked – he just did it.

The atmosphere improved tremendously and in a strange way, Mark almost enjoyed working there. Karen, for her part, seemed to have stopped making those remarks that annoyed him and the three of them sat and chatted pleasantly while they worked. The work was still boring, but he considered that Thursdays and Fridays would be boring in the Wages office anyway, so he decided a change of scene was no bad thing. And after all, wasn't one of his objectives to get used to female company. Well, he was doing that with Karen. He still didn't relish a trip to the Typing Pool, though.

Bob was always keen to interject some humour into the proceedings. He told Mark about an article he'd read.

'In a survey, it was found that forty per cent of all males masturbated in the bath, whilst the rest sang in the bath.

And what's more, the ones who sing invariably sing just one song. Do you know what it is?'

'No,' said Mark, innocently.

'Oh, no, of course you wouldn't.'

Karen creased up with laughter and pointed to Mark, who decided to keep a perfectly straight face. 'Come on, Mark,' she said. 'You've got to admit it's funny.'

'Well, no, it's not. The reason I didn't know the answer to the question is that we don't have a bath and I don't think it's nice making fun of underprivileged people.

'Oh, I'm sorry, ' she said. 'I never realised.' Then she looked at him, suspiciously. 'Are you making that up?'

'I might be,' he said, suddenly releasing a grin. Of course, it was true, but she didn't need to know that.

They were now a happy little group of three – even more so when someone like Gail or Penny paid them a visit. Mark observed that Karen enjoyed Bob's little jokes. He'd heard that a lot of women are attracted to men with a sense of humour and these three ladies all seemed to warm to Bob. Mark decided that when he got home that night he would dig out some old University Rag magazines and memorise a few jokes for slipping into the conversation to see if he got the same reaction.

He realised that he was now interested in creating a good impression with Karen. That didn't make sense.

The next day, he had a couple of very good jokes lined up and he waited for the right opportunity. It came mid-way through the morning, when they were all having a convivial chat about nothing in particular. He started with his favourite.

'There was this chap who went to see his doctor. The doctor said "I have very bad news for you. The results of all our tests show that your condition is terminal. You have less than twenty-four hours to live. You'll probably go in your sleep, tonight."

The man was devastated and went home to tell his loving wife. They agreed there was no time to organise any special event for his last few hours on Earth, but he would like to make mad passionate love one more time. So they did.

A few hours later, he asked her if they could do it again. And they did it again.

When it was time to go to bed, they made love a third time. His wife rolled over exhausted and went to sleep, but the man couldn't sleep. He only had a few more hours to live and if he fell asleep, he would probably never wake up again.

At three o'clock in the morning, he was still wide-awake, so he woke his wife up to ask her for another love session. She was very tired and angry and said "Listen! I've got to get up in the morning. You don't!"

They all laughed loudly. So much so, that Penny came in to hear what all the laughter was about. So Bob told one of his and Mark followed up with his second joke. 'Do you know Vic Burns?' he asked.

They all shook their heads. 'It does if you get it on your private parts!'

It took a few seconds before they all got the joke.

Karen gave him a very friendly smile and said 'Very good, Mark. I can't tell jokes. I can never remember them.'

'Of course, you can. Here's a very short joke. Try to remember it and tell it to someone else, later.

Did you hear about the architect who had his house-maid backwards, so he could watch television?'

Bob and Penny laughed, but Karen looked puzzled. 'No, why what happened?'

'No, Karen, that's the joke.' Still nothing.

'You see, it's a play on the word "house-maid" as opposed to "house made", see?'

'No, I'm sorry. I don't get it.'

'Well, you know what a "house-maid" is? And you know what it means to have a "house made" of bricks or whatever?'

'Oh, yeah. Sorry I was a bit slow, there.'

'Of course, it's not funny, when you have to explain a joke.'

'No. But I'll remember it and try it on someone else.'

During the afternoon, Ted came down to speak to Bob. Karen interrupted and said 'Ted. Did you hear about the architect who had his house built backwards, so he could watch television?'

Bob and Mark fell about laughing. Ted didn't get it, which was hardly surprising. Bob and Mark then spent a few minutes explaining to both Ted and Karen where it had all gone wrong.

Karen tried to recover the situation by asking Ted 'Do you know a chap named Vic Burns?'

By now Bob and Mark were practically rolling about the floor.

Mark said to Karen, 'I'm sorry. You were absolutely correct.' Then hesitated a few seconds. 'You can't tell jokes!'

She looked offended, so he added 'But we like it when you laugh at our jokes, don't we, Bob?'

A week earlier, he would have been perfectly happy for her to be offended, but now he felt differently about it. He wanted her to enjoy his jokes and he didn't want her to be offended in any way. And she appreciated his attempt to avoid being offensive. At this rate, they might even end up as friends.

The next day was Saturday and Mark was due to put in another Saturday morning appearance. When he arrived, he was surprised to see Karen there, but no Bob. The dress code for Saturdays was that anything goes. Mark was wearing jeans and a T-shirt, which seemed to be standard for the men on a Saturday. Karen was wearing black trousers and a thin yellow sweater. She also had (as usual) a thin cardigan draped over her shoulders.

They did very little work, preferring to sit and talk for most of the time. Karen even offered to fetch the coffees. Perhaps she felt that different rules applied on a Saturday. Or maybe she wanted to have a nose round to see who else was working that day.

Later on, Mark swivelled his chair round to say something to her, only to see her reaching across Bob's desk with her back towards him. He never got round to saying anything.

His eyes were drawn to the fantastic sight of her full but firm buttocks swelling her trousers. He had never imagined that she had such a wonderful feature. 'Even better than Blodwyn,' he told himself. He turned back to face his desk again before she could see him looking at her. How he would love to get his hands on that! But that wasn't going to happen. Karen wasn't Blodwyn, so he wasn't going to get an invitation. And he certainly didn't want to go out with her.

Mark now started wondering what her thighs were like. She had great calves and a wonderful bum. It stands to reason that her thighs would be worth looking at. After all, she used to be good at sport, so they ought to have an athletic appearance. Then he thought about Bill Connell and he considered if he wasn't careful, he would turn into a dirty old man like Bill.

Karen announced that she would have to be on her way. She had arranged for a neighbour to give her a lift home at 11.30, so she tidied up her desk. Mark decided he'd done enough by putting in an appearance and said he'd be off as well. They walked down the corridor together.

Mark realised that Karen was walking properly. She wasn't wearing her high heels. She still couldn't be described as elegant, but she was at least able to walk at Mark's pace. It felt good to walk beside a girl – even one he didn't fancy! They said 'goodbye' at the door. It was a particularly friendly 'goodbye' as though they were sorry to see each other go. Karen's lift was already waiting and Mark couldn't resist a last look at her bottom as she walked away from him towards the car. Unfortunately, he couldn't see very much of her shape at that point.

The next morning, Mark turned up at the 'kick-about'. Amazingly, Bob Walsh was there. He wasn't a bad player, but he was desperately unfit and admitted as much. Bob told Mark he was going to make a special effort to turn up every week from now on.

After the 'warm-up,' but before the 'kick-about', Nobby announced that they had a friendly lined up for next Sunday. It was against the White Hart pub team, who were planning to join the league themselves. He'd managed to borrow a football strip from another club.

In the 'kick-about', Nobby asked Mark to play out of goal, as there was another goalkeeper he wanted to see. Mark had never seen this chap before. His name was Terry and he was about thirty and quite a bit overweight. Everyone else seemed to know him and many of them called him "Tel."

Mark didn't think Tel was particularly good, so he wasn't too perturbed. Tel seemed to make unnecessary and extravagant full-length dives when Mark would have just moved his feet and caught the ball, ready to release the ball quickly. However, Mark enjoyed playing out of goal for a change. He scored a couple of goals, but he avoided heading the ball because of his glasses. His eyesight was not good enough to play without them.

At the end of the game, Nobby announced that he would select the team by Tuesday and let everyone know at the gym.

By now everyone was starting to lose interest in 'kick-abouts' and training at the gym, so this friendly was long overdue. As he rode home to his Sunday lunch of roast beef, Yorkshire pudding and marrowfat peas, Mark was looking forward to playing a proper game next week.

His life was starting to take shape. He certainly wasn't missing school. He was enjoying his work in the Wages Department and he was earning a little money. He was meeting a few girls and had a few new clothes. He was due to get his second pay packet in a few days. This time, there was no 'sub' to be deducted, so he would be ten pounds better off than last month. And now he would be playing in a proper football match.

Even the next day, when Josie told him off for making a mistake, it was very light-hearted. One of the labourers in the Despatch Department, a chap called Alf Seymour, had been underpaid by ten pounds. 'You got me into trouble with my old man!' she said. 'I had to lend him some of my own money.'

'Why did you get into trouble with your old man, because of Alf Seymour?' asked Mark.

'Alf is my old man. Didn't you know?'

'But your surname is Brocklehurst,' he said, looking puzzled.

'I'm not actually married to him. I just live with him. My daughters are from my previous marriage, so we've all kept that name.'

Mark wondered why this Alf lived with her, if he wasn't married to her. He couldn't imagine anyone choosing to live with her. He apologised for the mistake, but she didn't seem too upset. Although he still made the occasional mistake, he was certainly no worse than the other two, if not better.

He was now working at a very good pace and had got into the habit of pressing firmly with his pen. He had the makings of a callus on his finger. The number of employees on both payrolls had steadily increased over the weeks as business flourished. Mark's contribution was very important and was being appreciated.

On Tuesday afternoon, Karen came in for one of her chats. She said 'hello' to Josie and Penny, then turned to Mark and said 'Hello Mark.'

Mark turned to her and said 'Hello Karen. How are you, today?'

'Bleeding 'Ell!' said Penny. 'What's come over you two? Are you friends, all of a sudden?'

'We're very good friends, now. Aren't we Mark, darling?' and she walked over to him and sat on his lap.

He was totally taken aback by this move and blustered 'I didn't realise we were this friendly!'

He had never had a girl sit on his lap before and had no idea how pleasurable it could be. Karen was a lot heavier than he imagined she would be, but above all, he could feel those lovely firm buttocks pressing into his legs. She shifted to make herself more comfortable and he could sense her buttocks changing shape. He wasn't sure what to do with his hands. He just sat there for a few seconds with them dangling awkwardly in the air, while she stared at him to see his reaction.

Penny said 'Look at him. 'E's gone all unnecessary. I haven't seen 'im do that since he met Blodwyn.'

'Who's this Blodwyn?' asked Karen. 'You haven't got another woman, have you, Mark?'

'I haven't got any women.'

'Well, who was Blodwyn?' Karen addressed the question to anyone who was prepared to answer, so Penny chipped in again.

'She was just a young girl who wore skirts so short, that Mark's glasses kept getting steamed up.'

'Do you like short skirts, then, Mark?' He wasn't comfortable with this line of conversation – especially in front of three females.

'On the right person,' he replied, still showing some embarrassment.

'Do you think I'd be the right person?'

'I don't know. I haven't seen you in a mini-skirt. You'll have to wear one for me, one day.' He really wanted to say 'Yes, please!'

He was still looking uncomfortable, with his hands all superfluous to his needs at that time. He wanted to do something with them, but all the options seemed inappropriate.

'You look like you're cutting off his circulation,' said Josie.

'Am I too heavy for you?' Karen asked Mark, as though it wouldn't have made any difference, anyway. She wasn't going to move until she was ready to do so.

Mark answered her question by standing up, while gathering her up in his arms. After holding her like this for a minute, he put her down gently on her feet.

'No. You weren't too heavy, but you were making it hard for me!' he said with a suggestive grin.

'Mark Barker!' said Josie. 'Wash your mouth out! We don't expect that sort of talk from a seventeen year old!' Penny giggled.

'I don't know what you mean. I just meant it was hard to sit like that for very long.'

'We know very well what you meant, you dirty little devil.'

Penny said 'I fink it's since 'e starting working with Karen. I fink she's turning 'is 'ead.

'Am I turning your head, Mark?' asked Karen, looking at him in that way that always unnerved him.

'Sorry. I didn't quite hear the question. Are you doing what to my stomach?' Mark thought this was quite witty, but Karen didn't laugh.

'If you're going to start being horrible to me again, I'll have to come and sit on your lap again,' she replied, threateningly.

'I wasn't being horrible. I was just having a laugh. But you can sit on my lap, anytime.'

Although he had found this all rather embarrassing, he wasn't in any hurry to bring the conversation to an end and was sorry when Karen said she had to get back to work.

Later on, when Penny and Mark were alone, Penny told him she was pleased to see Karen and Mark getting along so much better. 'Ave you fort of asking 'er out?'

'The way we're always bickering. I don't think so, do you?'

'Well you weren't bickering earlier. She calls you "darling" and sits on your lap. I would say she fancies you. Do you fancy her?'

'No, not really.' He remembered the story of Pinocchio and how his nose grew whenever he told lies. Mark stroked his nose. He wouldn't mind her sitting on his lap again. He sat at his desk trying to remember the sensation. He'd never lifted a fully-grown woman before and was quite pleased that he'd managed it so easily. It could have been very, very embarrassing if he had dropped her. She was after all, a fully-grown woman – well apart from her bosom, of course.

He wondered if Penny was right about Karen fancying him. But that was what Bob had said about Blodwyn and look how well that turned out!

If he did go out with her, he would want to try to change a few things. He'd try to get her to stop wearing high heels for a start. And he would try to stop her draping a cardigan round her shoulders. He wondered what she would change about him. But no! He wasn't going to ask her out. Maybe if she asked him, he just might consider it.

When Tuesday evening came around, there was a better than usual turnout at the gym. Bob was there again. At the end of the session, Nobby announced the team for the match on Sunday. In the sixties, there were no such things as substitutes. A team turned up with eleven players and one reserve. The reserve was just that – a reserve in case someone failed to show. He didn't play. However, as it was a friendly, it had been agreed with the opposition that each team could swap up to six people at half-time.

The first name that Nobby called out was Terry as goalkeeper. Mark was furious. Mark's name was in the reserve six, but by then the red mist had descended. Bob Walsh was in the reserve six, which also seemed unfair to Mark. To make matters worse, the starting team included two people who hadn't bothered to turn up that night.

After Nobby had read out all the names, he added. 'I don't want anyone to be too disappointed if I pull them off at half-time.'

'Oh,' said a comedian from the back, in a very camp voice. 'I'm sure I won't be disappointed if you pull me off.'

And someone else added in an equally camp voice 'If you're going to pull me off, I'd rather I was first.'

'Now then, lads,' said Nobby. 'You know I don't do that anymore. Not since the court case, anyway.'

Everyone was giggling except Mark. He was not in the mood for laughing, and he didn't understand the joke anyway. As everyone else dispersed, Mark cornered Nobby. 'What's going on, Nobby?' he asked furiously. 'I've been to every bloody training session and every 'kick-about' and this chap Terry turns up once and goes straight into the team.'

'Woody and I have had a talk and we feel that Tel's got more experience at this level. He played for us in Balham. We've only ever seen you in a kick-about, so we don't know how you would cope in a real match. We're also concerned about you playing in glasses. Some referees might object. You're in the reserves, so you will definitely get half a game.'

Mark wanted to tell him to stuff his team, but he desperately needed to play and he didn't have anywhere else to go at that time, so he just stomped off.

That night in bed, he intended to have a fantasy about Karen squirming about on his lap, but he was still steamed up about the way he was being treated by Nobby and Woody.

The next day, being a Wednesday, meant he was locked in the Wages office nearly all day, so he didn't get to see Karen at all. He was very disappointed about this. What a turn-round from a few weeks earlier!

He did go on the Post Office run, but when he got back, it was after five o'clock and Karen had gone home by the time Mark wheeled his chair back into the Costing Department.

Never mind. He would see her tomorrow – and it was pay-day!

CHAPTER 9

Spoilt for Choice

Like Anne, Mark was not too happy about biking home in the dark. On one occasion, his rear light failed and he had to walk home, pushing his bike all the way. Not only that, but it was now late November and the weather was getting colder. He discovered that Margaret passed the top of his road on her way home. She got picked up at night by her husband, but still obtained a lift with George in the mornings. So Mark asked both Margaret and George if he could get a lift to and from work with them. George invariably worked late, which was why Margaret got her husband Alan to pick her up.

Alan was Irish and a very friendly chap, who worked various shifts as an ancillary worker at the local hospital, but most evenings he was able to fetch Margaret. The second time that Mark got a lift with Alan, he found a young lady already sitting in the back of the car. She was a neighbour of theirs, who worked at a clothing company down the road from Greshams. She was introduced as Jane.

Even though the interior light was on as Mark climbed into the back of the car next to her, it was really too dark to see what she looked like, but in the tiny Mini Countryman, he soon got a good idea what she felt like. He tried to keep to his side of the car, but Alan didn't hang about. Both Mark and Jane got thrown against each other by centrifugal force. It would have made more sense if Mark had sat in the front as he was much taller than Margaret, but that didn't happen. Not that Mark was complaining. Jane had quite wide hips and soft fleshy thighs and he loved every minute of it.

They hardly spoke to each other. Even when they did, it was only small talk and Mark wasn't very good at small talk. Unfortunately, Margaret and Alan didn't speak to Jane very much either. If they had done, Mark might have learnt more about her. Margaret and Alan mostly spoke to each other.

One evening, both Mark and Jane were ready before Alan and Margaret. They sat next to each other in reception. Mark wasn't sure if it was Jane, because they had never seen each other in good light. Neither of them spoke. 'If it is her,' he thought, 'she might not be sure it's me.' Sitting there did give Mark a better chance to have a quick look at her. She was quite tall and heavily built – perhaps a little overweight, but certainly not excessively so. She had long reddish-brown hair, high cheekbones, a sturdy chin and a slightly longer than usual nose. He could see no evidence of make-up, but Mark didn't like to see too much make-up anyway. She was not a stunning beauty, but she was certainly not unattractive either – perhaps "handsome" might be a more suitable word to describe her. Mark noticed she a slight moustache and a hairy mole on her left cheek, together with a good selection of freckles, but these did not detract from her appeal.

While they were waiting, he noticed another young lady waiting for a lift. She was blonde, slim and utterly gorgeous. She reminded Mark of a very young Kim Novak, whom he had always admired. He was particularly taken by her cute little turned-up nose. After a few minutes, she was collected by Fred Bland from the Buying Office.

After she had gone, Mark asked Ellie if that was Fred's daughter.

'Yes. That's Pauline. She's lovely isn't she?'

'Oh, I never noticed,' he replied, in a way that suggested he was deliberately lying.

'Well, I'm afraid she's spoken for. She's engaged. They're getting married next year.

'You're joking! She can't be any older than seventeen or eighteen.'

'I know. You have to be quick off the mark, if you want the good-looking girls, Mark.'

'She could have had *me*, if she had played her cards right. Oh, well! That's her loss!'

By now, Jane had recognised Mark's voice and was sure it was him, so she asked if he'd seen Margaret.

'I thought I heard her tidying up as I left my office,' he replied, glad that she had spoken. Mark thought that she just wanted to say something to break the ice.

'What do you do, here?' she asked.

Mark told her and asked her what she did. She started telling him, but Margaret appeared so they got up straight away, so as not to keep Alan waiting, who by now had parked his car outside the door.

Ever the gentleman, Mark opened the door for Jane. Jane was, indeed, quite tall – almost six feet, he thought. She had quite broad shoulders and a broad back. He had his usual sneaky look at her legs and they were much bigger than Karen's, but still very shapely. He averted his gaze as she climbed into the back of the mini, but her skirt had risen a little as she sat down and he couldn't resist a quick glimpse of her thighs as he climbed in next to her. They were definitely on the heavy side, but because she was so tall, he thought they were in proportion.

They continued their conversation in the car and she explained that she worked in a busy office that took orders for fashion items from big chain stores like Debenhams and John Lewis. Mark wanted to learn more about her, but despite the fact that she was the one who had earlier tried to break the ice, he now found he was forcing the conversation. And not too successfully, at that. The question he really wanted to ask was 'Do you have a boyfriend?' But that would have been too obvious. He still lacked self-confidence and preferred a more stealthful approach.

He did find out that she had been working for the clothing company for seven months and had lived in Sanford for eleven years. She was originally from Berkshire. This explained her lack of any obvious local accent.

Over the next few weeks, Mark was to find that she was much more talkative when she was waiting in Reception than when she sat in the back of the car with Mark. It was quite noisy in the Mini, so perhaps she found it hard work to talk in the car.

Mark now made a really big effort to leave on time each evening, so that he could see Pauline as often as possible. On one occasion, he found Jane and Pauline talking together when he arrived, so he felt entitled to join in the conversation. He considered Pauline to be the most beautiful girl he had ever met. The next evening, the conversation got round to music and Mark discovered that she liked Ben E. King, one of Mark's favourite artists. They talked about which of his records they both possessed, but Pauline only had two – "Stand By Me" and "Spanish Harlem."

Now he really fancied her. Not only was she the best looking girl he had ever met, but she had similar tastes in music. If only she wasn't engaged to be married. In any case, a beautiful girl like her wouldn't want to go out with someone like him.

The next time he talked to her about music, he found out that she actually liked lots of more mainstream pop artists and when Mark mentioned artists such as The Impressions or Jerry Butler, she hadn't got a clue who he was talking about. Still, she liked Ben E. King, which was more than any other girl he knew.

She was so lovely that Mark hardly noticed her figure, which was unusual for him. She was five foot seven inches tall and slim. Her legs were not especially shapely, and as far as he could tell, her bum and breasts were of quite moderate proportions, but she knew how to dress to maximise her appeal.

When he talked to Jane and Pauline together, he tried to give them equal attention, because he was still considering whether to try to date Jane. He knew there was no point in considering Pauline. He had asked Margaret if she knew whether Jane had a boyfriend, but Margaret confessed to knowing very little about her. She was just a neighbour.

During the few weeks after first meeting Jane and Pauline, Mark was constantly assessing his chances of getting a date with any of the girls he knew and which he would prefer, given a clear field.

Top of the list was definitely, by a very long distance, Pauline, but that wasn't going to happen. That left Jane and Karen. His relationship with Karen was improving all the time. He felt sure she would go out with him, if he asked her, but he still had misgivings about her looks and her lack of tact. If he didn't work with her, he would definitely give it a try. She had great legs and a wonderful bum – he told himself that these shouldn't be his main criteria in seeking a girlfriend, but they were definitely items to be considered.

Jane, on the other hand, didn't work in the same office, so there would be no complications if it didn't work out. She was better looking than Karen, but didn't have quite such a good figure. He found it easier to talk to Karen than he did Jane.

Whomever he chose, if any, he still had to pluck up courage to ask her – and he definitely needed the right opportunity.

While working in the Wages department, Josie and Penny had mentioned the Christmas Dinner and Dance. Tickets were subsidised by the newly formed Sports and Social Club. Mark had never been to a function of this nature. When Penny asked him if he was going, he replied that he didn't have the right clothes for such an event and he wouldn't want to go without a partner. They both suggested he should ask Karen, but he didn't display any enthusiasm for this, although he was secretly considering the possibility. He also considered asking Jane. After a lot of careful thought, he decided Jane was his first choice, if he got the right opportunity, but when would this be? He only ever saw her in Reception or in the close confines of Alan's Mini. He could do with bumping into her in town, but that hadn't happened, so far.

One evening, he decided he had to chance his arm. Mark approached the subject by asking Margaret if she and Alan were going to the dinner. They were and as he had hoped, Margaret asked Mark if he was going. He said 'I'd like to, but I have to find a partner.'

He left it for a minute before saying anything else, as though someone else might possibly solve his dilemma. Then he asked Jane if her company had a Christmas function of any kind. 'Yes, but I shan't be going. My boyfriend doesn't know anyone there, so he doesn't want to go and I'm not going on my own.'

'Damn and blast!' he said to himself. Well, at least he knew now that she had a boyfriend. He toyed with the idea of asking Jane if she would still like to accompany him to Gresham's function, just as a partner, but decided against it.

That just left Karen. He could make it clear that asking her was just for their mutual convenience to allow them both to attend without it having any great significance. He would have to give this a lot of thought. They had been getting on really well over the last few weeks. One particular incident had helped break down the barriers even more.

Late one afternoon, Karen was trying to find some items from the filing cabinet. She had her back to Mark and Bob was out of the office. Mark couldn't resist having a good long look at her excellent legs. Karen said, 'What do you think, then? Are they all right?'

This was late in the afternoon and it was very dark outside. Mark hadn't realised that although she had her back to him, she could see his reflection in the large window. In fact, she could see him very clearly, indeed. And she had seen him having a long look at her legs.

'Pardon?' he said, knowing full well, he had been caught out.

'You were having a good look at my legs. What do you think of them?'

He didn't know whether she really wanted to know what he thought or if she just wanted to embarrass him because she'd caught him out. This certainly had all the signs of a very embarrassing moment, but he thought that honesty would be the best policy.

'I'm very sorry,' he said. 'You really do have excellent legs, so I couldn't resist having a quick look.'

'Well, it was more than a quick look, but I am very flattered.' She often stared at him in a way that he found unnerving. He still hadn't got used to making lengthy eye contact, so he either had to say something or look away embarrassed.

He couldn't think of anything relevant to say, so just as he was about to do the latter, she said, 'We were talking a few weeks ago about mini-skirts and you said you had never seen me in a mini-skirt. I've been looking at buying one and I wasn't sure whether I've got the legs to get away with it. My friend Jean wears them all the time and she keeps telling me to get one. What do you think?'

'Well, if you buy one, I'll give it my honest and unbiased opinion.'

'No, I need to know before I buy one.' Then she lifted her skirt a few inches.

Unfortunately, it wasn't high enough to really form an opinion. 'If your skirt's going to be that length, no one's going to see very much, anyway.' He wanted to say 'Show me more,' but that might have sounded like a dirty old man.

She took the hint and raised her skirt another three inches. He still couldn't see an awful lot, but what he could see looked very promising. It was hard to compare her legs with Blodwyn, because Blodwyn's skirts were so much shorter. All he could honestly say was 'I think you could quite safely get away a mini-skirt if it's that length.'

'What do you mean "safely"? Do you mean my legs are too fat, to go any higher?'

Why did every girl seem to think her legs are too fat?

'No, I'm sure they're not too fat. What I meant was that I can't really tell from that.'

She raised her skirt another few inches. This time, he could get a better idea. They were a little bigger than he imagined, although not as big as Blodwyn's. There was definitely enough shape to satisfy Mark's tastes, but he really wasn't sure that others would share his views. He remembered Bob's unkind comments about Blodwyn and he didn't want Karen to suffer the same fate. He carefully considered his response.

After a few seconds, he replied 'Do you want my really honest opinion?'

'Yes,' she said, slowly, as though she thought she was about to hear something unpleasant.

'Well…' he said, slowly. 'From what I can tell, you've got a lovely pair of legs. They look very shapely.' She smiled at him as he said this. He continued. 'BUT ... They may be too good. What I mean by that is that the girls who mostly get away with wearing short skirts are those who don't have a lot of shape to their legs – skinny legs, if you like. I personally would love to see you wearing a short skirt, but your legs are probably so shapely that everyone would be staring at them all the time.

By all means, wear a skirt that is two or three inches above your knee, so that you're reasonably fashionable, but don't wear anything too short.

That's my view on the matter. And I hope you will appreciate my honesty.'

'Thank you, Mark. I think you have been very honest ... and helpful. I'm sure that what you're saying has a lot of truth in it. I know my legs are not thin. I thought men liked girls with slim legs.'

'Some do. But I reckon a lot more don't. Look at that new girl in Reception – Debbie. What do you think of her legs?'

Debbie had recently joined the company to share Ellie's workload. Debbie was very tall and slim and she was given to wearing very short skirts, but her legs were almost completely without shape. In fact, Debbie was completely without shape.

'I can't say I've taken too much notice of them,' was Karen's reply.

'Exactly! Neither have I, other than to dismiss them as not being very attractive. Now if your skirts were that short, I would certainly notice them – in fact, I wouldn't be able to stop looking at them. And the same would apply to other men. Maybe you would like to have men admiring your legs, but I've heard some of the remarks men make in those circumstances and they are not always pleasant – I won't go into details, so, please, just trust me on this.' Mark thought she would be offended if he mentioned the term "thunderthighs".

What could have been a very embarrassing moment seemed to have turned into a very friendly but frank discussion. Mark had not only been very keen not to say anything offensive, but he wanted to say something kind and helpful, as well. He had also been anxious not to let the conversation head in the same direction as those with Blodwyn. Moreover, he was surprised how well he had dealt with the situation, given his embarrassment.

This little episode seemed to improve their friendship even more. A few weeks later, Mark did see Karen wearing a mini-skirt, but it really was only a few inches above her knee, so his comments were obviously taken to heart.

★ ★ ★ ★ ★

Meanwhile, the football team was providing mixed fortunes for Mark. The first friendly had resulted in a heavy defeat for Greshams. Mark did play the second half, but as an inside forward, not in goal. He didn't get much chance to shine, as his team seemed to be defending most of the time.

On one occasion, he collected the ball in his own half and seeing no team-mates ahead of him, he set off on a solo run. He beat two defenders and drifted out towards the wing, from where he released a very good cross, but his colleagues were too slow and unfit to be up with play and the ball was easily cleared.

He felt secretly rather pleased that Tel had conceded eight goals. In fairness, he made a few good saves, but Mark felt that had he been in goal, he would have stopped some of the goals.

In another friendly, a week later, the team did a little better, losing 4-1, with Mark in the starting line-up. He was replaced at half-time. He couldn't see any signs of a settled team. There were a few people who were obvious candidates for a regular place, like Bob Nichols and Woody, but there wasn't much to choose between the rest. Despite all the fitness training, they were still not 'match-fit' and this showed in their results. Had it been a 'running-on-the-spot' contest, Greshams would almost certainly have come out as victors, because they'd been doing that for weeks, but football was a different matter.

For the third friendly, Mark played the whole game and scored a cracking goal from the edge of the box, as well as converting a good cross from the left wing. This time they drew 3-3.

When they played a return against the White Hart, they lost 12-1. Both teams had made improvements, but The White Hart's improvements were more successful. Mark was now holding down a regular place, but that was the last game before Christmas.

★ ★ ★ ★ ★

During December, everyone at Greshams was getting busier. The company was still expanding rapidly and the Wages bill had increased by nearly fifty per cent since Mark had started work. It was decided that Bob needed another full-time Costing Clerk and a bigger office, so there was to be a small office re-organisation. Mark was going to work in the Wages Department full time. He was pleased about this, but he couldn't help thinking he would miss working with Karen.

These changes would all happen sometime in the New Year. Meanwhile, Christmas was fast approaching, and so was the Dinner Dance. Mark still hadn't got a partner, nor any suitable clothes. He decided to take the bull by the horns, go into town to order a new suit and shirt and to ask Karen if she would partner him. He was fairly certain that she would say 'yes.'

He decided on a made-to-measure suit, which would take about ten days to be ready – just in time.

Now to ask Karen. He waited until he knew Bob would be out of the office for a while. He turned to face Karen and asked 'Are you going to the Christmas Dinner Dance?'

'No, I wasn't going to bother.'

'Why not?'

'I don't like that sort of thing.'

Mark wondered if it was because she didn't have a partner either, so he went for it. 'If you wanted a partner, I would be happy to go with you.'

'No thanks. I don't want to go.'

'Why not?' Her response was not what he expected nor hoped for.

'I told you. I don't like that sort of thing.'

Well that was that. There didn't seem any point in trying to persuade her. She could tell he was disappointed, so she added 'But thank you for asking me.'

Throughout all this, her body language had been so much different to what he was used to. She kept her head down, looking at her work, as though she viewed this conversation as an invasion of her time. Was this a matter of not wanting to go to the dinner or not wanting to go out with Mark? She didn't have a boyfriend and they had been getting along so well, lately, that he had assumed her answer would be 'yes.' Perhaps she didn't like to date people from her workplace. Perhaps he hadn't made a very good job of asking her. Had he made it sound like he would be doing her a favour by taking her? She gave all the appearance of not welcoming his invitation.

He felt very disappointed, rejected and very sorry for himself. If he couldn't get Karen to go out with him, what chance did he have of *ever* getting a girlfriend?

He had already ordered his suit and his ticket, but he wondered whether to bother to go on his own.

He didn't tell anyone else that he had asked Karen, but when he discussed the dinner with Penny, she persuaded him to go. 'There'll be plenty of people there you know and you can dance with lots of different people. You'll enjoy yourself, once you get there.'

So he went. He got a lift with George and his wife and sat at the same table, which also included Margaret and Alan, together with Margaret's new assistant and her husband. Her name was Jill. She was nothing like Blodwyn, much to Mark's disappointment. She was about Penny's age, dark-haired, chunky build and a very jovial lady. Mark liked her and often had a laugh with her in the office.

By the end of the evening, Mark was very pleased he had gone, although he would have loved to have shown off some pretty young girlfriend. Pauline was there with her parents and her boyfriend. Mark noticed that she didn't dance at all. She just sat there, next to her boyfriend, watching everyone else dance. She gave no signs of enjoying herself. Mark wanted to ask her for a dance, but he didn't think it right if she wasn't dancing with anyone else.

However, Mark did dance with lots of other people – Margaret, Jill, Penny, Ellie and George's wife. He and Penny won a box of chocolates in the 'spot-prize' and he threw himself into the 'Knees-up Mother Brown,' the Conga and the 'Hokey-Cokey.' He was equally keen to try a slow waltz as he was the twist or the jive (actually his 'jive' looked almost identical to his 'twist', which itself, wasn't that much like a 'twist'). Whenever he sat down, there was someone who didn't like to see him sitting on his own and who would drag him back onto the floor.

Several times, he tried to catch Pauline's attention to say 'Hello' or wave, but she seemed to be staring into space. He enjoyed all his dances, but he would have swapped every one for a single waltz with Pauline. There were lots of good-looking women there, in their evening gowns, but she stood out as by far the prettiest.

Mark had three glasses of wine, although having never drunk wine before, he could have benefited from some advice to help him decide whether to go for red or white. He thought that the red looked much nicer, but it tasted like vinegar to him, so he moved on to white for his second glass, which was more appropriate to his turkey. Jill told him not to go mad with it if he was new to wine. He was grateful for this advice when he started feeling just a little woozy after pacing his three glasses, but he recovered to carry on with the festivities.

He had had a wonderful time, but once he got home, the euphoria was replaced by a feeling of despondency and … well, yes – loneliness. He had been noticing this emotion more and more lately. There had been no contact with any of his old schoolmates since leaving school; no contact with Podge and he still hadn't made any proper friends at work. Yes, there was Anne, Penny, and even Bob, all with whom he was friendly. But they weren't friends, as such. And he didn't relate to anyone at home.

More and more he craved female company. She didn't have to be someone with glorious legs like Blodwyn or a beautiful woman like Pauline – just someone who enjoyed his company for what he was – a caring gentle young lad. Actually, someone who cared for him. That was it. As long as that someone was Karen.

No, he didn't mean that. She was no great catch. Someone like Janice, Jane or Blodwyn would be much better. Better still, Pauline. But these people all had boyfriends. Karen didn't. Why did she keep entering his thoughts? He considered some of those special moments over the past few weeks – the way she intimidated him into saying something nice to her; the way she had boldly sat on his lap; her lovely physical charms; most importantly of all, his desire to make her like him. Because she had rejected him, she now had the upper hand over him. He didn't like accepting defeat and he didn't like someone having the upper hand over him. It was as though she had thrown out a challenge to him – a challenge he just had to accept. He had to admit, she had gotten under his skin.

He mulled over the words to the Frank Sinatra song – "'I've Got You Under My Skin." Some of the lines seemed very pertinent.

He couldn't sleep at all that night. He was going to have to find out if her rejection was just for the dinner or whether it was for Mark himself. Whichever it was, he would have to win her round. He knew that he had taken her for granted and hadn't treated her very well to start with, but now that he realised the possibilities of their relationship, he was determined to do something about it. He formulated a couple of plans, but his favourite was to ride over to Aunt Louise's the next day, which was Saturday. He didn't know exactly where Karen lived, but he knew it was in Manningford, so there was a half chance he might bump into her. Then he could ask her out. Somehow, that seemed an easier way of dating her, as though fate was taking a hand.

Of course, he didn't see her. But Aunt Louise was glad to see him as usual. 'Is that the boy Mark?' she called in that lovely familiar Norfolk accent, as Uncle Fred told him to come in.

There was the usual pot of tea and a slice of fruit cake, together with further exploits of 'the girl Spencer.' Mark told her about the Dinner Dance and how much he was enjoying his new job. She had heard from George that he was doing well. That was nice to hear, because George certainly hadn't told Mark.

Just as he was thinking of leaving for home, George himself turned up with his wife, Tracy, so Mark stayed a little longer to relive some of their memories of the dance. Tracy called him "Old Rubberlegs" after his exploits on the dance floor.

Aunt Louise asked Mark to take some potatoes for his mother, but he pointed out that this would be very awkward to carry on his bike, so he took some carrots, instead. He wanted to get home before it was dark, so he thought better of his idea of riding around the village in the hope of getting a glimpse of Karen.

The next week was the week leading up to Christmas. With Christmas Day falling on a Friday, it was a four-day week, so it was expected to be a hectic week in the Wages Department. It was agreed that any timesheets lost or late due to the Christmas post would be substituted by a flat week payment and adjustments would be made next week. Not that the next week was going to be much easier, because New Year's Day also fell on the Friday. Because of the loss of a day, Josie had requested that Mark joined them all week to ensure they kept on top of the work.

Any other time, Mark would have been quite happy about this, but he was hoping for a good opportunity to speak to Karen. When she came in to the Wages office for a chat on Tuesday, Josie politely told her to come back another time. Before she left, Karen handed Mark a Christmas card. It wasn't a very big card, but she had placed some kisses against her name. He hadn't bought one for her, but he chuckled to himself at the thought of giving her some 'kisses on the bottom.'

Josie said 'I didn't get a card off Karen. Did you, Penny?'

'No. I didn't get a card off Karen.' Mark didn't say anything. He thought of mentioning the 'kisses on the bottom,' but he decided this might feed them some more ammunition.

Mark went to see Karen in his lunch period. Bob was there, so Mark confined his conversation to more general matters. Bob said he had seen Mark enjoying himself at the dance. Then he said 'It's a bit of a coincidence, but I read that the chap who invented the "Hokey-Cokey" died last month. His family was quite upset about it when they put him in the coffin. Because they started by putting his left leg in....'

Karen finished the joke by adding 'His left leg out...'

This prompted Mark to tell another of his own jokes from the Rag magazine and he was pleased to see Karen laughing. Then she said, 'Mark, darling. Are you going over to the canteen?'

'No, I've brought my own sandwiches, today.'

'You wouldn't like to go and fetch me a cheese roll, would you? All the men will be in there now and I don't like to go when they're all there. I'll be ever so grateful. I'll make it up to you, somehow.'

Of course, he agreed. How could he not with a promise like that? But to preserve some level of dignity, he said 'Well, actually, I wouldn't mind getting myself a bar of chocolate or something. Do you want anything, Bob?'

When he returned, she said, 'Thank you, darling.' She sounded very sincere.

Was she just using him, after he had revealed an interest in her? Or had she considered his interest as being worth some level of encouragement? Perhaps she might go out with him if he asked her out for a proper date. As it happened, of course, his invitation to partner him meant nothing to her and this was her normal behaviour. But Mark was now obsessed with a mission and was looking for signs in everything.

He went back to his desk to eat his lunch and consider his next move. Only he had lost his appetite and his sandwiches were as hard to digest as a piece of Aunt Louise's fruitcake.

The next day, being a Wednesday, he was locked in the Wages office all day and he didn't see Karen at all. As soon as Bob had taken the money to the Post Office, they all got stuck into their Thursday and Friday tasks.

Thursday was Christmas Eve and most people in the office were winding down for Christmas and some people had brought some mince pies and alcoholic beverages. But for the Wages Department, it was a day of hard work. They could hear other people laughing and relaxing, but they stuck to their task.

Mark did pay Karen a quick visit at lunchtime again. She and Bob had a bottle and some glasses on their desks and as Mark walked in, she grabbed his arm and pulled him onto her lap. She then offered him some whiskey, which Bob poured. Mark had a small glass. He didn't particularly enjoy it, but he did enjoy being so close to her, although he would much rather she was sitting on his lap.

'I can't stay for long,' he said. 'We've still got to get all our work finished by the end of the day.'

'Don't you want to stay with me, for a while?' she asked, obviously effected by the lack of blood in her alcohol stream.

'You know I do. If we get finished early, I'll come back and see you later.'

'I'll look forward to that.' He expected her to add a "darling" to the end of her sentence, but she didn't.

He stood up to leave. She stood up herself and told him to take her place on the chair, which he did. She then sat on his lap and it was every bit as enjoyable as before, except that this time, he put both his arms around her waist. She had a bit of a spare tyre, but it still felt nice to hold a real live woman in his arms. She seemed quite content to sit there and reached for her glass, finished its contents and replace the glass on her desk.

Mark was in no great hurry to move either, but no one seemed to know what to say. Bob must have found this equally embarrassing and he just sat there fiddling with his empty glass. Mark found the silence to be rather awkward, and he was afraid to move his hands anywhere else, so after a few more minutes of sheer enjoyment, he reluctantly stood up cradling her in his arms and placed her on her feet, like he had done before. 'I'll see you later,' he said and went back to his other office.

By 3.30, the payroll work was finished and Josie told Mark he could go off and enjoy himself. He naturally went next door to see Karen, but she wasn't there. Bob said he hadn't seen her all afternoon. Mark wandered round the building and exchanged good wishes with several people, but there was absolutely no sign of Karen. He asked Ellie if she had passed through Reception recently, but neither Ellie nor Debbie had seen her since the morning.

She still hadn't returned to her office by the time he left. He desperately wanted to see her one more time before the Christmas break, but he had to get a lift from George (Margaret had left mid-way through the afternoon, as had several other people). He couldn't help being concerned for her safety, but he needn't have worried. She was perfectly safe in the arms of Ron Hall, the Assistant Works Manager, in the back of his car, on a piece of secluded heathland near Fakenham.

This was the same Assistant Works Manager who had already availed himself of Gail's charms when they had both worked in London. He had a flash company car and was earning more money than Mark could dream of. He was also married and knew his way round a woman's anatomy. He knew exactly where to put his hands and he had no qualms about taking advantage of a young impressionable girl.

Mark went home, feeling very disappointed at not seeing Karen again, but he still retained some optimism of winning a date with her. If he had known the truth at that time, he would have been so utterly devastated.

CHAPTER 10

Never Rub a Sore!

Mark spent a very quiet Christmas at home with his family. Aunt Kate and Uncle Wally came round in the morning to bring them a bottle of sherry and have a couple of glasses themselves, before they moved on to visit some more relatives. Breathalysers hadn't yet been introduced, so Uncle Wally wasn't interested in abstinence and was already looking the worse for wear!

Then, Mark's sister and her husband came round to deliver and receive presents. Their visit overlapped with Aunt Kate and Uncle Wally, so for a while, the house was very crowded.

The family had a delicious and very large chicken for lunch, with home-made Christmas pudding to follow. In the Barker household, chicken was only eaten on special occasions. Beef, pork or mutton were more common fare for a Sunday roast in 1965. Fortunately, Mark's appetite had partially returned. For a pleasant change, Frank didn't go to the pub and he ate Christmas lunch at the same time as everyone else. It was almost three o'clock before lunch was cleared away and they sat down in front of the television to watch the Queen's Christmas message, with a cup of tea. Then they all fell asleep in front of the television.

When they all woke up, Mark's mother groaned that the washing-up still had to be done. Frank washed and Mark dried, while Brian made another cup of tea. It was their special Christmas treat to say 'thank you' for a delicious lunch. The men in the Barker household didn't help around the house as a general rule.

It was chicken sandwiches for tea, followed by a slice of Christmas cake washed down with another cup of tea. Although Mark didn't like fruitcake, there was so much icing and marzipan on his mother's cake that he had no trouble eating it. In any case, it wasn't as dry as Aunt Louise's. And they all spent the whole evening watching television.

Boxing Day revolved around a lunch of juicy boiled ham and chips, with Frank eating on his own, once he had staggered in from the pub. In the afternoon, Mark sat down to watch a circus on television. Everyone else groaned 'Oh no! Not another circus?' but Mark enjoyed them. He particularly liked to look at the female acrobats in their leotards. One of them reminded him of Blodwyn, with her strong meaty thighs.

All over the weekend, Mark couldn't help wondering what Karen was doing. Monday seemed a long way off. But it did eventually come round, only for Mark to discover that Karen was off sick. In fact, she was off for the rest of the week. Although he was very disappointed, Mark decided that absence might make her heart grow fonder. She would be really missing him, wouldn't she?

He especially missed her on New Year's Eve, when everyone else seemed to be going round shaking each other's hands or kissing each other. He would have dearly liked a New Year's kiss from Karen, especially if she was sitting on his lap at the time and calling him "darling."

That Sunday, there was a 'kick-about' down the 'rec.' There hadn't been any football training of any kind for more than two weeks, so Nobby insisted they work off their Christmas excesses.

It was a grey, cold misty morning, with a very poor turnout. There was no Tel, so Mark spent most of the time in goal and fluffed a few easy shots, but no one played particularly well.

Nobby informed them all that he was having difficulty organising friendlies. The teams that were already in the League had a backlog of fixtures, due to some waterlogged pitches earlier in the season. He hoped things would pick up again towards the end of the season, but they must keep up with their training. He was right. Even the short lay-off over Christmas had resulted in some very red faces from a modest 'warm-up,' mostly from the smokers among the team.

Toby 'agweed with him one hundwed per cent.'

Mark didn't see very much of Karen on Monday, Tuesday or Wednesday, but he was back in the Costing Department on Thursday. She had recovered from her illness and she was back to her old self, which included the occasional tactless remark, the occasional request for Mark to perform some menial task and the occasional 'Mark, darling. Will you fetch some coffees, please?' It was like turning back the clock several weeks, except that Mark went out of his way to be nicer than he would have done several weeks earlier.

In a few more weeks, he would be transferred permanently to the Wages Department, so he knew he had to make use of his time with her to worm his way into her affections, but he wasn't happy about his progress. He was determined to ask her out again, but he wanted everything to be just right to minimise the risk of another failure. What he needed was an invitation she couldn't refuse.

The following week, he came up with just the right solution. There was a new Charlton Heston film at the local cinema. Karen was a big fan of Charlton Heston, so this was a sure-fire winner. Mark waited until Wednesday, when Bob had gone off on the Bank run and went to see her in her office.

He said, 'I'm glad you're on your own. I wanted to ask you something. There's a new Charlton Heston film at the Regal, called "The War Lord." Would you like me to take you?'

'I've already arranged to go with someone else on Saturday.'

'Oh!' He was taken aback. Had she got a boyfriend all of a sudden? 'Anyone I know?'

'No. You wouldn't know them.'

He wanted to ask whether it was male or female, but for some reason, he couldn't bring himself to ask. She's said 'You wouldn't know *them.*' Was she being deliberately effusive?

'Perhaps another time, then?' he mumbled.

'I shouldn't think so, Mark.'

He didn't know what to say after that. It sounded so definite and he felt like his whole world was crumbling around him, so he went back to his other office, without saying another word. This time, she hadn't even thanked him for asking.

As he sat at his desk, he felt his stomach knotting up. His whole body seemed to ache to be with her. He would still be able to sit with her in the office for a few more Thursdays and Fridays, but that would only frustrate him. He wanted to be with her in the evenings and at the weekends. He hated the thought that someone else might be taking her out. They were just right for each other, weren't they? Neither of them could be described as the "catch of the day." Nobody else would appreciate her the way he did.

Throughout the day, he became more and more depressed. She must have a new boyfriend. That would explain her change of behaviour since Christmas and why she was so cold when he had asked her out. He couldn't accept defeat. He just couldn't.

By the time Saturday came round, Mark was totally eaten up with jealousy and was desperate to learn the truth. He decided he would go to the cinema on his own. He just had to find out if she had a boyfriend.

Mark arrived at the cinema in good time, so he could obtain a good seat near the back. He would then be able to see anyone who came in and hopefully not be noticed. He was assuming Karen wouldn't go in the upper circle. To his relief, she arrived with a girlfriend. They sat a few rows in front of him. He thought Karen had looked round at him as she came in, but she didn't show any signs of recognition in the half-light.

She had a vacant seat next to her and he considered sitting there, but decided she wouldn't welcome this. He enjoyed the film, which was about a Norman War Lord who had a right to any woman under his jurisdiction. So he availed himself of one particular young girl, which inflamed the locals. There were a lot of sex scenes. Mark had never before seen a film with sex scenes. He usually went to comedies such as "Privates Progress," which he'd seen three times. At that time, he had very old-fashioned views on sex outside of marriage.

At the end of the film, he determined to 'accidentally' bump into Karen on the way out, but the people in his row of seats seemed very slow at moving out. There were so many people milling about, that he wasn't sure whether Karen had got out before him or not. He hung about on the steps outside for a few minutes, but he didn't see her.

He then decided to race to the bus station, where he would catch his bus. There was a bus stop nearer to the cinema, but Karen would have to use the bus station for her bus to Manningford – if, of course, she was travelling by bus. But again, she was nowhere to be seen.

Still, at least he knew she didn't have a boyfriend. His feelings of jealousy could now be put aside. He just had to deal with this painful longing to be with her.

When Mark next saw Karen at work, he asked her if she had enjoyed the film. She said it was very good. Then he asked if she had seen him.

'No. Where were you?'

'I was just a few rows back from you.'

'Who did you go with?'

'I went on my own.'

'Did you enjoy it?'

'Yes, it was quite good. I can't see why you think Charlton Athletic is so wonderful, though.'

'Charlton Heston, Mark. He's a real man. You wouldn't know what that is, would you?'

'I think he's an ugly old man. He hasn't got anything the rest of us haven't got. Has he Bob?'

126

Before Bob could answer, Karen said 'When and if you turn into a man, you might be able to make such comments, but at the moment, you're just a boy. So don't be so silly.'

Well that showed what she thought of him, but who was she to think she could just dismiss someone of a similar age to herself in that way? He thought of making a comment about when she might become a woman, but he decided that might give her every opportunity to make some more caustic remarks, so he left it. One thing he had learnt about the opposite sex is that they are generally more accomplished at making hurtful remarks. And Karen had certainly never shown any concern for Mark's feelings.

Later that week, Bob asked Mark to take a white copy of a 'take-off' to Sally in Filing to ask her to do a "Xerox" The blue copy had gone missing.

'What's a "Xerox?"' asked Mark.

'It's a way of taking a copy of something. Haven't you seen the Xerox machine? It's in the room next to Filing. It's a smelly old process, so they have to keep the machine in a separate room. Go see Sally. She'll show what's involved. Here's the original copy.'

Sally had taken over from Anne during December. She was very quiet and Mark had hardly talked to her so far, but he had already found out that she had a boyfriend. He missed his little chats with Anne, who was now working in a little office in the Factory, so he didn't see her very often. Sally was slightly built; about five feet four inches tall, with ginger hair. She had a face full of freckles and was slightly buck-toothed.

When Mark got to the Filing Room, Sally was standing at the window looking out, with her back to him. 'Sally. Can you…?' He stopped what he was saying. She appeared to be wiping her eyes with a handkerchief.

'Are you all right?' he asked.

She composed herself, then turned and said 'Yes, of course. What did you want?'

'I needed a "Xerox" of this.'

She took the piece of paper off him, without saying anything and walked into the next room. Mark followed. She was still sniffling. He was by nature, a very caring person and couldn't help himself. 'Has someone been upsetting you?'

'It's the chlorine in the copying process. It makes my eyes water and my nose run.'

She was lying. He knew she had been crying.

'I think you've been crying.'

'I'm sorry. It's not your problem.' He thought about his own problem with Karen and how he often wished he had someone with whom he could share it.

'It sometimes helps to talk to someone about it,' he said very gently.

'It's just that I broke up with my boyfriend over the weekend. We'd been going out together for nearly three years… and I'm not coming to grips with it very well.'

'Why did you break up, if you don't mind me asking?'

'It was my choice. We were always arguing and he wasn't very nice to me. I've no regrets, but you just get used to someone being there all the time. I feel as though I'm starting life all over again.

I go home, expecting him to come round to take me out and he doesn't, of course. I suppose I'm just not used to being on my own.'

'It probably just takes time to get used to the situation. You'll get another boyfriend – one you're not always arguing with – then you'll be all right again. Just hang on and it will get better.'

'You sound as though you've been through this, yourself.'

'No. I've probably got that to look forward to. Show me how this machine works. I've never heard of a Xerox before.' He thought he'd said his few kind words. Now it was time for her to occupy her mind with something else.

'Well, basically, all you do is feed your original in here. Make sure the machine is loaded with this special heat-sensitive paper and press a button. Then wait a few minutes. It's a smelly old job and the copies are not very good, but it's convenient.'

The copy arrived after a few minutes. She was right. The quality was very poor. The writing was blurred. The paper was discoloured and felt very tacky. She warned him that sometimes the copy faded, particularly if left exposed to the air. These were the early days of photocopying and Gresham's machine was primitive by modern standards, but it was quite a revelation to Mark.

He thanked her and she thanked him for being so kind. 'Yeah, people are always saying "I know your kind" to me.' She didn't get his little joke. Or perhaps she didn't feel like laughing. Then he added 'If you're feeling down and want someone to talk to, you know where I am.'

'Thank you,' she said and gave a funny little half-hearted buck-toothed smile.

'No,' he thought as he walked back to his office. 'I couldn't possibly fancy her. And I certainly won't be diving in to ask her out in her vulnerable condition.' As far as Mark was concerned, she was nowhere near the same league as Karen.

★ ★ ★ ★ ★

A few weeks later, Mark moved into the Wages Department full time and the Costing department moved down the corridor into a slightly larger office. Mark's full-time replacement in Costing turned out to be Jean – Karen's old colleague and friend from Lemons.

Mark remembered her alleged comment about him getting his clothes from the jumble sale, so when he met Jean, he couldn't resist mentioning it to her.

'Karen told me you thought I bought my clothes from a jumble sale.'

She looked puzzled for a moment. Then she remembered the incident. 'Oh, no! Did Karen really tell you that? I don't believe that girl! I'm sorry, Mark. It was just a harmless remark. I can't believe she told you that. She hasn't got any feelings, you know, so she never considers other people's.'

Over the next few weeks, Mark got to know Jean a little better. He found out that she was engaged to Colin Greenwood, who Mark remembered from the Grammar School. He was the same age as Mark's brother and was always in trouble at school for wearing drainpipe trousers and winkle-pickers, both of which were banned from school. Colin received the cane as frequently as anyone Mark could remember.

Jean, herself, was much shorter than Karen and much thinner. When she stood next to Karen, she looked about half her size. She smoked very heavily and apparently could drink non-stop without ever feeling the effects. She had lived all her life in a pub and often worked in the bar, which was run by her parents.

She always wore a tight mini-skirt and her legs hung down like two pipe cleaners. She seemed to wear the same skirt every single day and Mark found that she constantly smelled of cigarettes and beer. He didn't dislike Jean, but she really wasn't his cup of tea.

However because she was Karen's friend, he would often sit and chat with her to see if she would reveal any interesting snippets of information about Karen. He tried very hard not to make it obvious that he had this interest, but Jean soon caught on. He assumed that Karen had probably told her that Mark had asked her out, which she had.

One day, when there was just the two of them together, Jean asked Mark 'You're really quite fond of Karen, aren't you?'

Mark hesitated, then said quietly 'Yes. Is it that obvious?' She nodded slowly. 'Do you know if she has a boyfriend?'

'She doesn't have a proper boyfriend,' was the reply.

'Do you mean she has an improper boyfriend, then?' asked Mark. This was meant to be an half-hearted attempt at humour, but it was a little too near the truth for Jean, who knew of Karen's affair with Ron Hall. In fact, nearly everyone at Greshams knew about the affair, except poor old Mark.

'No, I mean she doesn't go out with anyone regularly... as far as I know, anyway. She doesn't tell me everything.' Jean added the last little bit to cover herself for the time when Mark did eventually learn the truth, which he must surely do sometime. But she wasn't going to be the one to tell him. She knew it would break his heart.

'Why don't you find someone else to go out with? There's plenty of other girls around who would be glad to go out with you.'

'I suppose I've just set my heart on Karen and it may not be fair on someone else if I feel that way.'

'It's possible that Karen might view you a little differently if she thought you'd had more experience of other girls.' Jean had made this up. She didn't believe it for one minute, but she did feel that her comment might persuade Mark to try someone else. Mark considered her suggestion and decided there might be some truth in it. Karen might even feel a little jealous if she knew he was seeing someone else. He had a lot to learn about women like Karen.

But whom could he ask? Of course! There was Sally in Filing. She was available and needed someone to take her mind off her old boyfriend. Admittedly, he didn't fancy her, but he just needed to go out with her for a few weeks until Karen got the message.

He decided not to dwell on the matter. He would only get worked up about the prospect of asking someone out. He went to see her straight away.

As he walked into Sally's room, he said 'Hello Sally. I've come to ask you a little favour. Would you come out with me?' He hadn't thought about the right things to say, at all. He had just dived straight in and blurted it out.

Sally seemed very surprised and replied without hesitation 'Oh! I wondered what you were going to ask me for a minute. Yes, all right, then.'

'Great!' said Mark. At long last, someone had agreed to go on a date with him. 'Now what happens?' he thought. 'Oh, yes. I'd better make the arrangements.'

'What would you like to do?' he asked her.

'I don't know. The pictures, perhaps?' She sounded as flustered as he did.

'Yes, that would be nice. Do you know what films are on at the moment?'

'No, I haven't looked, lately.'

'Why don't I look in the local paper when I get home and come and see you again, tomorrow?'

'Yes, okay. I can look at my paper when I get home.'

'Great! I'll come and see you again, tomorrow.'

He was going on a date. At long last! She hadn't even hesitated. He wanted to tell everyone, but he thought he'd wait until it had actually happened. Penny observed that he was looking quite chirpy. 'You look like you've lost a penny and found a pound, Mark?' she said. He had been very morose, lately, so the contrast was instantly noticeable. He had sat there for the last hour, whistling and humming various happy tunes. Only last week, she had said to him 'You look like you've lost a pound and found a penny.'

'What's brought about this transformation?'

'Nothing. I'm just getting through the day.'

That night, when he checked the films, he couldn't get too excited about any of them, so he cut out the relevant page to take in to work to discuss with Sally.

The next morning before he had chance to see Sally, he saw Karen at the coffee machine and she said 'I hear you've been trying to date Sally?'

Mark couldn't believe that Sally had been bragging about this.

'How did you find out, so quickly?'

'She was in the ladies, yesterday, telling me what had happened and that she'd made a big mistake by saying 'yes'.

Good old Karen! Tactful as ever. Mark's jaw dropped and for a minute, he was lost for words. Then he said 'Is that really what she said? Are you just trying to be horrible, as usual?'

'Why would I do that? She told me that you had taken her by surprise and she just said 'yes' without thinking what she was saying. Why would I want to make that up? You've got a very low opinion of me if you think I would make up a story like that.'

'I'm sorry. You know I have a very high opinion of you. I'm just a little puzzled by her behaviour. If she didn't want to go out with me, she should have told *me*, not everyone else. I wonder how many other people know.'

'Are you disappointed?'

'No, not really. I would much rather go out with you, you know. Do you think there's any chance that could happen?'

'No. I don't think so. I prefer older men. You're too young for me.'

'You're only a year older than me!'

'But women like older men, Mark'

He knew he was wasting his time, but had been unable to resist another attempt to win her round. He knew that this latest attempt would only make him feel more despondent. As his mother always said 'Never rub a sore.'

He decided that he'd better go and see Sally as soon as possible to release her from her promise. He was actually most upset about the fact that Karen had witnessed his misfortune first hand and his inability to get a girlfriend – especially one whom he didn't particularly fancy! Not only had his efforts to date a girl not had the desired effect, he thought it had probably made matters worse as far as Karen was concerned.

When he saw Sally, she spoke first. 'I couldn't see anything at the pictures I want to see. Can we leave it for now?'

'Yes, of course. You didn't want to go anyhow, did you?'

'Well … Well, no. You took me by surprise, yesterday and I said 'yes' without thinking about it. I am sorry. Please don't take it personally.'

'No,' thought Mark. 'You don't want to go out with me. How can I not take that personally?' He hesitated for a few moments. He didn't really know the best way to respond. He didn't want her to think he was desperately disappointed, but he didn't want to appear rude about it either. He certainly couldn't disclose his true motives about trying to date her.

Eventually he asked her 'Are you back with your boyfriend, then?'

'No, I'm giving men a break for now. I've been catching up with some old girlfriends. If you want to go out with someone, I've got a friend who will go out with you.'

'Does she know me, then?'

'No, but I know she's looking for a boyfriend. Would you like me to arrange something?'

'Well, I don't know her and she doesn't know me. So how do we know that we will like each other?'

'I told her about you last night and she said she's willing to meet you, based on what I've told her. I know you'll like her. She's won a beauty competition – a local Young Farmers' contest or something. She's a very nice girl.'

'No, I don't think so. I like to get to know people before I ask them out.' Mark wanted to say 'yes' but he didn't want to look so desperate as to go out with a complete stranger, all arranged as a consolation by someone whom he didn't want to date in the first place.

'What have you got to lose? I know you'll like her. I think you'll both like each other.'

Mark sighed, then said 'I wished I'd never started this. It's a mistake to try to go out with people you work with.' The trouble was that his experience of girls was still confined almost exclusively to Greshams. At least this friend of Sally's didn't work there, so if it didn't work out, he wouldn't have to see her everyday in the office. And he wouldn't have to get all nervous about asking her out – someone was arranging it for him.

He gave another little sigh and said 'All right, then. What's her name?'

'It's Gillian Bowers. She lives at South Walton. Where do you live?'

'New Street, off Hall Lane.'

'Do you have a car?'

'No, I haven't even started learning to drive, yet.'

'I'll see her tonight. I'll talk to her about the best way for you to meet up.'

And that's how they left it. Mark had mixed feelings about this. He would certainly like to go out with someone, if only to take his mind of Karen, but he didn't like the idea of a blind date. Still, she had won a beauty contest – probably not a very prestigious event, but she must be reasonably attractive, mustn't she? It might work out. After all, she was a girl with legs and things – how terrible can that be?

Even if things didn't work out, it would give him valuable experience of going out with a girl. But why would she want to go out with him? He wondered how Sally might have described him to Gillian. Mark's own description would have been 'a four-eyed lanky seventeen year old with acne; very shy but with a very kind nature; a good sense of humour – just don't expect him to set your pulse racing on looks alone!'

Sally's actual description had been 'Tall and slim; wears glasses and looks intelligent; He's very quiet and a little shy, but kind hearted.'

He hadn't asked Sally for a description of Gillian. He would rather make up his own mind when he met her. He wondered if she was a 'young farmer' or perhaps a farmer's daughter?

It was now Friday, so he would have to wait until Monday at the earliest to find out how they would meet up.

That evening, he sat in Reception next to Pauline. She looked as lovely as ever. If only Gillian was half as lovely as Pauline, he would have fallen on his feet. However, he did consider that Pauline was not the happiest soul he'd ever met. She was always polite and friendly, and smiled at Mark's little jokes, but there was some kind of sadness lurking behind that lovely face. He often felt that he would like to talk to her about his concern for her, but this was never going to be the time or place.

As she left with her father, she said 'Goodbye' with a heavy sigh and Mark observed her body-language. She seemed to follow Fred with some reluctance, as though it was too much effort to walk to their car. Mark wanted to put his arms around her and ask what was troubling her.

Even though he still considered her to be the loveliest girl he had ever met, she was now relegated to second place behind Karen in his list of people he would most like to date. He couldn't explain that, but that's how it was.

It was now Mid-March and the nights were getting lighter. Mark had been contemplating going back to his bike. He didn't like having to rely upon other people for transport and he always seemed to be waiting for a lift. Although Alan's car was obviously much quicker than his bike, he didn't always get home any earlier. On the other hand, it was a lot easier to ride in the back of a car than pedalling the five miles home. And then there was the pleasure of seeing Pauline and being thrown against Jane's soft thighs.

Perhaps he would just wait until the clocks went forward in a few weeks.

CHAPTER 11

When is a blind date not a blind date?

When Mark arrived at work on the following Monday, he was anxious to see Sally as soon as possible. He didn't know if this blind date would work out or not, but he wanted to get things moving. And he was very curious to know what Gillian was like. So he offered to fetch some coffees for Josie and Penny and at the same time, he popped into the nearby Filing Room to see Sally.

Sally was busy talking to Ted, but she saw Mark and asked him to wait a few minutes while she attended to Ted. Ted engaged Mark in conversation, talking about various subjects, including football and working in the Wages Department instead of Costing. All the time, Mark wanted him to shut up and go away.

Eventually, he did go and Sally asked Mark 'Are you doing anything Friday evening.' Mark wasn't. 'There's a dance at the Village Hall in North Walton. Gillian and I will be going, so if you would like to buy a ticket, we can all meet up at the Hall.' North Walton was about five miles from Mark's home, so transport would be a problem. He might be able to get a bus part of the way, but as he had an aunt who lived nearby, he knew there was no direct bus service. But he didn't mention any of this to Sally.

Friday seemed to take forever to come round. Mark didn't tell anyone that he had a date. He'd pleaded with Sally not to tell anyone at work. His mother couldn't believe he was getting all dressed up in his best suit to go to a dance. She wanted to know all the details, but Mark just said 'I'm meeting a friend.'

The only suitable bus dropped him off at South Walton, about a mile and a half from the Hall, at 8.20. Sally had said that her and Gillian were going to get there about eight o'clock. Mark wasn't bothered about being late, because he certainly didn't want to arrive before them, not knowing anybody else at all. It was almost nine o'clock when he arrived.

Mark showed his ticket at the door and entered the hall, where he spotted Sally and went over to her. She was with some friends – male and female – and Mark wondered which was Gillian. None of them looked like a potential winner of a beauty contest.

Sally took Mark out into a side room where the music was a little less obtrusive.

'She hasn't come,' she said to an anxious Mark.

'Why not?' Mark replied, unable to disguise his anger.

'She's had second thoughts about it. I'm sorry. I had no way of letting you know. Why don't you stay, anyway? You might meet someone else.'

'No. I think I'll be off. I won't know anyone else apart from you. I've got a long walk home.' He knew he would be incapable of chatting up anyone else. He assumed that none of Sally's other friends would want to take Gillian's place or Sally would have suggested it. In any case, he was furious at having been stood up. After all, wasn't it Gillian who seemed keen to meet *him*?

Before he left, he said to Sally 'I was never very keen about this idea. Now look what's happened! I could have gone out with my mates, tonight.' This was a blatant lie, but it signified his indignity so much better than saying he could have been at home playing records. 'Now I've got a five mile walk home, having already walked all the way from South Walton.'

He stormed out.

Most of his walk home was going to be along dark country lanes and it was starting to rain. His best suit and shoes were going to be ruined.

Mark was halfway between North Walton and South Walton when a Triumph Herald sped past and braked suddenly, coming to a stop some fifty yards ahead of him. He recognised the car as being Jean's.

He ran to the car and opened the passenger door. She was on her own and asked where he was going.

'I'm going home. Are you going anywhere near to Hall Lane?'

'I go right past it. Get in.'

He squeezed in. His knees were hard up against the glove compartment. Triumph Herald's were not built for people of Mark's height. He said 'You don't know how pleased I am to see you. It was horrible walking along there in the dark, trying to avoid the puddles and the mud.'

'What on Earth are you doing out here?'

He decided to tell her the whole story. Jean knew Gillian Burrows from her school days and assured Mark he hadn't missed out on anything special. He mentioned the beauty contest and Jean laughed. 'The competition couldn't have been very fierce! That's all I can say.'

'Well, to be perfectly honest, I wasn't bothered what she looked like. In fact, I was never very keen on the idea anyway. Sally convinced me that we would like each other, so I went along with it. If looks were everything, I wouldn't be chasing after Karen.'

'That's true.'

'Anyway, what are you doing out here on your own?' he asked.

'Friday is my night off.'

'Night off from what?'

'From Colin. We have this agreement that we can both do what we like on a Friday, as long as we see each other every other night.' Mark wondered what she meant by 'what we like', but he didn't ask. She hadn't actually told him what she was doing out in the country on her own and he got the feeling he shouldn't pursue the subject.

'Can I ask you not to mention this to Karen? She already knows about my failed attempt to date Sally.'

'I wouldn't have told her, anyway. Sally's the one you should watch. She's always ranting away in the Ladies.'

'Really? She seems such a quiet girl. I'm glad I didn't get to go out with her. I never fancied her, anyway.'

Jean stopped at the top of Hall Lane and he thanked her profusely for turning up when she did. As he walked the last few hundred yards to his home, he was thankful that it was Friday and his mother wouldn't be home from Bingo yet. Otherwise, there would be an inquest into why he was home so early from a dance.

He contemplated where he went from here to get a date. He still believed that one day, he would go out with Karen, but for now, he had to bide his time. She would eventually see the light. He had to somehow put up with this horrible aching to be with her and dating someone else would help him get through it. He considered that his chances of getting a girlfriend would be improved if he had a car, so he decided to start driving lessons. There was a chap who worked in the Factory who gave lessons as a part time job. Mark would go and see him on Monday.

By now Mark was really getting into his full-time role in the Wages Department. They had recently completed the tax year-end procedure, which was quite traumatic, especially when none of the figures reconciled. After a lot of extra hours and delving back through the records, they got the figures to balance. All the year-end forms were completed and despatched to the relevant recipients. George came in to congratulate them all. According to Penny, last year's reconciliation had been a lot worse.

Greshams were continuing to expand and the payroll was increasing in numbers almost every week. One Thursday morning, Penny announced to Mark that they had twelve new starters to set up. 'You're pulling my wosname!' he said with genuine surprise.

'I wish I was,' Penny replied.

'Oh, I didn't know you felt that way about me,' he said and they both burst out laughing. 'You only had to ask,' he continued when the laughter had subsided a little. And they started laughing all over again.

'You've got a dirty mind, Mark Barker!' said Penny.

From then on, whenever anything unusual happened in the office, Mark would say 'Are you pulling my wosname?' and it invariably resulted in some amusing banter.

Mark was now dealing with all aspects of the job, including telephone queries from many of the site foreman. Josie had her favourite site foremen, so she still insisted on dealing with these (or as Mark would say 'handling their testy calls'). Mark was also getting to know all the Factory Foremen and Charge-hands, so soon after his unsuccessful blind date, he went to see the Joinery Foreman to ask his permission to go onto the Factory floor to talk to Lou Redmond to ask him about driving lessons.

It was agreed that Mark's first lesson would be after work on the first Wednesday after the clocks had been adjusted for British summertime, so that he could drive in daylight. Lou charged fifteen shillings for an hour's lesson. Mark had already obtained his provisional driving licence.

Lou Redmond wasn't a joiner himself. He worked as a labourer, mostly keeping the Joiners' Shop clean and tidy, as well as assisting with any heavy lifting, not that he looked capable of any heavy lifting. He was a small weaselly looking chap who didn't endear himself to Mark. He talked a lot without saying anything and his teeth seemed to be too big for his mouth, so that he spit a lot when he talked. Mark quickly learnt to keep a certain distance from him, which made it difficult to hear what he was saying in the busy Factory, but Lou didn't seem to have anything worth hearing anyway. Except that he was already giving lessons to Karen.

Mark hadn't been aware of that beforehand. Still, it gave him an excuse to go and talk to her about it, which he did later that afternoon.

Karen had been learning to drive for six weeks. According to Lou, she was nowhere near ready for a test yet. She told him that she too found it difficult to like Lou Redmond. He was not a very patient teacher and she felt he was always looking at her legs. Sometimes, his wife accompanied them in the back seat. When she did, the two of them were forever arguing. Lou and his wife lived near Manningford, so it was convenient for Karen to have a lesson straight after work and then finish up at home. She didn't think he was a very good teacher, but he was cheap and convenient.

Living in the same area, Karen had heard a few bits of gossip about both Lou and his wife. They didn't have any children and it was rumoured that both of them were inclined to having affairs. Karen understood that Mrs Redmond often accompanied Lou, but only when he gave lessons to females. Mark was to later confirm this, because he never met Mrs Redmond on any of his lessons.

Mark said he hadn't got time for people who had affairs. This was an innocent remark. In no way could it have been directed at Karen, but she thought it was and she became very angry with him. Bob and Jean sat there, in silence, both cringing and looking at Karen to see how she would react.

'It's got nothing to do with you what other people do with their lives! You should keep your nose out of it!'

'Hang on! You were the one who brought their affairs to my attention. What are you getting so shirty about? Are you defending them?'

'I'm not defending them. I couldn't care less what they do with their lives.'

'Well, why are you getting so annoyed with me?'

'I thought you were trying to make a point. Anyway, it's not up to you to sit in moral judgement about other people.'

'I'm entitled to my opinion.'

'You can set your own moral standards, but it's up to other people how they live their lives. There's no children involved, so they're only likely to hurt each other and they're both adults. So let them get on with it.'

Mark looked at Bob and Jean in turn. They both looked very sheepish and he wondered why. Then he really put his foot in it.

'So you think it's all right for people like Gail to go having affairs with married men like Ron Hall, who has a lovely wife and two children do you?'

Jean held her head in her hands, while peeping through her fingers to look at Karen's reaction.

'Mark. Go back to your work before I really lose control,' she said through gritted teeth and he could see she really was angry. He couldn't understand why.

Jean added 'I would leave it if I were you, Mark.' She gave a little movement of her head in the direction of Mark's office and he took her advice.

Back in his office, he thought of telling Josie and Penny what had just happened, but he thought he'd wait until he and Penny were alone. He had never really taken to Josie, but he valued Penny as a confidant in some matters, although he had never told her about his feelings for Karen.

It was another hour and a quarter before Josie left them alone. He told Penny what had happened. Penny's reaction was 'Oh, my Gawd! What 'ave you gone and done?'

'Why? What's so terrible?'

'Don't you know about Karen and Ron?'

'Karen and Ron?'

'They've been 'aving an affair for monfs. I fought everyone knew.'

Mark was standing next to Penny's desk at the time and he felt his knees buckle under him. His head starting swimming round. He didn't know what to say next. Now he certainly didn't want Penny to know about his feelings. Things suddenly made sense. Why Karen's behaviour had changed a few months earlier, just when he was convinced she might go out with him.

He said 'No wonder she got so angry. Presumably Bob and Jean know. That's why they both looked so sheepish during our heated conversation.'

'I fink everybody knows.'

'But isn't Gail also having an affair with him?'

'Probably.'

'I can believe it of Gail – but not Karen! I would have thought she had more sense.'

'Obviously not.'

Mark went back to his seat. He needed to hide his true feelings. He had never felt so unhappy in his life. He decided he didn't want anything else to do with Karen. She was now 'soiled goods.' Why would Ron Hall want her, when he had such a lovely wife? Perhaps they were just friends? Mark was so utterly mixed up and confused.

He stayed away from the Costing Department for the next few days. Life was Hell for him. He couldn't sleep and he'd completely lost his appetite.

A week after the incident, he saw Jean in the corridor. 'Why didn't you tell me about Karen and Ron?' he asked.

'I knew how badly you would take it and I didn't want to be the one to tell you. I've spoken to Karen and told her that you hadn't known about her and Ron. She now realises that you weren't having a 'go' at her. I think she regrets her outburst. She wants to be friends again.'

'Well, I don't think I want anything to do with her.'

'I can understand that. She's just a silly girl. I think she's flattered by Ron's attentions. I keep telling her she's not doing herself any favours, but I can't get through to her. I'm no saint, but I've never messed around with married men. I don't see the point. When he's finished with her, no one else will want her.'

'Well, I certainly won't,' said Mark.

'Yes, but don't let her see that it's gotten to you. Just act normally when you see her.' Mark nodded. Then Jean added 'Did you hear what happened when Gail came into our office on Thursday?'

'No. Why, what happened?'

'Well, she came to see Bob, but he wasn't there. She talked to Karen instead. I didn't hear exactly what was said, but the two of them were talking in a low voice. I heard Ron's name mentioned, but that was all I really heard. Anyway, I saw Karen get up slowly from her desk, walk round to Gail, physically pick her up and dump her in the waste paper bin and said "That's where the rubbish belongs!"

Gail just sat there in the bin with her tiny little bum stuck fast and her legs wriggling in the air. I had to help her out.'

'I'd like to have seen that,' said Mark. Gail was very slightly built and Karen was quite a bit bigger and heavier, so it would have been no contest. 'Did you ever find out what they had said to each other?'

'No. Karen wouldn't speak about it, but there's obviously some rivalry there.'

'So if he's still seeing Gail and he's married, that can't leave a lot of time for him to see Karen?'

'I've got no idea. She's my friend, but she never talks about it and to be honest, I don't want to. But I have told her she's a silly girl. You need to forget about her and get yourself another girlfriend.'

'I know that. I thought it might be a bit easier if I learnt to drive and become more mobile. I've got my first lesson on Wednesday. I'm going to start saving up for a car.'

'I don't know how I would manage without mine. Anyway, I must get back to work.'

The next time Mark saw Karen, he just behaved normally. He didn't mention their heated exchange and she was quite friendly to him. She even tried the old 'Are you going to the canteen?' line. He said he wasn't. He felt pleased that he hadn't jumped to her request like he used to, but afterwards he felt bad about not going for her. He liked waiting on her hand and foot. Who was he kidding? He was still utterly besotted with her. He had now managed to convince himself that her affair with Ron might be platonic.

The next day, he made a point of going into her office at lunchtime to say he was going to the canteen if anybody wanted anything. Nobody did want anything, but he saw Jean sat at her desk shaking her head in disbelief at Mark's actions. After all she had said to him earlier.

Mark had reverted to biking to work. He had given Alan a small bottle of Irish Whiskey to thank him for all the lifts over the winter period. Alan said he would gladly help Mark to find a car when he was ready to buy one, which Mark thought was a very nice gesture. He knew he would miss sitting next to Jane in the back of the mini, but he had never really come to know her that well. He had no great feelings for her, but he did find her physically attractive and often wondered about his chances with her. For all he knew, she might have broken up with her boyfriend, but she was hardly likely to tell him and he was hardly likely to ask.

Most evenings, he made a point of leaving the office by the front door so that he might see Pauline or Jane in Reception, even though the rear fire escape would have been more convenient for his bike.

On the first Wednesday after the clocks had gone forward, Mark had his first driving lesson. Lou's car was a grey 'C' registered Ford Anglia. It didn't have dual controls like those from proper driving schools, so most of the first lesson was conducted with the car parked; with the remainder on very quiet roads. Mark must have stalled the car about twenty times. He just couldn't manage the necessary co-ordination of applying a few revs, while gently releasing the clutch and the handbrake all at the same time. That was three things to perfect. He could manage any of the two actions together, but not all three at the same time. Especially as Lou insisted on reminding him to check behind him, before signalling and moving off. Just as he thought he'd got the hang of it all, the lesson came to an end.

When it came round to the next lesson in a week's time, it was like starting all over again. This time, he did go a little further, but Lou was constantly shouting at him not to keep steering the car towards oncoming traffic. The nearest Mark had come to driving before was at the dodgems, so he was obviously applying a similar driving technique.

Mark soon came to the same opinion as Karen that Lou Redmond was not a very good teacher. He was not very good at explaining things and had very little patience. Mark was to find out later that he was also teaching him some very bad habits. For instance, he insisted that Mark used the gears to slow down whenever possible and to only use the brakes in an emergency.

★ ★ ★ ★ ★

The football season was drawing to a close. There had only been one more friendly and on that occasion, Mark played the whole game. He felt that interest was waning. Training sessions were no longer cost-effective, with only five or six people attending on most nights, so Nobby abandoned them. He convinced himself that once the team was playing regular league matches every weekend, the interest would be rekindled.

At that time, football was as near as Mark got to having a social life, so he would miss it. However, the club organised an end-of-season dance to generate some additional funds and he felt obliged to attend, although that left him the usual problem of not having a partner. One of the people going round to sell tickets was Daniel Peterson – a charge-hand in the Metal Shop. He had nothing to do with the football team, but he liked getting involved in social activities.

When Mark told him he only needed one ticket, Daniel asked why he wasn't taking a girlfriend. Mark's answer prompted Daniel to tell him about his niece who was attending. She could do with a partner.

Mark remembered his bad experience with Gillian and didn't want another blind date, so he declined. But Daniel was a determined fellow. He suggested that as Mark wasn't attending with any friends, he could go with Daniel and his wife and the four of them could sit together. It wasn't a blind date at all. They would be four friends together.

Mark had to admit that he didn't want to sit on his own. George wasn't going, nor were Penny, Jill or Margaret. So it made some kind of sense. And Daniel would give him a lift, so he went along with it. Especially as Daniel seemed like a nice chap and it might be a good night.

Daniel's niece turned out to be just the sort of person you might expect on a blind date (not that this was a blind date!). She was five foot six, with glasses and she was fat – not obese, mind, but still fat. She was not totally unattractive, but she had a chubby face that never seemed to smile. Mark got the impression that she had been 'persuaded' to come along to meet someone. She was very quiet and throughout the evening, she and Mark barely exchanged twenty words. The band was far too loud and as conversation was very difficult, neither of them made the effort. It didn't help that she was sitting opposite him at the table instead of next to him.

At one point, Mark did ask her to dance with him, but she couldn't hear him and after repeating the request twice, he gave up. He wasn't too upset by this. It wasn't that he had anything against fat girls with glasses, but he had no chance to find out whether she had a nice personality or not. As he returned from a visit to the toilet, he looked at her perched on her seat like a miniature Humpty-Dumpty with her hands tightly clasped upon her plump lap, wanting her to have some physical appeal, but there was none. He hadn't built up any hopes of meeting someone special, so he wasn't to be disappointed, except that the evening hadn't been much fun.

Jenny from the Metal Shop dragged him onto the floor to do the Monkey and they ended up waving their arms around like a couple of demented chimpanzees. Everyone else joined in the antics. At the end of the dance, she gave him a big hug and a kiss. He remembered her telling him that her husband wasn't very big and she was right. He was about five foot three and built like a little whippet.

Mark also had an enjoyable waltz with Anne. As it was a quieter tune, he was able to talk to her. She glanced towards Mark's table and asked if he had a little girlfriend. 'No, that's Daniel's niece. I'm sitting with them because he gave me a lift. We're not together.' He felt ashamed of his answer, but it was the truth, after all.

This was the first time Mark had seen Anne with her fiancé and he had only just realised that he was Bill, who had been along to football a few times. Bill looked so much older than she did, probably because he was losing his hair. Mark thought he must be at least thirty years old, while she couldn't be any older than twenty.

Mark asked if she was also going to revert to her bike now that the days were lighter and longer. 'No, I've got used to being ferried around. The only problem is that Gary is inclined to forget to leave off work and I have to wait around a lot, but when I get married later this year, we'll be living the other side of town, so I'll have to make other travel arrangements then.'

As he walked back to his seat, Daniel's niece deliberately avoided looking at him, as though she had disapproved of him dancing with Anne.

On the way home, Mark sat in the back of the car with Daniel's niece. It suddenly occurred to him that he couldn't remember her name. They had been introduced when he was first picked up, but the name had never registered with him. He kept thinking he ought to try and engage her in conversation now that they had a better chance of hearing each other speak, but the only thing he could think to say was to ask her where she worked and what she did. She gave the briefest of answers and Mark had the impression that she had already washed her hands of him. She probably thought he was like all the other boys who didn't like fat girls with glasses. Mark really wanted to get to know her better, but he wasn't going to make the effort if she wasn't, so they sat in silence for most of the journey. He considered that it was also quite possible that she didn't fancy Mark anyway. Or maybe she was having an affair with one of her colleagues.

'Now you're getting paranoid, Mark,' he told himself.

A few weeks later, on a Saturday afternoon, Mark literally bumped into her in town. She was coming out of a bookshop just as Mark was going in. A young lady wearing a mini-skirt had distracted him and he wasn't looking where he was going. He said 'Hello' (he still couldn't remember her name). She didn't recognise him at first, but then she realised who he was.

'It's Mark. Sorry, I didn't recognise you. How are you?' She seemed remarkably friendly, he thought.

'I'm fine, thank you. How about you?'

'I'm a little stressed at the moment. I've just been all around town, looking for a present for my brother and I'm really struggling to know what to buy him. Have you got any ideas for a sixteen year old?'

'Well, it depends upon his interests.' While she was considering her response, he decided that he felt like being friendly, so he asked 'Do you fancy a cup of coffee? Then we can discuss it. You look like you could do with a rest.'

She smiled at him. 'Thank you. Yes, I could do with a sit down and a drink. Where shall we go?'

That was a tricky question. Mark had never had a cup of coffee in town. There had never been anyone with whom to have a coffee before. If he was ever in town and felt like a drink, he would pop in to see his Aunt Norma who lived near the quay. He certainly wasn't taking what's-her-name round his Aunt's. He must find out her name.

He looked both ways up and down the High Street. He saw a Wimpey bar. 'Well, there's always the Wimpey, but I'm sure we can do better than that.'

'No, the Wimpey is fine. I like their expresso,' she said.

As they walked the thirty yards towards the Wimpey, he said 'I'm very sorry, but I never really caught your name.'

'It's Rachel. It wasn't very easy to talk at the dance, was it? Did you enjoy yourself?'

'Umm. Well, some of it. I found the music too loud. And it wasn't my sort of music either. What about you?'

'The same really. To be honest, I didn't like being dragged along to a dance where there was no one I knew. Uncle Dan seems to think he has to look after my social life. He's my godfather and he acts as though that gives him some extra responsibility for my well-being. He's always doing things like that. He doesn't believe me when I tell him I'd rather stay at home and read a book.'

That confirmed to Mark that she hadn't seemed too happy about being there. Then she added 'At least you knew a few people you could dance with.'

'I did ask you to dance, but I don't think you heard me.'

'That was what you were trying to ask me, was it? I'm sorry. I just couldn't hear a word you said from the other side of the table. Thank you, anyway.'

They sat down at a table. Mark declined her suggestion to sit near the window. He didn't want to be on public display. He said they would get a draught being near the door, which was rather lame, because it wasn't a cold day. They both ordered an expresso. Mark had never tried an expresso before and he wasn't particularly impressed. As he sat there, he contemplated whether he wanted to ask her for a date. Although she seemed so much friendlier now and might be good company, he still couldn't find anything remotely attractive about her. He wouldn't mind being her friend, but he couldn't see how that could work.

'So what am I going to get my brother?' she asked.

'Well, what are his interests?

'He's a typical teenager. We don't talk very much, but I know he likes pop music. However, I wouldn't want to guess what records to buy him. I'd be bound to get it wrong.'

'I know. I wouldn't want anyone to buy my records for me. I'm the only one who really knows what I like. You could always get him a record voucher. Then he could get exactly what he wanted.'

'I've never heard of record vouchers. Are they like book tokens?'

'Yes, but obviously, you buy them from record shops instead of bookshops.'

'That would be ideal. That's a wonderful idea. Thank you.'

'I'm glad to have helped.' They had finished their coffee and again, he considered whether he should ask her out. He was in desperate need of a friend. He wondered if having a girl for a friend would inhibit his chances of getting a girlfriend. Not only that, she would probably be very offended if he asked her to go out with him as a friend.

He asked 'What sort of thing do you do in your spare time?'

'I don't go out much. I read a lot. I visit the library regularly. I usually get through a book a week – mostly the classics – Jane Austen and the like.'

'You don't play any sport, at all?' He was thinking he might ask her to play tennis.

'No, I've always been useless at sport. I can't run and my eye-to-ball co-ordination is very weak. I hated sport at school.'

He had to admit he couldn't imagine her running very far.

He said 'I've been playing football for the Works' team – hence the end of season dance. Now that the football season's almost over, I'm going to look out for a cricket team… or possibly a tennis club. You don't know of one do you?'

'No. I've never had any interest in tennis.'

So much for that wonderful idea. They might have joined a club together as friends.

'Do you buy records for yourself?' he asked.

'A few – mainly folk music.' So they didn't even like the same music. There didn't seem to be any point at all in pursuing any kind of relationship.

'Anyway,' he said, 'I'd better let you get on with your shopping.'

Outside, Rachel looked at him and said 'Thank you for the coffee.'

'It was my pleasure. Thank you for the company. I hope your brother likes his present.'

She didn't seem to be in a hurry to say goodbye, but Mark started walking away from her, saying 'Bye, then. I'll see you around.'

'Goodbye, Mark,' she said, watching him walk away.

He felt terrible. He got the definite impression that she wanted to see him again.

He didn't dare look round, in case she was still looking at him. He was not proud of himself, but he had to be honest about the fact that he really didn't fancy her. He remembered the conversation he'd had with Gail and Bob in the office, when Gail had asked what he was looking for in a girlfriend. His answer had been first and foremost, a nice personality. Well, Rachel seemed to have a nice personality, yet it wasn't enough. If only she had a nice pair of legs, it would be something. But there was nothing.

He could just go out with her for a while to gain more experience of girls. He might get to kiss her – possibly even more, but he was not the kind of person to take advantage of someone like that. Maybe, if they were to meet in town again, they could have another coffee.

In fact, they never met again and Mark never knew what became of Rachel.

CHAPTER 12

Getting a Social life

It was now the middle of May. Mark had found a tennis club, but it was way over the other side of town. The club night was Wednesdays from 6.30. The logistics of getting there from work and getting home again on a pushbike made it a non-starter. Not only that, but there was a registration fee of seventeen pounds ten shillings, plus an annual fee of ten pounds. And you were expected to provide your own tennis balls. So on Mark's limited income, he had to dismiss this option. He had actually been given a very small rise in April taking his salary to a giddy £350 per annum. This was a pleasant surprise, because he had been led to believe he wouldn't get a rise that year, because he hadn't been there long enough. Nevertheless, money was still very tight. He had saved very little towards his new car.

He placed a notice on the notice board at work to see if anyone was interested in making up a foursome and hiring a tennis court at the 'rec.'. He got some half-hearted interest, but nothing concrete. He was a little surprised when Karen told him she would like to play, but she would have had transport problems. Just when Mark was about to give up, Dave Taylor came to see him. He had heard of Mark's interest and told him that there was a little group of people who already played on a Friday night. These were mostly people that Mark did not know, but he recognised the name of Gary Collins. He was the chap from the Drawing Office who had been giving a lift to Anne.

Mark really appreciated Dave coming to invite him to play. He told Dave that he hoped he would be up to their standard. He had only 'messed around' at school, but Dave assured him that he would be welcomed. 'We all had to start somewhere,' he said, encouragingly.

The first time Mark played with them, there were six people altogether, so they hired two courts and everyone took turns at playing doubles and singles. They were all male and everyone without exception was of a very much higher standard than Mark, but no one complained. Indeed, he was given a few tips and lots of encouragement, so by the second and third week, there was a considerable improvement in his game. Several of the group went for a drink afterwards, and he was invited. The rest were all drinking beer or lager, but Mark had a small glass of cider. He hadn't yet developed a taste for beer. Being the shy person he was, he didn't contribute much to the conversation. Except when John Woodston, who was one of the Contracts Managers, told a joke. Then Mark followed up with one of his. He wasn't very good at small talk, but he liked telling jokes, especially if they were well received, which this one was.

When they went for a drink after the second week's tennis, the conversation inevitably got round to women. Four out of the six people were married, while Mark and Gary were both single and neither of them had girlfriends, so the married men had great fun in pairing them up with girls from the office. Gary seemed to be every bit as uncomfortable about this as Mark was, even though Gary was several years older than Mark, with his own car and earning very much more money. John seemed determined to fix up Mark with Karen. Even to the point of offering to put in a good word for him. Mark said very little, but showed some obvious embarrassment. Dave kept saying 'Leave the lad alone. He can sort out his own love life, can't you, mate?'

'I can't afford women,' said Mark, dismissively and that seemed to gain universal agreement.

Mark kept wondering if he was expected to buy a round of drinks, which he could ill afford, but he wanted to pay his way, so he made the offer. Gary was the only one who wanted a second drink, as long as Mark was having another one. So the two of them stayed behind and Mark felt he had paid his way.

Gary's car was parked near to Mark's bike and as they walked back to their contrasting modes of transport, Gary asked Mark if he would like to put his bike in the back of Gary's car, which was a Singer Gazelle Estate. As it was starting to get a little dark, Mark gratefully accepted his kind offer and they rode home together.

Gary picked up on the conversation about girls in the office. 'So you haven't got a girlfriend, at the moment?'

'No. I'd certainly like to find one, but I don't come into contact with many girls outside of Greshams.'

They then discussed all the girls they knew of at work and each gave their considered opinion. When Karen's name cropped up again, Mark had to admit to being very keen on her. 'I don't know why. She's not very attractive and she's got a very prickly personality, but she's gotten under my skin.'

'I know what you mean. I feel the same about Anne. Although, I'd have to say that Anne does have a lovely personality.'

Mark agreed with him about her personality, but it surprised him that Gary felt this way about her. Mark thought that Gary would have been a good catch for a girl. He had a car, was obviously earning decent money and was quite good looking (at least he didn't wear glasses!). Mark expected Gary to have his pick of the girls and here he was fancying Anne, who despite being a very nice person, was not much better looking than Karen.

Gary continued 'I've been giving her a lift to work for several months and I've really got to know her. I find I can sit and talk to her for hours. I've tried to talk her out of getting married, but it's no good. I find it hard to look at another girl. Do you know her very well?'

'We used to bike home together. I agree about her being a very nice person, but I have to say that I don't find her to be very attractive.'

'I do and she's got a cracking figure. Don't you think so?'

'Well, no. She's a bit too thin for my tastes.'

'What about Jean? Do you like her?'

'I get on all right with her. But I couldn't fancy her. She's even thinner than Anne. Do you fancy her, then?'

Oh yes. I think she's lovely.' This also surprised Mark. 'She's Karen's mate isn't she?'

'Yes. I think Karen helped her get a job here.'

'Perhaps we could arrange a double date with them both.' Mark couldn't see that happening in a million years. But it was a nice notion. He warned Gary about Jean's boyfriend.

By now, they were outside Mark's house, but Gary was in no hurry to leave. He carried on talking about Jean and Anne. It occurred to Mark that Gary was a little lonely. He was a Londoner and was still new to the area. He lived with his parents. By co-incidence, his father had also come up to Sanford with an overspill employer. Gary's parents had moved up some months earlier and Gary had lived on his own for a few months in London. All his friends were still in London.

He asked Mark what he did in his spare time. When Mark told him that he didn't go out very much, Gary asked him if he'd like to go out together one night.

This was the last thing Mark expected. Gary was a few years older than Mark and he was surprised that he would want a seventeen year-old cramping his style, but he was only too happy to accept the invitation. They agreed to go out for a drink or two on Tuesday. 'Perhaps we'll meet a couple of girls,' added Gary, while they were unloading Mark's bike. 'I'll pick you up here at 7.30.'

'I'll look forward to that. Thanks for the ride.'

Over the next few months, Mark and Gary went out together at least once a week – often twice. This was as well as the tennis on a Friday night. So suddenly, Mark had a social life of sorts. Their nights out mostly followed the same pattern, which was for Gary to fetch Mark from his home and they would visit two or three local hostelries. Once in a pub, they would each buy a round of drinks and sit at a table until a pair of likely young ladies appeared to whisk them away from their lives of celibacy. Of course, this never actually happened, but they both anticipated each new public house with optimism.

Even when they found a pub with two such ladies, neither Gary nor Mark had the courage to approach them. They tried all the pubs and hotels in town, those on the outskirts of town and lots of little village pubs. They seldom stayed for long in the village pubs, due to the unnerving habit that Norfolk villagers have of staring at strangers as they enter their local. Gary and Mark sometimes played darts or dominoes, and they sometimes played the jukebox, taking turns to select a record. It wasn't a scintillating social life, but it helped Mark deal with his loneliness. He eagerly looked forward to each night out, thinking each one would be the night he would meet some nice young girl.

Gary's favourite pub was the Ship Inn at North Sanford. It wasn't a particularly salubrious pub, being near to the docks and attracting a very mixed clientele, but it just happened to be the pub run by Jean's parents. On one occasion, Jean joined them for a drink and it was clear to Mark that Gary would rather sit and talk to her than play darts with him. During their conversation, Gary persuaded Jean to join them for tennis on the following Friday.

Much to Mark's delight, when Friday came round, Jean brought Karen. They had a very enjoyable game of tennis. Although the lads had to take it easy with their heavy serves, there was still a healthy level of competition, especially when Mark and Karen played against Gary and Jean. Gary and Jean won, mostly thanks to Jean's wicked forehand, but also due to Mark being distracted by Karen's wonderful legs beneath a mid-length tennis skirt.

As neither Karen nor Jean had played for a long while, they didn't want to over-exert themselves on their first night of tennis, so it was still early when they finished playing. There were still four other people playing on the other court, but they had only just started a set, so Gary and Mark decided they would finish early as well. This being a Friday (her 'night off'), Jean was quite happy to accept Gary's invitation to a trip to the seaside. Karen wasn't too sure, but Jean managed to persuade her to come as well and off they all sped to Old Hunstanton. Mark sat in the front of the car and the two girls sat in the back. Karen was adamant that Mark couldn't sit in the back seat with her and that attitude really set the pattern for much of the evening as far as Mark and Karen were concerned. Everytime Mark said something nice to her, she managed to deflate him. Jean told her to stop being so horrible to Mark and just enjoy herself.

None of this stopped Gary and Jean from making the most of each other's company. When they got to the beach, Gary laid down an old car blanket and the two of them playfully fought for a bigger share of it to sit upon. There wasn't room for all four of them on the blanket, so Mark sat on the sand.

He had brought his tennis racquet and a ball, so he suggested a game of French Cricket. No one else had heard of this game before, so he explained that the object of the game is to get the batsman 'out' by tossing the ball onto his or her legs, below the knee. He or she could also be caught out. The batsman must not move his or her feet, which must be kept together. The fielders had to throw the ball from wherever the ball landed after the batsman had hit it away. The game started out in good spirits, but before long there were good-humoured accusations of cheating. Mark was last to bat and being the only person to have played the game before, he demonstrated the best technique to avoid getting dismissed.

When Karen had her second innings, there was a big dispute as to whether the ball hit her above or below the knee. She refused to 'walk' and carried on her innings. During her fourth innings, she hit the ball behind her and Mark quickly gathered the ball and threw it firmly at her calves before she had chance to turn round. 'You can't do that!' she shouted.

'Of course I can. You're out. Give me the bat. It's my turn.'

'If you want the bat so bad, Mark, you're going to get it' and she raised the racquet as though she was going to hit him with it. Of course, she wasn't really going to hit him, but he instinctively pulled back to avoid her non-existent blow and his right foot sank into some soft sand causing him to lose his balance. As he fell over onto his back, Karen dropped the racquet and pounced on him. Before he knew what was happening, she was kneeling on his chest and holding his arms down in the sand. He was a little winded from the fall, but he was in no hurry to throw her off. She still wore her tennis skirt and all he could see in front of him were her knees and her delectable thighs, which were almost in his face. At this range, they seemed surprisingly large and firm.

'Now what are you going to do?' she said menacingly.

'I'll throw you off when I'm ready, but this is quite nice for the time being.'

'I bet you can't throw me off.'

This sounded like a challenge. After another minute of enjoying the view, he gave a big jerk, expecting to push her back, but she was a lot stronger than he realised and after lifting himself up a few inches, she pushed him back with her hands. Being on top, he had expected her to have an advantage, but he was amazed how strong she was. She was also quite heavy. He was eleven and a half stone. He estimated she must be nearly as heavy as he was and yet she certainly wasn't fat.

He tried again with the same result. He tried bucking his hips and twisting at the same time, but to no avail. Then he tried bringing his legs up to wrap round her head, but she just leant forward to avoid them. He had to do something. He was determined that she would not defeat him. Especially with the other two watching them. 'You're never going to throw me off, Mark,' she said. She'd obviously done this before and was very confident of her strength and her wrestling ability.

Mark sighed as though he was about to admit defeat, but just when he thought the time was right, he suddenly thrust upwards, taking her by surprise. This time, he caught her off-guard and she lost her balance. He had gained enough ground so that her positional advantage no longer existed. His slightly superior weight now made a difference and although she was still putting up a lot of resistance, he managed to force her over, so that he was now on top of her, but it had been touch and go for a while. He would have been mortified if he had had to accept defeat. He held her hands down.

Now she was the one determined to throw him off. Again, he was amazed at her strength. She was able to lift up her arms a few inches, but he now had the weight advantage. She tried bucking and writhing and Mark felt like a bucking bronco. It was a very close battle. He was hoping she might try his tactic of trying to wrap her legs round his head. That would be nice, but she disappointed him.

After a few minutes of this, she said 'Mark, you're hurting my bosom.' He had forgotten that he was on top of her bosom, it being practically non-existent. He said 'Sorry,' and let her up straight away. 'Are you all right?'

'Of course, I am. I was just about to throw you off, but it was getting very uncomfortable.'

They were both covered in sand, so they stood up and brushed themselves down with their hands. Then they sat down on the blanket to regain their breath and watch a glorious sunset. Meanwhile, Gary and Jean were frolicking about, throwing the ball at each other in a semi-violent way and teasing each other.

'I enjoyed that,' said Mark.

'Did you, Mark?' she replied as though she didn't really care.

'I was surprised how strong you are,' he added.

'I was surprised how strong you were,' she said. 'I thought I'd beat you easier than that.' This sounded to Mark as though she was under the impression that she had won. 'I'm used to wrestling with my older brother. He's mentally handicapped, you know, so I'm sometimes regard him as my younger brother.'

'And do you beat him?'

'Well, it's always very close. It keeps you fit and strong.' She pulled her sleeve up and showed him one of her biceps. He thought it was nearly as big as his. He was about to pull up his sleeve and compare his arm to hers, but decided against it, just in case hers was the bigger of the two.

He looked at her as she sat there with her skirt halfway up her thighs, which, although not overtly muscular, looked very strong. She looked strong. Now he knew why she had intimidated him that day in the office, when she perched herself on the desk in front of him. She was very sure of herself. Now, he wanted her more than ever and wondered if they could start another little wrestle. It occurred to him that she might even enjoy it.

He said 'Anytime you want a re-match, let me know.'

'I don't think so, Mark.' It was as though she suddenly remembered that she didn't want to give him any encouragement.

'You keep doing that, don't you?'

'What's that?'

'One minute we're on good terms and having a bit of fun. Then the next, you close the door on me, determined to hurt my feelings. You know I'm nuts about you and would give anything to take you out on a date.'

'I'm sorry, Mark. I just don't feel that way about you and I don't want to mislead you.'

'Are you still seeing Ron Hall?'

'Who says I'm seeing Ron Hall?'

'Everybody. At least everybody thinks you are – and that's just as bad. I don't like it that everyone has this view of you. Even if you don't ever come out with me, I wish you'd stop messing about with him. He's only using you. He's had loads of affairs and always goes back to his wife and children. Please don't kid yourself that you're any different to the rest.'

'I know,' she said, chewing her lip.

'I know you think this is none of my business, but I care so much for you. You're the one who's going to get hurt, not him. It's got to end sometime, so don't let him be the one to dump you. I don't want to see you getting hurt.'

She didn't say anything else. Mark had either struck a chord or she just didn't want to hear anymore. He wasn't sure which. Maybe she didn't have any feelings to get hurt.

By now, the sun was already below the horizon and the sky had changed from red to a light pink. Despite being on the East Coast, Hunstanton faces west across The Wash and lovely sunsets are a frequent occurrence on this stretch of the coast. Now the sky was a paler imitation of its earlier glory.

Gary and Jean had decided that they needed a drink, so they came over to collect their things together. Mark stood up and gathered up his racquet and ball. Karen was still lying on the blanket and she said 'Mark, I can see right up your shorts. It's gruesome!'

'No it hasn't, but it certainly "grew some" when we had our little wrestle.' He knew she had deliberately set him up for the old joke and he duly obliged. But she would still have the last word.

'Don't be so dirty, Sid. Anyway, it's more like a little piece of gristle!'

She had heard someone in the office call him "Sid" and she knew he didn't like it. She often used that name to indicate her displeasure at something he said or sometimes, just to annoy him. The 'gristle' remark was meant to keep him in his place.

They all walked back across the sand and up the road a little way to the car. Mark and Karen didn't say very much, but Gary and Jean were full of themselves.

The pub they decided upon was the Le Strange Arms, which was just round the corner. Everybody had just one drink each and as they were all thirsty, it didn't take long to finish. Then, they were on the road again.

This time, Jean insisted on sitting in the front next to Gary. Karen wasn't happy about this, but Mark said 'What the Hell do you think I'm going to do in the back of the car?' So she relented and Mark made a point of keeping well to his side of the bench seat. Jean didn't follow his example in the front.

Gary asked Mark 'I've got to go right past your road, shall I drop you off on the way back?'

'No, my bike's still at the tennis court. Do you mind bringing it back with me after we've dropped the girls off?'

And that's what they did. Mark wondered whether Gary intended to drop off both Mark and Karen so that he could be alone with Jean. But he wasn't going to leave his bike unattended at the tennis court. Jean's car was still near the tennis court and she gave Karen a lift home. As Gary drove back to Mark's house, he said 'You seemed to be getting on well with Karen. Did you get yourself fixed up?'

'You must be joking. She's still seeing Ron Hall. Even if she isn't, she's made it plain she won't ever go out with me.'

'I'm sorry, mate. She'd be much better off with you. Apart from that, it was a good night, wasn't it?'

'Apart from that small thing – yeah. You and Jean were certainly enjoying yourselves. You want to watch out for her boyfriend. He can get a bit nasty.'

'I'm not too bothered about him. We'll have to see if we can't get them both to play tennis again next week. You'd like that wouldn't you?'

'Yes, I suppose I would. It's the only way I can get to go out with Karen. Don't be surprised if she doesn't come, though. Are we going out for a drink over the weekend?'

'I can't this weekend. I've got some work to catch up on. I'll give you a call about going out one night during the week.'

Mark was disappointed about this. Karen had upset his equilibrium again and he didn't want to mope about the house all weekend.

When he got to bed that night, he relived their little wrestle on the beach and got excited all over again. He started to question why he had found it all so stimulating. It wasn't just the physical contact. It was the challenge that she presented. He had found her physical strength to be something of a 'turn-on.' He liked the idea of a petit, demure, feminine young lady that he could protect. He also found voluptuous, round-hipped ladies like Sophia Loren to be of enormous attraction, but Karen was something different again.

If only he had asked her out when they had first met, things might have been so different. He'd heard that women like to be swept off their feet. In that respect, he had only himself to blame. He had made up his mind about her at their very first meeting. Although, in retrospect, his first impressions of her still stood up. She *was* self-opinionated, unaware of others' feelings and not particularly attractive. And that hadn't changed. But now that he had got to know her better, there was so much more to her. He certainly found her physically attractive. He ached to be with her. He felt his stomach knotting up at the thought that she didn't care about him at all. He had to do something about it, but it all seemed so hopeless. He felt so unhappy. He didn't sleep at all that night.

The next day, he went into town and bought himself a new record. He often found this cheered him up. It was an LP of hits by Garnett Mimms and the Enchanters. It was full of lovely soulful ballads, culminating in the haunting and wistful 'I Keep Wanting You,' with lyrics that mirrored his feelings. It talked of sleepless nights and the pain of wanting someone..

Somebody had been through the same feelings as Mark. He played that one track several times. Each time, it hit home, but in a strange way, it helped… for a little while, at least. Mark's music was very important to him.

Just before teatime, Gary knocked on the door. He was on his way home from work and like Mark, didn't fancy staying in that night, so they arranged to go out a little later.

When Gary called round again to fetch Mark, it was no surprise to Mark that Gary suggested the Ship Inn as their first port of call. When they walked in, being a Saturday, the place was heaving. They managed to find a seat, but there was no way they could get near the dartboard. Gary kept looking round to see if Jean was about. In the end, he asked her father who was serving behind the bar, if she was around. She wasn't. She was out with Colin, so they moved on to another pub. This time, Mark suggested the Globe Hotel off the market place in the middle of town, simply because it was a little more upmarket and he was wearing his suit, which seemed out of place in the Ship.

Once seated with a drink in the Globe, Mark asked Gary why he had been putting in so many extra hours at work.

'I'm working on this new product called "curtain-walling." It's erected on the outskirts of a building like an extra skin. It will be the new big thing in modern architecture. The company wants to expand into new areas and this will build on our expertise in aluminium products.'

'I hope you're getting well paid for all this extra work?'

'I don't get any extra, but I'm on a thousand a year, so I can't complain. Next week, we'll be building a 'mock-up' on the side of our offices, so you'll see what it's all about.'

'What's a muck-up?'

'It's a mock-up. Don't make fun of it. It's going to make a lot of money for the company.'

Mark thought his 'muck-up' comment was witty, so he added 'They say "Where there's muck, there's money", don't they?'

Gary wasn't very amused. He had put a lot of hard work into this project. Mark decided to reserve 'cock-up' for a better moment. He changed the subject and they started talking about girls, as usual. It wasn't long before they were discussing Jean and Karen, which made a change from Anne and Karen.

Mark suggested to Gary that he was in danger of falling for another girl who already had a boyfriend. It didn't seem to bother Gary. Anne was getting married next month and Gary was now resigned to losing her. In fact, Mark thought he was now much more obsessed with Jean than he ever was with Anne. What's more, Jean seemed to be encouraging him... at least on a Friday night. If Jean brought Karen along again, then Mark certainly wouldn't mind, although he knew it would be much healthier if both Mark and Gary each found themselves a proper girlfriend.

Gary asked 'What have you been doing today?'

'I went into town to get a new LP, and then took it home to play it a few times. It's by Garnet Mimms. You won't have heard of him, but he's got a superb voice.' Gary hadn't heard of him. Like most people, he liked chart music, but he didn't buy many records. 'Apart from that, not very much,' continued Mark. 'Mostly moping about the house… wondering whether Karen will come to tennis again, next week.'

'Yes, it seems funny that it was only last night we were all larking about on the beach. I'll give Jean a call during the week to see if they're both coming on Friday.'

Mark said 'I'll be amazed if Karen comes next time.'

He looked round the bar and there were two nice looking young ladies sitting two tables away. One of them glanced towards them and said something to her friend. It might have been 'Look at those two nice looking lads' or possible 'What's he looking at?' or just as likely, 'Shall we get out of here and go home.' Mark indicated their presence to Gary by a nod of his head in their direction.

Gary said 'Go on, then. Go ask them if they want a drink.'

'No, you do it. I'm sure this nearest one looked at you. I'll settle for her mate.' The nearest one was the thinner of the two, so Mark thought that would suit Gary better. The other one wore glasses, but she still looked quite pretty and she appeared to have more curves. Mark considered Gary to be the better looking of the two lads, so he thought Gary would stand more chance of a successful outcome. Anyway, wasn't he older and more experienced in these matters?

'I'll do it in a minute,' said Gary.

A minute passed and still they sat there. Ten minutes passed. Wouldn't it be nice if girls could make the first move? Eventually, the girls left. The problem was that neither Mark nor Gary would be happy about dating girls who could be picked up in a bar. There had to be a better way of meeting girls.

A few minutes later, Mark and Gary moved on as well – this time to a small pub in the country. Mark observed Gary's driving skills. He drove a little too fast for Mark's liking. And he kept using the brakes to slow down, instead of the gears. Mark thought that Gary would be unlikely to pass his driving test if he drove like that! As they drove out into the country, Mark said 'I might put in for my driving test, soon. If I pass, I can get a car and take a turn at taking us out. Do you want me to give you anything towards your petrol?'

'No. You keep your money for your new car.' Gary knew Mark didn't earn very much.

Once inside the pub, they ordered their drinks. Neither of them could be described as hardened drinkers and they still hadn't established a favourite drink. They'd tried bitter, mild, pale ale, brown ale, Guinness, cider and lager. None of them were to their taste, although they found a lager and lime was successful at quenching their thirsts after a game of tennis. This time, they tried milk stout, which they'd seen Ena Sharples and Minnie Caldwell drinking on 'Coronation Street.' This wasn't much better. They always drank half pints, so even though they weren't used to drinking, there was little chance of them getting intoxicated.

Gary asked Mark if he'd ever been ten-pin bowling. He hadn't. 'Is there a bowling alley around here?'

'I think the nearest is probably in Norwich' replied Mark. 'There may be one in Peterborough, which is a littler further away. I've never played, but I'd like to try it sometime.'

'We'll have to give it a try. I used to go regularly when I lived in London. There were always lots of things to do with my mates in London. There was a skating rink, dance halls, loads of cinemas and theatres. Apart from a couple of cinemas, there's nothing around here. Still, at least we've got the tennis. Do you play badminton?'

'I had a few games at school. I enjoyed it.'

'We'll have to see if we can find a club. It's a very good way to meet people.'

'Yes, I'd like that,' said Mark. 'It would be nice to do that when it's too dark or too cold to play tennis.'

The dartboard became free, so they had a game, which Mark won after both of them had been stuck on double one for five minutes. Neither of them could be described as a brilliant player. A couple of men in their early twenties had been watching them while emptying their pint glasses and when the game finished, they got up and challenged Gary and Mark. Our two friends would have preferred to play on their own, but they reluctantly agreed to the challenge. The strangers won quite quickly. As neither Gary nor Mark enjoyed it, they said they'd have to be leaving. 'Don't you want a chance to get even?' one of them asked.

'No,' said Gary. 'We've got to get off home, now.'

'Aren't you going to buy the winners a drink?' asked the other stranger.

'No,' said Gary, surprised at his impertinence.

'It's customary for the losers to buy the drinks,' said the first one.

Mark was happy to let Gary do the talking. He had more experience of drinking in pubs than Mark and Mark wasn't sure if they were telling the truth or just trying it on.

'Where I come from,' said Gary, 'any agreement like that is stipulated before the game commences, not after.'

It was obvious that the two strangers had been watching the standard of play before issuing their challenge, so neither Gary nor Mark had any intention of buying any drinks.

'Well,' said the second stranger, 'we'll play another game. This time, it will be stipulated.'

'No, it won't,' Mark and Gary said, almost in unison. 'We're going home,' added Gary, finishing his drink.

As they prepared to leave, the second one said 'Don't come using our dartboard, unless you're prepared to do the right thing.'

It sounded like a threat. Mark looked at the two men. They looked as though they might be used to brawling, but nevertheless, he didn't want to be seen skulking away. He also finished his drink, but a little more slowly and deliberately than Gary. Then he took their two glasses back to the bar. He was feeling a little nervous, but he was determined not to show it. Gary was waiting for him near the doorway and they both left with as much dignity as they could manage. Neither of them said anything until they got into the car.

Gary's car swept out of the car park with a shower of loose gravel, but then he always drove like that. 'That was interesting,' said Mark.

'Yes, they were either looking for a free drink or looking for trouble. They got neither. I wasn't sure whether you were up for a 'bundle' or not, so I thought we'd just leave with our dignity intact.' Mark didn't respond. He couldn't imagine Gary being up for a 'bundle', any more than he was.

Neither of them spoke again until they arrived at Mark's house, when Gary said 'I'll probably be busy again this week, so I'll see you at tennis on Friday.'

Mark said 'If I get a lift to work that morning, will you be able to take me home when we've finished tennis? It would save me messing about with my bike after the game.'

'Yes, of course I will, mate. I'll speak to Jean to see if she and Karen will play again. Cheers, mate.'

'Bye,' replied Mark.

He was pleased that he now had a friend and a social life. He wasn't sure that he had a lot in common with Gary, but it was a step in the right direction.

CHAPTER 13

Frayed Tempers

On Monday, Margaret came to tell Mark that her husband Alan had seen an ideal car for Mark. Mark explained that he hadn't saved anywhere near enough money and his driving instructor didn't think he was ready for his test, yet. Margaret suggested he could get a 'sub' from the company and then once he had a car, Alan would be perfectly willing to take him out for a few rides to give him more experience. Mark had to admit that he wasn't really learning anything new with Lou and what he really needed now was more hours behind the wheel. An hour-long lesson, once a week, wasn't enough, but Mark couldn't afford any more than that.

He told Margaret that he would think about it. The more he thought about it, the more he wanted his own car. He was sure that having his own transport would open up his life in all sorts of ways. So, later that same day, he went to see Margaret to make the arrangements to view the car with Alan.

A few days later, Alan picked Mark up after work and they went into town to see the car. Mark's potential new vehicle was a bright blue 1956 Standard 8. Alan considered that the price, sixty-five pounds, was very good for a car in this condition. It had four doors and four good tyres. The garage owner would give him a three-month warranty. As it was just over ten years old, it would need an MOT certificate (the three-year rule was not introduced until the following year). Alan said the car would be very economical. Cars of this era had very few of the little extras that we now take for granted. There was no radio; no wing mirrors; no heated rear window; no windscreen washers; no reversing light; no dipping rear-view mirror. There wasn't even a parcel shelf. You could see into the boot through the rear seats. But Mark liked it. After Alan took Mark out for a quick test drive, Mark told the salesman that he would buy it, subject to him raising the money.

He went home that night full of excitement. He couldn't wait to tell everyone, including Karen, who still hadn't taken her test, even though she had been driving a little longer than Mark. The next day, George agreed to the sub and even helped Mark organise his third party insurance. Unfortunately, Mark had to wait another ten days before the garage could do the MOT and he could collect the car.

When he spoke to Karen, he asked her if she was going to play tennis again that week. He was overjoyed that she said she was, but she was quick to point out that she didn't want to go to the seaside again. She had enjoyed the tennis and was hoping that they would play a little longer this time. Mark was still pleased about it. That was two events to anticipate with relish – collecting his new car and another game of tennis with Karen.

Much to Mark's dismay when he woke up on Friday, it was raining and it looked like the rain was going to last all day. He had already arranged a lift to work with George, so ever the optimist, he went to work prepared for a game of tennis.

Just after lunch, Gary went to see Jean. He was just as unhappy as Mark was about not playing tennis, but for slightly different reasons. He was on a mission to pursue Jean and he didn't want to lose this opportunity. After all, who was to say it wouldn't be raining again, next week? Karen was sitting next to Jean, but Mark was still in his office, unaware of the discussion that was about to take place. Gary suggested that as they couldn't play tennis, the four of them could go to Norwich to try the Ten-pin Bowling Alley. Karen didn't want to go and she was relying on Jean to give her a lift home from work.

Jean said she would still give her a lift home first, but she wasn't going to Norwich with just the two lads. Gary thought that Mark might care to drop out as well, but he kept this thought to himself. Jean was very keen. Unlike Karen and Mark, she had been bowling before and had enjoyed herself. Moreover, she was the only one of the four who knew how to find the Bowling Alley in Norwich. But Karen was adamant. She would still play tennis in the unlikely event that the weather improved, but she didn't want to do anything else.

Gary and Jean looked at each other, desperately trying to think of a way to get her to change her mind, while Karen looked down at her work. Jean gestured to Gary with a movement of her head for him to leave them alone. Jean thought she stood a better chance of persuading her if they were alone.

After Gary had left, she said 'What's the real reason you don't want to go?'

'I don't want to go out in a little foursome. Mark might get the wrong idea for one thing. I've never been bowling, so I don't think I would be very good.'

'I think you've already made Mark aware of your feelings, so I'm sure he wouldn't get the wrong idea. I'm sure you would enjoy the bowling. It's good fun. No one's going to make fun of you if you're not very good to start with. You'll never be any good if you don't give it a try. Mark's never been before either.'

Karen didn't say anything else, so Jean carried on, 'There's three of us who would really love to go and have a good time, but we can't go unless you join us.'

'Can't you find someone else to be your gooseberry?' said Karen. She had a good inkling that Jean and Gary were attracted to each other – not that it took much of a genius to work that out.

'You know damned well that we're not going to find anyone else at such short notice. You won't be a gooseberry if there are four of us. You're just being selfish. Why don't you think of someone else for a change? You're supposed to be my friend. I don't ask you for many favours… just this one… please?'

Karen could see that Jean was letting her desperation turn to anger. And she was practically begging her.

As an afterthought, Jean added 'Have you got anything else to do tonight?'

'No.'

'Well, then. It's better than sitting at home, isn't it?'

Karen hadn't spoken to Ron Hall for three weeks. He hadn't contacted her and she hadn't contacted him. She had to admit that she didn't want to stay at home on her own. After another minute of looking thoughtful, she said 'I would need to go home first to change, but this is a one-off.'

'Thank you,' said Jean. 'I'm sure you'll enjoy it. I should think the men will probably want to change first as well, so I'll take you home straight from work and we'll all meet back at the pub. It will give us time to get some food inside us before we go out.'

She 'phoned Gary to give him the good news and make the arrangements. Gary then 'phoned Mark to tell him. Mark was still feeling very despondent about not playing tennis, so this cheered him considerably, but he wasn't sure why Karen was joining them. He felt a little confused. He knew she had already made it plain that she didn't want to go anywhere with them after the tennis, so why the change of heart? He didn't dare build up his hopes, because they had been dashed so many times before.

For once, Gary left work on time and he dropped Mark off at the top of his road, while he continued to his own home to get a change of clothing.

Mark bolted down a sandwich and had a shave. He was still only shaving once a week, but this was a special occasion. He borrowed his father's safety razor and managed to cut himself in two places, so he had to keep wiping the blood from his face and dabbing some Old Spice onto the wounds to heal them as best he could before he went out again.

When they all met up at the pub, Karen had changed into a pair of trousers and a thin pale orange sweater. She didn't look like she had made any special effort to look smart. In fact, Mark thought she had looked better dressed during the day, except that now she wasn't wearing those awful high heels. Jean on the other hand, was wearing exactly the same outfit she had been wearing all week at work. Gary was wearing a very smart brown suede jacket.

Karen, of course, noticed Mark's shaving cuts. 'I didn't realise you had started shaving,' she said. He ignored her – he wasn't going to tell her that he'd only been shaving for six months.

And off they sped to Norwich, with the two girls in the back. They were soon passing through Swaffham. Gary had trouble pronouncing the name of the town, so the other three, who were all local, laughed at him. Mark helped him by quoting the local expression 'They off 'em at Swaffham and they don't wear 'em at Dereham,' putting on an exaggerated Norfolk accent.

Jean said 'You don't go to Swaffham for narthin',' making Swaffham rhyme with 'narthin' and meaning 'You don't go to Swaffham for nothing,' which of course doesn't rhyme when spoken correctly'

Then they had a discussion about some of the strange pronunciations of local place names, including Happisburgh, Weybourne and Wymondham. When they passed through Costessey on the outskirts of Norwich, they all asked Gary how to pronounce that. He tried to pronounce it as it's spelt. 'No, Gary it's pronounced "Cossey,"' said Karen.

'But it's got all those extra letters in it,' he said. 'Why?' Nobody knew why.

They were soon at the Bowling Alley. It looked very busy. Gary went up to the desk to sort out a lane, but he returned to the group to announce that all the lanes were booked up until ten o'clock, mostly for league matches. It was only just eight o'clock and no one fancied hanging around for two hours. It would be very late before they would be finished and even later before they got home, so they all decided to abandon the idea of bowling for that night. Gary said that next time, they'd make a point of booking a lane beforehand. Mark thought that judging by the look of disgust on Karen's face, there wouldn't be a 'next' time.

They discussed what they might do instead. Jean and Gary came up with loads of suggestions, but they couldn't enlist any co-operation from Karen at all. In the end, they agreed to head back home, but they would stop somewhere on the way back for a quick drink. Tempers were a little frayed. Mark was as disappointed as anyone, but back in the car, he tried to lift their spirits by telling a few jokes. They didn't go down very well and Karen told him to give it a rest.

As they headed back towards Sanford, they had difficulty agreeing which pub to stop at. Some pubs looked too 'seedy', whilst Karen didn't feel she was suitably dressed for the better-looking establishments. They would soon be home, so they eventually stopped at a pub in Narborough, called co-incidentally 'The Ship Inn.'

While Gary fetched some drinks, Mark put some money in the jukebox. He asked Karen to help him select some music. She picked out both sides of a Jim Reeves record and one by Roy Orbison. Mark selected 'Stand By Me' by Ben E. King and another song by Roy Orbison.

'I didn't think you liked Roy Orbison?' queried Karen.

'Yes, I've always liked Roy Orbison. I used to buy some of his records before I discovered soul music. I used to like a few Country And Western records. Bobby Bare; Johnny Cash. I never liked Jim Reeves, though. He's your favourite, isn't he?'

'Him and Eddy Arnold.' Mark considered this to be old people's music, but he didn't dare tell her that. He watched her listening to the first Jim Reeves song, which was 'Welcome To My World.' She closed her eyes and looked totally immersed in the record. Meanwhile, Gary and Jean came back from the bar with all the drinks.

'What records have you put on, mate?' asked Gary of Mark. Mark told him. Then Gary asked Jean if she wanted to pick anything out. She was quite happy listening to any old record.

When the Ben E. King record was half-way through, Karen said 'I prefer the original version.'

'What do you mean? This is the original,' said Mark, indignantly.

'No, Mark. Kenny Lynch had the original. This is just a copy.'

Mark wasn't sure if she was trying to wind him up or not, but he still rose to the bait. 'Not only did Ben E. King have the original version, he also had a hand in writing the song!' he said quite firmly. 'And his version was issued three or four years before Kenny Lynch's version. Not only that, it's ten times better.' He raised his voice for the last sentence. He was getting annoyed.

She replied 'Don't be silly, Mark. I happened to know I'm right.'

'I don't know if you're trying to wind me up, or not, but you're talking a load of old squit.'

'What's a load of old "squit" mean?' asked Gary.

'It's a Norfolk expression for "Karen's talking out her backside." But as usual, she's convinced she's right and everyone else is wrong!' Mark had lost patience with Karen's tendency to be waspish whenever there was a danger of them chatting away nicely.

It all went quiet. It was unusual for Karen not to try to have the last word. After a few more seconds, Mark added 'Why do you always do it? Why do you always want to…?' He clenched his fists and gritted his teeth and just sank back in his chair, seething.

Over the last few months, he had tried everything to win her over. He'd tried telling her jokes, because he thought she was attracted to men with a sense of humour. He'd tried paying her lots of complements. He'd tried waiting on her hand and foot. He'd even had a spell of a few weeks when he led her to believe that he'd lost interest. But now was the first time he had got really angry with her. His anger was perfectly genuine, but he still wondered if it might have a positive effect. She certainly seemed a little subdued now. Wouldn't it be nice if she said that she was sorry? But that wasn't in Karen's nature.

He turned to the other two and said 'Somebody say something to change the subject. We came out to enjoy ourselves, didn't we?'

Jean said 'Well, I thought some of us did. We're having a good time, aren't we, Gary?'

'Yeah. It's a shame about the bowling, but these things happen. When do you pick up this new car, mate?' Gary usually called Mark 'mate' – in fact, Mark couldn't remember Gary ever using his name.

'Next Saturday.' He couldn't think of anything else to add. He'd already told everybody all the details and he was still trying to calm down.

'I'll look forward to having a ride in it,' said Gary. 'Aren't you going to get a car, sometime, Karen?'

'I keep thinking about it. But I want to pass my test first... And I think I would want something a little newer.' Mark gave her another angry look. She was doing it again. But this time she realised her remark might have caused offence, so she added, 'Or to be precise, my father thinks I should have something newer and totally reliable. He doesn't want me breaking down in the middle of nowhere.'

At least she had made some effort to recover from her inappropriate remark.

By now, the jukebox had finished playing their records and they'd all finished their drinks, so after a quick visit to the toilets, they were on their way again. Out of devilment, Jean asked Mark if he wanted to sit in the back, but before Karen could say anything, he said 'No, I'm fine in the front, thank you' and climbed in. He didn't speak to Karen throughout the journey back. He realised that it looked like he was sulking, but he couldn't see any way to break out of it.

As Manningford was just a slight detour off the road back to Sanford, it was agreed to drop Karen off first to save Jean getting her car out again. Karen gave Gary directions and by the time they pulled into her cul-de-sac, it was dark. Mark had been interested to see where she lived in case he might decide to bike over to see Aunt Louise again. Karen's house was the other end of the village and was the middle house of a block of three. They looked like council houses and they were in the rougher part of the village. Karen told Jean she would see her on Monday. She thanked Gary for dropping her off. Then she turned to Mark and said 'Bye, Mark. See you next week.'

Mark just said 'Bye.' He was still angry. He thought about totally ignoring her, but he already had difficulty assuring her of his maturity, without giving her further ammunition. As they drove off, Jean asked 'Are you still angry, Mark?'

'I suddenly feel a bit better. I'm sorry about my behaviour, but she's done things like that too many times and I just lost it, I'm afraid.'

'I'm surprised you haven't lost your temper before. She doesn't seem to want to enjoy herself. I don't think she's been seeing Ron lately, so I don't know if that's part of her problem at the moment.'

'Has she packed him in or has he dumped her?'

'I don't know. I think she was always at his beck and call, so who knows? She's changed so much in the last few months. We're just not as friendly as we used to be.'

When they arrived back at the other Ship Inn, Gary suggested they should go in for another drink. The three of them sat down together. Now Mark did feel like a gooseberry. Most of Gary's conversation was directed at Jean and hers at Gary. At closing time, they hung around to get another 'out of hours' drink 'on the house' courtesy of Jean's father and when everyone else had left, the three of them helped with the clearing up. While Mark stacked the chairs on top of the tables, Gary and Jean disappeared into the kitchen with all the glasses. Mark finished his chore and waited around for the other two to return. They seemed to be taking a long time.

Eventually Mark heard them returning, or so he thought, but they stopped in the lounge bar, which was separated from the saloon bar where Mark was waiting, by a dingy yellow frosted glass partition. He could see their silhouettes through the glass. They must have been totally unaware that he could see them, because they started to embrace each other. Then they were embracing each other passionately. Mark didn't know where to look. This went on for several minutes and Mark considered whether he should tap on the glass, but he didn't want to be a killjoy.

Mark was desperately hoping their embraces didn't lead to anything else. Jean looked liked she was eating Gary alive. Mark just stood there, waiting and looking in the other direction for what seemed an eternity. He couldn't have been much more embarrassed if they had been in the same room as him. Eventually, he heard their voices again and they came back into the saloon bar. Mark looked up, and seeing a guilty look on Jean's face, said 'Have you finished?' He intended it to sound like he meant 'Have you finished the clearing up?' but Jean replied 'We weren't doing anything,' as though she was afraid they'd been caught out.

Mark didn't appreciate being lied to, but Gary was a little more composed. He just said 'We'd better get off, mate' and they did, after a very quick 'Goodnight' to Jean.

In the car, both Gary and Mark were quiet. As they came within a half mile of his house, Mark said 'Just drop me at the top of Hall Lane. I feel like a little walk.'

'But it's still raining.'

'A little rain won't hurt me.'

'Are you all right, mate?'

'No. It hasn't been a good day. First, the rain stopped us playing tennis; then the Bowling Alley was all booked up; then I lost my temper with Karen.' He also felt uncomfortable about what he had just witnessed at the pub, but he didn't mention this.

'You take these things too much to heart.'

'Well, that's how I am. I'm also a little envious that you seem to be doing so well with Jean and I'm getting nowhere with Karen – not that I approve, mind you. I always thought Jean was quite serious about Colin, so someone's going to get hurt.'

'I'm sure we can look after ourselves.'

'If you say so. Anyway, are you working again this weekend?' Mark wasn't too sure whether he wanted to go out himself that weekend, so he was serving up an excuse for Gary.

'Yes, I've still got a lot to do. We had a few problems with the 'mock-up' so I've got to do some more work on it. I'll give you a call during the week.' By now, they were at the top of Hall Lane, so Mark got out and walked the last few hundred yards in the rain. He considered whether he really wanted to go out in these foursomes again. He never got anywhere with Karen and it just made him miserable. He still couldn't understand why she had come with them that night. Perhaps it did have something to do with her breaking off with Ron Hall.

Before he went to bed, he played 'I Keep Wanting You' again, with the sound turned low, so as not to wake the rest of the household.

The pain in the lyrics hit home again, just as before.

★ ★ ★ ★ ★

The next week seemed to drag on forever for Mark. He was so looking forward to picking up his new car and he didn't go out at all until Friday. Gary had 'phoned him on Thursday to ask him not to rely on him for a lift on Friday. He wasn't too sure whether he would be playing tennis or not. He told Mark he was still very busy. Mark wasn't sure if this was the truth. He considered it highly likely that Gary would be out with Jean on Friday as it was her 'night off.'

George had started playing tennis with them, so Mark arranged for a lift to work and home again after the tennis on Friday. But when they got to the tennis courts, there was Gary, Jean and Karen. Mark's first two games were with George, Dave and John. It wasn't until the third game that he got to play with Karen and Jean. He partnered Karen against Jean and George. During the game, Karen said 'I haven't seen you all week. What have you been doing?'

'I've been very busy.' Mark hadn't been any busier than usual, but he just couldn't be bothered to go out of his way to speak to Jean or Karen that week.

'You won't have heard that I've got another job, then?'

'You mean you're leaving Greshams?' Mark's eyes were glaring as he asked her.

'Yes, I'm going to work at a farm just outside Manningford. It's just general office work – typing and admin. work – a bit of book-keeping.'

'Why?'

'It will be a lot more convenient. The money's not very good, but it's right on my doorstep.'

Before he could pursue the conversation, George was getting impatient to serve, so they took up their positions. Mark watched Karen return George's serve to Jean, who volleyed the ball straight to Mark, who hit a glorious forehand into the far corner out of George's reach. 'Nice shot, Mark,' said Karen. It was nice to hear her pay him a complement, so he decided to concentrate on the tennis. He had a hundred and one questions to ask her, but, at that moment, he wanted them to play well together and win their match. Mark's game had improved tremendously over the last few weeks, to the point where he could give any of the other men a competitive game, while still being the weakest of the men. Jean was a slightly better player than Karen, so if Mark and Karen could win this match it would be quite an achievement.

They had already lost the first game of the set off Karen's serve and despite a fierce battle, they proceeded to lose this next game off George's serve. Now it was Mark's turn to serve. His first serve to Jean was a wicked sliced serve that took her completely by surprise. He had seen Dave Taylor execute this same slice serve and had been gradually trying to introduce it into his own game. When it worked, it was usually very successful. When it didn't, it went spectacularly wrong. His next serve to George was a power serve; as good as any Mark had ever served. Again

Karen complemented him 'Nice serving, Mark. Keep it going.' He would certainly try. He tried another sliced serve to Karen, but he hit the ball off the frame of his racquet and it ended up in George's court. His second serve was a safe dolly of a serve and Jean executed her delightful forehand to return the ball straight to his feet and although he got his racquet to the ball, he returned into the net. 30-15.

His next serve was another good power serve, but this time, George did return it, but it wasn't a good return and Karen was able to place her volley wide of Jean into the tram lines. 'Nice shot, Karen.'

'Nice serve, Mark.' This felt good. 40-15.

Mark didn't like serving too hard to a lady, so his next serve was another sliced serve. This time, it started way out wide and looked like it was going to be a 'fault,' but it swerved in the air and landed on the line. Jean had already decided it was going wide so she left it and when she saw it bounce on the line, she let out a little squeal, shouting 'Mark! That's not fair!' but Karen and Mark gave each other a very satisfied grin.

As they changed ends, Mark asked Karen if she was going for a drink after the tennis. 'I don't know. Jean's car is out of action, so Gary is taking us home. I believe he needs to get off sharp.'

Mark replied 'I'll bet you anything you like that he drops you off before Jean.'

Karen looked at him for a few seconds and then said 'Oh, I see what you mean. Well, we'll see.'

Now it was Jean's turn to serve. Karen seemed to be just as determined to win as Mark and she played several good shots against Jean's serve. She impressed Mark with her ability to cover the court. She couldn't have done that in her high heels. They won that game as well. It was now 2-2.

Now it was Karen's serve again. Mark considered that as she was so strong physically, she ought to have a power serve, but she didn't have Mark's height and seemed content to concentrate on a good length. They won three points serving to Jean, but lost three points serving to George. Karen said to Mark 'How do you do that swervey serve of yours?'

'It takes a lot of practice and a bit of trial and error. I wouldn't try it now. Just carry on the way you are. Let them make the mistakes.' For once, Karen took notice of him and they won the next point, serving to Jean. Her next serve to George was an attempt at a power serve. It was nearly successful. It wasn't quite as fierce as some of Mark's serves, but it still took George by surprise. Unfortunately, it was just too long, but it nearly hit George's leg. If it had done, it would have hurt. He looked at Karen as though he couldn't believe a woman could hit a serve as hard as that. Her second serve was weak and George shaped up to hammer it as if to show that the blokes should have the monopoly on power shots. However, he applied far too much power. Mark ducked and it sailed over his head and out of court. Karen and Mark were now 3-2 up.

George won his serve quite comfortably, as did Mark. It was then 4-3. They won against Jean's serve. 5-3. Karen was determined to win her serve. She had lost one service game and won one. She consulted Mark about tactics. They were consistently winning points serving to Jean, but George was mostly punishing her serve by standing quite close, so Mark suggested she didn't change anything when serving to Jean. But for her first serve to George, she should really send one down. Even if it was a 'fault,' it might persuade him to stand back a bit further, especially after her previous power serve.

She did as Mark suggested and her first serve to George slammed ferociously into the net, but again, George was taken aback by the sheer force of it. Even so, he punished her second serve. They won the next point, so it was now 30-15. This time, when she served to George, he did stand back near the baseline and when she went for accuracy instead of power, Mark had more time to anticipate George's return and ran across to put it away. It was now 40-15. Karen's serve to Jean was another accurate serve. Jean employed her wicked forehand and she sent the ball straight back to Mark at the net. He had no time to pick out his shot, but he did get his racquet to the ball and it flew off the frame at an angle, away from both his opponents. It was a fluke, but it was the match winning shot.

Mark and Karen turned to each other and hugged. It wasn't a passionate hug, but it was delivered by both parties with genuine joy. Mark didn't want to let go, but after a few seconds, Karen gently pushed him away.

Jean said 'I don't mind losing if it means you two are going to end up on such good terms.'

Karen said 'I don't think we expected to win that one, so we're just overjoyed.'

'You both played very well,' said George, magnanimously.

The other four had finished their game and were waiting to mix up the pairs again. However, Gary and Jean said they'd have to be going, which meant that Karen had to go as well. How Mark wished he could offer her a lift, himself. He had the impression that she was enjoying herself and wanted to stay. None of the others lived in her direction, so she had to go with Gary. That left an odd number. Mark suggested he could miss out the next game and get a lift home with Gary, but Gary said he was going back to work as soon as he had dropped off Karen and Jean. Mark thought it highly unlikely that Gary was going back to work at that time of night and no one else really believed him, either. But by then the other four were all ready to start another game, so Mark had to sit it out, anyway.

He sat patiently on the grass outside the courts. He had very mixed emotions at that moment. He had just heard the devastating news about Karen leaving, but he had also just had an immensely satisfying game with his heart's desire. He could do with having games like that every week. The two of them would take on the world. He felt an almost sexual satisfaction when they performed so well as a team. He hadn't even bothered to eye up her legs while they were playing. Mind you, he did have a good look during the previous game when she was on the adjacent court. 'What a woman!' he thought.

His little loss of temper was now confined to the past. She hadn't been at all waspish all night. Who knows, she might have gone for a drink in their little foursome, that evening, if it wasn't for the fact that Gary now had his own private agenda to consider. Mark had conveniently forgotten that he had decided that he had resolved never to go out in their foursome again.

CHAPTER 14

Getting Mobile

Mark was up very early on Saturday. Alan's son, Mick, was giving them a lift into town to collect Mark's car and he would come back to pick up Alan from Mark's house a little later. They were all very punctual. Mark had sixty-five pounds in cash in his pocket, which was the most money he had ever carried (except for the payroll run). He had also brought some 'L' plates, so that he could drive home.

The car was all ready, together with the MOT certificate and half a tank of petrol. It didn't take long to sort out the paperwork. The car wasn't yet taxed, but Mark had his insurance cover note with him. He attached the 'L' plates at each end of the car and he was all ready to go. Alan sat in the passenger seat, while Mark reminded himself of all the controls. He pulled out the choke, switched on the ignition and reached for the starter knob. The car started first time.

As he engaged first gear, he couldn't help feeling a little apprehensive. It was a busy Saturday morning in town and he had to turn right out of the garage across the road. Alan asked if Mark would prefer it if he drove them out of town, but Mark knew he had to do this. He was soon on his way. Alan suggested a few detours, not only to avoid the worst of the traffic, but also to give Mark more time behind the wheel. It took them twenty minutes to get home, by which time Mark's palms were sweaty and unable to get a firm grip on the plastic steering wheel. As he approached his house, he could see Mr Pettit trying to manipulate his car into the closest possible position to his gate. The car had been in his drive overnight, but he was going out in a little while, so he was getting it ready. That involved parking right outside his gate. Mark carried on to the end of the road and turned round, so that he could park behind Mr. Pettit on the same side of the road as him, but as Mr Pettit was still manoeuvring his car back and forward, Mark parked his car five yards behind him.

Alan watched in amazement at Mr Pettit's antics. Mark said 'Oh, he'll be doing that for another ten minutes, yet.' Then he added 'Margaret said you'd be able to come with me for a ride, sometime. When would be convenient?'

'Not this weekend, I'm afraid and I'm working nights all this week. I'll have to find out if I'm free next weekend. I'll get Margaret to let you know.'

'That's great,' thought Mark. 'I've got a new car and I can't use it at all.' Perhaps he could ask his sister or brother-in-law if they could sit with him sometime. Then there was Gary, if he wasn't too busy, which seemed to be the case all the time these days. He didn't want any of them to necessarily teach him – just sit with him and enjoy the ride, if that was possible. He had cancelled his lessons with Lou Redmond to save himself money.

Once Alan and his son had departed, and Mark had thanked him profusely, he rushed indoors to tell everyone that the car was there. His father couldn't be bothered to look, but his mother came out and told Mark that it was a nice colour. 'You'll be able to take me to Bingo, now.'

'I can't take you anywhere 'til I pass my test!' replied Mark.

Throughout the weekend, Mark kept going outside to sit in his car or look under the bonnet (not that he knew what he was looking at!). He felt very frustrated that he couldn't go anywhere in it. He cycled round to see his sister to ask if she or her husband could go for a ride with him, but they were too busy that weekend. He never heard from Gary. He certainly wouldn't be losing his trusty old bike just yet!

Mark's family didn't have a telephone, so he had to wait until he was back at work on Monday to talk to Gary to ask if they could go out for a drink one night during the week and Mark would drive. But Gary announced that he was now going out with Jean, who had broken off with Colin, so he would be going out with her nearly every night that week. Gary added that he wasn't sure when he would be able to go out with Mark again. Mark had effectively been dumped! He vowed to himself that when and if he ever did get a girlfriend, he wouldn't just abandon any friends he might have – not that he had a friend, anymore!

Throughout the early part of the week, he waited patiently for Margaret to come and tell him when Alan could take him for a ride, but no such visit materialised. However, George had a very good suggestion. It was the week of the firm's Sports Day, when staff from both the London and the Birmingham offices would compete for a trophy against the Sanford office. There would be a cricket match and, depending on numbers, a tennis match. George's suggestion was for Mark to drive them both to the venue, which was the Hunstanton Recreation Ground.

Mark was very grateful for the suggestion. However, he pointed out that George had already said that only one of the Wages staff could attend and Josie had stated her intention to go. Mark had been excluded from the cricket team because of this. Josie obviously wasn't participating. She only wanted to go to socialise with the Londoners, whom she knew quite well and hadn't seen for over a year.

George's response was that he would tell Josie that preference would be given to people taking part in the sports events. If she was willing to play tennis (and George knew she wouldn't), then she could still go. Otherwise Mark was required to attend to make up the numbers for tennis. George invited her to his office to tell her. The news was received like a declaration of war, with Josie storming out of George's office and making Mark's life Hell for the rest of the week, except for Thursday, which was the day of the big event. Penny was also in the thick of it and she didn't help by stating that she had just as much right to go as Josie did. But for Mark, it was worth it.

Mark would have liked a game of cricket for a change, but the team had already been selected. This included a good mixture of people from both the Factory and the Office. In any case, he thought there might be a chance of some girls playing in the tennis.

When the day arrived, he and George headed out to the coast. It was a slow journey on a lovely sunny day. Mark felt like a king driving along the coast road, until he was overtaken near Ingoldisthorpe (pronounced Ingolsthorpe!) by a Triumph Herald. It was Jean… and was that Karen with her? They probably wouldn't have recognised Mark in his new car. He could show Karen his car when he got there!

There were a surprising number of people milling around at the playing field. Both the London office and the Birmingham office were predominantly sales oriented, so they were able to attend in force, leaving only a skeleton staff behind. Everybody seemed to know everybody else, except Mark who still didn't even know a lot of the Sanford staff. There was a lot of standing around and talking and no one seemed to be in a hurry to get things moving. Mark decided that as he couldn't see Karen anywhere, he would find the changing rooms. He was more interested in playing tennis than standing around talking about nothing in particular.

In the changing rooms, he saw Ron Hall. They said 'Hello' to each other. Mark wondered if Ron knew of Mark's interest in Karen. The two rivals had never actually spoken to each other before. Mark had to admit that Ron could be considered good-looking, but in a 'smarmy' way. Penny had once described him as 'greasy,' whatever that meant.

Ron stood there in a pink shirt with a blue neck-scarf, like a modern day Noel Coward. Mark thought 'This chap really loves himself.' He was known not to mix very much with other men, much preferring female company. He was very slightly taller than Mark, with broad shoulders and a deep chest, yet even so, Mark couldn't imagine him as a sportsman. His hair was thickly curled and appeared to Mark to be permed. 'I bet he spends a lot of money at the Hairdressers,' thought Mark.

'I didn't see your name on the team list?' questioned Ron.

'That's because I'm playing tennis, not cricket... hence the... er... tennis racquet.' Mark couldn't resist one of his trademark sarcasms. He didn't have any great desire to befriend this chap. It occurred to Mark that he had never seen Karen and Ron together. There was every likelihood that he would today and he didn't know how he would handle it.

Naturally, Ron had his own immaculate cricket whites and cricket shoes. He also took great care in the placement of his box. Mark had never worn a box in his life. He couldn't help thinking it would just get in the way of free movement when running, but he could see a man like Ron wouldn't be without one. They carried on changing in silence. Mark kept hoping someone else would come in. Eventually, a tall, slightly bald and well-tanned gentleman came in. He was in his late-forties, had a neatly trimmed moustache and he too was immaculately dressed.

'Ah,' he said to Mark. 'Another tennis player. I'm Ted Barnes from the Birmingham office.' Mark could have guessed he was from the Birmingham office by his accent.

'I'm Mark Barker,' came the reply and they shook hands. Or to be precise, Ted shook Mark's hand. Mark had just held his hand out to be crushed.

Ron held his hand out. 'Hello, Ted. How are you?'

'I'm fine, thank you. Have we met?'

'Ron Hall – Assistant Works Manager. We met last year in the Balham office.'

'I don't remember,' Ted replied, looking carefully at him. Mark found this amusing.

Before they could follow up on that mysterious meeting, George came in to get ready. Ted and George recognised each other instantly and shook hands warmly. They proceeded to chat away like a couple of old friends, while Mark and Ron finished changing in silence.

Ted and George talked about a whole range of subjects including Ted's golfing handicap, England's success in the World Cup (which Ted had attended), and whether George had finished calculating this quarter's sales commission. From their conversation, Mark was able to work out that Ted was in charge of the Birmingham office, which was mainly responsible for Sales in the North and Midlands and not much else. There were only four people working in Birmingham and three of them were there that day.

Ted asked 'So what's the score with the tennis?'

George replied 'As far as I know we're waiting to see how many are playing from the London office. Is it just you from Birmingham?'

'Myself and Grace. She's a useful little player, you know,' said Ted.

'We weren't sure if there were going to be any ladies or not. I can't think of any from London, in which case we've brought one of our own ladies, just in case.'

'Which one's that?' interjected Mark, hoping it was Karen.

'It's Jean,' came the reply. 'I think they want to start both the cricket and the tennis about eleven o'clock. There'll be lunch – a light buffet – at one.' Mark looked at his watch. It was 10.15. Forty-five minutes to kill. He decided to go and have another wander round to see if he could find Karen and show her his car. He still couldn't find her, but he did find Jean. She still wasn't sure whether she was playing or not. Mark told her what George had said. 'Was that Karen in the car with you, when you came thundering past me near Ingoldisthorpe?'

'Oh, I didn't see you. Yes, that was Karen. Have you got your new car, here?'

'Yes. Do you want to have a look at it?'

'I will later. I'd better get changed if I'm playing.'

'Is Gary here?'

'No. He has to work on his curtain-walling. They're having lots of problems with water leaking in on the "mock-up".

'So it was a "cock-up", thought Mark to himself.

'He's hoping to play tomorrow night, though,' continued Jean.

Mark continued to wander round. At last he found Karen. She was standing beside the pavilion, talking to a couple of chaps that Mark recognised from the Drawing Office. She was wearing a tight knee-length turquoise dress that really suited her wonderful figure. It was sleeveless, so he could see, for the first time, her shapely shoulders and arms in all their lightly-tanned glory. The dress also wrapped tightly round her glorious rear-end, beneath which were those full and shapely calves. Mark had never seen her looking so lovely. He wondered whether he should interrupt them to say 'Hello.' At that moment, he was quite content to stand a few yards behind her and admire her impressive form from where he was standing, but he noticed Barney Briggs, the spiv look-alike from the Buying Office – obviously not involved in filming any Ealing comedies that week. Barney spotted Mark and said 'Hello Mark. Are you playing, my old son?'

'Yes. I'm playing tennis.'

Karen heard Mark's voice and turned to look at him. Barney and Mark exchanged a few pleasantries, and when Barney had moved off, Karen stumbled over awkwardly in her high heels to where Mark was standing. 'Hello Mark. I didn't think you were coming, today?'

'I'm glad I did. Just to see you. You're looking absolutely gorgeous.'

'Do I usually look horrible, then?'

'No, of course not. But that dress looks stunning.'

'You can have it when I've done with it.'

'I'm trying to pay you a compliment. Just say "Thank you, Mark" and accept the compliment.'

'Thank you, Mark. It is very nice of you.' Unbeknown to Mark, she considered giving him a little kiss on the cheek, but decided it was too public.

Mark said, 'At least seeing you in that dress makes up for you not playing with me. I really enjoyed our game last week. Are you playing tomorrow?'

'I will if I can get a lift. I enjoyed the game last week. Jean may not be playing, as she's playing today.'

'I know Gary is hoping to play, tomorrow, if that helps. I'd happily give you a lift, but I would need another driver to sit with me. I've got my new car here, today, if you'd like to look at it. It's in the car park.'

'Yes, I'll go and have a look a little later. You haven't said anything about me leaving.'

'There's not much I can say, is there? You know I would dearly like you to stay, but my views aren't going to change the price of sprouts. I really hope it all works out for you, but you know I'm going to miss you like Hell. Even more, now that I've seen you in that dress. When do you go?'

'At the end of August.'

'Well I hope you can play tomorrow. I'd like to see you as much as I can before you go, because I don't suppose I'll see you, once you leave. This farmer hasn't got any other vacancies, has he?'

'Are you any good at mucking out the cows?'

'I'd gladly muck out cows to be near you.' Mark wasn't sure if he meant that. He probably did, but it wasn't going to happen anyway.

'As soon as I leave, you'll have your eyes on someone else,' said Karen.

'Well, I hope so. But it's going to take someone special to help me get over you.'

'I wish it had worked out differently. You're a very nice chap, Mark.'

'I hate being called "nice." It seems to me that women prefer nasty chaps.'

'I don't.'

'But you like Ron Hall. What he does to women is nasty.'

'You don't know the whole story, Mark.'

'No. I'm just a nice innocent boy, aren't I?'

'You won't always be.'

'No. I'll be eighteen next month. My life's just flashing by.' He actually thought his life was dragging along and he couldn't wait to get out of his teens. Somebody might start taking him seriously, then. But that would be too late for Karen.

'Anyway,' he added, 'I'd better go round to the tennis courts to see if anyone's interest in playing yet.'

'Do you know who you're playing with?' she asked.

'No idea. No one seems to know what's happening. It's not very well organised. I hope the cricket goes a bit better. Are you watching the cricket or the tennis?' In other words 'Will you be watching Ron or me?' he thought to himself.

'I'll have a look at both. I wish I was playing, but they only wanted one lady. Jean and I tossed for it, and she won. I don't think anyone has really catered for women at this event. They could have had a game of Netball. Jean and I both played Netball at school. Anyway, have a good game. I'll see you later.'

Mark reluctantly turned away and walked towards the tennis courts. He couldn't resist turning round to have another look at Karen. Aagh! Those high heels! And the grass was making it even harder than usual for her to walk with any degree of elegance. Nevertheless, it was still an awesome sight, with her shapely shoulders narrowing to her waist, her calves straining and her buttocks swelling each side of her dress in turn.

There had been many occasions when she had stirred his sexual awareness – sitting on his desk in front of his face; bending over Bob's desk in her tight trousers; sitting on his lap and, of course, their little wrestle on the beach (especially their little wrestle on the beach!). But the sight of her in her tight sleeveless dress was the ultimate. She was so perfect. Well apart from her looks, her flat-chest, her high heels and her occasional waspishness. Apart from all that, she was perfect.

At the tennis courts, there was still no sign of anyone actually playing tennis, nor even warming up. Mark just wanted to get on with things. He found George and asked if he knew what was happening. This prompted George to spring into life. It was almost eleven o'clock. He found one of the London salesmen to ask him whom they had brought. It transpired that they only had two men who wanted to play tennis, so with the two people from Birmingham, that made a total opposition force of three men and a lady. Greshams had booked three courts for the day and Sanford had brought eight people, including one lady. After further protracted discussions, it was decided that they wouldn't bother too much about a serious match. They would let everyone rotate and play with different partners. Much to Mark's delight his first partner was the lovely Grace from the Birmingham office. Ted introduced them to each other and Ted partnered Jean.

Grace was a peroxide blonde, in her late twenties, who wore a lot of make-up, but had a lively personality and was very chatty to Mark. She and Ted seemed to be the best of friends. It was no surprise to Mark, when, he later learnt from George that Ted and Grace had a 'thing' going on, although they were both married (to someone else) and Ted must have been almost old enough to be her father. There seemed to be so much of this sort of thing going on that Mark had stopped being judgemental about it. Grace was a very competent player and had a natural athleticism to go with her fine array of shots, but she seemed incapable of applying any great power to those shots. She made up for this with consistency and an ability to return almost anything that came her way.

Ted was also a very fine player. He did have the power to go with his shots, particularly his serve. He had no compunction about serving as fiercely to Grace as he did to Mark. Grace didn't seem to expect any special treatment. Nevertheless, Mark chose not to blast Jean off the court, relying instead, on the occasional slice serve.

It was an enjoyable game, which Ted and Jean won comfortably 6-2.

While they waited for the other games to finish, the directors' secretary came to talk to them. She had only been with the company for six weeks and Mark didn't know her that well. She was about thirty years old, a little overweight and not particularly good-looking. She had a nervous habit of flickering her eyelashes and making her eyeballs disappear in their sockets. She also seemed to be smoking all the time and removing bits of tobacco from her tongue with her fingers. She was single and didn't currently have a boyfriend. Not that this was of any interest to Mark, because as well as the huge age difference, he didn't find her the least bit attractive. She told Jean and Mark that she would have liked a game, but no one had asked her. They both suggested she could join them on a Friday night and they gave her directions. She said she'd be along the next evening after work.

By now George had finished his game and he came over to join the conversation. 'Hello Wanda,' he said. 'Is the catering all in hand?' It seems Wanda had been responsible for a lot of the organisation of the day's events, so she must have known there would be a tennis match. Mark wondered why she hadn't previously asked someone if she could play.

'Well, I hope we've got enough food to go round. There seems to be more people here than I was told about,' replied Wanda. 'I would have liked to have included some alcoholic drinks, but Mr Wilcox was adamant that he didn't want anyone getting "blotto." I wouldn't be surprised to see a few people sloping off to the nearest pub at lunchtime, especially all these salesmen. I might even join them, if I get the chance!'

At least she had a sense of humour, but Mark didn't take to her at all. He remembered the last time he had made an instant judgement on someone – and look how that turned out!

A few minutes later, all three games were finished, so they all swapped round. The plan was for everyone to play with as many different people as possible. Mark found himself partnering Dave Taylor against the two London salesmen, who hadn't been introduced. They weren't very good and Mark and Dave won so easily that they played a second set while the others were still playing their one set.

As the tennis was expected to last all day, everyone decided they should pace themselves and break at that point to have a drink, look at the cricket or 'mingle.' Mark would have preferred to carry on, but he was happy to have a drink and watch some cricket before lunch. He just wasn't happy to 'mingle' – unless it was with Karen.

He grabbed a glass of orange squash and went to see how the cricket was progressing. Sanford were batting and he could see Ron wearing his pads, waiting to go into bat. Karen was just a few yards away, talking to someone whom Mark didn't recognise. As he walked past her, he couldn't resist putting his hand on her hip and giving her a gentle squeeze. Her hips felt very firm. She turned with surprise and when she saw who it was, she smiled at him, but didn't say anything. Ron had seen this, but didn't respond in any way. On another occasion, Mark might have got a more negative reaction from Karen. They seemed to be friends, at the moment.

Mark tried to find someone to talk to, but the only people he recognised were busy talking to someone else and he had always felt it was rude to interrupt. He sat on the grass to watch the cricket and soak up some sun. It was a very warm day, despite the gentle breeze coming off the sea. He stayed there until the lunch break, when everyone trooped into the pavilion to fetch their lunch, which consisted of a small selection of sandwiches, sausage rolls and a few chicken drumsticks. Mark duly queued for his food and then took it outside onto the grass to enjoy it. He was very hungry. Still no one spoke to him. He kept looking round for someone he knew to join him, but there was no one.

When he had finished, he went inside to return his plate and get another drink. On his way out again, he saw Karen talking to Ron. She looked quite agitated and Mark heard her say 'No, Ron,' in a very firm voice. He wondered about being the hero and going over to say 'Is this man bothering you?' like they do in the films, but he didn't need to, because she walked away, leaving Ron lost for words.

Ron looked round to see several people staring at him, including Mark. He didn't look unduly worried by this and fetched himself a glass of squash. Mark followed Karen out of the pavilion and caught up with her as she headed towards the car park. 'Are you all right?' he asked her.

'Yes, I'm fine, thank you. I was just going to have a look at your new car. Where is it?'

'I'll show you. Are you sure you're all right?' He had to admit she did look all right, but he was curious to know what had just happened.

She replied 'I am a little bored. I don't seem to know many people. The only people who want to talk to me are the London people... and you, of course. How are you getting on? Are you winning your tennis?'

'I've won two games and lost one. It's not a proper match anymore. It's more like our Friday nights with a couple of extra people. It's hot work though. This is my little car.'

'Nice colour. My uncle had one of these, years ago. You know I've passed my test.'

'You kept that quiet. When did this happen?'

'Last week. I didn't tell anyone, in case I failed. I packed up Lou Redmond and went to a proper driving school. I'm glad I did. I don't think I would have ever passed with Lou.'

'I could give you a lift tomorrow night, then.' Mark's eyes lit up. Then he thought about the logistics of it all. 'Hang on, though. I'd still have to get the car to work and home again after dropping you off. Oh, dear. That was a nice thought for a minute. I'll be glad when I pass my test. Are you going to get a car now?'

'No, not yet. Shall we walk back, now? When do you start the tennis again?'

'Who knows? I heard the two Londoners saying they were going to find a pub. Everyone seems more interested in standing around talking, rather than playing. Are you coming to watch?'

'Yes, why not? There's Jean. Let's go and have a chat with her.' Mark had been looking for a way to bring up Karen's little dispute with Ron, but now he had lost the chance. He was desperately curious to know what it was about. It certainly sounded as though Karen was turning him down for something, but what? Was she ending their relationship? Or had it already been ended?

'What are you two up to?' asked Jean, knowing full well that it would be nothing.

'I went to have a look at Mark's car. Are you enjoying the tennis?'

'Yes. It's a pity that there's only one other lady. You could have played, Karen. That new girl, Wanda, wanted to play, so we could have had four ladies.'

They could see the cricketers taking up their positions again, so Mark suggested going to the tennis courts to see if there was any likelihood of another game. Some of the tennis players were returning, but there was no sign of the Londoners, so George organised two games of doubles and one of singles. Mark, being the youngest and fittest, volunteered for singles and he played against John Woodston. Despite being the weaker of the two players in doubles, Mark was far more mobile than John and he ran out the winner at 6-4.

Karen had watched some of the tennis, but there were no seats near the courts, so she moved off to watch the cricket again. Nobody else felt like playing singles, so Ted said he and Grace ought to be getting back to Birmingham. The rest decided on one more game of doubles each before calling it a day. After that, Mark didn't really want to hang around doing nothing, but fortunately, George said he would like to get back to the office to do a few jobs. His car was at Mark's house and he said that Mark didn't have to go back to work with him.

After getting changed and having another drink, Mark had a quick wander round to say 'goodbye' to Karen and Jean, but he couldn't find either of them. It occurred to Mark that he would never see Karen in that lovely dress again. He had been so pleased to have the opportunity to drive his car, but now he wished that he hadn't. Then he might have got a lift home with Jean and Karen.

On the way home, Jean overtook him again, but this time she sounded her horn as she went past and Karen waved. He tried to keep up with them for a while, but when Jean overtook another car, Mark decided to concentrate on getting home in one piece and he let them disappear into the distance. He was just pleased that he had seen so much of Karen that day and without them both falling out. He was hoping she would be at the tennis the next evening. He asked George if he would be playing, but George didn't want to play two days in a row. Mark decided that he would take his bike to work the next day. It would be awkward carrying his racquet on his bike, but he wasn't going to miss the chance of a game of tennis with Karen.

As they drove along, George asked Mark if he had enjoyed the day. 'Oh, yes. It was much better than sitting in a sweaty office with Josie. It was nice to see a few new faces, as well. I thought Karen looked stunning in that dress.' He didn't know why he had said this – perhaps because she was uppermost in his mind.

'Karen? What, Karen from Costing?' George sounded very puzzled. Was Mark the only one to find anything attractive about her? He knew her looks were nothing special, but surely George could see she had a great figure? How could anyone not notice that, today?

'Yes, Karen from Costing.' George didn't comment and Mark decided not to pursue the subject. In a way, it made it all the more frustrating that he felt this way about her when everyone else dismissed her attraction so easily. He had been resigning himself to the fact that she would soon disappear from his life and he would never win her over, but she had looked so gorgeous that day, that he still longed to find a way. And she had been nice to him recently.

When they got near to Mark's house, George said he would be happy to take Mark for another ride soon. Mark thanked him and tried to firm up a time, but George said it would be a week or so and he'd let him know. Nevertheless, Mark said he was very grateful not only for the ride, but also for swinging it with Josie. George said 'That woman's got a rude awakening coming to her.' Mark wondered what he meant by this.

Mr Pettit came out of his garden to speak to Mark. 'Hello Mark. Are you going to leave that car there for long?'

'Probably all weekend. Why?'

'I won't be able to get out of my drive.'

Mark looked at Mr. Pettit's car and his drive. He had loads of room to get out.

'Do you want me to drive it out for you? I haven't passed my test, yet, but my granny could drive that out.'

'Now then, Mark. There's no need for that attitude. I asked nicely.'

'If I obstruct your driveway, you can complain. But I don't consider this to be blocking your driveway. I'm on my side of the road, outside my house and that's where I'm staying. And if you hit my car, you can pay for the damage.'

This was the first of many little spats with Mr. Pettit. Mark was always rude to him and Mr. Pettit was always polite. Sometimes, Mrs. Pettit would get involved as well. She wasn't always so polite, which suited Mark. To him, it was payback time for all those occasions when she had made a fuss about his football going into her garden.

Mark had enjoyed the day, particularly his time with Karen. The problem was that whenever he enjoyed her company, he paid for it afterwards. He now felt all those old feelings of despair and loneliness all over again. He yearned to be with her; to talk to her; to see her; to feel her – especially to feel her. And to make matters worse (as if they could be any worse), he had lost his so-called friend, so he couldn't even go out to take his mind off her.

The next day at work, Mark 'phoned Gary to see if he was playing tennis or not. He wasn't, so there didn't seem to be any point in asking Karen either. She couldn't play unless Gary or Jean gave her a lift. Late in the afternoon, he caught a glimpse of Karen walking down the corridor. She was wearing that dress! He wondered if his comments had influenced this in any way.

After work, he headed off to the tennis courts. There was no sign of anyone else. He waited for ten minutes. He was about to go home, when Wanda turned up. Fortunately, she had brought a few old tennis balls (Mark couldn't carry any on his bike), so they played singles for three-quarters of an hour. It was a very uneven game. She hadn't played for a few years and wasn't the least bit athletic. In fact, Mark considered her to be a very lazy player. If the ball wasn't within her reach, she couldn't be bothered to move. She missed more shots than she hit and never knew what the score was. Mark found it a very annoying game. He apologised to her for the absence of all the others. He said there was usually a much better attendance than that and the Sports day must have been the reason for their absence.

Much to his surprise, she asked him to go with her for a drink. He had a slight thirst and she insisted on paying for the drink, so he obliged. She did most of the talking. How ironic that everytime he found himself alone with a woman like Wanda or Rachel, it was someone who had no appeal whatsoever. Was it his imagination or was she coming on to him. Surely a woman of her age couldn't be interested in a person of his age? He dismissed the idea as being too absurd.

Out of politeness, he asked her if she wanted another drink. 'Oh, go on, then,' she replied. 'I'll have a gin and tonic.' That seemed like a strange drink to have when you've been running around and getting thirsty. But then he remembered that she hadn't actually run around at all. He didn't have one himself. He hadn't built up that much of a thirst, either.

She seemed to take forever to finish her drink. He wanted to get home, but he couldn't get up and leave her drinking on her own. She lit another cigarette and removed some bits of tobacco from her tongue. Smoking seemed to make her eyes disappear into her sockets for even longer. She only did this thing with her eyes when she was doing the talking, but then she always seemed to be talking. It wasn't a conversation. She was just talking. She didn't necessarily involve Mark in the discussion.

But then she asked 'How often do you play tennis?'

'We play every Friday... when it's not raining.'

'What do you do if it is raining?'

'Nothing. There's nothing worse than getting your balls soggy.'

'So I've heard,' she laughed, snorting as she did so and putting her hand on his knee. What a horrible laugh! Mark wanted to leave, but she was just playing with her drink. He decided he'd had enough.

'I need to get going, I'm afraid.'

'Oh, I'm sorry,' she said, gulping down her gin and tonic. 'I forget that some people have homes to go to.'

'Don't you have a home to go to?'

'Yes, of course. It's just an expression. So we'll do it again, next week, then?'

'Yes. I hope there'll be some other people here.' This had a double meaning and he meant both of them!

As they walked back to her car and his bike, he had a horrible feeling that she was going to ask to see him again. It didn't happen. It was probably just his imagination.

As he rode home, he decided she was just being friendly. Perhaps she was lonely and just wanted to be friends. That remark about having a home to go to – did that mean she didn't like going home? It can be lonely living on your own like she did. It could also be lonely living with your parents and your brother.

When Mark's mother returned home from bingo that night, she told him that his sister wanted to go to see Aunt Louise on Saturday afternoon, so if he was free, Mark could drive them over to Manningford. Of course Mark was free. He'd have to remember to get some petrol on the way over. His mother was coming as well. His father wasn't. Frank still hadn't shown any interest in Mark's car. Mark hadn't expected any.

It was raining on Saturday, so Mark drove very carefully. Barbara hadn't made any comments or suggestions about his driving, so when they were nearly there, he asked what she thought about his driving skills. 'I think you should put in for your test. You seem all right to me, except perhaps for being a little tense. You'll relax more once you've passed and get used to driving.' So he decided he would apply for his test.

Aunt Louise thought it was marvellous to see them all. 'Is that the boy Mark's car?' she said looking out of the window. 'I'll go and have a look if it stops raining. Fred's car is blue, as well. I'll just put the kettle on and then we'll have a natter.' The conversation followed the usual lines, except that Mark played an even smaller part in the proceedings than if he had visited on his own. They left loaded up with jam and vegetables from Uncle Fred's garden.

Mark was tempted to drive round to Karen's end of the village, but he wouldn't have wanted Karen to think he was stalking her, so they went straight home. It was still raining. Having driven twice in the last three days, Mark was gaining in confidence and Barbara's comments had helped.

However, the next few days, his car was left in the road, going nowhere. He had to pass his test. He had to get mobile.

CHAPTER 15

Big Game Hunters and New Opportunities

Over the last few months, Greshams had continued to expand. Plans had been drawn up to build an extension to both the Office block and the Factory. The Despatch Bay was to be enlarged; two new lorries were on order and there was to be a new Panel Making Shop, so that Greshams could manufacture their own panels. This involved a major investment in new machinery and skilled staff to operate it. To finance the expansion, Mr Gresham and Mr Wilcox, both joint owners, had sold 48% of the company's holdings to their aluminium suppliers – a company called Alcom.

Almost every department had taken on additional staff. Even before Karen's announced departure, the Costing Department had taken on another clerk. His name was Paul Sturridge. He was in his early fifties and had never risen to any great heights in his career. But he had accumulated a lot of experience in similar roles. He had lived in several different countries, including Rhodesia, South Africa and more recently, Peru. He was married and had no children. He was a very unimpressive five foot three inches tall, wore glasses and crept around the building as though he was stalking big game, which he claimed he used to do. In fact, he claimed to have done almost everything. Jean and Karen considered him to be the most boring and ineffectual person they had ever encountered. They both took great pleasure at ridiculing him at every opportunity.

He also had some weird little habits. One day, Jean looked up from her desk to find him staring at her. 'What's the matter?' she asked. There was no reply. He just carried on staring. She wondered if she had done something or said something to upset him, but still he carried on staring, as though he was in some kind of trance.

Karen intervened. 'Paul? Jean's talking to you. Are you all right?' He still didn't respond. His eyes weren't even blinking. Karen walked over to him and snapped her fingers beside his ear.

He looked at her with a puzzled look on his face. 'Is there something wrong?' he asked.

'That's what we want to know,' said Karen. 'You've been sat there staring at Jean for ages as though you're in some kind of trance.'

'Oh, was I? It's this little form of meditation I do. It helps me concentrate when I have a problem to resolve. Don't take any notice of me. I learnt the technique from a fakir in India.'

They didn't believe him. He was weird!

'A bit of a daft fakir, if you ask me,' Jean said quietly while returning to her work.

'He wasn't daft!' exclaimed an indignant Paul.

'Not him. You!' she said.

On another occasion, Mark had to visit the Costing Department to look at the previous week's timesheets for a query. The timesheets were on Paul's desk. Karen asked Mark to tell them a joke. Mark thought for a few seconds and then started his joke –

'A lion tamer in a circus was called before the circus boss to tell him he was being sacked.

"Why" asked the lion tamer. "Is there something wrong with my act?"

"Yes," replied the boss. "Your act is stale. Audiences have been spoiled with television and these days, they want something a little different. I'm taking on an exotic female lion-tamer. She's rehearsing at the moment. Come and have a look."

In the ring, the new lion-tamer was going through her act. She was beautiful and was dressed in a very skimpy outfit that revealed all her feminine charms. She lay down on the floor and called to the largest of the male lions.

The lion jumped down from his stool and majestically strolled over to her. He proceeded to gently lick the woman along her thighs, then up to her midriff and then licked the top of her breasts. All the circus staff were watching with open mouths.

"There," said the boss. "Can you do that?"

"You bet. Just get those damned lions out of there!"

Karen, Bob and Jean laughed. Paul didn't. He just said 'That's an old one.'

Karen said 'When you're as old as you are, you're bound to have heard them all before.'

Paul replied 'You're a very rude young lady. When I was your age, I was taught to respect my betters.'

She replied 'There's just one problem. You're hardly my better. In fact, you're probably nobody's better.'

Paul was furious. 'I think it's time someone taught you some manners, my girl.' If that was a threat, he had chosen the wrong person to threaten.

Karen stood up slowly and walked over, looking menacingly at him. 'Come on, then. Teach me some manners!' She was like a cat that raises its fur to make itself look larger to its enemy. She must have had two stones advantage over Paul and her intimidating presence was worth another two. Paul was having second thoughts about his ill-advised comments. He would have been safer stalking big game.

Bob said 'Come on, Karen. Let's get on with some work now, shall we?'

Karen and Paul looked at each other for a minute or so. Then she turned round and went back to her desk.

Paul suddenly recovered some of his courage and said to Bob 'Is she allowed to behave like that?' Then thinking that Bob would stop things getting too physical, he added 'If I had a daughter who behaved like that, I'd put her over my knee!'

Jean said 'If you carry on, Paul, you might find Karen putting you over her knee.'

Paul was trying to thinking of something else to add, when Mark intervened. 'I should leave it, if I were you, Paul. She'd have you for breakfast. In any case, if you laid a hand on her, I'd knock your block off!'

'Thank you, Mark,' said Karen. 'But I can handle him, any day!'

'I'm very pleased that you're leaving,' added Paul. Mark thought it was just as well for Paul that she was, because if he carried on like that, it would be just a matter of time before he ended up in the waste bin like Gail – only this time, Jean probably wouldn't bother to help him out of it!

Mark would miss little incidents like these when Karen left, which was only two more weeks away. She never did play tennis again. The next Friday, Gary and Jean had a special date and couldn't give Karen a lift. The week after that, it was raining. It didn't look like Mark would ever again go out with her in one of their little 'foursomes.' No more wrestles on the beach and no more games of tennis.

Karen's last day was Monday 31st August. As that day rapidly approached, Mark considered any 'last throws of the dice.' He had *almost* resigned himself to losing her forever, but it wasn't in his nature to totally give up trying. She had made it plain to him that she considered him to be too young for him. After her affair with an older man, he could see nothing but a mountain to climb. But he wouldn't always be a teenager. At what age could he expect to be 'old enough?' Next year? When he was twenty-one? Twenty-five, even? Maybe if he could have a heart-to-heart talk with her, he might be able to leave the door open.

Every time he tried to visit her during her last few days, there was someone else in the office. Now that there were four people working in the Costing Department, that was always going to be the case.

He decided to write her a little letter that he wouldn't pass on until the last minute. Then if he didn't get to have his little talk with her, he would hand it to her just before she left.

On the last Tuesday before she left, he returned home from football training (which had recently re-commenced ready for the new season) and sat down to draft out his letter.

My dearest Karen.

Before you leave my life forever, I felt compelled to write down some of my last thoughts. If you receive this letter, it is because I have been unable to find the opportunity to share these thoughts with you, face to face. Since you entered my life, I have been unable to look at another girl. You are everything I desire in a woman, but my aspirations have been cruelly thwarted.

My attempts to win you over have met with no success, but I like to think that we have maintained a friendship of sorts and had you stayed at Greshams, I would have treasured that friendship. You have made it clear to me that my age has been something of a barrier, but I won't always be seventeen and I cling to the hope that one day I will be old enough for you. I appreciate that that day may be some way off and we both have a lot of water to flow under our respective bridges. It is always possible that I may meet someone else who will occupy my thoughts in the way that you do at the moment (although she'll have to be someone very special!)

The reason for writing this note is to say to you, that if at any time you have a change of heart, please don't hesitate to call me.

He stopped writing at this point and read it back before proceeding. No, it was no good. That wasn't going to achieve anything. 'respective bridges?' – what did that mean? He tore it up into little pieces, ready to start again. His second attempt was no better. He decided to sleep on it. He didn't want to come across as some pathetic lovesick youth – even if that was exactly what he was! His message had to be mature and have a positive effect. Otherwise it would do more harm than good.

Right up to the weekend and indeed, all through the weekend, he continued his quest for some meaningful words, without success. He had no difficulty expressing his affection for her; no difficulty in expressing his desire for her, but he wasn't sure in his own mind what it was that he was trying to achieve with the letter and that's where all his attempts fell down. In any case, she was leaving and there was nothing he could do to stop her. And yet he couldn't just sit back and do nothing.

All too soon, Karen's last day arrived. Mark was very subdued throughout the morning. Just before lunch, Karen came into his office to tell everyone she was going to the pub at lunchtime if anyone wanted to join her. Mark looked round to see that she was wearing that dress! Penny said 'That's a nice dress, Karen. Is it new?'

'Thank you. I've had it a few months.'

Penny could see that Mark liked it. 'Put your eyes back in, Mark. It's just a dress.'

Mark had kept his feelings for Karen a secret from Penny and Josie, but now he couldn't resist saying 'No, it's a lovely dress and it looks perfect on Karen.'

Karen grinned. She already knew his opinion of her dress and was in one of her more friendly moods. She walked over to him and plonked herself on his lap. 'Are you coming down the pub, Mark?'

He thought that he had moved beyond all these silly moments of embarrassment, but he had only dreamed of this happening again. He was still surprised how heavy she felt on his lap and how delightful were her lovely firm buttocks as she fidgeted about to get more comfortable. He put one arm round her waist and the other round her shoulders, pulling her into him. She nestled her head into his neck and he stroked her shapely arm and shoulder.

'Can't we just sit here all lunchtime?' he replied. 'Then you can tell me how much you're going to miss me.'

'No, Mark,' she replied lifting her head up to look at him. 'I've just invited a few people down the pub and I've still got to go and see a few more people before lunch. Are you coming?'

'Not yet. Just a few more min…'

'Mark!' interrupted Josie. 'Don't say it!'

'Say what?' He said, looking as innocent as he could while failing to suppress a big grin.

'I know what you were going to say. And you stop encouraging him, young lady. We've got to work with him this afternoon!'

'Whose car are we going in?' Mark asked Karen.

'Jean's taking hers and Bob's taking his, so there's plenty of room,' replied Karen

'Have you invited your mate Paul?' he asked.

'Oh. Do you know? I forgot to ask him.'

'In that case, I'll join you.' He tried to think of something else to say so that he could continue to enjoy this wonderful sensation. As he continued to stroke her lovely arms, he remembered one of the lines from 'Alfie' and trying to mimic Michael Caine, he said 'Do you know, you're in lovely condition?' Then asked 'What time are we leaving?'

'We're all going at half-past twelve. I'll have to get on,' and she removed his hand from her waist and stood up. He tried to make the most of those last few seconds of contact, but she was up and out of the door. He looked round to see Penny and Josie both staring at him.

'What?' he asked. They didn't answer, but looked at each other with a grin.

Both Josie and Penny went into town at twelve o'clock, leaving Mark on his own. For the next twenty-five minutes, he kept looking at his watch, willing time to pass quickly, but just as he was thinking about wandering down the corridor to Karen's office, Nobby came in with a query relating to a payment to one of his fitters. By the time Mark had finished dealing with the query and Nobby had taken time to remind Mark about the friendly football match on Sunday, it was 12.37. He rushed down the corridor, only to find everyone had gone. He went outside in case they were waiting for him, but there was no sign of Bob's car, nor Jean's. He considered his bike, but he realised he didn't know which pub they were going to.

He went back to ask Paul Sturridge if he knew where they were going, but Paul said he didn't know anything about it. Mark was very angry to have missed out on a lunchtime drink with Karen when she was in one of her more friendly moods.

He had been asking himself if it was possible that she had worn that dress for his benefit. And could she actually be mellowing? She didn't seem quite so dispassionate, lately.

Mark slumped into his chair and tried to eat his packed lunch. His appetite had deserted him again. He pushed his half-eaten lunch to one side. He picked up a piece of paper and a pen to have one final attempt at writing his letter. After fifteen minutes, he finally abandoned his attempt. He decided that he might manage to finish his lunch if he had a cup of coffee to wash it down, so he headed off to the coffee machine, passing Ellie in Reception on the way. She was looking as lovely as ever and gave him a lovely smile as he approached.

'Hello, Mark,' she said. 'Didn't they invite you to the pub?'

'Yes, but I got tied up with work and missed my lift. You don't know where they went do you?'

'I think they were going to the Feathers at Broadby.'

'That's a bit too far for me to bike. Never mind,' he sighed. In fact, he did mind very much. He had hoped they might have waited for him or even come to find him.

'I've got some news for you,' continued Ellie. 'Pauline has broken up with her boyfriend.'

'Really? Weren't they supposed to have been married by now?'

'Yes. She called off the wedding. They still went out for a while. But now it's all off.'

'Is she upset about it?' he asked.

'It's hard to tell with Pauline. But I thought I'd tell you, because I know you like her.'

'I doubt whether I would stand much chance,' he said, feeling sorry for himself as usual.

'I don't see why. You've got nothing to lose by asking her out. She can only say "no," can't she? She's better looking than Karen.' Ellie gave him a 'knowing' look. She knew about Mark's infatuation. She knew everything about everyone. She wasn't a gossipmonger. It was just that she heard everything, working in Reception.

There was no denying that Pauline was much better looking than Karen, but on that day, at that time, his thoughts couldn't get beyond Karen. In any case, the chances of Pauline wanting him were very slim. She could have any chap she wanted.

Late in the afternoon, Mark saw Karen in the corridor. 'Where did you get to, lunchtime?' she asked.

'I got bogged down with a payroll query. I thought someone might have waited for me.'

'Jean thought you were going with Bob and Bob thought you were going with Jean. We didn't realise until we got to the pub. It was too late by then.'

'Did you have a good time?' asked Mark, hoping they hadn't.

'Yes, it was all right, but it didn't really get warmed up until it was time to leave. I'm sorry you weren't there. I wanted to say 'goodbye' properly. I will miss you.'

'Really?'

'Of course.'

'Can I just ask that if you ever do change your mind about going out with me, you will just give me a call?'

'Yes, Mark. I will.'

'Do you want to change your mind, now?'

'No, Mark.' She looked genuinely sorry about her reply. She was mellowing.

'Well, if you ever need a friend for anything, you know where I am.' Mark's voice was going. He was starting to feel very emotional. She gave him a little kiss on the cheek. He put his arms around her and gave her a hug. She didn't hug him back, but that didn't stop him. He felt her strong back; then moved his hands further down to her firm hips. He considered moving down still further. This was his last chance to touch that most wonderful pair of firm buttocks. What did he have to lose? But he still lacked the confidence to try his luck. He let her go and said 'Goodbye and good luck.'

She said 'Goodbye, Mark' and he went back to his office, knowing that he might never see her again. He had expected this to be a traumatic day and it was. At least they'd left on good terms. Moreover she had sat on his lap one more time, so he could have a fantasy about it all that night. After all, he wasn't expecting to get any sleep.

In fact, he slept surprisingly well and during the next few days, he coped better than he thought he might, although he didn't relish having to visit the Costing Department to see her empty desk and chair. When he did go to see them, Bob announced that he, too, was leaving. His wife had been feeling very homesick, so when Bob received a very interesting offer of work in the London area, he had no hesitation in accepting. Mark later learnt that Bob and George had been interviewing for Karen's replacement, but no decision would be made until Bob's successor was found. Mark was disappointed about this, because he also heard that there were a couple of very pleasant young ladies amongst those being interviewed. Ellie had suddenly become a valuable source of information.

Now that Karen had left for good, Mark had been watching out for new arrivals at Greshams. Most of the females were married. If not, they were either much too old or they already had boyfriends. Mark had recognised the new Trainee Surveyor. He was Dougie Davis, whom Mark knew from his days at the Grammar School. Dougie was a year older than Mark and they hadn't had much to do with each other at school. Dougie had been something of a gang leader – a gang that was always getting into scrapes, although he managed to avoid getting into trouble himself. The one thing that Mark remembered about Dougie was his footballing ability. Not only had he always represented his school, he had also been selected to represent a Sanford Schools Area team. He was quick and was a natural goal scorer. Mark pointed this out to Nobby, even though this might mean an additional barrier to his own chances of a regular place in the team.

Dougie turned up for the first friendly and was selected to play the full ninety minutes. It was no surprise to Mark to find him selected to play in the first league match the following Sunday. Mark was asked to turn up as the reserve. The first match was an away fixture. As Dougie lived just a few streets away from him, Mark asked for a lift. For most of the previous away matches, Mark had relied on Nobby to come out of his way to pick him up. Nobby had an enormous Vauxhall Cresta, complete with American style fins and chrome. The Cresta would easily accommodate six people – three in the back and three on the front bench seat. On one occasion, Mark had banged his knee on the corner of the wrap-round windscreen. The edge of the windscreen formed a sharp corner that necessitated a cut-out in the front passenger door. Mark had been in such pain, that he couldn't play when they arrived at the venue.

Dougie had a mini which he drove like a rally driver. It only had a small engine, but that didn't stop Dougie from taking on everyone who blocked his way. Mark was glad he didn't have a mini. On the early models you had to keep double-declutching. Mark had enough trouble changing gear as it was.

Dougie remembered Mark from school as a goalkeeper and after the match, which they lost 3-1, he commented that he thought Mark would have been better than Tel in goal.

Mark hadn't played this time. He told Dougie that if he couldn't get a regular game, he would try to find another team, which prompted Dougie to ask if he would like to play for Dougie's Saturday team – Northfleet United. They had lost their regular goalkeeper at the end of the last season and had been struggling to find a replacement.

Mark said he was definitely interested. Dougie said he would speak to their manager and let him know the outcome.

Considering that Mark hadn't played that morning, he had enjoyed himself. Dougie was different from the person he remembered from school – or perhaps he had never really got to know him properly. The two of them didn't have deep and meaningful conversations, but they got on really well and enjoyed recalling some of the characters from their school days, particularly the teachers.

Mark learned that Dougie had a regular girlfriend. They were 'sort of engaged' and had been going out together for years, but that didn't stop Dougie from eyeing up every female they passed. What's more, they mostly looked back at him. He was extremely good-looking with bright blue eyes and a slim athletic build. He was certainly not lacking in self-confidence. He swaggered as he walked and always looked smartly dressed, without seeming to make any effort at all.

Later in the week, Dougie came to tell Mark that he could play for Northfleet Reserves that Saturday, if he wanted. He just had to sign a registration form and Dougie would get it to the team manager by Saturday. Dougie said if he played well, he could be in the first team the following week. That all seemed too easy for Mark. Northfleet were a First Division side and their reserves were in the Second Division. Both teams regularly won their respective league titles.

Saturday came round and Mark cycled round to North Sanford where Northfleet played their home matches. He didn't know anyone, so he stopped one of the players outside the changing room to ask him to point out the team manager. The manager had not been told that Mark would be playing. In fact, they had a goalkeeper already getting changed! It suddenly dawned on Mark that he was talking to the opposition's manager. He was so used to playing in a tangerine strip, for Greshams, that when he saw someone with the same coloured shirt, he had jumped to conclusions. Northfleet Reserves played in yellow, with green shorts and socks, just like Norwich City. The Reserves' manager handed him his goalkeeper's strip, which included a green jersey. Goalkeepers nearly always played in green in 1966.

Nobody spoke to Mark in the changing room. He felt very

apprehensive. There was no 'team talk' and no introductions, so Mark knew nobody's name except for the captain, who was Les. It was a very one-sided game. Mark had no shots to save at all, three back-passes, which he dealt with quite adequately and one corner, which he came out to catch, comfortably. 'Give us a shout, Mark!' ordered Les, but Mark replied that he didn't know any names. 'Just say "Keeper's," then!'

And that was his first game for Northfleet. They had won 9-0, with three of their regulars having been loaned to the first team. Mark hadn't put a foot wrong, but he hadn't done anything to impress anyone, either. Nevertheless, Dougie came to see Mark later in the week to tell him that he was playing for the first team next Saturday. The first team had won their fixture 7-2 and Dougie said their goalkeeper was at fault for both goals. Mark found it ironic that he could get straight into a First Division team without really having to prove himself and yet he couldn't get a regular game for a Fourth Division Sunday League team. But he wasn't complaining. Dougie obviously had a lot of influence. Mark just hoped he didn't let him down.

Saturday's game was against a team from Norwich. It was in the Norfolk Junior Cup – a competition open to all teams from leagues in Norfolk, including King's Lynn, Thetford, Great Yarmouth, Norwich and of course, Sanford.

It had long been a dream of the Northfleet players to win this prestigious competition, but they knew it wouldn't be easy. No team from the Sanford league had ever won it. Northfleet had got to the semi-finals back in the forties, but that was the best anyone had ever achieved. The club had hired a coach to transport the team and their many supporters to Norwich. Dougie picked Mark up from his house and drove them to the Ship Inn, where the coach was waiting. Mark still didn't know anyone other than Dougie, but the two of them sat in the back seat and it wasn't long before a game of three-card brag was in progress. Mark didn't know the game, so he watched. He soon got to know the people in the card school. As well as Dougie, there was Teddy Walker, Lennie Ward (who turned out to be the brother of Les from the Reserves) and Mick Baker. Mark was glad he didn't know the game. There was quite a lot of money changing hands. Dougie came out on top, mostly at the expense of Mick. By the time they got to Norwich, they were all totally relaxed (except Mick!) and ready to turn their attention to football.

The standard of football was much higher than Mark was used to. He didn't think any of the Gresham players, except Dougie, would get into the Northfleet team – probably not even the Reserves! The team won 3-1. Mark had made a few saves and could not be blamed for the goal he did concede. This was all helped by a very solid defence. Everyone was saying 'This was the year.' It was very pleasing to be able to play for a team with such confidence and such good team spirit.

The opposition very kindly provided a light tea and suggested a local hostelry, but many of the Northfleet players already had plans, so they all agreed to go straight home and those who desperately wanted a drink could do so at the Ship. The journey back was much noisier than the outward trip, with some very interesting lyrics being sung to some old familiar songs.

Back at the Ship, Dougie and Mark decided to have a quick drink. Jean was there and was surprised to see Mark. It had been several weeks since Gary had 'dumped' him. She told Mark that she had seen Karen, who now had a new boyfriend. Jean seemed to think it was quite serious. Ron Hall was definitely consigned to the past.

As Dougie drove Mark home, he asked Mark what he was doing for the rest of the evening. Mark replied that he had no plans to do anything. Dougie suggested that Mark could join him and his girlfriend for a night in town. 'Won't I be in the way if you're with your girlfriend?'

'No. She'll be glad to see a new face. When you've been going out as long as we have, we need some new company occasionally.'

So it was agreed that Dougie would call on Mark at 9.00, after they'd washed and changed. When they both arrived at Dougie's girlfriend's house, Mark wasn't at all sure she was happy to see Mark there. In fact, she didn't seem too happy to see either of them. Her and Dougie spent the evening snapping at each other, which made Mark feel very uncomfortable. She was a very slightly built lady with a permanent scowl on her face and answered to the names of Anita or 'Old Ratbag'. Mark called her Anita. He had expected someone like Dougie, who obviously had a way with women, to have a much more attractive girlfriend.

As the night wore on and he found Anita laughing at some of his jokes, Mark realised that she wasn't angry with him, she was angry with Dougie (or 'Scumbag' as she called him). Dougie seemed used to this treatment.

They visited three different establishments in town. At each of them, they ran into people Dougie knew. Sometimes these people were in a group of men, talking about football. Sometimes, there were couples (also talking about football). Sometimes, they were Northfleet players. Dougie would often introduce Mark as Northfleet's new 'keeper, as though he was some wonderful new signing. Everywhere they went, Mark was aware of women looking at them. The more they looked, the angrier Anita became.

At the Boar's Head, a fight broke out. This was the first time Mark had seen a fist fight in a pub and it looked like turning quite nasty, but Dougie carried on talking as though it was normal behaviour. Towards the end of the evening, Anita disappeared to talk to a few of her friends (who weren't introduced to Mark). When the pub closed, and they all headed towards Dougie's car, one of these friends had joined them. She sat in the back of the car with Anita. Mark gathered that her name was Marlene. She looked like a Marlene. She had a very coarse manner. She swore a lot, she smoked a lot and she treated Dougie the same way that Anita did. Mark was hoping that this wasn't some sort of ploy to pair him up with Marlene, because he would rather remain celibate for the rest of his life than go out with her.

They all went round Anita's house where her mother and father sat in front of the television. Here the atmosphere worsened. Dougie treated Anita's mother like a servant, calling her by her first name (Aggie) and issued orders for cups of coffee for him and his mate. 'Don't you come round here, ordering me around, you little shite, you!'

'I'll make it myself, then. Do you want a coffee, Mark?'

'Well if that's all right with Aggie,' Mark replied. He was starting to feel really uncomfortable and wouldn't mind leaving. At least Anita's father wasn't joining in with the nastiness. He just sat there trying to listen to the television.

Dougie turned on Marlene. 'You're the one who started all this with your big mouth!'

'She's my friend and I'm not going to stand by and let you fucking walk all over her.'

'We can sort our own problems out. So you keep out of it,' came back Dougie.

At that juncture, Anita burst into tears and starting slapping Dougie about the head. 'I'm gonna cut your balls off!' she screamed, as he put his hands up to protect himself. Mark had never seen anyone rain in so many blows before. No one raised a finger to stop her. Eventually, Dougie managed to push her away and she collapsed in a heap on the floor, still in tears.

Dougie turned on Marlene again 'I've half a mind to smash your face in, you nasty old cow.'

'Don't you call me a fucking cow, you fucking twat. And don't threaten me or I'll get my brother on to you again.'

'I don't care about your brother. And I don't want you interfering with me and my girlfriend.'

'I'm not your girlfriend!' screamed Anita. 'You can sod off out of my house. And don't come back! And take your friend with you.'

'Right! That's it! Come on, Mark'

'So, no coffee, then!' thought Mark, though he was extremely pleased to be leaving. They left to the accompaniment of some more choice swearwords from all three women. Anita's father still didn't have anything to say.

Back in the car, Dougie asked if Mark needed a lift the next day.

'No, it's a home match. I'll bike down. Then if I'm not playing, I can go straight home.'

Mark had just witnessed the outbreak of World War III and here was Dougie, acting as though nothing had happened. It was just a normal Saturday night out for him. Mark thought his own household had their share of 'ups and downs,' but this was on a different scale altogether. He suspected that Marlene had seen Dougie with another girl and reported the news to Anita, but he didn't like jumping to conclusions.

'It was a good result today, Markie boy.'

'Yeah. Do you think I'll get in the team next week?'

'Course you will. You played all right, didn't you?'

'I don't know. It's not for me to judge.'

'Nah! You'll be all right. We can win some silver, this year. It's been a fucking good day. And I'm a free agent now. Do you want to go out tomorrow night?'

'Yeah, why not? Where are we going?'

'Well I don't want to go anywhere where I might bump into Anita. How about the Ship? It's usually a bit quieter on a Sunday. We can play darts… or crib. Do you play crib?'

'No, I've never played.'

'I'll show you. Jean'll probably be there. She's looking nice, these days.'

'Oh no!' thought Mark. 'Not another one chasing after Jean.' He had to admit she was looking a little more attractive since she'd been going out with Gary. She'd put on a little weight and got some new clothes. And Mark couldn't remember seeing her with a cigarette lately.

'You know Gary's going out with her, don't you?'

'Yeah. She could cope with both of us. He's looking really knackered these days. I have this image of her lying back and polishing her nails, while he's trying to do the business.' Mark had to admit that he'd never had that image before, but Gary was looking a little worn. Mark had put it down to hard work.

Sunday turned out to be an equally eventful day. Mark had been asked to be the reserve player, yet again, so he turned up ten minutes before the kick-off. Nobby was very pleased to see him. 'Have you got your kit, Sid?' he asked.

'Of course.'

'Right! Get changed. You're in goal. Tel hasn't turned up.'

Mark didn't need telling twice. He had no time for a warm-up. The referee held up play long enough for him to run onto the pitch and then blew his whistle for the kick-off. After a shaky start while Mark got his eye in, he ended up having an excellent game. They lost 3-1, but it was still a good team performance against their old enemy, The White Hart. Nobby thanked him for helping them out. Mark didn't say anything. He felt he should be in the team on merit, as well as the fact that he was far more reliable than Tel.

In the afternoon, Mark's brother-in-law went for a ride with him in his little blue car. It was much more of a driving lesson than when Barbara or George had accompanied him and William was happy to make some constructive comments to help him. And they tried some reversing manoeuvres and emergency stops. William suggested using the brakes to slow down the car rather than the gears. 'But that's what my instructor taught me.'

'Well, he was wrong. Brakes are cheaper to replace than gearboxes and clutches! The other thing is that this car has a very poor turning circle. This is not going to help you on your test. Your three-point turns are always going to be five-point turns.'

'Well I can't get another car at the moment,' said Mark.

William thought about this for a few minutes, then suggested 'You could get a couple of lessons with a proper driving school, a week or two before your test. And then use their car for the actual test. If he's a professional instructor, he'll be much better at preparing you for the test than Barbara or myself.'

'That's an excellent suggestion,' Mark replied. But he wouldn't use Lou Redmond again. Mark's mother had told him about a man who lived nearby, who ran a proper driving school. His car had dual controls and she had heard one or two very good recommendations about him. He charged a pound an hour, which was much more than Lou, but it was only going to be for a few lessons. Mark decided to go and see this chap as soon as they got home. His test was only three and a half weeks away and he would dearly love to pass at the first attempt.

That evening, Dougie drove them over to the Ship and he taught Mark how to play cribbage. Mick Baker came in after a while with his mate, who was introduced as Wally, so they both joined in just as soon as Dougie had explained how you play crib with four people instead of two. Mark picked the game up quite quickly. He enjoyed it because there was a certain element of skill involved, rather than just luck. And you had to do a little mental arithmetic to work out your score.

Mick was a very jovial chap who laughed at anything. He made Mark feel as though he was now one of a group of friends. Both Mick and Wally were married, but they were happy to ogle a pair of young ladies, who were enjoying a quiet drink on their own. When one of the ladies went up to the bar, Dougie joined her and offered to pay for her drinks. Mark couldn't help comparing his technique to that used by Gary and Mark – or to be precise their total lack of technique.

When Dougie returned to his seat, Mick asked 'How did you do?' as though this was a regular activity.

'They're both married. I don't do married women.' Mark was disappointed. He quite liked the look of one of them, but he was pleased that Dougie stared clear of married women. In any case, he didn't think it would be too long before Dougie struck gold. Mark thought he might pick up some useful tips from Dougie.

He was feeling very pleased with himself. He suddenly had a social life again and what's more, it looked like being far more interesting than when he was going out with Gary. Now if he could just pass his driving test and get a good raise next time. Even the news about Karen hadn't hit him as hard as he might have expected.

'I wonder if Pauline would go out with me,' he thought to himself in bed that night. He'd love to take her to the Christmas Dinner Dance. It would be a huge feather in his cap.

CHAPTER 16

I Don't Fancy Yours

During the next few weeks, Mark continued to expand his social life. Not only did he go out with Dougie several evenings a week, the pair of them often went down to their local during their lunch breaks, playing darts or playing on the pinball machine. Friday nights and Saturday nights were spent in King's Lynn (to avoid the possibility of bumping into Anita). Other nights, they could usually be found at their local – the Cock Inn. Dougie's favourite joke was that he liked the old 'Cock Inn.'

A frequent visitor to the Cock Inn was a young lady who Mark came to know as Mary. He found her to be very attractive, but he wasn't on speaking terms with her yet. She was dark-haired, of medium build and of great importance to Mark, had very shapely legs. More to the point, she didn't appear to have a boyfriend. She often came into the pub with her father, but sometimes on her own. Mark hoped that Dougie's influence with women might help him break the ice with her, but Dougie insisted that Mark should steer clear of her. 'She's a prick-teaser,' Dougie would say.

Mark thought to himself, 'So what? I just want to go out with her.' Dougie's criteria for a date were different to Mark's. Dougie was quite happy to go out on one-night stands. Mark wanted something longer lasting. He guessed that Mary might have been one of the few women to have rebuffed Dougie and that's why he called her a 'prick-teaser.' Mark decided that when the time was right, he might ask Mary for a date, but not when Dougie was around.

Such was Dougie's record with women, that it was just a matter of time before he was chatting up a couple of girls in the Maid's Head – the place to go in King's Lynn in the sixties. Dougie possessed a built-in radar system that alerted him to unaccompanied young girls. He had spotted one very attractive slim young lady across the dance-floor. She, in turn, had returned his gaze, so he was in there like a shot from a gun. She was with a friend, but unfortunately for Mark, her friend was the complete opposite in appearance. She was short and dumpy and very plain. Dougie persuaded the two girls to join him, Mark and Mick Baker, across the Tuesday Market Place at the much quieter Riverside Bar. There, they were able to sit and talk in relative comfort and peace. The Riverside Bar was decked out with fishing nets, lobster pots and other paraphernalia associated with the sea. The two girls – Dawn and Sylvia – lived in Swaffham. Dawn was the centre of attraction. Both Dougie and Mick expended a lot of energy chatting to her, to the exclusion of Mark and Sylvia. Mick was not interested in dating Dawn – he just enjoyed the thrill of the chase and watching Dougie go into action.

Mark felt sorry for Sylvia. She must have realised that she presented no attraction to Mick and Dougie, but she just sat there, quietly listening to the conversation. Nobody asked her what she did with her spare time; nor asked about her taste in music. Mark could have done this, but he didn't want to mislead her into thinking that he was interested in her. When Dougie invited Dawn to go out with him the next night, she insisted that she wouldn't go out with him on her own. She didn't know anything about him. After all, she'd only just met him in a bar. She asked if Sylvia could join them. Mark agreed to make up a foursome (Mick was excluded from the arrangement due to his marital status). Mark didn't tell anyone, but he only agreed out of friendship to Dougie. He doubted whether Dougie would do the same for him, but he wasn't too unhappy about sharing Dawn's company.

Mark didn't enjoy the next evening. He and Sylvia had to watch Dougie and Dawn making overtures to each other, while not advancing their own relationship at all. Dawn was not going to be a complete pushover for Dougie. If he was to have his wicked way with her, he was going to have to be patient. She insisted that Sylvia had to accompany them on their next date as well. This was to be the following weekend. Mark reluctantly agreed to another foursome, but he was determined that this would be the last time and told Dougie so, as they drove home alone. Dougie didn't always want Sylvia and Mark with them, anyway. Mark's only fear was that if Dougie and Dawn got too serious, he might find himself being 'dumped' again.

Dougie joked to Mark that he would love to wake up at the 'crack of Dawn.' Mark said he thought this was in very poor taste, whilst secretly wishing he had thought of it first.

★ ★ ★ ★ ★

Mark had organised his additional driving lessons, which had proved very useful He was ready for his test on the Tuesday of that week. He simply had to pass first time. The clocks had just gone back and he was having to depend on George and Alan for lifts again.

He scraped through his test. He went back to work and wanted to tell everyone, but as it was a Tuesday, he was stuck in the Wages Department for almost all of the remainder of the day, making up for the time he had lost.

Once the payroll was completed, Mark went to tell Dougie, only to find that Dougie wasn't at work that day. Mike told him that he had gone to Manchester with Greg to visit one of Gresham's customers to 'measure up,' whatever that meant. When Mark told Mike he had passed his test, Mike said 'That's really pissbodical, mate. Now the World's your lobster.'

Mark was going to say 'Don't you mean "oyster?"' but then he realised it was meant to be a joke.

After work, Mark was pleased to find both Jane and Pauline waiting in Reception and soon told them both of his good news. He also told them both that if they ever needed a lift, he would be happy to oblige. Pauline was surprisingly pleased about his news. It still occurred to Mark that she was a troubled soul. He would love to talk to her in more intimate surroundings to find out why she always looked so sad. A girl as lovely as she was should not have a care in the world.

Mark relished the pleasure of squeezing next to Jane in the back seat of Alan's mini for the last time. He still considered her to be a possibility for a date if she no longer had a boyfriend. Having his own transport suddenly made him feel a little bolder about asking her out, but this wasn't the right time. He might even chance his arm with Pauline. As Ellie had rightly said – 'You've got nothing to lose by asking.'

Mark told Alan the good news and thanked him for his help in getting mobile (although Alan never did make himself available to help with Mark's driving practice). Alan said he was pleased to have helped. Just then, he threw his car round a sharp left-hand bend and Mark found himself thrust against Jane's lovely soft hips and shoulders. She didn't seem to make any effort to avoid him. Yes, he'd definitely like to ask her out.

That evening, after tea, Mark got into his car and drove it on his own for the first time. He went round Dougie's house, but Dougie still wasn't home from Manchester. Mark asked Dougie's father to give Dougie the news about his driving test.

Dougie's father, Tim, was a motor mechanic by trade, so he asked to have a look at Mark's new car. After looking under the bonnet, he asked Mark where he got it serviced. 'I haven't had a service, yet. How often do I need to do it?' He replied.

'It will be in your handbook. It's probably every six thousand miles.' That sounded like a lot to Mark. He was sure he hadn't done anything like that amount of miles, so he wasn't too worried. He didn't remember seeing a handbook.

Mark was feeling a great sense of freedom, so he took his car for a drive round town, taking great care to look at every bus stop to see if there was anyone he recognised, which wasn't easy in the dark. He didn't see anyone.

He called in at The Cock Inn to see if Mary was there. She was, but so was her father. Nevertheless, Mark stood at the bar to drink his half-pint of beer, close to where Mary was sitting. It was the first time he had ever entered a bar on his own, although he was becoming a bit of a regular at the Cock Inn and the Landlord now knew him quite well. Mark thought if he stood there long enough, he might end up in conversation with Mary, but it didn't happen. He told the landlord he had passed his test that day and he had his new car outside, thinking this might impress Mary, but she showed no signs of even acknowledging his presence.

After a while, Mark finished his drink and left. He still didn't want to go home, so he headed for the road where he knew Jane lived. He wasn't sure exactly which house she lived in, but he drove past the nearest bus stop – and there she stood! He braked suddenly and opened the passenger door to ask her if she needed a lift. She was heading into town to meet a friend and said she would be very grateful for a lift. Jane asked what he was doing down her road and Mark said he was just enjoying the freedom of driving around on his own. 'Are you going into town?' she asked.

'No, but it's no trouble. I'll be glad of some company. My mate's not around, so I was just killing some time.' He hoped she didn't think he was driving down her road just on the offchance of seeing her – even though he was!

This felt great. He was alone in his car with a woman he fancied. 'Are you meeting Sammy?' he asked. Sammy was the name of the boyfriend she had been dating.

'No, I split up with Sammy a few months ago.' Mark's heart suddenly starting beating faster. She'd split up with Sammy and was going out that night to meet a friend! Would he have the courage to ask her out? He didn't want to dive straight in, as though his only motive for giving her a lift was to ask her out. He carried on talking to her about her plans for the night and she made some comments about his car.

As they got a bit nearer to town, he decided to go for it. With a trembling voice, he asked, 'Now that I've got a car, would you like to come out with me?' The bit about the car was meant to indicate a reason for not having asked her before.

'It's a pity you didn't ask me a couple of weeks ago. I've just started going out with someone else,' she replied sounding genuinely disappointed, but she was nowhere near as disappointed as Mark was. It seemed he had missed the boat by a few weeks and it sounded as though she might otherwise have said 'yes.' Of course, it was also possible that she was just pretending to be disappointed, but he preferred to think not.

'Never mind,' said Mark. 'Perhaps another time.'

'Yes. Thank you for asking me and thanks for the lift.' By now, they were at the Bus Station, where Jane was to meet her friend, who wasn't there, yet.

'It's cold outside,' said Mark. 'You can wait in the car until your friend turns up if you like'?

'No. I'll be fine, thank you. I've already taken you out of your way.' She got out before he could insist.

Yet another disappointment. Now, he really would have to ask Pauline. But when? He decided to go the long way home via North Sanford, where Pauline lived. He hadn't a clue where she lived, except that it was on the new estate, so he drove all the way round, passing all the bus stops, but with no luck.

This was to become a regular pattern for Mark over the next few months. Whenever he took his mother to Bingo, he would return via the bus station and North Sanford. When he was at a loose end in the evenings or weekends, he would take a little ride – all to no avail. He still had a social life of sorts. Dougie would see Dawn at the weekends, but during the week, he would also find time to go down the local with Mark or sometimes The Ship Inn. So Mark hadn't been 'dumped' by Dougie. But Mark still didn't have a girlfriend. Dougie's influence with women hadn't helped him. Nor had his little car. And the Christmas dinner was rapidly approaching. He didn't want to go without a partner two years in a row.

Mark decided to confide in Ellie and asked if she knew whether Pauline currently had a boyfriend. 'I don't think so, but you'll have to be quick if you want to go out with her. They're emigrating to Australia in the New Year.'

Now what was he to do? Was there any point in asking her out if she was going to live the other side of the world? Well yes, there was. He still had this ambition to show her off to everyone at the Christmas dinner and no one in his right mind would object to dating such a beautiful girl for a few months. But the only time he saw her was in reception, surrounded by other people, often including Jane. He had to speak to her alone.

Then his luck changed. He was driving past the bus station one Saturday morning and there she stood waiting for a bus. He stopped and asked her if she would like a lift and she said 'yes' but it was with a certain reluctance and she seemed even more subdued than ever. During their journey, he discovered that she was very unhappy about going to live abroad. Eighteen months earlier, she had been dragged up from London, leaving all her friends behind and just when she was starting to get used to living in Norfolk, her parents decided to move again. She couldn't contemplate staying behind on her own, but she certainly wasn't looking forward to living in Australia. Mark was full of sympathy for her and told her he would miss her. He asked if she had a boyfriend at the moment.

'No,' she said. 'There's doesn't seem to be any point. I would hate to get involved with someone and then have to leave him behind.'

'Are you going to Gresham's Christmas dinner?' he asked.

'No. We're not going this year.'

'Would you come with me?' Why did his voice always seem to tremble when he asked someone out?

'No, I'd rather not get involved with anyone.'

'It could just be a one-off date?'

'No. I really would rather not go. It's not my sort of thing. I didn't enjoy myself last year.'

Then she pointed out her house and Mark stopped the car, feeling thoroughly dejected. He couldn't think of anything else to say, except 'Goodbye. I hope it all works out for you. I'm sure you'll be all right once you settle down.'

'Good-bye. Thanks for the lift,' she said, with a huge sigh.

Mark couldn't help but feel sorry for himself. Would he ever get a girlfriend? As Penny often said, 'Everything in my favour is against me' and 'As one door shuts, another door closes.'

As he drove past the Cock Inn on his way home, he saw Dougie's car in the car park, so he decided to call in. There was no football match that afternoon. Dougie's father was also there and a friend of his made up a four for a game of darts. Dougie and Mark got thoroughly thrashed. So after the game they sat down to finish their drinks. Dougie asked Mark to join him and Anita for a night out in town.

'Anita?' queried Mark.

'Yes, I saw her last night. Someone told her I'd be at King's Lynn and we ran into each other. We're back together.'

'What happened to Dawn?'

'She got her father to come and pick her up.'

'That can't have been very nice for her.'

Dougie just shrugged his shoulders. He wasn't one for caring about women's feelings. 'So, are you going to join us?' asked Dougie.

Mark wasn't sure if he wanted to tag along and listen to Dougie and Anita bickering at each other, but he'd just had a huge disappointment with Pauline, so he didn't want to stay at home either. After all, he was never going to meet anyone sitting at home. So far, there hadn't been any nice young girls knocking on his door to ask him out.

'Yes, all right. As long as Marlene isn't there. Do you want me to drive for a change?'

'No, we'll get the bus. Then we don't have to worry about how much we drink. Meet me at the bus stop at 7.30. I'm meeting Anita at the bus station. She's getting into town with her cousin. I wouldn't be going if Marlene was there – bleeding old cow!'

And so it was all arranged. Mark had assumed that Dougie meant that Anita was getting a lift with a male cousin, but it turned out to be her female cousin, Mandy and Mandy certainly didn't have a car. As the evening developed, it was clear that Anita and Dougie were trying to match Mark with Mandy. Mandy was not unattractive, but she was barely sixteen years old. Although Mark was desperately in need of a girlfriend, he resented other people picking them out for him and Mandy certainly wouldn't have matched Mark's selection criteria. She was reasonably attractive, but apart from her lack of years, she seemed to lack everything else – a bust; a shape; intelligence; conversation; a sense of humour. She might develop these things in years to come, but at that moment, she was hardly a substitute for Pauline, Jane or Karen.

Mark tried to engage Mandy in some meaningful conversation, all to no avail and she didn't show any great enthusiasm herself. Dougie and Anita were not a great advertisement for close relationships. Despite their recent reconciliation, they were still bickering most of the time, but this seemed to be their normal behaviour, because they were also capable of having a laugh or two together.

In one bar, towards the end of the evening, Mark met his Aunt Kate, Uncle Wally, their daughter Carol and their two sons, both in their early twenties. As it was getting near to Christmas, they all exchanged season's greetings and Mark bought them all a drink. A few minutes later, he found all five of them placing a whiskey and orange on his table in front of him.

Uncle Wally had asked Dougie what Mark was drinking. Mark had just experimented with his first whiskey and orange. All five of them had insisted on buying him a drink in return, so now he had five more whiskeys to drink! And he wouldn't be allowed to leave until he had finished them. Closing time was approaching, so he couldn't even pace himself. In any case, Dougie, who had far more experience of these things than Mark, had always impressed upon Mark that you don't leave a pub until your glass is empty. It's not the done thing!

But it was no big deal. He knocked them back, a few minutes apart, until ten minutes after closing time, there was just the one left. He wasn't feeling too bad, despite the four drinks he'd had before the whiskey, so when Dougie said it was time to go, Mark finished the last one and said 'goodbye' to his relatives. He felt fine, until he got outside and the cold night air hit him. Suddenly his head started swimming round and his knees buckled from under him. He fell against a wall and slumped to the ground. The other three had seen him downing all these whiskeys and were not surprised at the outcome. They all stood around him laughing. After a few attempts to get up, he said 'I'll be all right. Just leave me, here.'

With a little help from Dougie, Mark staggered down the High Street in the direction of the bus station and when they took a short cut through Sykes Alley, he found himself bouncing off the buildings like a ball in a giant pinball machine. His head continued to swim around, but by concentrating very carefully, he found he could gradually manage an approximation of the process of walking, even though he had no feeling whatsoever in his legs. By the time they got off the bus, things were starting to make a little more sense. They were going into Anita's house. Mark's house was the other side of town and there was no way they would get a bus home at that time of night. Mandy was no longer with them. Mark wasn't sure when they parted company. He didn't remember saying goodbye to her. Dougie ordered Aggie to make Mark a strong black coffee. 'With a little drop of whiskey in it!' demanded Mark.

Mark started singing some of the songs he had learnt from his coach trip to Norwich, but the only words he could remember were the rude bits. Aggie was not impressed by his behaviour, but Anita's father continued to watch the television. After a few minutes of singing and after drinking his coffee, Mark started to feel sorry for himself, moaning that he 'needed a woman.' Apparently any woman would do. He said he could even fancy Aggie at that moment.

At that point, Aggie decided it was time for them to go. She wasn't going to be insulted like that in her own house. Mark wasn't sure what he'd done to upset her. He thought he'd just paid her a compliment, but he was ready to go, anyway. At least he'd had a coffee before he was thrown out this time.

Dougie and Mark had no alternative but to walk the five miles home. This wasn't as bad as it might seem, because Mark still didn't have a lot of feeling in his legs and Dougie was used to this little walk.

As they walked home, Dougie asked 'What did you think of Mandy?'

'She's seems a nice quiet girl, but she's too young for me.'

'I thought you wanted a girlfriend? You're too fussy. You could have had Sylvia. I know she wasn't much to look at, but she would have done for a little practice.' Dougie's attitude to women appalled Mark.

Then Dougie asked 'Have you ever had sex?'

'Not with another person!' was Mark's reply and they both staggered about the pavement, laughing.

Dougie told Mark he would pick him up for the football the next morning. Mark had forgotten about the football. He hadn't even been picked as reserve for the last two games, but due to various injuries, he was due to start this game. He didn't think he would be in a fit state to play football.

This wasn't helped by the fact that when he got to bed, he couldn't sleep. He collapsed on the bed and expected to drop off straight away as it was now nearly two o'clock in the morning, but his head was still swimming round. Was it his imagination or was the bed moving up and down? Every time he changed position, it took another ten minutes for everything to settle down again. Then just as he was entering that beautiful world of blissful sleep, his right calf seized with pain. All this walking had given him cramp. He tried to leap out of bed, but his head was still swimming and instead of standing up to put some weight on his foot, he fell over and in the dark, he lost all sense of direction. By now, he was screaming with agony and had woken up the whole household. His mother came racing into his bedroom, certain that someone was trying to murder her son. She was closely followed by his brother. The light suddenly went on and Mark managed to see enough to get to his feet.

At last, he was able to put some weight on his foot and the pain started to subside a little, but by now, his leg had been wracked with so much pain, he couldn't get rid of the last little bit of residual pain. Now the pain was making him feel queasy and he decided he had better visit the outside toilet. Quickly, he grabbed some extra clothes to protect him from the cold air outside, but as he pulled a thick sweater over his head, his arms got stuck and he lost his balance again, falling onto the bed in a heap.

'If you can't handle a little drink, perhaps you ought to leave it alone!' shouted his mother.

'It's your sister's fault. Her and her family kept plying me with whiskey!'

He found his way outside, but it was all a false alarm. Perhaps the cold air had helped.

It was another hour and a half before he finally went to sleep. He didn't think he was going to be in a fit state to run around a football pitch in the morning.

When they got to the venue, just a few hours later, Mark was surprised to find himself no worse for wear, except for being a little tired. Nobby greeted him with the news that there was still no sign of Tel and Mark might be playing in goal. Mark grabbed the goalkeeper's jersey. He didn't fancy doing a lot of running around, so he was very pleased when Tel still hadn't shown by the kick-off.

This was the quarter final of the Division Four Knockout cup – the one chance Greshams had that season of any sort of glory, since they were currently languishing in the bottom three of the league. Mark was determined to make the best of his opportunity and no one was going to score a goal past him that day. Greshams were favourites to lose this game against The Victory, a pub team, who were third in the league. Greshams were defending for most of the game, but the opposition failed to take advantage of their numerous chances to score, due to a combination of some poor finishing, as well as some excellent saves from Mark. It was still nil-nil with five minutes to go, when Dougie received a long ball out of defence and headed towards the opposition's goal, leaving two defenders in his wake. As the goalkeeper advanced out of his goal to narrow the angle, Dougie chipped the ball over his head. For a moment, it looked as though the heavy mud in the goalmouth would stop the ball, but it just trickled over the line before a defender could get to it.

The opposition threw every man into attack and Gresham pulled everyone back to defend. In the last minute, Mark dived to save a comparatively easy shot, only to see his right-back reach out a foot to deflect it. Somehow, Mark managed to twist in mid-air and clear the shot with his trailing leg. It was a wonderful save and as the referee blew his whistle for fulltime, Mark was surrounded by his team-mates. He was the hero, even putting Dougie's wonderful solo goal into the shade.

Nobby spoke to him in the changing room. 'From now on, Sid' he said, 'you're our goalkeeper. You've won your place on merit – and that's not just because Tel keeps letting us down!'

Mark felt very pleased with himself. Now he would be playing regularly on both Saturdays and Sundays. Northfleet were doing very well in their league, but there were only two other teams in their league who could give them a decent game, so he didn't have a lot of chance to shine, but he would always be busy when playing for Greshams. He might make a point of getting drunk every Saturday night if it meant he would play like that on a Sunday.

★ ★ ★ ★ ★

It was now just one week away from the Christmas Dinner Dance and Mark still didn't have a partner. Penny had told him that Wanda was looking for a partner. This idea did not appeal to Mark. His last chance was with Mary, but he didn't see her at all that week, so the Dinner Dance was almost a repeat of the previous year's dance. He danced with several different people, but secretly bemoaned the absence of a partner of his own. Moreover, he resented the fact that everyone could see he didn't have a partner. He resolved not to go next year if he didn't have a partner.

Over Christmas, his social life quietened down as Dougie spent a few days round his girlfriend's. Mark had been told to stay away from Anita's house. Her mother would not allow him into their home.

He spent the Christmas period re-evaluating his set of objectives. He felt that he had achieved those he had set himself when he first left school. Now it was time to set himself some fresh objectives.

To get a date during 1967.

And that would do. He could have added some more relating to his career aspirations, but he was enjoying his work and would surely get a decent rise in April, despite the recent legislation enforcing a pay freeze – that wouldn't apply to a junior on such a low wage. He had to concentrate his energies on a love life. 1967 was going to be the year when all his wishes came true.

CHAPTER 17

Crashes and Crushes

During December, the new cost Accountant had been installed at Greshams. His name was Arthur Capstick. He insisted that both Jean and Paul should call him Mr. Capstick – not Arthur. Jean had decided to call him Mr. Dipstick, although not to his face. Paul, in turn, said he would call him Mr. Chopstick (it was in Paul's nature to be different!). Mark thought Jean's name was far more appropriate.

Mr. Capstick was different to Bob Walsh in almost every way. He was taller, older and more serious. When Josie asked him to organise the payroll run as Bob used to do, he declined on two counts. Firstly, he didn't feel comfortable about the idea of carrying all that money about and secondly, he avoided riding in a car driven by anyone other than his wife. She was the driver in their family and he considered her to be a much better driver than he was. This did not endear him to the other men at Greshams. They all felt that no man should ever admit that his wife is the better driver!

Arthur Capstick convinced George that he needed two new Costing Clerks to replace Karen, so both of the two attractive young ladies, previously interviewed, were employed. They started work during January, with Debbie Pope starting two weeks after Lizzie McKay.

Lizzie was from Dundee and despite being in her very early twenties, she was married. Nevertheless, Mark considered her to be delightful. She was full of fun and mischief. She and Jean soon hit it off and formed an alliance against the two men in the department. She was blonde, of medium height and medium build. She had a very thick Scottish accent and some wonderful little Scottish words and phrases. 'Och, Mark Barker! You're a blether.' Mark tried to look up 'blether' in his dictionary. He found 'to blather' was to talk a load of nonsense, so he assumed a 'blether' was a Scottish pronunciation and meant someone who talked a load of nonsense, but when Lizzie said it, it sounded like something much more acceptable.

Debbie was single. She was Mark's age, with dark hair and gorgeous green eyes. She also had the most delightful little turned up nose, which turned up even more when she smiled. She was a very similar build to

Lizzie, which meant she had a very nice figure – except for her legs! She had very thick ankles and knees, which made her legs look almost shapeless. This was a big disappointment to Mark, because in every other respect, she was lovely and she soon attracted the attentions of every red-blooded male in the building. But she was painfully shy.

Jean had told her that Mark was unattached and looking for a girlfriend, so whenever he entered their office, Debbie would colour up and look embarrassed. Mark had little opportunity to talk to her, since Jean and Lizzie dominated the conversation whenever he visited and he was, at first, unaware of their little mischief. They often made remarks that flew over his head, but he began to suspect something was going on.

One day, Jean informed Mark that Debbie kept small birds. 'Oh really,' said Mark. 'What birds do you have?' It was one of the few occasions that he had actually spoken to her.

Debbie went red, but mumbled that she had some canaries, budgies and a pair of lovebirds. Lizzie sniggered, but Mark said he couldn't see why that was amusing. Then Jean said 'She's got a pair of Great Tits, you know.'

And Lizzie added 'She might let you go round to handle them.'

Jean completed the mischief with 'And she's had a cockatoo!'

As the pair of them burst into hysterical laughter, Debbie got up and ran out of the door, trying to hide her face. Mark was very annoyed at them both and told them not to embarrass Debbie like that. It was always significant when Mark started to stick up for someone. He was developing an attraction for her and he wanted to ask her out, but this behaviour by Jean and Lizzie meant he would have to be very discrete about it. He decided to find out where she lived to see if there was any likelihood of passing her bus stop.

This might have been a very good plan except for a minor disaster that befell him in late February. Mark and Dougie were returning from the pub one night in Mark's car. As Mark pulled out of the pub car park and stopped before proceeding onto the road, he noticed the brakes didn't feel right. He mentioned this to Dougie, who suggested his father could check them for him. Mark still hadn't driven six thousand miles since buying the car, so the only maintenance the car had received since then was for the occasional pint of oil and some anti-freeze, although lately, he had noticed a certain reluctance to start in the mornings.

Two hundred yards down the road, they approached a junction. Mark duly applied the brakes, only nothing happened. He tried again and was now starting to panic. The vehicle in front was rapidly getting larger and larger. Mark shouted out 'My brakes! They don't work! Shi – i – i – it!' They both braced themselves as they went straight into the back of the van already waiting at the junction. There was a loud crash and the sound of breaking glass. Fortunately, they were only doing 15 m.p.h. at the time.

Mark checked that Dougie was unhurt and then got out to inspect the damage. There was fluid all over the road and he could hear a hissing sound.

The driver of the van got out as well. Mark asked if he was hurt and was very relieved to see that he wasn't. The van seemed to be untouched, but despite the low speed, Mark's car was in a very sorry state. One headlamp was badly damaged, the bumper was hanging loose and the front had been pushed into his radiator. The leaking fluid was from his radiator. The van driver said that as his vehicle wasn't damaged, he wasn't interested in taking insurance details. Mark only had third party cover, so he wouldn't be able to claim anyway.

They were about a half a mile from Mark's home, so he decided to risk crawling home, using the gears and the handbrake to slow them. It was a tortuous journey and Mark was very relieved when he parked his car outside his house. Apart from the risk of not being able to stop in any emergency, he could see the needle on his temperature gauge creeping up and the car felt very juddery.

The next morning, in daylight, Mark could see that the damage was even worse than he had thought the night before. He went round Dougie's to ask his father to have a look at it. When Tim came round to inspect the car, he said he didn't think it would be cost effective to repair it. Apart from repairs to the radiator, bumper and front-end, the car needed new brakes and probably a service. He advised Mark to take the car to a breaker's yard and he might get five pounds for it. This is what Mark did and he did get five pounds for it, but now he was without transport again. He still owed twenty pounds of his original sub, so he thought he'd better pay that off before buying another car.

Ever since the company's formation in 1960, Greshams had enjoyed a consistent programme of growth, and since moving to Norfolk, the number of staff employed at Sanford had more than doubled. However, they were part of the construction industry, which is always the first industry to suffer whenever a recession hits the country. The orders started drying up and it became necessary to lay off staff and workers. Initially, this meant the loss of just a few site workers, but this was soon followed by a few people from both the factory and the office.

Morale suffered and everyone was wondering if they would be next. Mark wasn't too worried, because making him redundant would not save the company very much on the wage bill, but he and Penny knew their workload had tailed off quite dramatically. Josie wouldn't admit this. She told George that they were still very busy.

But George knew the score and saw this as an ideal opportunity to get rid of his biggest headache and as Josie was the highest earner in the department (and the least productive), he decided she was the one to go. Both Mark and Penny were secretly pleased to see the back of her, but they still felt very sorry to see her dismissed in this way, especially as Alf Seymour had also been made redundant a few days earlier. They had two teenage daughters to raise and it would not be easy for them.

One benefit of Josie's departure was that Mark now had a proper desk, with proper drawers.

★ ★ ★ ★ ★

By mid-March, Northfleet United were running away with the League title. There was only one other team with any chance of catching them and that would require a huge slump in form from Northfleet, which didn't seem very likely. They had reached the quarterfinal of the Norfolk Junior Cup, but they lost after a replay to a very good side from Norwich. Most league matches saw them dominate the opposition and Mark was seldom called into action.

The opposite was true on Sundays, where Greshams were still languishing near the bottom of their league, and Mark was always very busy. But they had somehow made their way through to the final of the Division Four Cup, where, at the end of April, they were due to meet their old adversaries, The White Hart. Mark had played in every game since the occasion when Tel had failed to show up and was really enjoying himself. Not only that, but everyone who worked at Greshams was talking about their successful run in the Cup. Nobby was drumming up a lot of support for the final.

★ ★ ★ ★ ★

Mark, with Dougie's help, had spent a few weeks looking at the second-hand car market and had seen a nice little 1959 Ford Anglia 100E. It was a very clean little two-door saloon and the garage were advertising it for seventy-five pounds, but Mark had negotiated a five pound discount for paying by cash. It was an unusual car in that it only had three forward gears, but that didn't bother Mark. When cold, the side-valve engine made a horrible hissing noise, but this soon disappeared when the engine warmed up. It was a very wet day when Mark took it for a test drive and one thing he really didn't like about the car was the vacuum operated windscreen wipers. These drew their power from the engine, so when the car was struggling up a steep hill, the wipers also started to struggle. The garage owner said that some people who owned this model had converted them to electric wipers. Dougie said his father might help with that.

Mark approached George for another sub, which was granted after Mark agreed to pay off the outstanding ten pounds of his original sub. Mark reminded George that he was due for a good pay increase in April. 'Haven't you heard that there's a pay-freeze?' asked George.

'Yes, but that surely can't apply to me?'

'It applies to everyone, except in exceptional circumstances. That's the law.'

'Well, surely these are exceptional circumstances. I was seventeen when you took me on as a junior and now I'm doing practically the same job as Penny.' Mark was sounding very indignant.

George replied 'The directors have said they are not prepared to budget for any pay increases this year.'

'Can't you tell them about my situation?'

'It wouldn't make any difference. Do you still want this sub?'

Mark thought carefully for a minute and then replied 'Yes. I've got to get some transport. I'll have to make some savings some other way. Can you let me have the money on Friday? I've arranged to pick up the car on Saturday morning.' Then he stormed out of George's office.

That night, in the Ship Inn, Mark told Dougie about his conversation with George. He said 'By the time I start to make ends meet, they move the ends!'

'Why don't you come and work in our department?' asked Dougie. 'I get paid a lot more than you. We need a new trainee. Mike's leaving soon. He's buying a pub.'

'I don't know,' said Mark. 'I enjoy my work. I don't want to go back to filing and fetching coffees again. I'll think about it.' Mark did enjoy his work and he knew he was good at his job. He also couldn't be sure if he would get a raise for changing jobs, but he liked the idea of getting out of the office to visit customer sites. He hadn't been to very many places in his life and he was envious when Dougie told him about his little trips to Newcastle or Manchester.

Jean was working behind the bar and when Mark went to buy a round of drinks, she told him that she had seen Karen. She was getting married soon. 'That was quick!' exclaimed Mark. 'She's not ... You know, is she?' He patted his stomach.

'No, I don't think so. She seems very happy, actually. She was with him when we last met. He looks about thirty!'

'Well, she always said she preferred older men. Anyway, I'm very pleased for her. When you see her again, tell her I sent my best wishes.'

'You're not upset about it, then?'

'No. I've got my thoughts on someone else, now.'

'Are you after Debbie?'

'No. I don't want to go out with anyone from work.' Mark stroked his nose to make sure it wasn't growing. He didn't like telling lies, but he knew that sometimes there was no choice.

Lately, he had been inventing more and more excuses to visit the Costing Department. He knew that Debbie would be too shy to go to the canteen on her own, so he often poked his head round the door to see if anyone wanted a bread roll. Debbie certainly didn't relish going to the canteen on her own, but she also found it difficult to ask Mark to go for her, so most times, she muttered a polite 'No, thank you,' but if he was fetching something for someone else, she felt happier about taking him up on his offer. Mark knew that she didn't want to exhibit any signs of encouragement in front of her colleagues, but that didn't necessarily mean she wasn't interested in him, did it? On the occasions when she did want something from the canteen, she gave him a lovely little smile, which certainly made it all worthwhile. Jean remembered how Mark used to wait on Karen, so she recognised the signs.

The more Mark saw of Debbie, the more he decided she was the one for him. She was more like the young girl he had hoped Karen was going to be when he learnt she was coming to work with him, nearly eighteen months ago. Debbie was quiet and unassuming, and very attractive. Her legs were not too brilliant, but otherwise, she had a very pleasant figure.

And she did have a bosom. She really was the complete opposite of Karen in almost every respect. He would have to get to know her *very* well before *she* would be sitting on his lap.

On Saturday, Mark fetched his new car and was so pleased to be mobile again, that he drove out into the country for a prolonged ride, but not without first driving around Debbie's housing estate. He didn't see her. He returned via the bus station and then again went round Debbie's estate. Still no sign of her.

Even when he went to play football that afternoon, he went the long way round via her estate. He told himself that this was a silly waste of petrol, but he saw it as the only way to meet her away from the office. At least the next morning, he had arranged to give Dougie a lift to the away match, so even Mark couldn't justify a diversion past her road.

This was the last match before the big final and everyone was keen to play in order to secure a place in the team for the final. They lost as usual, but the team was definitely showing signs of improvement.

When Mark went into the Costing Department during the week, he tried to persuade a few people to come and watch the big game. It was really only Debbie he was interested in, but he had to appear to be asking everyone. He was pleased to hear Lizzie and Debbie discussing whether they would go together, although they seemed more interested in watching Dougie and Woody, than watching Mark.

Both girls lived quite close to the venue, so Mark was very pleased to see them on the touchline when he ran out onto the pitch. This more than made up for the fact that his father had shown no interest in attending. Dougie's father was there to watch. In fact Dougie's father often turned up to watch the local Saturday matches.

Mark was all fired up for this match and despite feeling quite nervous, he was soon in action, making two good saves in quick succession and cleanly collecting several high crosses. But Greshams were not making any progress in the opposition's half of the pitch. Dougie was getting very frustrated at the lack of service he was receiving. At the interval, it was still 0-0, but it seemed just a matter of time before The White Hart scored, even though they were missing their top scorer.

After ten minutes of the re-start, they did go ahead. Toby attempted a pass back to Mark, but his pass was severely under strength. Although Mark was out of his goal quickly, the opposition's inside-forward was able to intercept the pass and he turned the ball into the path of their centre forward, who made no mistake with an empty goal ahead of him.

In previous games, this would have been the start of a collapse as heads went down, but this was a final and there were lots of people watching, including Mr Gresham, himself. As long as it remained 1-0, there was always a chance of scraping some kind of fluke result. The White Hart were still doing all the attacking, but no one in the Gresham team was going to give in. At last, Dougie did receive a decent pass, but with the rest of the team struggling to get out of their own half, his lone attack came to nothing.

With just two minutes to go, there was a scramble in the Gresham goalmouth. Woody's attempted clearance struck his own player and was rebounding slowly towards the goal. Mark lost sight of the ball, until it was already past him. Instinctively, he reached out behind him and somehow got his hand to the ball. It was a miraculous save and he had kept the team in the game a little longer. He got up and quickly threw the ball out to Dougie, who went on one of his solo runs. This looked very similar to the situation in the quarterfinal when Dougie had scored the winning goal. Mark and the supporters were sure this was the big moment, when having saved a certain goal, he had set up Dougie for the match saving equaliser. Alas it was not to be. Dougie was suddenly surrounded by three defenders and although he beat the first, the other two gave him nowhere to go.

A minute later, it was all over. The Gresham players sank to their knees in despair. Everyone was saying that at least they hadn't disgraced themselves in front of all their supporters, but at that moment, that was no consolation. Toby sloped over to say 'Sorry lads,' but there were no recriminations. They had to admit that the better team had won.

Mark glanced over to the touchline to see Debbie's reaction, but she was already walking out of the gate with Lizzie. He was desperately hoping that his performance had impressed her. There had been no opportunity to speak to her. Although he was disappointed that the team had lost, he was very pleased with his own performance and he received many congratulations as he made his way to the changing rooms.

The next day, Mark made a point of visiting the Costing Department to see if he could elicit some kind of reaction from Debbie. Lizzie said she had enjoyed the game, but that was all that was said on the subject. Debbie didn't say a word and Mark didn't feel it was his place to ask her for any comment.

Mark asked Jean if she would be playing tennis when the evenings were light enough. She said she probably would. 'What about you two ladies?' he asked of Debbie and Lizzie. 'Do you play?'

'No. I canna play,' replied Lizzie. 'I suffer from tennis elbow.'

Mark saw an opportunity for one of his witticisms. 'I've never suffered from tennis elbow, but I have got tennis balls!'

'Whas that like?' asked Lizzie with a snigger.

'They're soft and furry and I have to keep them in a box.' Everyone was laughing, except Debbie who was, at least, smiling.

'What about you, Debbie?' Mark asked, hoping with all his heart for a positive response.

'I can't play tennis,' she mumbled.

'Of course you can. We're not professionals. We just play for a bit of fun. We have a good evening, don't we, Jean?'

Jean was about to reply, but Debbie responded first. 'No, I'm not interested, thank you' and her face turned a pinky colour. Mark didn't want to embarrass her any further, so he left. Another brilliant idea had come to nothing. He'd have to pursue the old 'driving past her bus stop' routine. He couldn't help feeling that the longer he went without asking her out, the less chance he had of success. He could sense that Jean and Lizzie were aware of his interest in her and their silly little remarks were not helping his cause one bit. The more he visited their department, the more Debbie seemed determined to ignore him and the harder it became to engage her in conversation.

And the longer this situation went on, the stronger his infatuation grew. Until by the time he eventually did see her at the bus station, he was desperate to go out with her. As she got into his car, he was feeling extremely anxious and couldn't think straight. He had spent so many hours rehearsing what he was going to say when he got the opportunity, but now that it had arrived, none of the things he intended to say felt appropriate. And he didn't want her to think he was just giving her a lift so that he could ask her out. Otherwise, she might never accept a lift again. By the time he arrived at her house, he had abandoned his plans to ask her out, contenting himself with enjoying her company.

As he drove away from her house, he thumped the steering wheel angrily and shouted to himself 'YOU STUPID PRAT!' He had just wasted a golden opportunity to date her. Who knew when he would get another?

In fact, two weeks later, he did see her again at the bus station, but this time she was with her mother, who was very grateful for the lift. He had probably won her mother's approval for him to date Debbie, but that didn't help him unless he could actually ask Debbie.

CHAPTER 18

Time's Running Out

It was now June 1967. Despite all the cutbacks, a new Chief Accountant had been brought in above George. George was not happy about this. It was explained to him that this was no reflection on his ability. It was rumoured that the new man, Alfred Southgate, was a member of the same Round Table as Mr. Wilcox. Alfred Southgate insisted that everyone should call him Mr. Southgate and he disapproved of people using first names at work.

He was a very tall austere looking figure, not unlike a bespectacled Abraham Lincoln, complete with a goatee beard. He always wore a three-piece dark-grey pin-stripe suit, with a grey or medium-blue shirt. He usually had a pipe in his mouth. It wasn't always lit, but when it was, it left a foul stench everywhere he went. He was not popular with anyone, except for Mrs. Hetherington, whom he had brought in after only two weeks in his job, as a Senior Ledger Clerk above Margaret. Needless to say, Margaret was most put out. Nobody bothered to explain to Margaret that Mrs Hetherington's appointment was not a reflection on Margaret's ability. Mrs. Hetherington didn't appear to have a first name either. She and Mr. Southgate were *very* good friends. They shared the same sense of humour.

Mr. Southgate wasted no time in introducing several changes to the administration of the company and was very keen on modernisation. This included the introduction of an NCR Accounting machine, in which Mrs. Hetherington was already skilled. Jill was to be trained to use it as well. Margaret wasn't. It was a very noisy machine. Ledger cards were fed into the machine and as calculations were performed, the carriage shuddered across backwards and forwards as information was printed onto the card, with the updated card being ejected on completion, ready for the next one.

Another innovation was the introduction of Sumlock Comptometers. These machines were, in many ways, the forerunners of the modern calculator, but were far more bulky and needed specialist skills to operate them. So Greshams employed a team of three 'Comps'. The machines were capable of quite complex arithmetic calculations and were suited to large volume repetitive tasks.

It wasn't long before Mr Southgate insisted that 'comps' were used on the payroll calculations. Mark felt that some of his work had been taken away from him, so after careful consideration, he went to see Dougie's boss, Reg Stanmore, about becoming a Trainee Surveyor. Reg was very keen on the idea, because with the cutbacks, his staff budget had been cut. Yet he still wanted to replace Mike who had already left.

Mark was insistent that he would only transfer if he received a substantial pay increase. He explained how he had been badly affected by the pay freeze. Reg didn't seem to think that would be a problem and two days later, he offered Mark the new position on a salary of £450 per annum. Mark felt he had to accept. He was struggling to keep up his payments on the car and would dearly like to buy some more clothes. He also considered that becoming a surveyor was a big career move, although he appreciated that the move meant that he had to go back to something resembling a 'junior' status.

Unfortunately, this all took time, because Mark had to wait until a replacement Wages clerk was found and then he had to spend two weeks showing her the ropes. Her name was Wendy and she knew Debbie from her days at the High School. Wendy was engaged to be married, so Mark felt able to relax and enjoy her company, while he passed on his knowledge.

While he was waiting for his transfer to take place, Mark managed to arrange a date with the lovely Pauline. Although Debbie was now the main object of his desires, an opportunity presented itself that he just could not ignore.

On a Wednesday evening in June, he had been talking to George's younger sister, Maureen. Maureen regularly visited the Gliderdrome in Boston on a Saturday night. This venue was very popular in the sixties and early seventies for its success at attracting live acts from all over the world – until 'Disco' killed off that success. Maureen knew Mark was a big fan of Ben E. King and she told Mark about his forthcoming appearance at the Gliderdrome. Maureen didn't have a car. She usually caught a bus to King's Lynn, where a coach was laid on every Saturday to take people to the Gliderdrome. Mark said he would give her a lift and she could bring one friend. Mark told Maureen that he was expecting to bring somebody.

His first thought, of course, had been about Pauline. Someone once

231

told him that you could get a date with any woman if you can make the date sound interesting enough. When he didn't see Pauline in Reception the following evening, he drove round to her house to see her. Luckily, she was at home and he was able to speak to her. She was very excited at the prospect of seeing one of her heroes and she said 'Yes' but she pointed out that it was only one week before she was due to emigrate. Mark said that didn't matter and they agreed he would pick her up at six o'clock on Saturday.

At long last he had a date; not a blind date with someone he'd never met and didn't fancy; not making up a foursome; a real date with someone he had fancied since the very first time he had set eyes on her. Someone who would make him the envy of every other bloke at the Gliderdrome. It knew it wouldn't lead to anything, because she would be leaving the country in a few days time. But this was *it*.

He couldn't resist telling everyone – Penny, Ellie, Dougie, Maureen, Gary and Jean (but not Debbie!).

He went into town on Saturday to buy Pauline a Ben E. King record. The only record in stock at the record shop was an EP. It contained the original version of 'I (Who Have Nothing)' and three other tracks. This was going to be a night to remember and he was going to pull out all the stops to make it so.

He called round Pauline's house as arranged and was met at the door by her father, who by now had left Greshams to prepare for his move.

'Hello Fred. I've come to pick up your daughter,' said Mark with a huge grin.

Fred looked very serious. 'I'm afraid she's not coming. I'm sorry, but we didn't know where you live, otherwise I'd have let you know.'

Mark thought he was joking. Fred was known to enjoy a little practical joke, but it gradually dawned on Mark that this might not be one of them. 'You are joking, aren't you, Fred?'

'No, I'm sorry. She's been moping about the house for weeks. I was really pleased when I heard you'd been round to take her out. She seemed to perk up for a little while, but then she started thinking about it and changed her mind. We've been trying desperately to make her come with you, but when she's made up her mind, that's it, I'm afraid. Don't take it personally. She's got herself in a little rut.'

'Can I see her?'

'She won't come to the door. I told her to tell you herself, but she can't face you. I'm so sorry, Mark.'

Mark sloped back to his car. He looked at her present lying on the seat beside him. He thought about going back to give it to her, but decided to keep it for himself. Now he was committed to driving Maureen and her friend all the way to Boston without his date.

As he got to the outskirts of Boston, he asked Maureen if she minded making her own way home. She could still catch the coach, so it was no great hardship. She tried to persuade him to stay. 'You don't want to go home feeling sorry for yourself,' she said, sympathetically.

"It's what I do best,' he replied, with a half hearted smile. 'I've got GCE's in "feeling sorry for myself". Maureen understood his disappointment and didn't mind being abandoned. In fact, she said she often enjoyed the coach journey back. Mark had really wanted to see Ben E. King, but at that moment, he didn't feel in the mood.

The ride home seemed to take forever. The road across the Lincolnshire Fens is not the most interesting in the world and as the sun sank on the horizon, he could feel himself getting drowsy. He decided to sing to himself to keep awake. He chose one of his favourite songs by Jerry Butler – 'Need to Belong'. It summed up his mood perfectly, reflecting on the need to find a soulmate and how much it hurt not to have someone to bring love into his world.

He knew his voice couldn't match Jerry Butler's, but he sang it with just as much feeling. He consoled himself with the fact that it hadn't been Debbie who had rejected him and as far as he knew, she still didn't have a boyfriend.

★ ★ ★ ★ ★

Later on in June, Dougie informed Mark that he and Anita were going to marry. Anita was with child. It surprised Mark that someone with Dougie's experience of the opposite sex could slip up like this. It was always assumed that they would get married at some point, but their plans had been brought forward by some considerable margin. They had found a little terraced house the other side of town and the sale was proceeding quite rapidly. In fact, everything was happening quite quickly and Dougie was far too busy to socialise.

Consequently, Mark's social life took a downward spiral, except for the occasional lunchtime drink. Mark and Dougie had transferred their allegiance from the Cock Inn to Mike's pub, which was a few hundred yards down the road from the Cock. It was called the Bricklayer's Arms. Hence Mike's little joke that he was always finding his wife in the Bricklayer's Arms.

The great attraction of the Bricklayer's, apart from Mike's witty banter, was the pinball machine. Mike had modified the 'tilt' switch, so that it would hardly ever activate, no matter how much you shook the machine. Mike had found that when he first moved into the pub, he was getting numerous complaints about the switch being too sensitive, so he tampered with it. Now he didn't get any complaints at all. When Mike wasn't looking, Mark and Dougie would lift the machine and force the ball to repeatedly hit the 'Free Game' button, so that for the modest outlay of one bob (normally three games), they could rack up a bank of ten games to keep them occupied all lunchtime. If they then legitimately won some free games, it made them late back for work. Mike offered a prize for the highest game score of the week, which was suspiciously always won when he wasn't looking!

Mark still had his tennis on a Friday. He tried to encourage some of the other tennis players to play a second night, but the only person who was agreeable to this was Wanda, so he declined.

But at least he had his car and he spent most weekends driving around and exploring the Norfolk countryside. And, of course, he would usually return via the bus station. Twice he saw Jane and gave her a lift home. On the second occasion, he asked her if she was still going out with her new boyfriend. She was, but she didn't seem to mind Mark asking her the question. He had the feeling that, one day, he would go out with her, but not at this time.

The downside of switching allegiance from the Cock Inn was that Mark didn't see Mary again, but by now he only had thoughts for Debbie.

His encounters with Debbie at work were less and less promising.

One day, just before he transferred to the Surveyors', Mark was in the Costing Department, thumbing through the previous week's timesheets to resolve a payroll query, when Jean, quite out of the blue, said 'If you want to impress Debbie, Mark, you should tell her you've got twelve finches.'

'If he's got twelve finches, he could impress me!' said Lizzie, with a little squeal of laughter. Everyone in the room was laughing, except Debbie and Mark. Mark was furious, but before he could bring himself to say anything, Debbie ran out of the office. Mark followed her down the corridor, after first giving everyone else a very hard stare and angrily asking Mr Dipstick to keep his staff under control. He caught up with Debbie. He had to speak to her now. Matters had been brought to a head and he decided he had to seize the moment or the situation would deteriorate beyond the point of no return.

'I know you hate all this silliness and I can assure you that it is not of my making. I promise you that I have never said anything to anyone about fancying you. However, I have to confess that I do and I would dearly like to take you out. So will you come out with me? I promise that no one else would learn about it.'

'No. People *would* learn about it and the situation in the office would be even worse if I went out with you. I would never date anyone from work.' And she walked off towards the Ladies. It was one of the longest conversations Mark had ever had with Debbie, but it was all over in a flash.

But at least he'd finally got round to asking her. Mark ought to have been getting used to being rejected, but all it did was make him even more determined to win her over, just as it had done when Karen first rejected him. He'd leave it a few weeks to see if she had a change of heart after she'd got to know him better. He would have to wear her down.

On Mark's last day in the Wages Department, he invited several people out for a lunchtime drink. This included Wendy and everyone in the Costing Department. Mr. Dipstick and Paul didn't accept the invitation, but the three girls did. It gave Mark the chance to sit next to Debbie in the pub. He chatted freely and told a few jokes and made himself the centre of attraction. By now, he was gaining in self-confidence and was not as shy as he was when he first left school. But Debbie and Lizzie still seemed to be more interested in Dougie, who wasn't telling any jokes. Whenever Debbie wanted to laugh, she gazed across to Dougie to see if he was laughing as well.

Surely, she couldn't have designs on him? She must know that Anita was expecting and that they would be getting married in a few weeks. When they were all ready to return from the pub, Debbie refused Mark's offer of a lift. She had already accepted Dougie's offer.

That evening, Dougie and Mark went to the Bricklayer's. Dougie was very subdued. He told Mark that he was having second thoughts about getting married. There were so many other young ladies around and he wasn't ready to settle down yet. 'Lovely young things like Debbie,' he said.

Mark didn't know what to say. He didn't approve of Dougie marrying Anita if he was going to carry on playing the field, but he had assumed that he might settle down once he was married and had a child to raise. And Mark certainly wasn't going to give his blessing for Dougie to steal Debbie from him. All he could think to say was 'I can't help you, mate. You know how you feel about things and it has to be your decision. I do know you think the world of Anita. That was obvious when you ditched Dawn to go back to Anita.'

He wondered whether Dougie had already taken advantage of Debbie's obvious interest in him. It was clear that Mark now had even less chance of winning Debbie for himself.

★ ★ ★ ★ ★

A few weeks later, the wedding went ahead. Mark was relieved that Dougie hadn't asked him to be his best man. That honour fell to Mick Baker. Mark didn't attend the actual wedding, which was conducted in the Registry Office. But he did attend the reception – a rather subdued affair, held in the backroom of a small hotel in town.

You could almost draw a line across the middle of the room to separate the two families. Although both families were from a working class background, there was still a distinct class divide. Dougie's father drove a Ford Cortina, had a trade and their council house was on a modern estate. None of Anita's immediate family owned a car. Her father was a labourer in a local factory and they lived on the worst council estate in town, where many of the town's local criminals were housed. Moreover, Dougie's mother worked at the local Marks & Spencer, whereas Anita worked in Woolworth's – both as shop assistants. M & S employees traditionally looked down upon those from Woolies.

Mark felt his family background placed him somewhere in the middle of the two class divides. His father was a craftsman and they lived in their own house, but financially, they were inferior to Dougie's family. Mark's father had never owned a car.

Mark steered clear of Anita's side of the room, which included Marlene and Mandy. Aggie gave him a very dirty look and didn't speak to him throughout the afternoon.

The couple disappeared to get changed (or 'to put their things together,' as Mick described it) and then they were off on their honeymoon. The reception broke up around six o'clock. It had been nothing like Mark's sister's wedding reception, where everyone was still dancing away at two o'clock in the morning.

Now that Dougie was married, he did, indeed, settle down. His new house needed a lot of work and he seldom went out in the evenings, so Mark's social life suffered even further decline.

By now, Mark had started work as a Trainee Surveyor. This was a mixed blessing. The benefits were that he was starting out on a more lucrative career. He would be able to get out of the office several times a month and he was working with a group of men who enjoyed their work and constantly engaged in some very interesting banter – some of it quiet educational for a young lad who had led a sheltered life.

The down side was that, although he was classed as a Trainee rather than a Junior, the five surveyors believed that their time was more valuable than his. This meant he had to fetch the coffees and do a certain amount of filing. Reg Stanmore had his own adjoining office and his own secretary, who did some filing, but it was considered part of a Trainee's training to perform all the menial tasks. Dougie was still classed as a Trainee, but he had now jumped up the hierarchy, so he only got the menial tasks when Mark was out of the office.

Although Mark was effectively at the beck and call of any of the surveyors, he was assigned to specifically work with Ian Beddington – a very outspoken right-wing person, who sported a thick ginger beard, which he constantly stroked. He also wore suede shoes and a green and yellow checked jacket – just like those that Mark's schoolteachers used to wear. Ian rolled his own skinny little cigarettes and would often spend half an hour rolling a small supply to see him through the day. He had very strong views on everything and would argue with anyone about anything just for the fun of it. His favourite expression was 'I blame the Labour Government!' He was also most vociferous about Mr. Southgate who had insisted that all company cars would be Volkswagen Beetles. 'We didn't win the war, just to have them forcing their bloody "people's car" on us.' Ian was hoping to get a company car soon. He reminded Reg about it several times a week, but he didn't want any German rubbish.

He didn't suffer fools gladly and Mark found he had to be on his toes all the time. But Mark liked Ian (most of the time) – even when he called Mark a "brown hatter." Mark wasn't sure what that was, but it didn't sound like a compliment. Mark learnt a great deal from Ian – some of it about surveying! Ian maintained that all young trainees were guilty of spending their time playing with themselves under the desk. 'Is that what you did, at my age?' Mark would ask him when these accusations were flying around. Ian also insisted than when you went to the toilet, more than three shakes constituted "playing with yourself."

Dougie also had a mentor in Greg Tully, who was senior to Ian and already had a company car. He deputised for Reg when Reg wasn't around, much to the disgust of Ian who considered himself to be the better Surveyor. Greg had been with the company much longer than the other Surveyors and was by far the oldest at fifty-one years old.

Next in the pecking order after Ian was Noel Bunter – also known as Billy. A slightly overweight individual (though not as overweight as the Billy Bunter of Frank Richard's novels – and a little taller). Noel was an out and out socialist, so the conversations between him and Ian were often very ripe. Several times a week, Reg would call out from his office 'Keep the noise down, you two!'

The fifth Surveyor was Sam Baggeley. Sam had joined the company after Dougie, but he was an experienced Surveyor, not a Trainee. Mark didn't know what to make of Sam. He was a divorced Londoner, with a very greasy complexion, a dark goatee beard and long dishevelled black hair, which showered dandruff all over his black suit. He never took off his jacket and had a problem with personal hygiene. He smoked a lot, so when Ian lit up at the same time, the office could get very smoky.

Sam was forever talking about his love life. At first, nobody believed his tales, but then Ian saw him in town one day with a beautiful willowy blonde. The other Surveyors couldn't understand his success with women, because he was an ugly individual with some disgusting habits. One of which was to cough up a mouthful of phlegm from the back of his throat and then appear to savour it in his mouth, before swallowing it. It was a horrible noise and a nauseating sight, but he didn't seem to realise he was doing it.

He was also partially deaf in one ear and wore a hearing aid (they were quite bulky in the sixties). Someone could be halfway through telling him something, when he would suddenly interrupt them and talk about something completely unconnected, as though he hadn't heard a word of what was being said. Mark thought that Sam sometimes just pretended to be deaf to suit his needs.

The conversation in the office was a complete contrast to those Mark had been used to in the Wages Department and some of it, particularly the sexual innuendoes, went over his head, but he gradually assimilated enough information to improve his knowledge. He learnt about 'going down,' 'giving head,' 'doggy-fashion' and 'sixty-nines.' He also got to read 'Eskimo Nell.'

Ian and Sam took great delight in embarrassing Reg's secretary, Pat.

Ian asked her 'Do you like "sixty-nines", Pat?'

'That's none of your business,' she replied.

'I prefer sixty-eight,' added Ian.

'What's that?' she asked, wondering whether she should encourage him or not.

'Well, it's very much like sixty-nines, but you do it to me, and then I owe you one.'

'Ooh, you men! You're terrible.' But Mark could see her grinning as she bustled back to her office, which she shared with Reg.

Pat was in her late thirties and had two daughters. She was of very stocky build, with thick calves, sturdy thighs, wide hips, a medium-large bosom and very broad shoulders. Mark thought she would probably have had a very good figure when she was younger and before she started putting on weight. In fact, she still had a certain appeal to a young impressionable teenage lad and he wasn't averse to having a little harmless flirt with her from time to time. If he wanted some typing done, he would put his arm round her surprisingly firm hips and she would say 'Oh, hello. What do you want? I can always tell when you want something.'

Mark could always tell when she was entering the office by the sound of her tights rustling as she bustled around. She enjoyed working in an office full of men, but she never let the men know that. She had a lot to put up with and she was a very patient lady.

Mark's first trip out of the office was to Croydon. Ian needed someone to 'hold his rod'. The finished work on a site did not always match the original drawings. If, for example, the ceiling height was five per cent greater than the original estimates, it meant the partitioning was five per cent higher, which in turn, meant almost five per cent extra on the invoice, so site visits were very important. If there was less partitioning than estimated, the original estimate usually stood, unless the client was really on the ball.

Ian liked an early start and told Mark he would pick him up at his house at six o'clock in the morning. The customer was Wellsey Insurance. It was a brand new office block and by the time of the site visit, the building was already in use. Ian sought out the Office Manager to get permission to wander round the building with his 'measuring stick'. There was a Board meeting that day, so they were told not go into the Boardroom. Ian was disappointed with this as he wanted to view the Boardroom's partitions, which were veneered panels to match the hefty doors.

Ian had to keep telling Mark to concentrate on his measuring and not to keep looking round at all the pretty young girls working in the offices. 'It's not professional. You're here as a representative of Gresham Installations, so you have standards to maintain.' That didn't stop Ian from entering into conversation with one over-friendly lady.

'That's a big one,' she said, referring to Ian's measuring stick, which Mark was holding.

'Mine's only twelve inches, but I don't use it as a rule,' said Ian, as he noted down some measurements in his little book. Mark tried to think of a reference to his twelve finches, but he couldn't make it work, so he kept quiet.

Ian was very thorough and went round the whole building, using his site drawings to find his way round, knocking on any closed doors and being very polite to the occupants of each office. To Mark, it seemed a very long and very exhausting day, but they had finished by 1.30. After a quick pub lunch, they made their way back to Sanford. 'Was that a typical site visit?' asked Mark, in the car.

'There's no such thing as a typical visit. They're all different. The other week, I had to go to Fort Dunlop, outside Birmingham. There were only a few partitions to measure up, but they were dotted about all over the site – some in the offices, some in the factory. And it was additional partitioning, so I had to differentiate between the new and the old. That's when you need to study the drawings and work with the Contracts Manager or Site Foreman. A good site visit can pay dividends. I'm always making extra money for the company.

Our old mate, Billy Bunter, on the other hand, just goes on site for a "jolly." He whizzes round and does as little as he can get away with.'

Mark was to discover this first hand a fortnight later, when he and Noel went to a site in Manchester. Noel arranged to fetch Mark at eight o'clock, but was thirty-five minutes late, so it was lunchtime by the time they got to Manchester and Noel was hungry. So they found the building, looked at it from the outside and he said 'Yeah, I can see some partitioning through the window. Let's go get some lunch.' And that was it. They didn't even enter the building.

'How do you know what's there?' Mark asked, remembering Ian's comments.

'I had a chat with John Woodston. The contract all went according to plan and the original estimate, so that's what we'll bill them.'

After lunch, they returned through the attractive Derbyshire Peak District. It was the first time that Mark had seen proper hills. As it was a nice day, Noel took a few diversions. He liked to drive down a side road, get lost and then find his way back, relying on his superior 'sense of direction.' At one point, they saw a group of people gazing over a wall and pointing, so he stopped the car and they both got out to view the attraction. What Mark saw, took his breath away.

Over the wall, was a steep drop down to a valley, with a lovely little river winding its way around a steep hill on the other side of the valley. Across the river, stretched a beautiful railway viaduct. It was a perfect setting and Mark was filled with awe. He had never owned a camera, but at that moment, he resolved to buy one. He didn't want to leave, but Noel said they had to get going.

Back in the car, Mark grabbed a map and tried to work out where they were. He spotted a roadsign, pointing towards Great Longstone. After more studying of the map, he decided that the beauty spot must have been Monsal Head. One day, when he had a girlfriend, he would return. You needed to be with someone special to really appreciate this wonderful location. Billy Bunter certainly didn't fit the bill.

Mark spent a lot of time out of the office, because Ian, Noel and Sam all liked someone to 'hold my rod.' Greg always used Dougie to hold his.

However, back in the office, he found work to be a bit of a drudge. He didn't have any sites of his own and he had no responsibility to speak of.

His love life was definitely not showing any signs of improvement. It was now September, so he had four months in which to achieve his big objective of getting a proper date. Dougie was no longer part of his social life, so Mark wasn't sure how he would turn things around. But all of that was due to change. All thanks to a chance remark.

CHAPTER 19

Getting 'Off the Mark'

The football season had started again. Mark was still playing for Northfleet on Saturdays and Greshams on Sundays. Dougie had abandoned Greshams. He wasn't enjoying playing for them and he had used his contacts in the game to find a First Division team – another high-riding team known simply as 'The Reds.' But he had stayed with Northfleet. They had, after all, won their league the previous season and he had been the top scorer in the league. Dougie had tried to get Mark to sign for 'The Reds.' Mark was tempted, but preferred to play for at least one team that was going to keep him busy, even if it meant losing nearly every week.

Tennis had fizzled out at the end of summer, due to lack of interest. When Mark had found himself playing singles with Wanda, he decided to tell her that the season was over. During the summer, he and Gary had discussed the possibility of playing squash or badminton. Mr. Gresham had his own squash court in one of his out-buildings and had told the Social Club that they could use it, so when the tennis finished, Mark and Gary decided to take him up on his offer.

Mr Gresham lived at Broadby Manor, six miles outside Sanford. Jean joined them, but she was the only female. Of course, Debbie couldn't be persuaded to play. It was the first time that Mark had played squash. He considered it to be a reasonably enjoyable evening, but Gary was much better than both Mark and Jean. There was only one court and three other people turned up, so there was a lot of waiting around.

The next day, Mark went to chat to Jean. He no longer had a reason to visit the Costing Department for work purposes, but he still popped in for the occasional lunchtime chat – provided Debbie was there! He asked Jean if she had enjoyed the squash. She hadn't and said she wouldn't be going again. Mark agreed with her and said he would prefer to play badminton. Paul was listening and he said 'Why don't you come to our badminton club?'

'You play badminton?' asked Mark. He couldn't imagine Paul doing anything remotely energetic, nor, for that matter, doing something that might involve pleasure of any kind.

'You don't have to look so surprised. I've been playing badminton for years. It was very popular when I was in the Far East.'

'Where do you play?' asked Jean.

'At Hunstanton.' Mark remembered that Paul lived in Hunstanton. He was always talking about the sea view from his bungalow.

'Is it a big club,' asked Mark.

'It's quite small. The numbers vary. We usually have about six or seven people turn up, but there are about a dozen members. We don't play in a league or anything. It's more of a social evening than anything too competitive. We play every Thursday, if you're interested.'

Mark was definitely interested, but Jean wasn't too keen and Debbie was still not interested. So later that day, Mark asked Gary if he would join him for a game. Gary was happy to give it a try. He just happened to own two old racquets, so Mark could borrow one of them.

On the Thursday evening of that same week, Gary and Mark made their way to Hunstanton. The club played in a school hall, with only one court set up for use, although there was space for more courts.

When they arrived, Paul was sitting out watching a game of mixed doubles that was already in progress. Paul introduced Mark and Gary to everyone. There were three ladies and three men, as well as Mark and Gary. When the first game had finished, Paul partnered Gary against Mark and a middle-aged lady called Rose. Rose asked Mark if he liked to play 'front and back' or 'sides.' Mark hadn't got a clue what she was talking about. He'd only ever played a few games at school and those had been mostly singles. Rose could see he was struggling with the question, so she said 'Would you rather I stayed at the net or do you want me to come back?'

'You choose,' he replied. 'I don't mind.' That sounded better than 'I haven't got a clue what you're talking about, lady!'

Rose said, 'We'll play "sides", then.' And Mark kept to his side of the court. He was still a bit rusty and had trouble remembering the rules of the game and the way you scored points, but it soon came back to him. Gary was even rustier. So for once, Mark felt himself to be the better player. Paul wasn't the best player in the world, despite having played for years and Rose had, at one time, played league badminton, so although Rose was not the swiftest player around, she and Mark ran out comfortable winners.

By now, another middle-aged lady had arrived, so she and one of the ladies who had been waiting went on with the other two men. Everyone was very friendly and the badminton wasn't too competitive – just as Paul had said. In fact, everyone was more interested in talking than playing – except Mark, that is, although he was quite happy to chat to the two younger ladies. They were probably both a few years older than he was, but they were both very pleasant to look at. Tonya was the one who was still sitting out and she was very talkative to both Gary and Mark. During the conversation, she informed them that one of the other men was her husband. But Mark's attention kept wandering to Jenny who was on court.

Jenny was fair-haired, five feet eight inches tall, of medium build and was the more attractive of the two younger ladies, especially when she smiled, which was most of the time. She wore a knee length tennis skirt, so Mark couldn't assess the shape of her legs, although her calves were slim. In fact her calves seemed a little out of proportion to the rest of her, because she seemed to be just a little overweight, but she was still quick on her feet. She carried her large bosom very well and she had wide hips. There was no one particular feature about her that attracted Mark. It was her general persona; her presence. She seemed to make everyone enjoy themselves.

If Mark had passed her on the street, he might not have given her much of a second look. But on the badminton court, laughing and running around, she looked lovely. But she was probably a few years older than him and possibly married. He wasn't going to get involved with married women.

Nevertheless, he thought while he was talking to Tonya and Paul, he would fish for information. 'Do you all live locally?' he asked of no one in particular.

'Yes,' replied Tonya. 'We all live within a few miles radius of Hunstanton. Jenny lives in Heacham.'

'And are you all a collection of friends – and husbands and wives?' That sounded like a messy question, but it kept the conversation going.

Tonya and Paul thought for a few seconds and then Paul answered 'Yes. I suppose we are really. Tom there, is my neighbour and Jenny met you, Tonya, through your husbands.'

Well that had answered the question Mark had really wanted to ask. Jenny was married. Never mind. They were still a friendly bunch of people. Even Paul seemed more acceptable in this very social environment.

Mark and Gary played a few more games, mostly against each other. The standard of play was to Mark's liking. Most players were better than he was, but not so much so that he felt overawed and his game improved during the evening as he got his eye in. Before they knew it, it was 9.30 and time to go. The caretaker appeared to signify that their two hours were up. He stared at them disapprovingly when Tom asked if they could just finish their game. He reminded Mark of the caretaker at his old school. He was a miserable old soul, as well. Perhaps it's a pre-requisite for the job!

Tonya asked Gary and Mark if they wanted to join some of them for a drink, which they did. They went to the Golden Lion, overlooking the pier. Mark was never very sure of himself with strangers, but everyone went out of their way to be friendly to the two newcomers and insisted that they return the next week.

When it was time to go, Paul turned to Gary and Mark and said 'You go past Heacham, don't you?'

'Yes,' said Gary, who was driving that night.

'Would it be possible for you to drop off Jenny? I normally give her a lift, but if you're going that way, it would be a big help to me.'

'Of course,' replied Gary. 'We'll be happy to do so.'

Mark certainly wasn't complaining. He was just a teeny little bit smitten with Jenny. All night, he had been gazing at her and wishing she had been single and perhaps a little younger (or to be precise about it, he a little older, because she was lovely just as she was). In the car, he tried to engage her in conversation. Normally, this would have been a struggle for Mark, but Jenny was a delight to talk to and she made it easy for him. He could have talked to her all night long and he was disappointed when they reached her house. As she got out of the car, she said 'I hope I see you both again, next week.'

Mark had no doubts that he would come back the following week, but after they drove off, Gary said he would prefer to play squash. Jean wasn't going to play either game, so Gary wouldn't be allowed to play both. Mark preferred to play badminton, so they agreed to do their own thing. It was just as well that Mark now had his own transport.

He still lacked confidence with girls, not helped by his various rejections, but he was now nineteen years old and had filled out a little. His acne was a lot better these days, as well. He remembered how he had been when he first left school and started work. How he was unable to look people in the eye; unable to answer a telephone without sounding abrupt and how he struggled to talk to any female without turning red. But now he had just enough self-confidence to turn up at the badminton club alone.

But on Monday, Ian told Mark that he would be going to Leeds with him on Thursday, to 'hold his rod'. It would be a very long day, and Mark wondered if he would miss out on his badminton. Fortunately, Ian was as keen as ever to make an early start, so they arrived on site just after ten o'clock, got round their building quickly and had a quick lunch. Mark was home again just after six o'clock. So armed with a new wooden racquet, which he had bought at the weekend, he made his way to Hunstanton.

Everyone was pleased to see him again. Tonya and her husband were not there this time, but there was a new man who hadn't played the first week, so there were still enough people to make the games varied.

If anything, this was an even more enjoyable evening and Mark's game was definitely improving. Mark got to play with the lovely Jenny and they seemed to be getting on really well together, both on the court and off it. What a pity she was married. But her being married allowed Mark to relax a little more than if she had been single. He still tended to get a little tense when around single girls. Especially ones he fancied.

After a drink at the Golden Lion, Paul again asked Mark if he would take Jenny home. This time, as Mark dropped her off at her house, he suggested he could pick her up on the way to next week's badminton to save Paul having to fetch her. 'Oh, that's kind. You're definitely coming again, then?' she asked.

'Of course. It's good fun and everyone is very friendly. It's a very good way to make friends and meet people. My social life has taken a dip, recently. I used to go out regularly with Gary, but he's courting heavily, so he's not allowed out now. My other mate's just got married and doesn't have a lot of spare time, either.'

'Surely you have a little girlfriend tucked away?'

'Not at the moment, but I don't need one if I can come and see nice people like you and Tonya.' That sounded a bit lame, but he never liked admitting that he didn't have a girlfriend.

'That's a nice thing to say,' she replied. 'I'm sure we're all pleased to see you – some of us more than others.' That last statement was delivered in a soft seductive voice and it made Mark feel a little uncomfortable. Not only was the conversation getting a little awkward (partly of his own making), but they had been parked outside her house for a few minutes and Mark wondered if her husband would have spotted them arriving.

'Anyway, I mustn't keep you,' he said, a little abruptly. 'I'll pick you up next week.'

'Oh, all right then. Are you in a hurry to get home?'

'Well, I've been in Leeds all day. I had to leave at six o'clock this morning and it is starting to catch up on me.'

'Oh, I'm sorry. I didn't realise. It sounds like you have an interesting job. You can tell me all about it next week. I'll look forward to seeing you, then. Thanks for the lift. I'll see you at seven fifteen, next week. Goodnight.'

'Goodnight.' She had made next week's meeting sound like a date.

Mark was starting to wonder if he had done the right thing in offering to pick her up next week. She really seemed to be showing some sort of unhealthy interest in him. But then she didn't seem like the sort of girl who would fool around with other men. This didn't make sense. Why couldn't he just meet a nice attractive single girl and get a nice uncomplicated date? The only women who seem to be interested in him were the ones he didn't find attractive – like Wanda or Rachel. And now a married woman, for Heaven's sake!

He questioned whether he could bring himself to take advantage of Jenny's possible attraction to him. She was certainly lovely and under normal circumstances, he would be after her like a shot, but she was married. Even if her marriage wasn't a happy one, he didn't want to get involved. No, he decided it just wasn't worth the hassle. Next week, he would try to keep the conversation on a polite level. If she said anything untoward, he would not offer to pick her up again. This wasn't the way he wanted to fulfil his objective of getting a date before the end of 1967.

All through the next week, Mark couldn't stop thinking about Jenny. Even Debbie was relegated to the back of his mind and when he went into town on Saturday, he couldn't even be bothered to drive past the bus station. He toyed with the idea of asking Paul to give Jenny a lift, but he had to admit that he was looking forward to seeing her. He would just have to deal with whatever came up. In any case, the more he thought about it, the more he realised that she couldn't possibly be interested in him. He must have misinterpreted what she had said and the way she had said it.

When Mark turned up at Jenny's house the next week, he sat outside in his car for a few minutes. He didn't really want to go to the door to see her husband, but after a few more minutes, he began to wonder if she knew he was there. Her house was totally surrounded by a high hedge, so she wouldn't be able to see his car.

Eventually, when she didn't appear, he decided he had to knock on her door. Jenny answered the door and said 'Please step inside a few minutes. I'm having some problems with my badminton dress. The one I normally wear has got a mark on it and I'm just ironing my old one. Sorry to keep you.'

Just then, a middle-aged woman came down the stairs and Jenny said, 'Oh, mum. This is Mark. He's the chap who's taking me to badminton, tonight.'

'Hello, Mark,' said her mother and they shook hands. 'Are you a keen player?'

'I've only been playing a couple of weeks, but I'm keen to improve.'

'Jenny joined to meet more people. It looks like it's done the trick.'

'Yes, it is a good way to make new friends,' replied Mark.

Jenny was ready and said 'See you, later, mum.'

'You've got a key, in case you're late back, haven't you?' Jenny checked while her mother added 'Goodbye, Mark. It's nice to have met you. I hope we'll see you again, sometime.' It sounded as though her mother approved of Jenny getting lifts with strange men. Mark was a little puzzled. Something didn't seem right.

When they were in the car and on their way to Hunstanton, Mark asked 'Does your mother live with you, then?'

'Well, to be precise, I live with her.'

'Are you and your husband looking to find a place of your own?'

'I'm divorced Mark. Didn't you know?'

'No.' He felt very pleased at this news, but didn't think he should show it. 'I heard Tonya mention your husband and it never occurred to me that you could be divorced.' Of course it didn't. He had heard the term "husband" being used and jumped to conclusions, just as he always did.

But she would still have been sexually experienced and a little older than he was, so would she want to go out with a younger inexperienced teenager?

He added 'You must have been quite young when you married?'

'I was just eighteen. My experience is a good example of why you should never marry young. We lived together in a council house for less than a year. One day, I found a pair of ladies' knickers under the seat of his car – and they weren't mine! When I confronted him about it, he confessed – well, the evidence didn't leave him a lot of choice. He told me that he had been working very closely with this young girl at the bank and they just fell for each other. He couldn't envisage life without her, so I told him he could have her as far as I was concerned. They've rented a small cottage in Grimston.'

'That must have all been awful for you?'

'Well actually, it wasn't as bad as it could have been. He didn't contest the divorce and living in a council house meant there wasn't too much to split up. I just wanted to get on with my life. Mum and Dad were very supportive, so it's all in the past now.'

'You must feel like you can't trust men again?'

'Only a certain type of man, Mark. He was always a bit of a ladies' man. It was as well that I caught him out when I did. I'm glad we didn't have any children.'

She went quiet for a few minutes. Then added 'So that's really why you were in a hurry to get rid of me, last week. You thought I was still married.' She was a very perceptive young lady.

By now, they were at the school, so that was the end of the conversation. Mark hurriedly changed and entered the hall to find that several people were already playing, so he took a seat beside Tonya, who asked 'Did you bring Jenny?'

'Yes. She's just getting changed.' Jenny must have told Tonya that he was giving her a lift. Or maybe it was Paul, because he was already on court and he normally fetched her.

Then Jenny came into the hall. Her 'old' skirt was a little bit shorter than her normal one and Mark could see a little of the shape of her legs above the knee. He liked what he saw. Her legs were quite full and out of proportion to her calves, but they were very shapely.

Mark was now filled with trepidation. He had decided that he was going to ask her for a proper date, but not until they were on their way home. Unfortunately, that gave him plenty of time to get worked up about it. He had been disappointed so many times with girls, that he feared something was bound to go wrong. She would probably tell him that he was too young for her. Or that she just wanted to be friends or something. But he still had to ask. And it had to be that night. He couldn't wait another week.

After the badminton, they joined the others for a drink as usual and then on the way back to Jenny's house, she said, 'I'll see you again, next week, will I?'

'Definitely. You won't keep me away.'

'And can you pick me up, again?'

'Of course.' And then after a few seconds, he added 'I don't suppose you would like to see me sooner than that, would you?'

'Gosh! What did you have in mind?' She was trying not to sound too eager, but she wasn't successful.

'I was hoping you might like to go for a drink one evening. Just the two of us, that is.'

'That would be nice.'

'Really?'

'Really! I was hoping you might ask, but I was afraid you wouldn't want to go out with a divorcee.'

'It's better than thinking you might be developing an attraction for a married woman!'

'I suppose that would be unfortunate,' she laughed.

'When would you like to make it?'

'How about Saturday?' she replied.

'Saturday's fine by me. What time?'

'How does eight o'clock sound?'

'Just great. I'll pick you up here at eight.' By now they were outside her house and he had parked the car. She reached over and gave him a little kiss on his cheek and ran out like an excited schoolgirl. He knew how she felt because he couldn't have been more excited himself.

'Was this really it?' He thought.' Have I really got a date? No. Wait until it actually happens. Don't tell anyone. Just keep your feet on the ground.' But all the way home, he kept singing happy songs.

At work the next day, he was bursting to tell someone, but he somehow managed to keep it to himself. Pat came close to getting him to tell her, because she could see that he was in a particularly good mood all day. Ian said, 'I think he's on a promise.'

'Are you on a promise, Mark?' asked Pat. Mark had never heard the expression before, but he guessed its meaning. He didn't reply, so Sam joined in the fun.

'Who's the lucky fellow?' he asked. 'If it's a girl, give her one for me, would you? Unless it's Wanda. It's not Wanda, is it? 'Cause don't you two play tennis together?'

'No, it's not Wanda!' said Mark.

'Oh, so it is someone, then?' observed Pat. Still Mark didn't respond. He was pleased with his self-control.'

'He hasn't got a woman,' said Ian. 'I keep telling you all that he's a brown hatter.'

Now Mark really wanted to say something, because he had worked out what Ian had meant by a 'brown hatter,' but he still contained himself.

Mark spent most of the next morning washing and polishing his car. Then he went into town to buy himself a new shirt and tie. He would wear them that evening with his suit, which hadn't seen a lot of use, lately. He was tempted to buy Jenny a little gift, but he remembered what had happened with Pauline and decided that would be too much like 'tempting fate.'

As it got nearer and nearer to the evening, Mark kept imagining all the things that would go wrong. Jenny's reaction to his invitation convinced him that she probably wouldn't get cold feet like Pauline did, but she might still go down with a cold. Or perhaps something else had cropped up – a family crisis, for example. And he would have to drive all the way over to Heacham to find out, because he wasn't on the telephone and she had no way of contacting him. Then he'd have to drive straight home again.

It was soon time to leave. He left with plenty of time to spare and was very relieved when the car started first time. He drove very carefully all the way and arrived at the top of Jenny's road with fifteen minutes to spare. After deciding he was too early, he drove around the village for a few minutes, looking for a nice pub to take her to; then he went back to her road. It was still a little early, so he drove down to the bottom of her road to turn round and parked the car outside her house, so that the passenger side was nearest her gate. Then he could open the door like a gentleman. After sitting there for a few more minutes, he slowly got out. He was feeling very apprehensive. He ambled to her door and knocked.

Her mother answered the door and said 'Hello Mark. She's almost ready.'

'It's all right. I am a little early,' said Mark, as Jenny came down the stairs. He gazed up at her and said 'Hello Jenny.' She was even lovelier than ever. She had just a little make-up and gave him one of her lovely smiles.

'Hello, Mark. You look smart in your suit. Are we going somewhere special?'

'I don't know where we're going. I was hoping we could use your local knowledge to find somewhere nice.' He was still a little anxious.

'I don't want to go anywhere in Heacham, thank you. We'll discuss it in the car, shall we? I'm all ready. 'Bye mum. I'll see you later.'

Her mother replied 'Bye. Have a nice time. 'Bye Mark.'

'Goodbye,' replied Mark and off they went down the path, with Mark stepping in front to open the gate and then do the same with his car door. She thanked him.

Once inside the car, he said 'You look really lovely.' She was wearing a simple black sweater, which hugged her bosom to great effect, and a matching knee-length skirt, which also showed off her hips to great effect. She had a tartan shawl draped round her shoulders. 'So where would you like to go?' he asked.

'Do you know the Lifeboat at Thornham?'

'No. I'm not too sure I even know where Thornham is,' he replied.

'The Lifeboat is a lovely little place. It gets very busy with tourists in the summer, but this time of year, there's a nice atmosphere. If we're lucky, we can play "penny-in-the-hole." Have you ever played that?'

'I've never heard of it. Where do we go?'

'Just head out along the coast past Old Hunstanton. I'll show you which way to go.'

He was starting to relax. He was actually on a date! She directed him to the Lifeboat and he was able to park right outside the pub. 'You should come here in daylight,' said Jenny. 'It's all creeks and salt marshes along that end of the village. The road sometimes gets flooded when there's a high spring tide.

Inside, he was very pleased at what he saw. It was a very traditional looking bar with a large log fire. At one end of the bar, sat an old man with an old dog curled at his old feet. 'We're in luck. We can play 'penny-in-the-hole', said Jenny, pointing to a long bench. 'We'll have a game before the bar starts filling up.'

Mark ordered their drinks and when he paid for them, Jenny asked the landlord if they could have the 'pennies.' The landlord brought a pile of coins – only they weren't real coins. They were copper discs, just slightly larger than a halfpenny, but smaller than a penny.

'Right,' said Jenny. 'We each take a turn to throw the pennies at that metal plate on the back of the bench, so that they fall into the hole below. We have to get as many as we can into the hole in one turn. But we have to stand over here next to the fire, so you'll want to take your jacket off. I'll go first to show you.'

After playing this for just a few minutes, Mark found himself roasting, with his back to the fire. Jenny beat him every time, as he struggled to get the right technique. He seemed to spend most of his time scrabbling about on the floor to pick up his coins, which had rebounded off the bench, but he enjoyed watching Jenny go into action. He even found the fact that she had beaten him to be something of a 'turn-on.'

As a few more people came into the pub, it became clear that their game was becoming an inconvenience to everyone else, so they finished their game and returned the 'coins.' Mark was pleased to sit down and recover from his roasting. Jenny seemed able to cope with the heat better than Mark, despite wearing black.

Mark ordered some more drinks. The heat had made him very thirsty.

They both sat down and started talking. Mark had prepared a few jokes in case there were any embarrassing gaps in the conversation, but he needn't have bothered. At no point did the conversation flag. Jenny told him about her job at a school in Dersingham, where she 'assisted' the teachers. This included nature rambles with the children, which she particularly enjoyed. She considered herself to be very much an outdoor sort of person and she liked to be out in the countryside as much as possible. Mark told her about his little stop at Monsal Head and her obvious interest convinced him that he would love to take her there, one day.

Mark asked her about her taste in music. 'I don't particularly like pop music,' she replied. My husband seemed to like everything in the charts and that put me off pop music. I'm a bit of an old romantic. I like people like Tony Bennett and Nat King Cole. Although, lately, I've come to like some of this Tamla Motown stuff, like The Temptations and The Four Tops. What about you?'

Mark replied, 'Well, I like The Temptations and The Four Tops, but you probably won't have heard of most of the records I buy. Have you heard of Jerry Butler?'

'No, I don't think so.'

'What about The Impressions?'

'No.'

Major Lance or Gene Chandler?'

'No.'

Mark reeled off a list of his favourites, which all met with the same response. Then he added 'Ben E. King and The Drifters?'

'Oh, I like them,' she responded.

'Well, you would probably like some of the others – especially if you like The Temptations and The Four Tops. You just don't know you do, because you haven't heard of them. I could lend you some of my records, if you like.' Mark wouldn't trust his precious records with anyone, unless he was really sure of that person, so this was an important gesture.

'We don't have a record player. My husband took ours when we split up.'

'Good Heavens! I couldn't imagine being without a record player,' Mark replied.

Mark had never before sat down and talked with one single person for so long. He also found himself sexually aroused. He couldn't understand that, because Jenny wasn't revealing any part of her anatomy. He just liked looking at her and talking to her. The time just flew by and there was still so much to talk about when the landlord signalled 'time.'

Whenever Mark had been out with Gary, the conversation would have reached a natural lull and they would have moved on to another pub to perk things up, but there was no need of any such action that night. Even with Dougie, there was often a need for a game of darts or cribbage to keep the evening flowing. But with Jenny, he could have sat there all night long.

As they got to the car, Jenny said 'Thank you, Mark. That was a lovely evening.'

'Thank you. That was the most enjoyable evening I've ever had.' If this was what dating was like, he wanted some more of it.

As they came into Heacham, Jenny said 'I don't really want to go home, just yet. Can we just drive down to the beach? Just follow this road down and it takes you right down to the beach.'

The road ended just where the shingle started. Mark opened the window to hear the waves. 'Shall we just get outside to listen to the sea?' suggested Jenny.

As they got out, a cold wind hit them. They walked over the brow of the shingle beach to see and hear the sea, but the wind was even fiercer there and it was much too dark to see anything, so they abandoned this idea and returned to the car. Mark wanted to put his arm around her to keep her warm, but he didn't know if this was 'too forward'. Instead, he rushed to open Jenny's door again. 'Cor! That was bracing,' he said.

He was starting to feel apprehensive again. Everything he was doing that night was for the first time. He had just had his first date ever and his priority was to ensure that there would be further dates, so he didn't want to overstep the mark. At the same time, he didn't want to ruin things by *not* doing something that was expected of him. Perhaps the first thing was to ensure she wanted to see him again. So he went for it.

'Can I see you again?'

'Yes, I'll see you at badminton, won't I?' she replied, mischievously.

'Oh! Is that it?' disappointment obvious in his voice.

'I'm teasing, Mark. Of course you can see me again. I've had a great time.'

'Wow! How about tomorrow? You can show me Thornham in the daylight.'

'I'd better not make it tomorrow. We've got relatives coming round. But Tuesday or Wednesday I can make.'

'I've got to go up to Newcastle on Tuesday. I probably won't be back till about nine or ten at night. But Wednesday would be great. Shall I pick you up at eight o'clock again?'

'Yes. I'll look forward to that.'

Now it went a little quiet and they just sat there. Mark was aware that Jenny was looking at him in the dark. Was she expecting him to do something? Should he try to kiss her? He'd never kissed a girl before. He'd practised on the back of his hand, but that was different. Suppose he made a bog-up of it. He might ruin everything. She'd already said he could see her again. Perhaps he would try on Wednesday. There was no point in spoiling it all now.

'I'd better get you home,' he said as he started the car and then did a three-point turn.

Jenny was very quiet as they headed back to her house. He would love to know what she was thinking at that moment. Perhaps he should have kissed her back at the beach. After all, hadn't she already given him a little kiss on Thursday? Outside her house, he turned off the engine and said 'Can I kiss you?'

'I would think so,' she whispered. He leaned over and kissed her gently on the mouth, then took his lips away.

'That felt nice,' he thought and she hadn't really moved. So he repeated it, only this time, he lingered a little more. She put her arms around his neck and held him there.

He didn't know whether he was doing this right or not, but Jenny was going for it and it felt good to him. Now what about this French kissing lark? Should he try that? Things seemed to be going so well, he thought he'd risk it, so he put his tongue in her mouth and she responded likewise. He wasn't too sure about this bit. Perhaps there was more to it than that? But Jenny was still going strong, so he carried on, until she pulled away and softly whispered 'You're not doing me any good, Mark!'

So he wasn't doing it right. She would have been used to someone who did know the ropes. Perhaps if she knew he was inexperienced she might help him learn how to do it properly. 'I have to tell you I'm a virgin!' he blurted, without thinking.

'You'll have to do something about that,' she replied in a soft voice, but it sounded like an order. 'I'd better get going. Thanks again for a lovely evening. Goodnight. ' Then she gave him another little peck on the cheek. And she was gone.

Mark felt really wretched. It had all been going so well, but it was ruined by his lack of experience. Not only did Jenny regard him as a lousy kisser, but she also indicated that he needed to lose his virginity if he was to get anywhere with her. How was he to do that? And why did she dash off like that?

The next day, he had a football match. It was just as well, because he was busy throughout the game and for a couple of hours, it took his mind off his concerns about Jenny. But afterwards, he still felt sorry for himself.

At work on Monday, Pat could see that he was no longer in a jovial mood and he had to endure several jibes from the others, but just before lunchtime, Ian's telephone rang. Ian said 'Mark. It's for you. It sounds like your bit of stuff.'

Mark took the telephone and said 'Hello?'

He heard Jenny's voice and recognised it immediately. 'Hi. It's me,' she said.

Various thoughts went through his head. He thought she was going to tell him she didn't want to see him on Wednesday. Mark had told her where he worked and she must have found the number from the 'phone book. Perhaps she preferred to end it over the 'phone rather than tell him to his face.

He replied 'Oh, hello,' without showing any great enthusiasm.

She detected this and said 'Do you still want to see me on Wednesday?'

'Of course! Why wouldn't I?' He still didn't display any enthusiasm. Apart from anything else, everyone in the office was listening.

'I thought you might have thought I sounded a bit tarty.'

'Why on Earth would I have thought that?'

'Well, I talked about helping you to lose your virginity. I don't know how you thought that sounded. And how you were getting me all excited.'

Mark hesitated before he replied. 'I'm a little confused. That's not how I saw things, but I can't really talk about it at the moment. I can assure you that I am definitely looking forward to seeing you again.'

Everyone in the office went 'Aaaah!'

Jenny replied 'Well, I'm looking forward to seeing you again. We'd better have a little heart to heart talk when I see you.'

'Yes,' said Mark. 'I'd like that. I can't really say anything else at the moment. I'm working in an office full of idiots, here.'

'Yes, I can hear. I hope I haven't caused you any embarrassment.'

'Nothing I can't handle. It's because their own lives are lacking something.'

'Ooooh!' went everyone in the office.

Mark continued, 'I'll see you on Wednesday, then. Thanks for calling. 'Bye.'

'So you're not a "brown-hatter" then,' said Ian. 'I'm glad to hear it. I hope she's got plump milky-white thighs. I like plump milky-white thighs.'

Mark ignored him and went back to work. He felt a whole lot better, now, although he had exchanged his feelings of self-pity for a state of some confusion. She had just said that he had been getting her excited. That didn't match with the things she had said at the time and the way she had almost run out of the car. The main thing was that she still wanted to see him again. Did he dare hope that he might still have someone to take to the Christmas Dinner Dance?

Wednesday was a long time coming. But when it arrived, Mark duly called at Jenny's house and she opened the door before he could knock on it. This time she was wearing a slightly shorter coffee coloured skirt beneath a brown coat. She kissed him on the cheek as soon as she had closed the door behind her.

Once in the car, she said 'Before we go anywhere else, shall we just drive down to the beach and have this little chat?' Mark thought that was a good idea and they were soon in position at the beach.

Jenny was first to speak. 'I didn't mean to sound tarty when I said you would have to lose your virginity. It just came out like that.'

Mark said 'I thought you meant you wanted me to go and lose my virginity elsewhere.'

'Good heavens! Why would I want you to go elsewhere to do that?'

'Perhaps I was just a little paranoid about my situation and expected the worst.'

'Well you can forget about seeing anyone else. We'll just see how things develop and not going rushing into anything.' That sounded to Mark as though she didn't want to have sex with him – at least not yet. But all he really wanted at that time was to keep seeing her.

Mark was still puzzled about her comments about not doing her any good, so he said 'That was the first time I'd ever kissed anyone properly.'

'You could have fooled me, Mark. You seemed to know exactly what to do.'

'But you said I wasn't doing you any good?'

'That's because I didn't want you getting me all worked up, only to leave me up in the air and unsatisfied. Not that you were no good, for Heaven's sake! Quite the opposite, in fact! I'd never have known you were new to all this. Are you really trying to tell me that you've never had a girlfriend?'

'I've never had a girlfriend. I'd never even had a proper date until last week. There's been a few foursomes and a couple of blind dates, but not a proper date.'

'That's incredible,' she said.

'I wish I had joined a badminton club before,' said Mark. 'So we're all O.K., now, are we?'

'Yes, Mark. Shall we go and have a drink?'

'I'm gasping for a drink. My mouth has been feeling dry since I left home. Do you want to go to the Lifeboat again?'

'We can do. Or we can try somewhere else. How about the Gin Trap at Ringstead?'

'I've never been there, but I'll give it a go.'

The Gin Trap was fairly quiet and they had a game of dominoes which Mark won, but only just. Jenny had a very quick mind and was good at working out the best tactics. She was in the lead for a while and Mark found this to be sexually stimulating. In fact, he was sexually stimulated all evening.

He couldn't help but keep looking up at her when he should have been studying the dominoes. She kept looking at him. He tried to take in the whole image of her – her lovely eyes, her fair hair framing her lovely cheekbones, her breasts, her arms – even her hands. He wanted to touch her. He wanted another one of those kisses.

After a few more games of dominoes, he made the excuse that he had to go to work the next day, so he didn't want to be too late, so they finished their drinks and left. Back in the car, he leaned over and they both kissed. After a few seconds of this, Jenny said 'Do you really have to get home early?'

'No, not really.'

'Shall we go somewhere quiet? Not down the beach. Somewhere a bit more secluded. I'll show you where.'

She directed him down a few lanes and they arrived at a quiet spot surrounded by trees. Mark hadn't a clue where they were, but he could see that they were unlikely to be disturbed. She told him to drive a little way off the road into a gap between the trees and he turned off the engine. It bothered him a little that she must have been there before.

They started kissing again. Mark was feeling a little bolder, so he put his hands on her shoulders; then ran them down her arms. They were lovely soft shoulders and arms. He continued to let his right hand wander over her hips and down the side of her thighs, whilst all the time, their kissing was getting more and more passionate.

Jenny pulled away and said 'Did you bring anything?'

'I did actually,' he breathed, hoping he knew what she meant. 'I just happened to see a machine in the pub the other day. I don't know if I got the right ones. I just shoved my money in and grabbed them before someone else came into the toilet. I've got a packet of three.'

'Well, that should be enough,' she laughed. 'At least for tonight! Shall we get in the back? I hope there's enough room.'

It was a two-door car, so they both got out into the cold night air and climbed into the back, closing their doors behind them. Jenny pulled her sweater over her head and then pulled down her skirt and tights, leaving herself in bra and panties. Mark removed his clothing, all except his pants and his socks. This was not an easy operation for either of them, due to the lack of space in the back of the car, but eventually, they made it. Then feeling a little cooler, they hugged each other to share their body heat, feeling each other's soft bodies with their hands. Mark was aware of Jenny's lovely breasts and reached down to cup one of them. He decided these warranted the attention of both hands – one per breast. At the same time, Jenny reached below to gauge Mark's interest. He was interested, so she pulled down his pants and starting stroking his manhood. This was a hundred times better than when he did it to himself.

Mark wasn't sure what to do next. There was so much to explore and he wanted to explore all of it. He turned his attention to her thighs. Ian would have been pleased with these. Although it was dark, Mark could tell that they were plump and milky-white – and oh, so soft!

Now he wanted to return to her breasts, so he reached behind to unfasten her bra strap, but after a few unsuccessful attempts, Jenny had to break away from her task to help him and suddenly her breasts were released in all their glory. He leaned over to kiss them, one after another. Then he felt her nipples and gently ran his finger round each of them in turn. Then kissed them and the rest of her ample breasts.

'You're like a kid with a new toy, Mark,' she said.

'Father Christmas never brought me anything like these,' he replied.

Now Jenny removed her panties and said, 'Let's see if we can get one of those things on you. There is a knack to it. You have to make sure you only let the inside come into contact with your little fellow. Otherwise, we'll have to throw it away. We don't want to take any risks. You hold the nipple to make sure there's no air in it and then you peal it down.'

Of course, in the dark, this was not easy, so he turned on the light to remove the wrapping. The sight of Jenny, sitting there, with nothing on, distracted him for a few seconds. What a wonderful sight. Her full breasts blazing away, with no sign of sagging, despite their impressive size – and then those wonderful milky-white thighs and hips, begging for his attention. But he went back to the task in hand.

He had the blessed thing out of its wrapper and applied it to his member, as Jenny had told him, but something didn't seem right. Then he realised it was inside out. 'You'd better throw that one away,' said Jenny. 'You can't turn it round, now. It's a good job, you bought three!' Mark thought Jenny was probably being over-cautious, but he did what she said.

The next one was dropped on the floor, so she told him to throw that one away, as well. This time, she suggested she handled the last one. She had obviously done this before and was more successful, although she thought he could have bought a better make. 'I just went for the first machine I saw', he said.

'These are a bit like having a bath with your socks on!' She laughed. 'They're thick enough to mend a puncture on your tyre. Never mind. It's on, now. Let's see how we do.'

Mark tried to manoeuvre into position. One of Jenny's legs was sticking out at an angle and there didn't seem to be enough room on the seat for his legs as well. He was almost kneeling on the floor, but somehow, with Jenny's help he was able to perform something resembling intercourse. After two minutes of this, they both decided it wasn't very satisfactory, so Jenny suggested she should be on top. Mark was beginning to wish he had bought one of those large Vauxhall Crestas or a Ford Zodiac, with their big bench seats, rather than a two-door Ford Anglia.

Their second position was slightly better, but the back seat wasn't wide enough for Mark and both of Jenny's legs, so they abandoned it. In any case, Mark said he couldn't feel very much wearing this French letter. 'It really is like having a bath with your socks on!' he said. Then added 'I'm sorry. I'm not very good at this, am I?'

'It's not your fault, Mark. We need a better place to do it in. Anyway, let me finish you off. Sit down properly.'

As she started stroking his manhood, he said 'Can I do something for you?' So she showed him what to do and he seemed to pick it up quite quickly. So much so, than when he said 'I'm coming,' it was enough to enable her to match his orgasm, almost simultaneously.

'Have you got a tissue or anything?' Jenny asked.

'No. You can do what I normally do, if you like and wipe it on my underpants. It's funny, but you never see James Bond offering his underpants for this purpose when he makes love to a beautiful woman, do you?'

She laughed. As she replaced her panties and tights, she said 'Do you realise that you've just lost your virginity, Mark.'

'Does that count?' he asked.

'Of course it does. You entered me and you satisfied me. That qualifies in anyone's book. What's more, you were a very attentive lover. You'll go far.'

'But it wasn't proper sex, was it?'

261

'Believe me, Mark. A lot of people would have been very satisfied with that performance. We need a better venue, though. I'll have to find out when my parents are going out for the night. And you need to get some better thingies, next time.'

Suddenly, they both felt very cold and quickly dressed – at least as quickly as they could in their close confinement, getting in each other's way. Before moving back into the front of the car, they embraced again, but as soon as the kissing got a little passionate, Jenny stopped him, saying 'No. Don't get me all excited again.'

They climbed out of the car and back into the front seats. After another quick kiss, Mark started the car. He suddenly realised he couldn't see a thing out of the back window. All the windows were misted up and it was very dark. They opened their side windows, but that did little to help. There were no such things as reversing lights or rear demisters on a 1959 Ford Anglia. He edged his car backwards, very gingerly, waiting to hit something, but he found himself back on the road and Jenny gave him directions back to her house.

'We're going to keep the badminton going, aren't we?' Mark asked,

'Yes. Will you pick me up tomorrow, as usual?'

'Of course I will.'

Back outside Jenny's house, they kissed again. Jenny said 'I don't really want to go.'

'I know,' said Mark, 'but I do have to go to work tomorrow.' So they had a final kiss and said 'Goodnight.'

On his way home, Mark felt himself to be a very happy man. He had not only fulfilled his objective of getting a date before the end of the year, but he had 'broken his duck.' He was finally 'off the mark.' 'Mark's off the mark,' he said out loud. And he couldn't have done it with a more wonderful girl. He no longer had any thoughts for Debbie, Karen, Pauline, Jane or Mary. He just wanted his lovely little Jenny. And he couldn't wait to show her off at the Christmas Dinner and Dance.

Then he started singing

'Grey skies are gonna clear up.

Put on a happy face.

Da da da da da dum

I must learn the words somehow

So I can spread sunshine all over the place.

Put on a happy face.'